Percival Keene

by

Captain Marryat

Percival Keene
by Captain Marryat

Copyright © 2024

All Rights reserved.

No part of this publication may be reproduced,
stored in a retrieval system, or transmitted in any
form or by any means, electronic, mechanical,
photocopying or Otherwise, without the written
permission of the publisher.
The author/editor asserts the moral right to
be identified as the author/editor of this work.

ISBN: 978-93-67146-27-9

Published by

DOUBLE 9 BOOKS

2/13-B, Ansari Road
Daryaganj, New Delhi – 110002
info@double9books.com
www.double9books.com
Tel. 011-40042856

This book is under public domain

ABOUT THE AUTHOR

Captain Frederick Marryat (an early innovator of the sea story) was a British Royal Navy Officer and novelist. He gained the Royal Human Society's gold medal for bravery, before leaving the services in 1830 to write books. He is mainly remembered for his stories of the sea, many written from his own experiences. He started a series of adventure novels marked by a brilliant, direct narrative style and an absolute fund of incident and fun. These have The King's Own (1830), Peter Simple (1834), and Mr. Midshipman Easy (1836). He also created a number of children's books, among which The Children of the New Forest (1847), a story of the English Civil Wars is a classic of children literature. A Life and Letters was processed by his daughter Florence (1872). He is recognized also for a broadly used system of maritime flag signalling known as Marryat's Code. Familiar for his adventurous novels, his works are known for their representation of deep family bonds and social structure beside naval action. Marryat died in 1848 at the age of fifty.

CONTENTS

Chapter One

A few miles from the town of Southampton there is an old mansion-house, which has been for centuries known as Madeline Hall, in the possession of the de Versely family. It is a handsome building, surrounded by a finely timbered park of some extent, and, what is more important, by about 12,000 acres of land, which also appertain to it. At the period in which I commence this history, there resided in this mansion an elderly spinster of rank, named the Honourable Miss Delmar, sister of the late Lord de Versely and aunt to the present earl, and an Honourable Captain Delmar, who was the second son of the deceased nobleman. This property belonged to the Honourable Miss Delmar, and was at her entire disposal upon her decease.

The Honourable Captain Delmar, at the time I am speaking of, commanded a frigate employed upon what was designated channel service, which in those days implied that the captain held a seat in the House of Commons and that he voted with the ministry; and further, that his vote might, when required, be forthcoming, the frigate was never sea-going, except during the recess. It must be admitted that H.M. ship Paragon did occasionally get under weigh and remain cruising in sight of land for two or three days, until the steward reported that the milk provided for the captain's table was turning sour; upon which important information the helm was immediately put up, and the frigate, in a case of such extreme distress, would drop her anchor at the nearest port under her lee. Now as the Paragon was constantly at Spithead, Captain Delmar was very attentive in visiting his aunt, who lived at Madeline Hall; ill-natured people asserted, because she had so fine an estate in her own gift. Certain it is, that he would remain there for weeks, which gave great satisfaction to the old lady, who liked her nephew, liked attention, and was even so peculiar as to like sailors. But it must be observed that there was another person at the mansion who also liked the captain, liked attention, and liked sailors; this was Miss Arabella Mason, a very pretty young woman of eighteen years of age, who constantly looked in the glass merely to ascertain if she had ever seen a face which she preferred to her own, and who never read any novel without discovering that there was a remarkable likeness between the heroine and her pretty self.

Miss Arabella Mason was the eldest daughter of the steward of the old Lord de Versely, brother to the Honourable Miss Delmar, and was much respected by his lordship for his fidelity and his knowledge of business, in the transaction of which he fell, for he was felling trees, and a tree fell upon him. He left a widow and two daughters: it was said that at his death Mrs Mason was not badly off, as her husband had been very careful of his earnings. Mrs Mason, however, did not corroborate this statement; on the contrary, she invariably pleaded poverty; and the Honourable Miss Delmar, after Lord de Versely's death—which happened soon after that of his steward—sent both the daughters to be educated at a country school, where, as everything that is taught is second-rate, young ladies, of course, receive a second-rate education. Mrs Mason was often invited by the Honourable Miss Delmar to spend a month at Madeline Hall, and used to bring her eldest daughter, who had left school, with her. Latterly, however, the daughter remained as a fixture, and Mrs Mason received but an occasional invitation. It may be inquired in what capacity Miss Arabella Mason remained at the Hall; she was not a servant, for her position in life was above that of a menial; neither was she received altogether in the saloon, as she was of too humble a grade to mix with gentry and nobility; she was, therefore, betwixt and between, a sort of humble companion in the drawing-room, a cut above the housekeeper in the still-room, a fetcher and carrier of the honourable spinster's wishes, a sort of link between the aristocratic old dame and her male attendants, towards whom she had a sort of old maidish aversion. However this position might be found useful to her mistress, it must be admitted that it was a most unfortunate position for a young, thoughtless, and very pretty girl, moreover, who was naturally very lively, very smart in repartee, and very fond of being admired.

As the Honourable Captain Delmar was very constant in his visits to his aunt, it was but natural that he should pay some little attention to her humble companion. By degrees the intimacy increased, and at last there were reports in the servants' hall, that the captain and Miss Bella Mason had been seen together in the evergreen walk; and as the captain's visits were continually repeated during the space of two years so did the scandal increase, and people became more ill-natured. It was now seen that Miss Bella had been very often found in tears, and the old butler and the older housekeeper shook their heads at each other like responsive mandarins; the only person who was ignorant of the scandal afloat was the old lady spinster herself.

I must now introduce another personage. The Honourable Captain Delmar did not, of course, travel without his valet, and this important personage had been selected out of the marine corps which had been drafted into the frigate. Benjamin Keene, for such was his name, was certainly endowed with several qualities which were indispensable in a valet; he was very clean in his person, very respectful in his deportment, and, after the sovereign of Great Britain, looked upon the Honourable Captain Delmar as the greatest person in the world. Moreover, Benjamin Keene, although only a private marine was, without exception, one of the handsomest men that ever was seen and being equally as well made and well drilled as he was handsome in person, he was the admiration of all the young women. But Nature, who delights in a drawback, had contrived to leave him almost without brains; and further, he was wholly uneducated—for he was too stupid to learn—his faculties were just sufficient to enable him, by constant drilling, to be perfect in the manual exercise, and mechanically to perform his duties as a valet.

Ben always accompanied his master to the hall, where the former was at one and the same time the admiration and laughter of all the servants. It hardly need be observed, that the clever and sprightly Miss Arabella Mason considered Ben as one much beneath her, that is, she said so on his first arrival at Madeline hall; but, strange to say, that two years afterwards, just at the time that reports had been raised that she had been frequently discovered in tears, there was a change in her manner towards him; indeed some people insinuated that she was setting her cap at the handsome marine: this idea, it is true, was ridiculed by the majority; but still the intimacy appeared rapidly to increase. It was afterwards asserted by those who find out everything after it has taken place, that Ben would never have ventured to look up to such an unequal match had he not been prompted to it by his master, who actually proposed that he should marry the girl. That such was the fact is undoubted, although they knew it not; and Ben, who considered the wish of his captain as tantamount to an order, as soon as he could comprehend what his captain required of him, stood up erect and raised his hand with a flourish to his head, in token of his obedience. Shortly afterwards, Captain Delmar again came over to Madeline Hall, accompanied as usual, by Ben, and the second day after their arrival it was made known to all whom it might concern, that Miss Arabella Mason had actually contracted a secret marriage with the handsome Benjamin Keene.

Of course, the last person made acquainted with this interesting intelligence was the Honourable Miss Delmar, and her nephew took upon himself to make the communication. At first the honourable spinster bridled up with indignation, wondered at the girl's indelicacy, and much more at her demeaning herself by marrying a private marine. Captain Delmar replied, that it was true that Ben was only a private, but that every common soldier was a gentleman by profession. It was true that Bella Mason might have done better—but she was his aunt's servant, and Keene was his valet, so that the disparity was not so very great. He then intimated that he had long perceived the growing attachment; talked of the danger of young people being left so much together; hinted about opportunity, and descanted upon morals and propriety. The Honourable Miss Delmar was softened down by the dexterous reasoning of her nephew; she was delighted to find so much virtue extant in a sailor; and, after an hour's conversation, the married couple were sent for, graciously pardoned, and Mrs Keene, after receiving a very tedious lecture, received a very handsome present. But if her mistress was appeased, Mrs Keene's mother was not. As soon as the intelligence was received, old Mrs Mason set off for Madeline Hall. She first had a closeted interview with her daughter, and then with Captain Delmar, and as soon as the latter was over, she immediately took her departure, without paying her respects to the mistress of the Hall, or exchanging one word with any of the servants; this conduct gave occasion to more innuendoes—some indeed ascribed her conduct to mortification at her daughter's having made so imprudent a match, but others exchanged very significant glances.

Three weeks after the marriage, the Parliament having been prorogued, the admiral of the port considered that he was justified in ordering the frigate out on a cruise. Ben Keene, of course accompanied his master, and it was not until three months had passed away that the frigate returned into port. As usual, the Honourable Captain Delmar, as soon as he had paid his respects to the admiral, set off to visit his aunt, accompanied by his benedict marine. On his arrival, he found that everything appeared to be in great confusion; indeed an event was occurring which had astonished the whole household; the butler made a profound bow to the captain; the footmen forgot their usual smirk when he alighted. Captain Delmar was ushered in solemn silence into the drawing-room, and his aunt, who had notice of his arrival received him with a stiff, prim air of unwonted frigidity, with her arms crossed before her on her white muslin apron.

"My dear aunt," said Captain Delmar, as she coldly took his proffered hand, "what is the matter?"

"The matter is this, nephew," replied the old lady—"that marriage of your marine and Bella Mason should have taken place six months sooner than it did. This is a wicked world, nephew; and sailors, I'm afraid, are—"

"Marines, you should say, in this instance, my dear aunt," replied Captain Delmar, insinuatingly. "I must confess that neither sailors nor marines are quite so strict as they ought to be; however, Ben has married her. Come, my dear aunt, allow me to plead for them, although I am very much distressed that such an event should take place in your house. I think," added he, after a pause, "I shall give Mr Keene seven dozen at the gangway, for his presumption, as soon as I return on board."

"That won't mend the matter, nephew," replied Miss Delmar. "I'll turn her out of the house as soon as she can be moved."

"And I'll flog him as soon as I get him on board," rejoined the captain. "I will not have your feelings shocked, and your mind harassed in this way, by any impropriety on the part of my followers—most infamous—shameful—abominable—unpardonable," interjected the captain, walking the quarter-deck up and down the room.

The Honourable Miss Delmar continued to talk, and the honourable captain to agree with her in all she said, for an hour at least. When people are allowed to give vent to their indignation without the smallest opposition they soon talk it away; such was the case with the Honourable Miss Delmar. When it was first announced that Bella Keene was safely in bed with a fine boy, the offended spinster turned away from the communication with horror; when her own maid ventured to remark that it was a lovely baby, she was ordered to hold her tongue; she would not see the suffering mother, and the horrid marine was commanded to stay in the kitchen, lest she should be contaminated by meeting him on the stairs; but every day softened down her indignation, and before a fortnight was over the Honourable Miss Delmar had not only seen but admired the baby; and at last decided upon paying a visit to the mother, who was now sufficiently recovered to undergo a lecture of about two hours' length, in which the honourable spinster commented upon her *in*decency, *in*discretion, *in*considerateness, *in*correctness, *in*decorum, *in*continence, and *in*delicacy; pointing out that her conduct was most inexcusable, iniquitous, and most infamous. The Honourable Miss Delmar having had such a long innings then gave it up, because she was out of breath. Bella, who waited patiently to make her response, and who was a very clever girl, then declared, with many tears, that she was aware that her conduct was *in*excusable, her faults had been *in*voluntary, and her sorrow was *in*expressible; her *in*experience and her *in*fatuation her only apology; that her *in*felicity at her mistress's displeasure would *in*evitably increase her sufferings; assured her that she was not *in*corrigible, and that if her mistress would only indulge her with forgiveness, as she hoped to *in*herit heaven she would never *in*cur her anger by committing the same fault again. Satisfied with this assurance, the Honourable Miss Delmar softened down, and not only forgave, but actually took the child into her lap that Bella might read the Bible which she had presented her with. Reader, the child who had this great honour conferred upon him, who actually laid in the immaculate lap, on the apron of immaculate snowy whiteness of the immaculate Honourable

Miss Delmar, was no other person than the narrator of this history—or, if you please it, the Hero of this Tale.

That my mother had so far smoothed things pretty well must be acknowledged; but it was to be presumed that her husband might not be pleased at so unusual an occurrence, and already the sneers and innuendoes of the servants' hall were not wanting. It appeared, however, that an interview had taken place between Ben and Captain Delmar shortly after my making my appearance: what occurred did not transpire, but this is certain that, upon the marine's return to the kitchen, one of the grooms, who ventured to banter him, received such a sound thrashing from Ben that it put an end to all further joking. As Ben had taken up the affair so seriously, it was presumed that if there had been anticipation of the hymeneal rites he was himself the party who had been hasty; and that now he was married, he was resolved to resent any impertinent remarks upon his conduct. At all events, the question now became one of less interest, as the scandal was of less importance; and as Ben had made known his determination to resent any remarks upon the subject, not a word more was said, at all events when he was present.

In due time I was christened, and so completely was my mother reinstalled in the good graces of her mistress, that as Captain Delmar had volunteered to stand my sponsor, the Honourable Miss Delmar gave the necessary female security; at the particular request of my mother, the captain consented that I should bear his own Christian name, and I was duly registered in the church books as Percival Keene.

Chapter Two

There is no security in this world. A dissolution of Parliament took place, and on the following election the Honourable Captain Delmar's constituents, not being exactly pleased at the total indifference which he had shown to their interests, took upon themselves to elect another member in his stead, who, as Captain Delmar had previously done, promised everything, and in all probability would follow the honourable captain's example by performing nothing. The loss of his election was followed up by the loss of his ship, his majesty's government not considering it necessary that Captain Delmar (now that he had leisure to attend to his professional duties) should retain his command. The frigate, therefore, was paid off, and recommissioned by another captain who had friends in Parliament.

As Ben Keene belonged to the marine corps, he could not, of course, remain as valet to Captain Delmar, but was ordered, with the rest of the detachment, to the barracks at Chatham; my mother, although she was determined that she would not live at barracks, was not sorry to leave the Hall, where she could not fail to perceive that she was, from her imprudent conduct, no longer treated with the respect or cordiality to which she had been previously accustomed. She was most anxious to quit a place in which her disgrace was so well known; and Captain Delmar having given her his advice, which coincided with her own ideas, and also a very munificent present to enable her to set up housekeeping, took his departure from the Hall. My mother returned to her room as the wheels of his carriage rattled over the gravel of the drive, and many were the bitter tears which she shed over her unconscious boy.

The following day the Honourable Miss Delmar sent for her; as usual, commenced with a tedious lecture, which, as before, was wound up at parting with a handsome present. The day after my mother packed up her trunks, and with me in her arms set off to Chatham, where we arrived safely, and immediately went into furnished lodgings. My mother was a clever, active woman, and the presents which she had at different times received amounted to a considerable sum of money, over which her husband had never ventured to assert any claim.

Indeed, I must do Ben Keene the justice to say that he had the virtue of humility. He felt that his wife was in every way his superior and that it was only under peculiar circumstances that he could have aspired to her. He was, therefore, submissive to her in everything, consenting to every proposal that was made by her, and guided by her opinion. When, therefore, on her arrival at Chatham, she pointed out how impossible it would be for one brought up as she had been to associate with the women in the barracks, and that she considered it advisable that she should set up some business by which she might gain a respectable livelihood, Ben, although he felt that this would be a virtual separation *a mensâ et thoro*, named no objections. Having thus obtained the consent of her husband, who considered her so much his superior as to be infallible, my mother, after much cogitation, resolved that she would embark her capital in a circulating library and stationer's shop; for she argued that selling paper, pens, and sealing-wax was a commerce which would secure to her customers of the better class. Accordingly, she hired a house close to the barracks, with a very good-sized shop below, painting and papering it very smartly; there was much taste in all her arrangements, and although the expenses of the outlay and the first year's rent had swallowed up a considerable portion of the money she had laid by, it soon proved that she had calculated well, and her shop became a sort of lounge for the officers, who amused themselves with her smartness and vivacity, the more so as she had a talent for repartee, which men like to find in a very pretty woman.

In a short time my mother became quite the rage, and it was a mystery how so pretty and elegant a person could have become the wife of a private marine. It was however, ascribed to her having been captivated with the very handsome person and figure of her husband, and having yielded to her feelings in a moment of infatuation. The ladies patronised her circulating library; the officers and gentlemen purchased her stationery. My mother then added gloves, perfumery, canes, and lastly cigars, to her previous assortment and before she had been a year in business, found that she was making money very fast, and increasing her customers every day. My mother had a great deal of tact; with the other sex she was full of merriment and fond of joking, consequently a great favourite; towards her own sex her conduct was quite the reverse; she assumed a respectful, prudish air, blended with a familiarity which was never offensive; she was, therefore, equally popular with her own sex, and prospered in every sense of the word. Had her husband been the least inclined to have asserted his rights, the position which she had gained was sufficient to her reducing him to a state of subjection. She had raised herself, unaided, far above him; he saw her continually chatting and laughing with his own officers, to whom he was compelled to make a respectful salute whenever they passed by him; he could not venture to address her, or even to come into the shop, when his officers were there, or it would have been considered disrespectful towards them; and as he could not sleep out of barracks, all his intercourse with her was to occasionally slink down by the area, to find something better to eat than he could have in his own mess, or obtain from her an occasional shilling to spend in beer. Ben, the marine, found at last that somehow or another, his wife had slipped out of his hands; that he was nothing more than a pensioner on her bounty a slave to her wishes, and a fetcher and carrier at her command, and he resigned himself quietly to his fate, as better men have done before.

Chapter Three

I think that the reader will agree with me that my mother showed in her conduct great strength of character. She had been compelled to marry a man whom she despised, and to whom she felt herself superior in every respect; she had done so to save her reputation. That she had been in error is true but situation and opportunity had conspired against her; and when she found out the pride and selfishness of the man to whom she was devoted, and for whom she had sacrificed so much,—when her ears were wounded by proposals from his lips that she should take such a step to avoid the scandal arising from their intimacy—when at the moment that he made such a proposition, and the veil fell down and revealed the heart of man in its selfishness, it is not to be wondered that, with bitter tears, arising from wounded love, anger, and despair at her hopeless position, she consented. After having lost all she valued, what did she care for the future? It was but one sacrifice more to make, one more proof of her devotion and obedience. But there are few women who, like my mother, would have recovered her position to the extent that she did. Had she not shown such determination, had she consented to have accompanied her husband to the barracks, and have mixed up with the other wives of the men, she would have gradually sunk down to their level; to this she could not consent. Having once freed herself from her thraldom, he immediately sunk down to his level, as she rose up to a position in which, if she could not ensure more than civility and protection, she was at all events secure from insult and ill-treatment.

Such was the state of affairs when I had arrived at the important age of six years, a comic-looking, laughing urchin, petted by the officers, and as fall of mischief as a tree full of monkeys. My mother's business had so much increased, that, about a year previous to this date, she had found it necessary to have some one to assist her, and had decided upon sending for her sister Amelia to live with her. It was, however, necessary to obtain her mother's consent. My grandmother had never seen my mother since the interview which she had had with her at Madeline Hall shortly after her marriage with Ben the marine. Latterly, however, they had corresponded; for my mother, who was too independent to seek her mother when she was merely the wife of a private marine, now that she was in flourishing circumstances had first tendered the olive branch, which had been accepted, as soon as my grandmother found that she was virtually separated from her husband. As my grandmother found it rather lonely at the isolated house in which she resided, and Amelia declared herself bored to death, it was at last agreed that my grandmother and my aunt Amelia should both come and take up their residence with my mother, and in due time they arrived. Milly, as my aunt was called, was three years younger than my mother, very pretty and as smart as her sister, perhaps a little more demure in her look, but with more mischief in her disposition. My grandmother was a cross, spiteful old woman; she was very large in her person, but very respectable in her appearance. I need not say that Miss Amelia did not lessen the attraction at the circulating library, which after her arrival was even more frequented by the officers than before.

My aunt Milly was very soon as fond of me as I was of mischief; indeed it is not to be wondered at, for I was a type of the latter. I soon loved her better than my mother, for she encouraged me in all my tricks. My mother looked grave, and occasionally scolded me; my grandmother slapped me hard and rated me continually; but reproof or correction from the two latter were of no avail; and the former, when she wished to play any trick which she dared not do herself, employed me as her agent; so that I obtained the whole credit for what were her inventions, and I may safely add, underwent the whole blame and punishment; but that I cared nothing for; her caresses, cakes, and sugar-plums, added to my natural propensity, more than repaid me for the occasional severe rebukes of my mother, and the vindictive blows I received from the long fingers of my worthy grandmother. Moreover, the officers took much notice of me, and it must be admitted, that, although I positively refused to learn my letters, I was a very forward child. My great patron was a Captain Bridgeman, a very thin, elegantly-made man, who was continually performing feats of address and activity; occasionally I would escape with him and go down to the mess, remain at dinner, drink toasts, and, standing on the mess-table, sing two or three comic songs which he had taught me. I sometimes returned a little merry with the bumpers, which made my mother very angry, my old grandmother to hold up her hands, and look at the ceiling through her spectacles, and my aunt Milly as merry as myself. Before I was eight years old, I had become so notorious, that any prank played in the town, any trick undiscovered, was invariably laid to my account; and many were the applications made to my mother for indemnification for broken windows and other damage done, too often, I grant, with good reason, but very often when I had been perfectly innocent of the misdemeanour. At last I was voted a common nuisance, and every one, except my mother and my aunt Milly, declared that it was high time that I went to school.

One evening the whole of the family were seated at tea in the back parlour. I was sitting very quietly and demurely in a corner, a sure sign that I was in mischief, and so indeed I was (for I was putting a little gunpowder into my grandmother's snuff-box, which I had purloined, just that she might "smell powder," as they say at sea, without danger of life or limb), when the old woman addressed my mother—

"Bella, is that boy never going to school? it will be the ruin of him."

"What will be the ruin of him, mother?" rejoined my aunt Milly; "going to school?"

"Hold your nonsense, child: you are as bad as the boy himself," replied granny. "Boys are never ruined by education; girls sometimes are."

Whether my mother thought that this was an innuendo reflecting upon any portion of her own life, I cannot tell; but she replied very tartly.

"You're none the worse for my education, mother, or you would not be sitting here."

"Very true, child," replied granny; "but recollect, neither would you have married a marine—a private marine, Bella, while your sister looks up to the officers. Ay," continued the old woman, leaving off her knitting and looking at her daughter, "and is likely to get one, too, if she plays her cards well—that Lieutenant Flat can't keep out of the shop." (My granny having at this moment given me an opportunity to replace her snuff-box, I did not fail to profit by it; and as I perceived her knitting-pin had dropped on the floor, I stuck it into the skirt of her gown behind, so that whenever she looked for it, it was certain ever to be behind her.)

"Mr Flat is of a very respectable family, I hear say," continued my grandmother.

"And a great fool," interrupted my mother. "I hope Milly won't listen to him."

"He's an officer," replied my granny, "not a private."

"Well, mother, I prefer my private marine, for I can make him do as I please; if he's a private, I'm commanding officer, and intend so to be as long as I live."

"Well, well, Bella, let us say no more on the old score; but that boy must go to school. Deary me, I have dropped my needle."

My grandmother rose, and turned round and round, looking for her needle, which, strange to say, she could not find; she opened her snuff-box, and took a pinch to clear her optics. "Deary me, why, what's the matter with my snuff? and where can that needle be? Child, come and look for the needle; don't be sticking there in that corner."

I thought proper to obey the order and pretended to be very diligent in my search. Catching aunt Milly's eye, I pointed to the knitting-needle sticking in the hind skirts of my grandmother's gown, and then was down on my knees again, while my aunt held her handkerchief to her mouth to check her laughter.

A minute afterwards, Ben the marine first tapped gently, and then opened the door and came in; for at that late hour the officers were all at dinner, and the shop empty.

"There are three parcels of books for you to take," said my mother; "but you've plenty of time, so take down the tea-things, and get your tea in the kitchen before you go."

"You haven't got a shilling, Bella, about you? I want some 'baccy," said Ben, in his quiet way.

"Yes, here's a shilling, Ben; but don't drink too much beer," replied my mother.

"Deary me, what can have become of my needle?" exclaimed my grandmother, turning round.

"Here it is, ma'am," said Ben, who perceived it sticking in her skirt. "That's Percival's work, I'll answer for it."

My granny received the needle from Ben, and then turned to me: "You good-for-nothing boy; so you put the needle there, did you? pretending to look for it all the while; you shall go to school, sir, that you shall."

"You said a needle, granny; I was looking for a needle: you didn't say your knitting-pin; I could have told you where that was."

"Yes, yes, those who hide can find; to school you go, or I'll not stay in the house."

Ben took the tea-tray out of the room. He had been well drilled in and out of barracks.

"I'll go down in the kitchen to father," cried I, for I was tired of sitting still.

"No, you won't, sir," said my mother, "you naughty boy; the kitchen is not the place for you, and if ever I hear of you smoking a pipe again—"

"Captain Bridgeman smokes," replied I.

"Yes, sir, he smokes cigars; but a child like you must not smoke a pipe."

"And now come here, sir," said my granny, who had the lid of her snuff-box off, and held it open in her hand; "what have you been doing with my snuff?"

"Why, granny, have I had your snuff-box the whole day?"

"How should I know?—a boy like you, with every finger a fish-hook; I do believe you have; I only wish I could find you out. I had fresh snuff this morning."

"Perhaps they made a mistake at the shop, mother," said aunt Milly; "they are very careless."

"Well, I can't tell: I must have some more; I can't take this."

"Throw it in the fire, granny," said I; "and I'll run with the box and get it full again."

"Well, I suppose it's the best thing I can do," replied the old woman, who went to the grate, and leaning over, poured the snuff out on the live coals. The result was a loud explosion and a volume of smoke, which burst out of the grate into her face—the dinner and lappets singed, her spectacles lifted from her nose, and her face as black as a sweep's. The old woman screamed, and threw herself back; in so doing, she fell over the chair upon which she had been sitting, and, somehow or another, tripped me up, and lay with all her weight upon me. I had been just attempting to make my escape during the confusion—for my mother and Milly were equally frightened—when I found myself completely smothered by the weight of my now almost senseless granny, and, as I have before mentioned, she was a very corpulent woman. Had I been in any other position I should not have suffered so much; but I had unfortunately fallen flat on my back, and was now lying with my face upwards, pressed upon by the broadest part of the old woman's body; my nose was flattened, and my breath completely stopped. How long my granny might have remained there groaning I cannot tell; probably, as I was somewhat a spoiled child before this, it might have ended in her completely finishing me; but she was roused up from her state of half syncope by a vigorous attack from my teeth, which, in the agony of suffocation, I used with preternatural force of jaw from one so young. I bit right through everything she had on, and as my senses were fast departing, my teeth actually met with my convulsive efforts. My granny, roused by the extreme pain, rolled over on her side, and then it was that my mother and aunt, who supposed that I had made my escape from the room, discovered me lifeless, and black in the face. They ran to me, but I still held on with my teeth, nor could I be separated from my now screaming relative, until the admission of fresh air, and a plentiful sprinkling of cold water brought me to my senses, when I was laid on the sofa utterly exhausted. It certainly was a narrow escape, and it may be said that the "biter was nearly bit." As for my granny, she recovered her fright and her legs, but she did not recover her temper; she could not sit down without a pillow on the chair for many days, and, although little was said to me in consequence of the danger I had incurred, yet there was an evident abhorrence of me on the part of the old woman, a quiet manner about my mother, and a want of her usual hilarity on the part of my aunt, which were to me a foreboding of something unpleasant. A few days brought to light what was the result of various whisperings and consultations. It was on a fine Monday morning, that Ben made his appearance at an unusually early hour; my cap was put on my head, my cloak over my shoulders; Ben took me by the hand, having a covered basket in the other, and I was led away like a lamb to the butcher. As I went out there was a tear in the eyes of my aunt Milly, a melancholy over the countenance of my mother, and a twinkling expression of satisfaction in my grandmother's eyes, which even her spectacles could not conceal from me: the fact was, my grandmother had triumphed, and I was going to school.

Chapter Four

As soon as I was clear of the door, I looked up into Ben's face and said, "Father, where are we going?"

"Well," replied he, "I am going to take you to school."

"School! What am I going to school for?" replied I.

"For biting your grandmother, I expect, in the first place, and to get a little learning, and a good deal of flogging, if what they say is true! I never was at school myself."

"What do you learn, and why are you flogged?"

"You learn to read, and to write, and to count; I can't do either—more's the pity; and you are flogged, because without flogging, little boys can't learn anything."

This was not a very satisfactory explanation. I made no further inquiries, and we continued our way in silence until we arrived at the school door; there was a terrible buzz inside. Ben tapped, the door opened, and a volume of hot air burst forth, all the fresh air having been consumed in repeating the fresh lessons for the day. Ben walked up between the forms, and introduced me to the schoolmaster, whose name was Mr Thadeus O'Gallagher, a poor scholar from Ireland, who had set up an establishment at half-a-guinea a quarter for day scholars; he was reckoned a very severe master, and the children were kept in better order in his school than in any other establishment of the kind in the town; and I presume that my granny had made inquiries to that effect, as there were one or two schools of the same kind much nearer to my mother's house. Ben, who probably had a great respect for learning, in consequence of his having none himself, gave a military salute to Mr O'Gallagher, saying, with his hand still to his hat, "A new boy, sir, come to school."

"Oh, by the powers! don't I know him?" cried Mr O'Gallagher; "it's the young gentleman who bit a hole in his grandmother; Master Keene, as they call him. Keen teeth, at all events. Lave him with me; and that's his dinner in the basket I presume; lave that too. He'll soon be a good boy, or it will end in a blow-up."

Ben put down the basket, turned on his heel, and left the schoolroom, and me standing by the throne of my future pedagogue—I say throne, because he had not a desk, as schoolmasters generally have, but a sort of square daïs, about eighteen inches high, on which was placed another oblong superstructure of the same height, serving him for a seat; both parts were covered with some patched and torn old drugget, and upon subsequent examination I found them to consist of three old claret cases without covers, which he had probably picked up very cheap; two of them turned upside down, so as to form the lower square, and the third placed in the same way upside down, upon the two lower. Mr O'Gallagher sat in great dignity upon the upper one, with his feet on the lower, being thus sufficiently raised upon an eminence to command a view of the whole of his pupils in every part of the school. He was not a tall man, but very square built, with carroty hair and very bushy red whiskers; to me he appeared a most formidable person, especially when he opened his large mouth and displayed his teeth, when I was reminded of the sign of the Red Lion close to my mother's house. I certainly never had been before so much awed during my short existence as I was with the appearance of my pedagogue, who sat before me somewhat in the fashion of a Roman tribune, holding in his hand a short round ruler, as if it were his truncheon of authority. I had not been a minute in the school before I observed him to raise his arm; away went the ruler whizzing through the air, until it hit the skull of the lad for whom it was intended at the other end of the schoolroom. The boy, who had been talking to his neighbour, rubbed his poll, and whined.

"Why don't you bring back my ruler, you spalpeen?" said Mr O'Gallagher. "Be quick, Johnny Target, or it will end in a blow-up."

The boy, who was not a little confused with the blow, sufficiently recovered his senses to obey the order, and whimpering as he came up, returned the ruler to the hands of Mr O'Gallagher.

"That tongue of yours will get you into more trouble than it will business, I expect, Johnny Target; it's an unruly member, and requires a constant ruler over it." Johnny Target rubbed his head and said nothing.

"Master Keene," said he, after a short pause, "did you see what a tundering tump on the head that boy got just now, and do you know what it was for?"

"No," replied I.

"Where's your manners, you animal? No 'If you plase.' For the future, you must not forget to say, 'No, sir,' or, 'No, Mr O'Gallagher.' D'ye mind me—now say yes—what?"

"Yes, what!"

"Yes, what! you little ignoramus; say 'yes, Mr O'Gallagher,' and recollect, as the parish clerk says, 'this is the last time of asking.'"

"Yes, Mr O'Gallagher."

"Ah! now you see, there's nothing like coming to school—you've learn't manners already; and now, to go back again, as to why Johnny Target had the rap on the head, which brought tears into his eyes? I'll just tell you, it was for talking; you see, the first thing for a boy to learn, is to hold his tongue, and that shall be your lesson for the day; you'll just sit down there and if you say one word during the whole time you are in the school, it will end in a blow-up; that means, on the present occasion, that I'll skin you alive as they do the eels, which being rather keen work, will just suit your constitution." I had wit enough to feel assured that Mr O'Gallagher was not to be trifled with, so I took my seat, and amused myself with listening to the various lessons which the boys came up to say, and the divers punishments inflicted—few escaped. At last, the hour of recreation and dinner arrived, the boys were dismissed, each seized his basket, containing his provisions, or ran home to get his meal with his parents: I found myself sitting in the school-room *tête-à-tête* with Mr O'Gallagher, and feeling very well inclined for my dinner I cast a wistful eye at my basket, but I said nothing; Mr O'Gallagher, who appeared to have been in thought, at last said—

"Mr Keene, you may now go out of school, and scream till you're hoarse, just to make up for lost time."

"May I take my dinner, sir?" inquired I.

"Is it your dinner you mane?—to be sure you may; but, first, I'll just look into the basket and its contents; for you see, Mr Keene, there's some victuals that don't agree with larning; and if you eat them, you'll not be fit for your work when your play-hours are over. What's easy of digestion will do; but what's bad for little boys' stomachs may get you into a scrape, and then it will end in a blow-up; that is, you'll have a taste of the ferrule or the rod—two assistants of mine, to whom I've not yet had the pleasure of introducing you—all in good time. If what I've hear of you be true, you and they will be better acquainted afore long."

Mr O'Gallagher then examined the contents of my basket; my aunt Milly had taken care that I should be well provided: there was a large paper of beef sandwiches, a piece of bread and cheese, and three or four slices of seed-cake. Mr O'Gallagher opened all the packages, and, after a pause, said—

"Now, Master Keene, d'ye think you would ever guess how I came by all my larning, and what I fed upon when it was pumped into me? Then I'll tell you; it was dry bread, with a little bit of cheese when I could get it, and that wasn't often. Bread and cheese is the food to make a scholar of ye; and mayhap one slice of the cake mayn't much interfere, so take them, and run away to the play-ground as fast as you can; and, d'ye hear me, Master Keene, recollect your grace before meat—'For what we have received, the Lord make us truly thankful.' Now, off wid you. The rest of the contents are confiscated for my sole use, and your particular benefit."

Mr O'Gallagher grinned as he finished his oration; and he looked so much like a wild beast, that I was glad to be off as fast as I could. I turned round as I went out of the door, and perceived that the sandwiches were disappearing with wonderful rapidity; but I caught his eye: it was like that of a tiger's at his meal, and I was off at redoubled speed.

Chapter Five

As soon as I gained the play-ground, which was, in fact, nothing more than a small piece of waste land, to which we had no more claim than any other people, I sat down by a post, and commenced my dinner off what Mr O'Gallagher had thought proper to leave me. I was afraid of him, it is true, for his severity to the other boys convinced me that he would have little mercy upon me, if I dared to thwart him; but indignation soon began to obtain the mastery over my fears and I began to consider if I could not be even with him for his barefaced robbery of my dinner; and then I reflected whether it would not be better to allow him to take my food if I found out that by so doing he treated me well; and I resolved, at all events, to delay a little. The hour of play was now over, and a bell summoned us all to school; I went in with the others and took my seat where Mr O'Gallagher had before desired me.

As soon as all was silent, my pedagogue beckoned me to him.

"Now, Mr Keene," said he, "you'll be so good as to lend me your ears— that is, to listen while I talk to you a little bit. D'ye know how many roads there are to larning? Hold your tongue. I ask you because I know you don't know, and because I'm going to tell you. There are exactly three roads: the first is the eye, my jewel; and if a lad has a sharp eye like yours, it's a great deal that will get into his head by that road; you'll know a thing when you see it again, although you mayn't know your own father—that's a secret only known to your mother. The second road to larning, young spalpeen, is the ear; and if you mind all people say, and hear all you can, you'll gain a great many truths and just ten times as much more in the shape of lies. You see the wheat and the chaff will come together, and you must pick the latter out of the former at any seasonable future opportunity. Now we come to the third road to larning, which is quite a different sort of road; because, you see, the two first give us little trouble, and we trot along almost whether we will or not: the third and grand road is the head itself, which requires the eye and the ear to help it; and two other assistants, which we call memory and application; so you see we have the visual, then the aural, and then the mental roads—three hard words which you don't understand, and which I shan't take the trouble to explain to such an animal as you are; for I never throw away pearls to swine, as the saying is. Now, then, Mr Keene, we must come to another part of our history. As there are three roads to larning, so there are three manes or implements by which boys are stimulated to larn: the first is the ruler, which you saw me shy at the thick skull of Johnny Target, and you see'd what a rap it gave him; well, then, the second is the ferrule—a thing you never heard of, perhaps; but I'll show it you; here it is," continued Mr O'Gallagher, producing a sort of flat wooden ladle with a hole in the centre of it. "The ruler is for the head, as you have seen; the ferrule is for the hand. You have seen me use the ruler; now I'll show you what I do with the ferrule."

"You Tommy Goskin, come here, sir."

Tommy Goskin put down his book, and came up to his master with a good deal of doubt in his countenance.

"Tommy Goskin, you didn't say your lesson well to-day."

"Yes I did, Mr O'Gallagher," replied Tommy, "you said I did yourself."

"Well then, sir, you didn't say it well yesterday," continued Mr O'Gallagher.

"Yes I did, sir," replied the boy, whimpering.

"And is it you who dares to contradict me?" cried Mr O'Gallagher; "at all events, you won't say it well to-morrow, so hold out your right hand."

Poor Tommy held it out, and roared lustily at the first blow, wringing his fingers with the smart.

"Now your left hand, sir; fair play is a jewel; always carry the dish even."

Tommy received a blow on his left hand, which was followed up with similar demonstrations of suffering.

"There sir you may go now," said Mr O'Gallagher, "and mind you don't do it again; or else there'll be a blow-up. And now Master Keene, we come to the third and last, which is the birch for the tail—here it is—have you ever had a taste?"

"No, sir," replied I.

"Well, then, you have that pleasure to come, and come it will, I don't doubt, if you and I are a few days longer acquainted. Let me see—"

Here Mr O'Gallagher looked round the school, as if to find a culprit; but the boys, aware of what was going on, kept their eyes so attentively to their books, that he could not discover one; at last he singled out a fat chubby lad.

"Walter Puddock, come here, sir."

Walter Puddock came accordingly; evidently he gave himself up for lost.

"Walter Puddock, I just have been telling Master Keene that you're the best Latin scholar in the whole school. Now, sir, don't make me out to be a liar—do me credit,—or, by the blood of the O'Gallaghers, I'll flog ye till you're as thin as a herring. What's the Latin for a cocked hat, as the Roman gentlemen wore with their *togeys*?"

Walter Puddock hesitated a few seconds, and then, without venturing a word of remonstrance, let down his trousers.

"See now the guilty tief, he knows what's coming. Shame upon you, Walter Puddock, to disgrace your preceptor so, and make him tell a lie to young Master Keene. Where's Phil Mooney? Come along, sir, and hoist Walter Puddock: it's no larning that I can drive into you, Phil, but it's sartain sure that by your manes I drive a little into the other boys."

Walter Puddock, as soon as he was on the back of Phil Mooney, received a dozen cuts with the rod, well laid on. He bore it without flinching, although the tears rolled down his cheeks.

"There, Walter Puddock, I told you it would end in a blow-up; go to your dictionary, you dirty blackguard, and do more credit to your education and superior instruction from a certain person who shall be nameless."

Mr O'Gallagher laid the rod on one side, and then continued—

"Now, Master Keene, I've just shown you the three roads to larning, and also the three implements to persuade little boys to larn; if you don't travel very fast by the three first, why you will be followed up very smartly by the three last—a nod's as good as a wink to a blind horse, any day; and one thing more, you little spalpeen, mind that there's more mustard to the sandwiches to-morrow, or else it will end in a blow-up. Now you've got the whole theory of the art of tuition, Master Keene; please the pigs, we'll commence with the practice to-morrow."

My worthy pedagogue did not address me any more during that day; the school broke up at five, and I made haste home, thinking over all that had passed in the school-room.

My granny and mother were both anxious to know what had passed; the first hoped that I had been flogged, the second that I had not, but I refused to communicate. I assumed a haughty, indifferent air, for I was angry with my mother, and as for my grandmother, I hated her. Aunt Milly, however, when we were alone, did not question me in vain. I told her all that had passed; she bade me be of good heart, and that I should not be ill-treated if she could help it.

I replied, that if I were ill-treated, I would have my revenge somehow or another. I then went down to the barracks, to the rooms of Captain Bridgeman, and told him what had occurred. He advised me to laugh at the ruler, the ferrule, and the rod. He pointed out to me the necessity of my going to school and learning to read and write, at the same time was very indignant at the conduct of Mr O'Gallagher, and told me to resist in every way any injustice or tyranny, and that I should be sure of his support and assistance, provided that I did pay attention to my studies.

Fortified by the advice and protection of my two great friends, I made up my mind that I would learn as fast as I could, but if treated ill, that I would die a martyr, rather than yield to oppression; at all events, I would, if possible, play Mr O'Gallagher a trick for every flogging or punishment I received; and with this laudable resolution I was soon fast asleep, too fast even to dream.

Chapter Six

When my aunt Milly called me in the morning, that I might be up and have my breakfast in time for school, I felt as if two years had passed over my head during the last twenty-four hours. I had never witnessed tyranny until the day before, and my blood was heated with indignation: I felt myself capable of anything and everything.

My anger was about as great towards my mother and grandmother for having sent me to such a place, as it was against Mr O'Gallagher. Instead of going up and kissing my mother, I paid no attention to either her or my grandmother, much to the mortification of the former and surprise of the latter, who said, in a very cross manner, "Where's your manners, child? why don't you say good morning?"

"Because I have not been long enough at school to learn manners, granny."

"Come and kiss me before you go, my child," said my mother.

"No, mother; you have sent me to school to be beat, and I never will kiss you again."

"Naughty, good-for-nothing boy!" exclaimed my granny; "what a bad heart you must have."

"No, that he has not," cried my aunt Milly. "Sister should have inquired what sort of a school it was before she sent him."

"I made every inquiry," replied my granny; "he can't play tricks there."

"Won't I?" cried I, "but I will; and not only there but here. I'll be even with you all; yes, I'll be even with you, granny, if I die for it."

"Why, you audacious wretch, I've great a mind to—"

"I dare say you have, but recollect I can bite; you'd better be quiet, granny, or, as the master says, 'it will end in a blow-up.'"

"Only hear the little wretch," said my granny, lifting up her hands; "I shall see you hanged yet, you ungrateful child."

"I'm not ungrateful," replied I, throwing my arms round Milly's neck, and kissing her with fervour; "I can love those who love me."

"Then you don't love me?" said my mother, reproachfully.

"I did yesterday, but I don't now; but it's time for me to go, aunt; is my basket ready? I don't want father to take me to school, I can do without him, and when I don't choose to go any more, I won't; recollect that, mother." So saying, I seized my basket and quitted the room. There was a long consultation, I found, after my departure: my mother, when my aunt had informed her of Mr O'Gallagher's conduct, wished to remove me instantly; my grandmother insisted upon it that there was not a word of truth in what I had said, and threatened that if I did not remain at that very school, she would leave Chatham, and take my aunt with her. As my mother could not part with aunt Milly, the consequence was, that my grandmother gained the day.

I arrived in good time, and took my seat near my master. I preferred doing this, as I had had a long conversation with Captain Bridgeman who told me that although Mr O'Gallagher had put the ruler down as punishment Number 1, the ferrule Number 2, and the birch as Number 3, and of course they were considered to be worse as the number rose, that he considered it to be the very contrary, as he had had them all well applied when he was at school; he ordered me, therefore, never to hold out my hand to the ferrule, by which refusal I should, of course, be flogged; but he assured me that the birch, especially when it is given often, was a mere nothing. Now I considered that the surest way to avoid the ruler was to sit close to my master, who could then have no pretence for sending it at my head; the fact was I had determined to save the more noble portions of my body, and leave Mr O'Gallagher to do what he pleased with the other: to do him justice, he lost no time.

"Come here, Mr Keene," said he, "where's your manners? why don't you say good morning to your preceptor? Can you read at all?"

"No, sir."

"D'ye know your letters?"

"Some of them—I think I do, sir."

"Some of them—I suppose about two out of six-and-twenty. It's particular attention that's been paid to your education, I perceive; you've nothing to unlearn anyhow, that's something. Now, sir, do you think that a classical scholar and a gentleman born, like me, is to demane myself by hearing you puzzle at the alphabet? You're quite mistaken, Mr Keene, you must gain your first elements second-hand; so where's Thimothy Ruddel? You, Timothy Ruddel, you'll just teach this young Master Keene his whole alphabet, and take care, at the same time, that you know your own lessons, or it will end in a blow-up; and you, Master Keene, if you have not larnt your whole alphabet perfect by dinner time, why you'll have a small taste of Number 2, just as a hint to what's coming next. Go along, you little ignorant blackguard; and you, Timothy Ruddel, look out for a taste of Number 3, if you don't larn him and yourself all at once, and at the same time."

I was very well pleased with this arrangement; I had resolved to learn, and I was doubly stimulated to learn now, to save poor Timothy Ruddel from an unjust punishment.

In the three hours I was quite perfect, and Timothy Ruddel, who was called up before me, was also able to say his lesson without a blunder very much to the disappointment of Mr O'Gallagher, who observed, "So you've slipped through my fingers, have you, this time, Master Timothy? Never mind, I'll have you yet; and, moreover, there's Master Keene to go through the fiery furnace." Just before dinner time I was called up; with my memory of many of the letters, and the assistance I had received from Timothy Ruddel, I felt very confident.

"What letter's that, sir?" said Mr O'Gallagher.

"A B C D E."

"You little blackguard, I'll dodge you; you think to escape, you?"

"V, X, P, O."

Much to Mr O'Gallagher's surprise I said them all without one mistake. Instead of commendation I received abuse. "By all the powers," exclaimed my pedagogue, "but everything seems to go wrong to-day; my hand has been completely idle; this will never do; didn't you tell me, Mr Keene, that you didn't know your letters?"

"I said I knew some of them, sir."

"If my memory is correct, Mr Keene, you told me that you knew two out of twenty-six."

"No, sir, you said that."

"That's just as much as to tell me, your preceptor, a classical scholar, and a Milesian gentleman to boot, that I lie, for which I intend to have satisfaction, Mr Keene, I assure you. You're guilty in two counts, as they say at the Old Bailey, where you'll be called up to some of these days, as sure as you stand there; one count is in telling me a lie, in saying you did not know your alphabet, when it's quite clear that you did; and, secondly, in giving me the lie, by stating that I said what you said. You thought to escape me, but you're mistaken, Mr Keene; so now, if you please, we will just have a taste of Number 2. Hould out your hand, Mr Keene: d'ye hear me sir? hould out your hand."

But this I positively refused to do. "You won't, won't you? Well, then, we must increase the punishment for our contempt of court, and at once commence with Number 3, which we intended to reserve till to-morrow. Come along, Phil Mooney, there's fresh mate for you to carry, and come out Number 3, here's fresh ground for you to travel over."

Phil Mooney and the birch soon made their appearance: I was hoisted by the one and scourged by the other.

The first taste of the birch is anything but agreeable; I could only compare it to the dropping of molten lead. I tried all I could to prevent crying out, but it was impossible, and at last I roared like a mad bull; and I was as mad as a bull, and as dangerous. Could I have picked up any weapon at the moment that I was dropped from the shoulders of Phil Mooney, it would have gone hard with Mr O'Gallagher. My rage was greater than my agony. I stood when I had been landed, my chest heaving, my teeth set fast, and my apparel still in disorder. The school was dismissed, and I was left alone with the savage pedagogue, who immediately took up my basket, and began to rummage the contents.

"Make yourself decent, Mr Keene, and don't be shocking my modesty, and taking away my appetite. Did you mention the mustard, as I desired you? Upon my faith, but you're a nice boy and do justice to the representations of your grandmother, and when you see her you may tell her that I did not forget the promise she exacted from me. You forgot all about the mustard, you little blackguard. If Phil Mooney was here I would give you another taste to freshen your memory for to-morrow; however, to-morrow will do as well, if the mistake's not corrected. Here, take your victuals, and good appetite to you, you little monster of iniquity."

Mr O'Gallagher tossed me some bread but this time reserved the cheese for his own eating. I had adjusted my dress, and I therefore left the school-room. I could not sit down without pain, so I leant against a post: the bread remained in my hand untouched; had it been the greatest delicacy in the world I could not have tasted a morsel; I was giddy from excess of feeling, my thoughts were rapidly chasing each other when I heard a voice close to me; I looked round, it was Walter Puddock, who had been flogged the day before.

"Never mind, Keene," said he, kindly; "it hurts at first, but the more you get it the less you care for it; I don't mind it a bit now; I cries, because he goes on flogging till you do, and it's no use having more than you can help."

"I didn't deserve it," replied I.

"That's not necessary; you'll get it, as we all do, whether you deserve it or not."

"Well, I'll try to deserve it in future," replied I, clenching my fist; "I'll be even with him."

"Why, what can you do?"

"Wait a little, and you'll see," said I, walking away, for an idea had come into my head which I wished to follow up.

Soon afterwards the bell rang, and we returned to the schoolroom. I was put under the tuition of another boy, and took care to learn my lesson. Whether it was that he was tired with the exercise, for he flogged and ferruled a dozen during that afternoon, or that he thought that my morning dose had been sufficient, I received no more punishment on that day.

Chapter Seven

As soon as school was dismissed, I went straight to the rooms of Captain Bridgeman, and told him how I had been treated. As soon as he heard it, he exclaimed, "This is really too bad; I will go with you, and I will consult with your aunt Amelia."

It so happened that aunt Milly was alone in the shop when we arrived, and after a detail of what had passed, she told Captain Bridgeman that my grandmother had put me to that school out of feelings of ill-will for the tricks I had played, and had threatened that if I were removed she would leave Chatham and take her away with her. My mother required assistance in the shop, and was afraid to affront my grandmother, who was a very dictatorial, positive old woman, and would certainly keep her resolution; but that rather than I should be treated in such a barbarous manner she would insist upon my mother taking me away, or would herself leave the place.

"It would never do for you to leave us, Miss Amelia," replied Captain Bridgeman, "there are but few attractions in this place, and we cannot spare you; the whole corps would go into deep mourning."

"I don't want to leave the school," interrupted I; "I would not leave it till I am revenged, for all the world. Now, I'll tell you what I want to do—and do it I will, if he cuts me to pieces. He eats my sandwiches, and tells me if there's not more mustard to-morrow, he'll flog me. He shall have plenty of mustard, but he shall have something else. What can I put into the sandwiches, so as to half kill him?"

"Not a bad idea, my little Percival," said Captain Bridgeman; "I'll just ask the doctor how much calomel a man may take without a coroner's inquest being required."

"Yes, that will do nicely," said my aunt; "I'll take care he shall have mustard enough not to perceive it."

"Well, I'll go to the barracks and be back directly," said Captain Bridgeman.

"And I'm ready for the flogging as soon as the sandwiches are down his throat," replied I, laughing, "I don't care a fig for it."

Captain Bridgeman soon returned with forty grains of calomel, which he delivered into aunt Milly's hands. "That is as much as we dare give the strongest man without running great danger; we'll try the effect of that upon him, and if he don't improve, I think I shall go up to the school myself and threaten him."

"As for that," replied aunt Milly, "I'm sure that sister, if she hears what's going on, as she cannot take Percival away, will order her husband, Ben, to go up and thrash him."

"Not a bad idea, Miss Amelia, we'll try that if we find it necessary; at all events, we'll see who can persecute most."

"Granny has told him to treat me ill," said I, "that's very clear, from what he said; never mind, I'll make her sorry for it."

"Oh Percival! you must not do anything to granny," said aunt Milly, looking very archly; "I must not hear anything of the kind."

The next morning I set off with a full conviction that I should be flogged before night, and notwithstanding that, as full of joy as if I was going to the fair.

The morning passed as usual; I said my lesson, but not very well; I was thinking so much of my anticipated revenge, that I could not pay attention to my teacher, who was, as usual, one of the boys.

"Master Keene," said Mr O'Gallagher, "we'll let the account stand over till the evening, and then I'll give you a receipt in full; I may have one or two lines to add to it before the sun goes down; you'll not escape me this time, anyhow."

The boys went out at the dinner hour, leaving me, as before, to wait for my basket, after the tyrant had helped himself. I stood by him in silence while he was rummaging its contents.

"Now, Mr Keene, I'll see if you've remembered my particular injunction relative to the mustard."

"I told my aunt to put more mustard, sir," replied I, humbly, "it she that cuts the sandwiches."

"Well, then, if your aunt has not complied with your request, see if I don't flay you alive, you little imp of abomination."

The sandwiches were pulled out of the paper and tasted. "Down on your knees, Mr Keene, and thank all the blessed saints that your aunt has saved you from at least one-half of what I intended to administer to you this blessed afternoon, for she has doubled the mustard, you tief," said Mr O'Gallagher, speaking with his mouth as full as it could hold. Down went sandwich after sandwich, until they had all disappeared. Oh! what joy was mine! I could have tossed up my cap and leapt in the air. Having received the bread and cheese, for he permitted me to have the latter on this occasion I went out and enjoyed my meal, delighted with Mr O'Gallagher's having fallen into the trap I had laid for him.

The bell summoned us in, and all went on as usual for the first two hours, when I thought Mr O'Gallagher changed countenance and looked very pale. He continued, however, to hear the lessons, until at last I perceived him pass his hand up and down and across his stomach, as if he had had a twinge; a few minutes afterwards, he compressed his thick lips, and then put his hands to his abdomen.

"Ah! he begins to feel it now," thought I; and sure enough he did; for the pain increased so rapidly that he lost all patience, and vented his feelings by beating with his ruler, on the heads of the whole class of boys standing up before him, till one or two dropped down, stunned with the blows. At last he dropped the ruler, and, pressing both hands to his stomach, he rolled himself backwards and forwards, and then twisted and distorted his legs till he could bear the pain no longer; and he gave vent to a tremendous Irish howl—grinning and grinding his teeth for a few seconds, and then howling again, writhing and twisting in evident agony—while the perspiration ran off his forehead.

"Och! murder! I'm poisoned sure. Lord save my sinful soul! Oh—oh—oh! eh—eh—eh! mercy, mercy, mercy, mercy, mercy! Oh holy St. Patrick! I'm kilt entirely:"—and so subdued was he at last by the pain, that he burst out into a flood of tears, crying and roaring like a child.

Again the paroxysms came on—"Murder, murder, murder!" shrieked the wretch at the highest pitch of his voice, so that he was heard at some distance, and some of the neighbours came in to inquire what was the matter.

Mr O'Gallagher was now in a fainting state, and leaning against the table, he could merely say in a low voice, "A doctor—quick—a doctor."

The neighbours perceiving how ill he was, led him out of the school-rooms into his own apartment, one going for a doctor, and the others telling the boys they might all go home, a notice of which they gladly availed themselves.

I need hardly say, that I made all the haste I could to communicate the successful result of my trick to Milly and Captain Bridgeman. The medical man who was summoned, gave Mr O'Gallagher some very active medicine, which assisted to rid him of the calomel; of his having taken which, of course, the medical man was ignorant. The violence of the dose was, however, so great, and left him in such a state, that Mr O'Gallagher could not leave his room for three days, nor resume his seat in the school until a week had elapsed, during which I remained at home plotting still further mischief.

Mr O'Gallagher resumed his occupations, and I was again sent off to school. When I entered the school-room I found him looking very pale and cadaverous; as soon as he saw me his lips were drawn apart, and he showed his large white teeth, reminding me of the grinning of a hyena; he did not, however, say anything to me. My studies were resumed; I said my lesson perfectly, but was fully prepared for punishment. I was, however, agreeably disappointed; he did not punish either me or any of the other boys.

I afterwards found out the reason was, that, although necessity compelled him to re-open his school as soon as he could, he was too weak to undergo the fatigue of following up his favourite diversion.

When the dinner-hour arrived, and the boys were dismissed, I waited patiently to see what he would do with my basket, which stood beside him. "Take your basket, and eat your dinner, Master Keene," said he, walking out of the school-room into his own apartments. I could not help saying, "Won't you have the sandwiches, sir?"

He turned round and gave me a look so penetrating and so diabolical, that I felt sure that he knew to whom he had been indebted for his late severe illness.

From this day forward Mr O'G never interfered with the contents of my basket and I had my dinner all to myself. The shock which had been given to his constitution was so great, that for three or four months he may be said to have crawled to his school room, and I really began to think that the affair would turn out more serious than was intended; but gradually he regained his strength, and as he recovered his vigour, so did he resume his severity.

But I was a great gainer during the three or four months of quiet which reigned during Mr O'Gallagher's convalescence. Since I have been grown up, I have often thought, and am indeed confirmed in my opinion, that we lose rather than gain by being educated at too early an age. Commence with one child at three years, and with another at seven years old, and in ten years, the one whose brain was left fallow even till seven years old, will be quite as far, if not further advanced, than the child whose intellect was prematurely forced at the earlier age; this is a fact which I have since seen proved in many instances, and it certainly was corroborated in mine.

In six months I could read and write very fairly, and had commenced arithmetic; true, I was stimulated on by the advice of Captain Bridgeman, the love I bore my aunt Milly, and the hatred which I had for my master, which made me resolve that I would not deserve punishment on that score.

It was in May that I administered the dose to Mr O'Gallagher; in September he was quite well again, and the ruler, the ferrule, and the rod, were triumphantly at work. It is useless to say how often I was punished, for it was every day; always once, sometimes twice; I became completely callous to it, nay, laughed at it, but my mind was ever at work upon some mischief, in the way of retaliation.

I put little pancakes of cobblers' wax on Mr O'Gallagher's throne, and he had the pleasure of finding himself stuck fast by the breeches when he rose up to punish. I anointed the handle of the ferrule and rod with bird-lime; put dead cats under the claret cases, which composed his seat of authority, so that the smell would drive him distracted before he found it out. I drew up with a squirt, all the ink which was in the inkstands fixed in the writing-desks, so as not to be taken out of the sockets, and made good the deficiency with water, which put him to no little expense.

I once made him almost frantic, by rubbing his handkerchief which always laid by his side, and with which he was accustomed to wipe his face every five minutes (for he was profuse in his perspiration), with what is called cow-itch: not being aware of what was the cause, he wiped his face more and more, until he was as red as a peony, and the itching became intolerable.

On such occasions he never inquired who was the party, but called me and Phil Mooney. I, on the other hand, never said a word in way of expostulation. I took my flogging, which was as severe as he could give it, as a matter of course, quite satisfied with the exchange.

As Walter Puddock had told me, and, as I have no doubt, the Eton boys will confirm, after a certain quantity of flagellations, the skin becomes so hard as to make the punishment almost a matter of indifference and so I found it. So passed the time until the month of November, when I was fully enabled to pay off my worthy pedagogue for all that I was indebted to him.

Chapter Eight

The boys had been saving up all their money to purchase fireworks for the celebrated 5th of November—a day on which it was said that certain persons, finding it impossible to reform the Lords and Commons, had determined to get rid of them at once: why they have not been in similar danger every year since the first attempt was made, I know not; certain it is, that it is the only reform measure that can ever be effectual. Guy Fawkes and his confederates, whether Popish or Protestant, from the disregard of human life, certainly proved themselves the founders of a party, still existing, whose motto is, "Measures and not Men."

But to proceed: Mr O'Gallagher had never before attempted to interfere with the vested rights of urchins on that day; being, however, in a most particular irascible humour, instead of a whole, he made it known that there would only be a half, holiday, and we were consequently all called in for morning lessons instead of carrying about, as we had intended, the effigy of the only true reformer that ever existed in this country.

This made us all very sulky and discontented in the first place, and our anxiety to get out of school was so great, that the lessons were not very perfect in the second. The ferrule and rod were called out and liberally administered; but what was our horror and dismay when Mr O'Gallagher, about an hour before dinner, announced to us that all the squibs and crackers, with which our pockets were crammed, were to be given up immediately; and that, as we had not said our lessons well, there would be no half-holiday, the whole school were in mute despair.

One by one were the boys summoned up to the throne of Mr O'Gallagher, and their pockets searched by Phil Mooney, who emptied them of their pyrotechnical contents, all of which were deposited on the daïs of Mr O'Gallagher's throne, which, I have before observed, was composed of two empty claret cases turned upside down, surmounted by another, on which Mr O'Gallagher sat, all three covered with old green baize.

By the time that the whole school had been rifled, the heap of fireworks was very considerable, and Mr O'Gallagher, to prevent any of them being recovered by the boys, lifted up the claret case on which he sat, and which was on the top of the other two, and desired Phil Mooney to put them all underneath it. This was done; Mr O'Gallagher resumed his seat, and the lessons continued till the dinner hour arrived, but, alas! not the half-holiday or the fireworks.

The boys went out; some mournful, some angry, some sulky, some frightened; a few, a very few, declaiming against such injustice.

I was in a rage; my blood boiled; at last my invention came to my aid, and, without considering the consequences, I determined how to act.

As it was an hour and a half before school would commence, I hastened home, and, having spent all my money, begged aunt Milly to give me some; she gave me a shilling, and with that I bought as much gunpowder as I could procure, more than a quarter of a pound.

I then returned to the school, looked into the school-room, and found it empty; I quickly raised up the claret case, under which the fireworks had been placed, put the powder under it, leaving only sufficient for a very small train, which would not be perceived in the green baize covering; having so done, I left the school-room immediately, and rejoined my companions. I had a piece of touch-wood, as all the boys had, to let off their fireworks with, and this I lighted and left in a corner until the bell should summons us into school.

Oh! how my heart beat when I heard the sound, so full was I of anxiety lest my project should fail.

Once more we were all assembled. Mr O'Gallagher surveying, with the smile of a demon, the unhappy and disappointed faces of the boys, was again perched upon his throne, the rod on one side, the ferrule on the other, and the ruler, that dreaded truncheon of command, clenched in his broad fist.

I had the touchwood lighted and concealed in my hand; gradually I moved downwards, until at last, unperceived by Mr O'Gallagher, I was behind him, and close to my train of gunpowder. I gave one look to ascertain if he had observed me; his eye was roving over the school for some delinquent to throw his ruler at; fearful that he might turn round to me, I no longer hesitated, and the touchwood was applied to the train.

Ignorant as I was of the force of gunpowder, it was with astonishment, mingled with horror, that I beheld, in a second, the claret case rise up as if it had wings, and Mr O'Gallagher thrown up to the ceiling enveloped in a cloud of smoke, the crackers and squibs fizzing and banging, while the boys in the school uttered a yell of consternation and fear as they rushed from from the explosion, and afterwards, tumbling over one another, made their escape from the school-room.

The windows had all been blown out with a terrible crash, and the whole school-room was now covered by the smoke. There I stood in silent dismay at the mischief which I had done. The squibs and crackers had not, however, all finished popping, before I heard the howling of Mr O'Gallagher, who had fallen down upon the centre school-room table.

I was still in the school-room, half-suffocated, yet not moving away from where I stood, when the neighbours, who had been alarmed by the explosion and the cries of the boys, rushed in, and perceiving only me and Mr O'Gallagher, who still howled, they caught hold of us both, and bore us out in their arms. It was high time, for the school-room was now on fire, and in a few minutes more the flames burst out of the windows, while volumes of smoke forced through the door and soon afterwards the roof.

The engines were sent for, but before they could arrive, or water be procured, the whole tenement was so enveloped in flames that it could not be saved. In an hour, the *locale* of our misery was reduced to ashes. They had put me on my legs as soon as we got clear of the school-room, to ascertain whether I was hurt, and finding that I was not, they left me.

I never shall forget what my sensations were, when I beheld the flames and volumes of smoke bursting out; the hurry, and bustle, and confusion outside; the working of the engines, the troops marched up from the barracks, the crowd of people assembled, and the ceaseless mingling of tongues from every quarter; and all this is my doing, thought I—mine—all mine.

I felt delighted that I had no partner or confederate; I could, at all events, keep my own secret. I did, however, feel some anxiety as to Mr O'Gallagher, for, much as I detested him, I certainly had no intention to kill him; so after a time, I made inquiries, and found that he was alive: and in no danger, although very much bruised and somewhat burnt.

No one could explain how the catastrophe occurred, further than that Mr O'Gallagher had collected all the squibs and crackers from the boys, and that they had exploded somehow or another—most people said that it served him right. My grandmother shook her head and said, "Yes, yes, gunpowder will go off, but—" and she looked at me—"it requires a match to be put to it." I looked up very innocently, but made no reply.

Mr O'Gallagher's favourite expression, to wit, "that it would end in a blow-up," proved, as far as his school was concerned, literally true. He had not the means of procuring another suitable tenement in Chatham, and as soon as he had recovered from the injuries he had received, he quitted the town.

It was not until he had left, that I ventured to make known to Captain Bridgeman, and my aunt Milly, the trifling share I had in the transaction; and they, perceiving the prudence of keeping my secret, desired me on no account to let it be known to any one else.

Chapter Nine

As soon as it was ascertained that Mr O'Gallagher was gone, my grandmother insisted upon my being sent to another school, and on this occasion my mother made the inquiries herself, and I was despatched to one much nearer home, and being treated well, not only played fewer tricks, but advanced rapidly in my education; so rapidly indeed, that my grandmother began to think that I was not so bad a boy as I used to be.

As she treated me more kindly, I felt less inclined to teaze her although the spirit of mischief was as undiminished as ever, and was shown in various ways.

I may as well here observe, that out of the many admirers of my aunt Milly, there were only two who appeared to be at all constant in their attention. One was Lieutenant Flat, who was positively smitten, and would have laid his pay and person at her feet, had he received anything like encouragement; but my aunt disliked him in the first place, and, moreover, had a very strong feeling towards Captain Bridgeman.

Mr Flat was certainly a very fine-looking soldier, being tall, erect, and well-made, but he was at the same time not over-brilliant; he was, as an officer, the very sort of person my father Ben was as a private.

But the other party, Captain Bridgeman, did not come forward; he appeared to be in doubt, and not at all able to make up his mind.

The fact was, that my mother being married to a private, made any match with the sister objectionable to the whole corps, as it would be derogatory that one sister should be the wife of a private, and the other of an officer. Ben would have been able to say, "My brother-in-law, the captain of my division," which would never have done; and this Captain Bridgeman felt, and therefore resisted, as well as he could, the inroads which my aunt's beauty and mirth had made into his heart. My aunt was exactly a person to suit Captain Bridgeman as a helpmate, had it not been for this unfortunate alliance of my mother's.

Lieutenant Flat was too stupid and indifferent to the opinion of the other officers, to care anything about what they thought; he would have married Milly long before, but my aunt, who had made up her mind to marry an officer, did not yet despair of obtaining the captain; and although she would not positively dismiss Lieutenant Flat, she merely kept him as a sort of reserve, to fall back upon when every other chance was gone.

I should like, if I possibly could, to give the reader some idea of my mother's circulating-library and sort of universal commodity shop: it was a low-windowed building, one story high, but running a long way back, where it was joined to a small parlour, in which we generally sat during the day, as it was convenient in case of company or customers, the little parlour having a glass door, which permitted us to look into the shop.

In the front windows, on one side, were all the varieties of tapers, sealing-wax, inkstands, and every kind of stationery, backed by children's books, leather writing-cases, prints, caricatures, and Tonbridge ware. In the other windows were ribbons, caps, gloves, scarfs, needles, and other little articles in demand by ladies, and which they required independent of their milliners.

At the entrance were sticks and canes; on the counter a case of gold and more moderate-priced trinkets. On the shelves of the millinery side were boxes of gloves, ribbons, buttons, etcetera. On the opposite side, perfumes, cigars, toothbrushes, combs, scented soaps, and other requisites for the toilet.

About ten feet on each side of the shop was occupied with the above articles; the remainder of the shelves were reserved for the circulating-library.

At the back of the shop were some seats round a small table, on which was laid the newspaper of the day, and on each side of the parlour-door were hoops, bats, balls, traps, skittles, and a variety of toys for children.

My mother usually attended to the millinery, and my aunt Milly to what might be termed the gentlemen's side of the shop; the remainder of the goods and circulating-library were in the hands of both.

There were few hours of the day in which the chairs at the counter and round the table were not taken possession of by some one or another, either reading the paper or a book, or talking, to pass away the time. In fact, it was a sort of rendezvous, where all who met knew each other, and where the idle of our own sex used to repair to get rid of their time. Captain Bridgeman and Mr Flat were certainly the two most constantly to be found there, although few of the marine officers were a day without paying us a visit.

Such was the *locale*; to describe the company will be more difficult, but I will attempt it.

My mother, remarkably nicely dressed, is busy opening a parcel of new books just arrived. My aunt Milly behind the counter, on the gentlemen's side, pretending to be working upon a piece of muslin about five inches square. Mr Flat sitting near the table, fallen back in his chair, apparently watching the flies on the ceiling. Captain Bridgeman, a very good-looking man, very slight, but extremely active, is sitting at the counter opposite to where my aunt is standing, a small black cane, with a silver head to it, in his hand, and his gloves peculiarly clean and well-fitting. He has an eye as sharp as an eagle's, a slight hook to his nose, thin lips, and very white teeth; his countenance is as full of energy and fire as that of lieutenant Flat is heavy and unmeaning.

"Miss Amelia, if I may take the liberty," said Captain Bridgeman, pointing with his cane to the bit of muslin she is employed upon; "what are you making? it's too small for any part of a lady's dress."

"It is quite large enough for a cuff, Captain Bridgeman."

"A cuff; then you are making a cuff, I presume?"

"Indeed she is not, Captain Bridgeman," replies my mother; "it is only to keep herself out of mischief. She spoils a bit like that every week. And that's why it is so small, Captain Bridgeman; it would be a pity to spoil a larger piece."

"I really was not aware that such a mere trifle would keep you out of mischief," said the captain.

"You know," replied Aunt Milly, "that idleness is the root of all evil, Captain Bridgeman."

"Flat, do you hear that?" says Captain Bridgeman.

"What?" replies Flat.

"That idleness is the root of all evil; what an evil-disposed person you must be."

"I was thinking," replied Flat.

"I suspect it's only lately you've taken to that. Who or what were you thinking about?"

"Well, I believe I was thinking how long it would be before dinner was ready."

"That's very rude, Mr Flat; you might have said that you were thinking about me," replied my aunt.

"Well, so I was at first, and then I began to think of dinner-time."

"Don't be offended, Miss Amelia; Flat pays you a great compliment in dividing his attentions; but I really wish to know why ladies will spoil muslin in such a predetermined manner. Will you explain that, Mrs Keene?"

"Yes, Captain Bridgeman: a piece of work is very valuable to a woman, especially when she finds herself in company with gentlemen like you. It saves her from looking down, or looking at you, when you are talking nonsense; it prevents your reading in her eyes what is passing in her mind, or discovering what effect your words may have upon her; it saves much awkwardness, and very often a blush; sometimes a woman hardly knows which way to look; sometimes she may look any way but the right. Now a bit of muslin with a needle is a remedy for all that, for she can look down at her work, and not look up till she thinks it advisable."

"I thank you for your explanation, madam; I shall always take it as a great compliment if I see a lady very busy at work when I'm conversing, with her."

"But you may flatter yourself, Captain Bridgeman," replied my mother; "the attention to her work may arise from perfect indifference, or from positive annoyance. It saves the trouble of making an effort to be polite."

"And pray, may I inquire, Miss Amelia, what feeling may cause your particular attention to your work at this present moment?"

"Perhaps in either case to preserve my self-possession," replied Amelia; "or perhaps, Captain Bridgeman, I may prefer looking at a piece of muslin to looking at a marine officer."

"That's not very flattering," replied the captain; "if you spoil the muslin, you're determined not to spoil me."

"The muslin is of little value," said Amelia, softly, walking to the other side of the shop, and turning over the books.

"Mr Flat," said my mother, "your subscription to the library is out last month; I presume I can put your name down again?"

"Well, I don't know; I never read a book," replied Mr Flat, yawning.

"That's not at all necessary, Mr Flat," said my mother; "in most businesses there are sleeping partners; besides, if you don't read, you come here to talk, which is a greater enjoyment still, and luxuries must be paid for."

"Well, I'll try another quarter," replied Mr Flat, "and then—"

"And then what?" said my aunt Milly, smiling.

"Well, I don't know," says Flat. "Is that clock of yours right, Mrs Keene?"

"It is; but I am fearful that your thoughts run faster than the clock, Mr Flat; you are thinking of the dress-bugle for dinner."

"No, I was not."

"Then you were thinking of yourself?"

"No, I wasn't, Mrs Keene," said Flat, rising, and walking out of the shop.

"I'll tell you," said he, turning round as he went out, "what I was thinking of, Mrs Keene; not of myself,—I was thinking of my bull pup."

My mother burst out a laughing as the lieutenant disappeared. "I was not far wrong when I said he was thinking of himself," said she, "for a *calf* is a sort of *bull pup*."

At this sally Captain Bridgeman laughed, and danced about the shop; at last he said, "Poor Flat! Miss Amelia, he's desperately in love with you."

"That's more than I am with him," said Amelia, calmly.

Here two ladies came in.

Captain Bridgeman made a most polite bow. "I trust Mrs Handbell is quite well and Miss Handbell—I hardly need ask the question with the charming colour you have?"

"Captain Bridgeman, you appear to live in this library; I wonder Mrs Keene don't take you into partnership."

"If I were not honoured with the custom of Mrs Handbell and other ladies; I fear that my shop would have little attraction for gentlemen," replied my mother, with a courtesy.

"Mrs Keene is quite correct in her surmise, Miss Handbell," said Captain Bridgeman, "now that I have seen you, I shall not think my morning thrown away."

"If report says true, Captain Bridgeman," replied Mrs Handbell, "you would be quite as often here, even if no ladies were to be customers of Mrs Keene. Mrs Keene, have you any of that narrow French ribbon left?"

"I think I have, madam; it was off this piece, was it not?"

"Yes; but I really don't know exactly how much I require; perhaps you will measure it and allow me to return what is left?"

"Certainly, madam; will you take it with you, or shall I send it?"

"I wish for it directly; will you be very long in measuring it, for I ought to be home now?"

"Perhaps you'll have the kindness to measure what you take off yourself, madam," replied my mother, "and then you need not wait."

"You put confidence in me, I observe, Mrs Keene," replied Mrs Handbell; "well, I will do you justice."

My mother smiled most graciously, put the piece of ribbon in paper, and handed it to Mrs Handbell, who, bowing to Captain Bridgeman, quitted the shop.

"I wonder whether you would trust me in that way?" said Captain Bridgeman to my mother.

"I don't think I should; Amelia says you will help yourself to cigars and that she is sure you cheat when you count them."

"Does she really say that? Well, I did think that if there was any one who would have upheld my character, it would have been Miss Amelia."

"Perhaps, Captain Bridgeman, she is getting tired of so doing."

"Or tired of me, Mrs Keene, which would be worse still. Here comes a fair young lady—Miss Evans, if I mistake not; I believe she is a good customer to your library?"

"She reads a great deal, and is therefore only a customer to the library."

"Ladies who are fond of reading are seldom fond of working."

"Good morning Miss Evans," said Captain Bridgeman; "you come for more food for the mind, I presume?" (Miss Evans gave a bob, and turned to my mother.)

"Have you anything new, Mrs Keene? I have brought back the three volumes of Godolphin."

"Yes, miss, I have some books down to-day."

While Miss Evans was selecting from the new books, enter Mr Jones, Mr Smith, and Mr Claville, of the marine corps, for cigars. Amelia comes out to attend them—they purchase a few articles, and are talking very loud, when three more ladies enter the shop, all for books.

It being now about three o'clock, the customers and loungers come in fast. Captain Bridgeman saunters away in company with his brother officers; other parties enter, who are succeeded by fresh claimants for books or the other articles to be procured in the repository.

This demand continues till about five o'clock, when the library becomes empty; I come home from school, my father slinks in from barracks, and my mother and sister return to the back parlour, where they find my grandmother, as usual, very busy with her knitting.

Such is a fair sample of what took place at our shop every succeeding day. My mother made few bad debts, and rapidly added to her savings. My aunt Milly still balancing between the certainty of Lieutenant Flat and the chance of Captain Bridgeman, and I dividing my time and talents between learning and contriving mischief.

Chapter Ten

About six months after I had blown up the school of Mr O'Gallagher, the company to which my father Ben belonged was ordered afloat again, and shortly afterwards sailed for the East Indies, in the Redoubtable, 74. That my mother was very much pleased at his departure, I do not scruple to assert; but whether she ever analysed her feelings, I cannot pretend to say; I rather think that all she wished was, that the chapter of accidents would prevent Ben's reappearance, as she was ashamed of him as a husband, and felt that he was an obstacle to her sister's advancement.

So one fine day Ben wished us all good bye; my mother was very generous to him, as she could well afford to be. I rather think that Ben himself was not sorry to go, for, stupid as he was, he must have felt what a cypher he had become, being treated, not only by my mother, but by everybody else, even by me, as a sort of upper servant.

It so happened, that about a month after Ben's departure, Captain Delmar had, through the interest of his uncle, Lord de Versely, been appointed to a ship which was lying in the Medway, and he came down to Chatham to join her. He had no idea that my mother was there, for he had lost sight of her altogether, and had it not been for me, might very probably have left the town without having made the discovery.

Among other amusements, I had a great partiality for a certain bull pup, mentioned by Lieutenant Flat in the former chapter, and which he had made me a present of; the pup was now grown up, and I had taught it many tricks; but the one which afforded me most amusement (of course, at other people's expense) was, that I had made out of oakum a sham pigtail, about a foot and a half long, very strong and think, with an iron hook at the upper end of it.

The sham tail I could easily hook on to the collar of any one's coat from behind, without their perceiving it; and Bob had been instructed by me, whenever I told him to fetch it (and not before), to jump up at the tail wherever it might be, and hang on to it with all the tenacity of the race.

As it may be supposed, this was a great source of mirth in the barracks; it was considered a good joke, and was much applauded by Captain

Bridgeman; but it was not considered a good joke out of the barracks; and many an old woman had I already frightened almost out of her senses, by affixing the tail to any portion of the back part of her dress.

It so happened, that one afternoon, as I was cruising about with Bob at my heels, I perceived the newly-arrived Captain Delmar, in all the pomp of pride of full uniform, parading down the street with a little middy at his heels; and I thought to myself, "Law! how I should like to hang my tail to his fine coat, if I only dared;" the impulse had become so strong, that I actually had pulled up my pinafore and disengaged the tail ready for any opportunity, but I was afraid that the middy would see me.

Captain Delmar had passed close to me, the middy at his heels was passing, and I thought all chance was gone, when, suddenly, Captain Delmar turned short round and addressed the little officer, asking him whether he had brought the order-book with him? The middy touched his hat, and said, "No;" upon which Captain Delmar began to inflict a most serious lecture upon the lad for forgetting what he had forgotten himself, and I again passed by.

This was an opportunity I could not resist; while the captain and middy were so well employed giving and receiving I fixed my oakum tail to the collar of the Captain's gold-laced coat, and then walked over to the other side of the street with Bob at my heels.

The middy being duly admonished, Captain Delmar turned round again and resumed his way; upon which I called Bob, who was quite as ready for the fun as I was, and pointing to the captain, said, "Fetch it, Bob." My companion cleared the street in three or four bounds, and in a few seconds afterwards made a spring up the back of Captain Delmar, and seizing the tail, hung by it with his teeth, shaking it with all his might as he hung in the air.

Captain Delmar was, to use a sailor's term, completely taken aback; indeed he was nearly capsized by the unexpected assault. For a short time he could not discover what it was; at last, by turning his head over his shoulder and putting his hand behind him, he discovered who his assailant was.

Just at that time, I called out "Mad dog! mad dog!" and Captain Delmar, hearing those alarming words, became dreadfully frightened; his cocked hat dropped from his head, and he took to his heels as fast as he could, running down the street, with Bob clinging behind him.

The first open door he perceived was that of my mother's library; he burst in, nearly upsetting Captain Bridgeman, who was seated at the counter, talking to Aunt Milly, crying out "Help! help!" As he turned round, his sword became entangled between his legs, tripped him up, and he fell on the floor. This unhooked the tail, and Bob galloped out of the shop, bearing his prize to me, who, with the little middy, remained in the street convulsed with laughter. Bob delivered up the tail, which I again concealed under my pinafore, and then with a demure face ventured to walk towards my mother's house, and, going in at the back door, put Master Bob in the wash-house out of the way; the little middy who had picked up the captain's hat, giving me a wink as I passed him, as much as to say, I won't inform against you.

In the meantime Captain Delmar had been assisted to his legs by Captain Bridgeman, who well knew who had played the trick, and who, as well as Aunt Milly, had great difficulty in controlling his mirth.

"Merciful heaven! what was it? Was the animal mad? Has it bitten me?" exclaimed Captain Delmar, falling back in his chair, in which he had been seated by Captain Bridgeman.

"I really do not know," replied Captain Bridgeman; "but you are not hurt, sir, apparently, nor indeed is your coat torn."

"What dog—whose dog can it be?—it must be shot immediately—I shall give orders—I shall report the case to the admiral. May I ask for a glass of water? Oh, Mr Dott! you're there, sir; how came you to allow that dog to fasten himself on my back in that way?"

"If you please," said the middy, presenting his cocked hat to the captain, "I did draw my dirk to kill him, but you ran away so fast that I couldn't catch you."

"Very well, sir, you may go down to the boat and wait for orders," replied the captain.

At this moment my mother, who had been dressing herself, made her first appearance, coming out of the back parlour with a glass of water, which aunt Milly had gone in for. Perceiving a gold-laced captain, she advanced all smiles and courtesies, until she looked in his face, and then she gave a scream, and dropped the tumbler on the floor, much to the surprise of Captain Bridgeman, and also of aunt Milly, who, not having been at the Hall, was not acquainted with the person of Captain Delmar.

Just at this moment in came I, looking as demure as if, as the saying is, "butter would not melt in my mouth," and certainly as much astonished as the rest at my mother's embarrassment; but she soon recovered herself, and asked Captain Delmar if he would condescend to repose himself a little in the back parlour. When my mother let the tumbler fall, the captain had looked her full in the face and recognised her, and, in a low voice, said,

"Excessively strange,—so very unexpected!" He then rose up from the chair and followed my mother into the back room.

"Who can it be?" said Aunt Milly to Captain Bridgeman, in a low tone.

"I suppose it must be the new captain appointed to the Calliope. I read his name in the papers,—the Honourable Captain Delmar."

"It must be him," replied Milly; "for my sister was brought up by his aunt, Mrs Delmar; no wonder she was surprised at meeting him so suddenly. Percival, you naughty boy," continued Milly, shaking her finger at me, "it was all your doing."

"Oh, Aunt Milly! you should have seen him run," replied I, laughing at the thought.

"I'd recommend you not to play with post captains," said Captain Bridgeman, "or you may get worse than you give. Mercy on us!" exclaimed he, looking at me full in the face.

"What's the matter?" said aunt Milly.

Captain Bridgeman leant over the counter, and I heard him whisper, "Did you ever see such a likeness as between the lad and Captain Delmar?"

Milly blushed a little, nodded her head, and smiled, as she turned away. Captain Bridgeman appeared to be afterwards in a brown study; he tapped his boot with his cane, and did not speak.

About a quarter of an hour passed, during which Captain Delmar remained with my mother in the parlour, when she opened the door, and beckoned me to come in. I did so not without some degree of anxiety, for I was afraid that I had been discovered: but this doubt was soon removed; Captain Delmar did me the honour to shake hands with me, and then patted my head saying, he hoped I was a good boy, which, being compelled to be my own trumpeter, I very modestly declared that I was. My mother, who was standing up behind, lifted up her eyes at my barefaced assertion. Captain Delmar then shook hands with my mother, intimating his intention of paying her another visit very soon, and again patting me on the head, quitted the parlour, and went away through the shop.

As soon as Captain Delmar was gone, my mother turned round, and said, "You naughty, mischievous boy, to play such pranks. I'll have that dog killed, without you promise me never to do so again."

"Do what again, mother?"

"None of your pretended innocence with me. I've been told of the pigtail that Bob pulls at. That's all very well at the barracks with the marines, sir, but do you know *who* it is that you have been playing that trick to?"

"No mother, I don't. Who is he?"

"Who is he, you undutiful child? why, he's—he's the Honourable Captain Delmar."

"Well, what of that?" replied I. "He's a naval captain, ain't he?"

"Yes; but he's the nephew of the lady who brought me up and educated me. It was he that made the match between me and our father: so if it had not been for him, child, you never would have been born."

"Oh that's it," replied I. "Well, mother, if it had not been for me, he'd never have come into the shop, and found you."

"But, my child, we must be serious; you must be very respectful to Captain Delmar, and play no tricks with him; for you may see him very often, and, perhaps, he will take a fancy to you; and if he does, he may do you a great deal of good, and bring you forward in the world; so promise me."

"Well, mother, I'll promise you I'll leave him alone if you wish it. Law, mother, you should have seen how the middy laughed at him; it was real fun to make a gallant captain run in the way he did."

"Go along, you mischievous animal, and recollect your promise to me," said my mother, as she went into the shop where she found that Captain Bridgeman, to whom she intended to explain how it was that she had dropped the tumbler of water, had gone away.

There was a great deal of consultation between my grandmother and my mother on that evening; my aunt and I were sent out to to take a walk, that we might not overhear what passed, and when we returned we found them still in close conversation.

Chapter Eleven

The Honourable Captain Delmar was now a frequent visitor to my mother, and a good customer to the library. He did, however, generally contrive that his visit should be paid late in the afternoon, just after the marine officers had retired to dress for dinner; for he was a very haughty personage, and did not think it proper for any officers of an inferior grade to come "between the wind and his nobility."

I cannot say that I was partial to him; indeed, his pomposity, as I considered it, was to me a source of ridicule and dislike. He took more notice of me than he did of anybody else; but he appeared to consider that his condescending patronage was all that was necessary; whereas, had he occasionally given me a half-crown I should have cherished better feelings towards him: not that I wanted money, for my mother supplied me very liberally, considering my age: but although you may coax and flatter a girl into loving you, you cannot a boy, who requires more substantial proofs of your good-will.

There were a great many remarks not very flattering to my mother, made behind her back, as to her former intimacy with Captain Delmar; for, somehow or another, there always is somebody who knows something, wherever doubts or surmises arise, and so it was in this case; but if people indulged in ill-natured remarks when she was not there, they did not in her presence; on the contrary, the friendship of so great a man as the Honourable Captain Delmar appeared rather to make my mother a person of more consequence.

She was continually pointing out to me the propriety of securing the good will of this great personage, and the more she did so, the more I felt inclined to do the reverse; indeed, I should have broke out into open mutiny, if it had not been for Captain Bridgeman, who sided with my mother, and when I went to him to propose playing another trick upon the noble captain, not only refused to aid me, but told me, if I ever thought of such a thing, he would never allow me to come to his rooms again.

"Why, what good can he do to me?" inquired I.

"He may advance you properly in life—who knows?—he may put you on the quarter-deck, and get you promoted in the service."

"What, make a middy of me?"

"Yes, and from a midshipman you may rise to be a post-captain, or admiral,—a much greater rank than I shall ever obtain," said Captain Bridgeman; "so take my advice, and do as your mother wishes; be very civil and respectful to Captain Delmar, and he may be as good as a father to you."

"That's not saying much," replied I, thinking of my father Ben; "I'd rather have two mothers than two fathers." And here the conversation ended.

I had contracted a great alliance with Mr Dott, the midshipman, who followed Captain Delmar about, just as Bob used to follow me, and generally remained in the shop or outside with me, when his captain called upon my mother. He was a little wag, as full of mischief as myself, and even his awe of his captain, which, as a youngster in the service, was excessive, would not prevent him from occasionally breaking out. My mother took great notice of him, and when he could obtain leave (which, indeed, she often asked for him), invited him to come to our house, when he became my companion during his stay; we would sally out together, and vie with each other in producing confusion and mirth at other people's expense; we became the abhorrence of every old fruit-woman and beggar in the vicinity.

Captain Delmar heard occasionally of my pranks, and looked very majestic and severe; but as I was not a midy, I cared little for his frowns. At last an opportunity offered which I could not resist; and, not daring to make known my scheme either to Captain Bridgeman or Aunt Milly, I confided it to Tommy Dott, the little middy, who, regardless of the consequences, joined me in it heart and soul.

The theatre had been opened at Chatham, and had met with indifferent success. I went there once with my aunt Milly, and twice with Mr Dott; I, therefore, knew my *locale* well. It appeared that one of the female performers, whose benefit was shortly to take place, was very anxious to obtain the patronage of Captain Delmar, and, with the usual tact of women, had applied to my mother in the most obsequious manner, requesting her to espouse her cause with the gallant captain.

My mother, pleased with the idea of becoming, as it were, a patroness under the rose, did so effectually exert her influence over the captain, that, in a day or two afterwards, play-bills were posted all over the town, announcing that the play of *The Stranger*, with the farce of *Raising the Wind*, would be performed on Friday evening, for the benefit of Miss Mortimer under the patronage of the Honourable Captain Delmar, and the officers of his Majesty's ship Calliope. Of course the grateful young lady sent my mother some tickets of admission, and two of them I reserved for Tommy Dott and myself.

Captain Delmar had made a large party of ladies, and of course all the officers of the ship attended: the house was as full as it could hold. My mother and aunt were there in a retired part of the boxes; Tommy Dott and I entered the theatre with them, and afterwards had gone up to what is, at the theatres at seaports, usually denominated the slips, that is, the sides of the theatre on the same range as the gallery. There was Captain Delmar with all his ladies and all his officers, occupying nearly the whole of the side of the dress circle below us, we having taken our position above him, so that we might not be observed.

The performance commenced. Miss Mortimer, as *Mrs Haller*, was very effective; and in the last scene was compelling the eyes of the company to water, when we thought we would produce a still greater effect.

We had purchased a pound of the finest Scotch snuff, which we had enclosed in two pasteboard cases, similar in form to those of squibs, only about six times the size, and holding half a pound of snuff each. Our object was, in doing this, that, by jerking it all out with a heave, we might at once throw it right into the centre of the theatre above, so that in its descent it might be fairly distributed among all parties.

There was no one in the slips with us, except midshipmen, and a description of people who would consider it a good joke, and never would peach if they perceived we were the culprits.

At a signal between us, just as *Mrs Haller* was giving a paper to her husband did we give our shower of snuff to the audience, jerking it right across the theatre. In a few minutes the effect was prodigious; Captain Delmar's party being right beneath us, probably received a greater share, for they commenced sneezing fast, then the boxes on the other side, the pit followed, and at last *Mr and Mrs Haller* and the *Stranger* were taken with such a fit of sneezing that they could no longer talk to each other.

The children were brought out to their parents to effect their reconciliation, but they did nothing but sneeze, poor things; and at last the uproar was tremendous, and the curtain was dropped, not to loud plaudits, but to loud sneezings from every part of the theatre.

Never was there anything so ludicrous; the manager sent officers up to discover the offenders but no one could tell who had played the trick; he then came before the curtain to make a speech upon the occasion, but, having sneezed seven or eight times, he was obliged to retire with his handkerchief to his nose; and the audience, finding it impossible to check the titillation of the olfactory nerves, abandoned the theatre as fast as they could, leaving the farce of *Raising the Wind* to be performed to empty beaches.

I hardly need say, that as soon as we had thrown the snuff, Mr Dott and I had gone down and taken our places very demurely in the box by the side of my mother, and appeared just as astonished, and indeed added as much as possible to the company of sneezers.

Captain Delmar was very furious at this want of respect of certain parties unknown, and had we been discovered, whatever might have been my fate, it would have gone hard with Tommy Dott; but we kept our own counsel, and escaped.

That I was suspected by Aunt Milly and Captain Bridgeman is certain, and my aunt taxed me with it, but I would not confess; my mother also had her suspicions, but as Captain Delmar had none, that was of no consequence.

The success of this trick was a great temptation to try another or two upon the noble captain. He was, however saved by the simple fact of H.M. ship Calliope being reported manned and ready for sea; orders were sent down for his going round to Portsmouth to await the commands of the Lords Commissioners of the Admiralty, and Captain Delmar came to pay his farewell visit.

The report from the schoolmaster had been very favourable and Captain Delmar then asked me, for the first time, if I would like to be a sailor. As Captain Bridgeman had advised me not to reject any good offer on the part of the honourable captain, I answered in the affirmative; whereupon the captain replied, that if I paid attention to my learning, in a year's time he would take me with him on board of his frigate.

He then patted my head, forgot to give me half a crown, and, shaking hands with my mother and aunt, quitted the house, followed by Tommy Dott, who, as he went away, turned and laughed his adieu.

I have not mentioned my grandmother lately. The fact is, that when Captain Delmar made his appearance, for some cause or another, which I could not comprehend, she declared her intention of going away and paying a visit to her old acquaintances at the Hall. She did so. As I afterwards found out from what I overheard, she had a very great aversion to the noble captain: but the cause of her aversion was never communicated to me. Soon after the sailing of the Calliope, she again made her appearance, took her old seat in the easy-chair, and resumed her eternal knitting as before.

Chapter Twelve

Another year of my existence passed rapidly away; I was nearly thirteen years old, a sturdy bold boy, well fitted for the naval profession, which I now considered decided upon, and began to be impatient to leave school, and wondered that we heard nothing of Captain Delmar, when news was received from another quarter.

One morning Captain Bridgeman came much earlier than usual, and with a very grave face put on especially for the occasion. I had not set off for school, and ran up to him; but he checked me, and said, "I must see your mother directly, I have very important news for her."

I went in to tell my mother, who requested Captain Bridgeman to come into the parlour, and not being aware of the nature of the communication, ordered Aunt Milly and me into the shop; we waited for some minutes, and then Captain Bridgeman made his appearance.

"What is the matter?" said Milly.

"Read this newspaper," said he; "there is a despatch from India, it will tell you all about it, and you can show it to your sister, when she is more composed."

Curious to know what the matter could be, I quitted the shop, and went into the parlour, where I saw my mother with her face buried in the sofa pillow, and apparently in great distress.

"What's the matter, mother?" said I.

"Oh! my child, my child!" replied my mother, wringing her hands, "you are an orphan, and I am a lonely widow."

"How's that?" said I.

"How's that?" said my grandmother, "why, are you such a fool, as not to understand that your father is dead?"

"Father's dead, is he?" replied I, "I'll go and tell Aunt Milly;" and away I went out of the parlour to Milly, whom I found reading the newspaper.

"Aunt," said I, "father's dead, only to think! I wonder how he died!"

"He was killed in action, dear," said my aunt; "look here, here is the account, and the list of killed and wounded. D'ye see your father's name— Benjamin Keene, marine?"

"Let me read all about it, Aunt Milly," replied I, taking the paper from her; and I was soon very busy with the account of the action.

My readers must not suppose that I had no feeling, because I showed none at my father's death; if they call to mind the humble position in which I had always seen my father, who dared not even intrude upon the presence of those with whom my mother and I were on familiar terms, and that he was ordered about just like a servant by my mother, who set me no example of fear or love for him, they will easily imagine that I felt less for his death than I should have for that of Captain Bridgeman, or many others with whom I was on intimate terms.

What did puzzle me was, that my mother should show so much feeling on the occasion. I did not know the world then, and that decency required a certain display of grief. Aunt Milly appeared to be very unconcerned about it, although, occasionally, she was in deep thought. I put down the paper as soon as I had read the despatch, and said to her, "Well, I suppose I must go to school now, aunt?"

"Oh no, dear," replied she, "you can't go to school for a few days now— it wouldn't be proper; you must remain at home and wait till you have put on mourning."

"I'm glad of that, at all events," replied I; "I wonder where Captain Delmar is, and why he don't send for me; I begin to hate school."

"I dare say it won't be long before you hear from him, dear," replied my aunt; "stay here and mind the shop, while I go in to your mother."

If the truth was told, I am afraid that the death of Ben was a source of congratulation to all parties who were then in the parlour. As for me, I was very glad to have a few days' holiday, being perfectly indifferent as to whether he was dead or alive.

When I went in I found them in consultation as to the mourning: my mother did not, in the first place, wish to make any a parade about a husband of whom she was ashamed; in the second, she did not like widow's weeds, and the unbecoming cap. So it was decided, as Ben had been dead six months, and if they had known it before they would have been in mourning for him all that time, that half-mourning was all that was requisite for them; and that, as for me, there was no reason for my going into mourning at all.

Three days after the intelligence, my mother re-appeared in the shop; the reason why she did not appear before was, that her dress was not ready—she looked very pretty indeed in half-mourning, so did my Aunt Milly; and the attentions of the marine corps, especially Captain Bridgeman and Lieutenant Flat, were more unremitting than ever.

It appeared that, as the death of Ben had removed the great difficulty to my aunt's being married to an officer, my grandmother had resolved to ascertain the intentions of Captain Bridgeman, and if she found that he cried off, to persuade Milly to consent to become Mrs Flat. Whether she consulted my mother or my aunt on this occasion, I cannot positively say, but I rather think not.

My mother and my aunt were walking out one evening, when Captain Bridgeman came in, and my grandmother, who remained in the shop whenever my mother and Milly went out together, which was very seldom, requested him to walk into the back parlour, desiring me to remain in the shop, and let her know if she was wanted.

Now when they went into the parlour, the door was left ajar, and, as I remained at the back part of the shop, I could not help over-hearing every word which was said; for my grandmother being very deaf, as most deaf people do, talked quite as loud as Captain Bridgeman was compelled to do, to make her hear him.

"I wish, Captain Bridgeman, as a friend, to ask your advice relative to my daughter Amelia," said the old lady. "Please to take a chair."

"If there is any opinion that I can offer on the subject, madam, I shall be most happy to give it," replied the captain, sitting down as requested.

"You see, my daughter Amelia has been well brought up, and carefully educated, as was, indeed, my daughter, Arabella, through the kindness of my old patron, Mrs Delmar, the aunt of the Honourable Captain Delmar, whom you have often met here, and who is heir to the title of de Versely; that is to say, his eldest brother has no children. I have been nearly fifty years in the family as a confidential, Captain Bridgeman; the old lord was very fond of my husband, who was his steward, but he died, poor man, a long while ago; I am sure it would have broken his heart, if, in his lifetime, my daughter Arabella had made the foolish marriage which she did with a private marine—however, what's done can't be helped, as the saying is— that's all over now."

"It was certainly a great pity that Mrs Keene should have been so foolish," replied Captain Bridgeman, "but, as you say, that is all over now."

"Yes; God's will be done, Captain Bridgeman; now you see, sir, that this marriage of Bella's has done no good to the prospects of her sister Amelia, who, nevertheless, is a good and pretty girl though I say it, who am her mother; and moreover, she will bring a pretty penny to her husband whoever he may be; for you see, Captain Bridgeman, my husband was not idle during the time that he was in the family of the Delmars, and as her sister is so well to do, why little Amelia will come into a greater share than she otherwise would—that is, if she marries well, and according to the wishes of her mother."

At this interesting part of the conversation Captain Bridgeman leant more earnestly towards my grandmother.

"A pretty penny, madam, you said; I never heard the expression before; what may a pretty penny mean?"

"It means, first and last, 4,000 pounds, Captain Bridgeman; part down, and the other when I die."

"Indeed," replied Captain Bridgeman; "I certainly never thought that Miss Amelia would ever have any fortune; indeed, she's too pretty and accomplished to require any."

"Now, sir," continued my grandmother, "the point on which I wish to consult you is this: you know that Lieutenant Flat is very often here, and for a long while has been very attentive to my daughter; he has, I believe, almost as much as proposed—that is, in his sort of way; but my daughter does not seem to care for him. Now, Captain Bridgeman, Mr Flat may not be very clever, but I believe him to be a very worthy young man; still one must be cautious, and what I wish to know before I interfere and persuade my daughter to marry him is, whether you think that Mr Flat is of a disposition which would make the marriage state a happy one; for you see, Captain Bridgeman, love before marriage is very apt to fly away, but love that comes after marriage will last out your life."

"Well, madam," replied the captain, "I will be candid with you; I do not think that a clever girl like Miss Amelia is likely to be happy as the wife of my good friend Mr Flat—still there is nothing against his character, madam; I believe him harmless—very harmless."

"He's a very fine-looking young man, Captain Bridgeman."

"Yes; nothing to be found fault with in his appearance."

"Very good-natured."

"Yes; he's not very quick in temper, or anything else; he's what we call a slow-coach."

"I hear he's a very correct officer, Captain Bridgeman."

"Yes; I am not aware that he has ever been under an arrest."

"Well, we cannot expect everything in this world; he is handsome, good-tempered, and a good officer—I cannot see why Amelia does not like him, particularly as her affections are not otherwise engaged. I am satisfied with the answer you have given, Captain Bridgeman, and now I shall point out to Amelia that I expect she will make up her mind to accept Mr Flat."

Here Captain Bridgeman hesitated.

"Indeed, madam, if her affections are not otherwise engaged—I say—are not engaged, madam, I do not think she could do better. Would, you like me to sound Miss Amelia on the subject?"

"Really, Captain Bridgeman, it is very kind of you; you may, perhaps, persuade her to listen to your friend Mr Flat."

"I will, at all events, ascertain her real sentiments, madam," said the captain, rising; "and, if you please, I will say farewell for the present."

As my grandmother anticipated, the scale, which had been so long balanced by Captain Bridgeman, was weighed down in favour of marriage by the death of my father Ben, and the unexpected fortune of 4,000 pounds.

The next day the captain proposed and was accepted, and six weeks from that date my aunt Milly became his wife.

The wedding was very gay: some people did sneer at the match, but where was there ever a match without a sneer? There are always and everywhere people to be found who will envy the happiness of others. Some talked about the private marine; this attack was met with the 4,000 pounds (or rather 8,000 pounds per annum, for rumour, as usual, had doubled the sum); others talked of the shop as *infra dig*; the set-off against which was, the education and beauty of the bride. One or two subs' wives declared that they would not visit Mrs Bridgeman; but when the colonel and his lady called to congratulate the new-married couple, and invited a large party in their own house to meet them, then then subs' wives left their cards as soon as they could.

In a few weeks all was right again: my mother would not give up her shop—it was too lucrative; but she was on more intimate terms with her customers; and when people found that, although her sister was a captain's lady, my mother had too much sense to be ashamed of her position; why they liked her the better. Indeed, as she was still very handsome, one or two of the marine officers, now that she was a widow, paid her very assiduous court; but my mother had no intention of entering again into the holy state—she preferred *State in quo*. She had no one to care for but me, and for me she continued her shop and library, although, I believe, she could have retired upon a comfortable independence, had she chosen so to do.

My mother, whatever she might have been when a girl, was now a strong-minded, clever woman. It must have been a painful thing for her to have made up her mind to allow me to go to sea; I was her only child, her only care; I believe she loved me dearly, although she was not so lavish of her caresses as my aunt Milly; but she perceived that it would be for my advantage that I should insure the patronage and protection of Captain Delmar, and she sacrificed self to my interest.

Chapter Thirteen

About a month after my aunt's marriage, a letter was received from Captain Delmar, who had arrived at Spithead, requesting my mother to send me to Portsmouth as soon as she could, and not go to the trouble or expense of fitting me out, as he would take that upon himself.

This was but short notice to give a fond mother, but there was no help for it; she returned an answer, that in three days from the date of the letter I should be there.

I was immediately summoned from school that she might see as much of me as possible before I went; and although she did not attempt to detain me, I perceived, very often, the tears run down her cheeks.

My grandmother thought proper to make me very long speeches every three or four hours, the substance of which may be comprehended in very few words—to wit, that I had been a very bad boy, and that I was little better now; that I had been spoiled by over-indulgence, and that it was lucky my aunt Milly was not so much with me; that on board a man-of-war I dare not play tricks, and that I would find it very different from being at home with my mother; that Captain Delmar was a very great man, and that I must be very respectful to him; that some day I should thank her very much for her being so kind to me; that she hoped I would behave well, and that if I did not, she hoped that I would get a good beating.

Such was the burden of her song, till at last I got very tired of it, and on the third evening I broke away from her, saying, "Law, granny how you do twaddle!" upon which she called me a good-for-nothing young blackguard, and felt positively sure that I should be hanged. The consequence was, that granny and I did not part good friends; and I sincerely hoped that when I had come back again, I should not find her above ground.

The next morning I bade farewell to my dear Aunt Milly and Captain Bridgeman, received a very ungracious salute from granny, who appeared to think, as she kissed me, that her lips were touching something poisonous, and set off with my mother in the coach to Portsmouth.

We arrived safe at Portsmouth, and my mother immediately took lodgings on the Common Hard at Portsea. The next day, having dressed herself with great care, with a very thick veil on her bonnet, my mother walked with me to the George Hotel, where Captain Delmar had taken up his quarters.

On my mother sending up her card, we were immediately ushered upstairs, and on entering the room found the Honourable Captain Delmar sitting down in full uniform—his sword, and hat, and numerous papers, lying on the table before him. On one side of the table stood a lieutenant, hat in hand; on the other, the captain's clerk, with papers for him to sign. My friend Tommy Dott was standing at the window, chasing a blue-bottle fly, for want of something better to do; and the steward was waiting for orders behind the captain's chair.

My mother, who had pulled down her veil, so that her face was not visible, made a slight courtesy to Captain Delmar, who rose up and advanced to receive her very graciously, requesting that she would be seated for a minute or two, till he had time to speak to her.

I have thought since, that my honourable captain had a mind to impress upon my mother the state and dignity of a captain in his Majesty's service, when in commission. He took no notice whatever of me. Tommy Dott gave me a wink of his eye from the window, and I returned the compliment by putting my tongue into my cheek; but the other parties were too much occupied with the captain to perceive our friendly recognition. Captain Delmar continued to give various orders, and after a time the officers attending were dismissed.

As soon as we were alone, my mother was addressed in, I thought, rather a pompous way, and very much in contrast with his previous politeness before others. Captain Delmar informed her that he should take me immediately under his protection, pay all my expenses, and, if I behaved well, advance me in the service.

At this announcement, my mother expressed a great deal of gratitude, and, shedding a few tears, said, that the boy would in future look up to him as a parent. To this speech Captain Delmar made no reply; but, changing the conversation, told her that he expected to sail in about three or four days, and that no time must be lost in fitting me out; that, all things considered, he thought it advisable that she should return at once to Chatham, and leave the boy with him as she could not know what was requisite for me, and would therefore be of no use.

At the idea of parting with me, my mother cried bitterly. Captain Delmar did then rise off his chair, and taking my mother by the hand speak to her a few words of consolation. My mother removed her handkerchief from her eyes and sighed deeply, saying to Captain Delmar, with an appealing look, "Oh! Captain Delmar, remember that for you I have indeed made great sacrifices; do not forget them, when you look at that boy, who is very dear to me."

"I will do him justice," replied the captain, somewhat affected, "but I must insist upon inviolable secrecy on your part; you must promise me that under any circumstances—"

"I have obeyed you for thirteen years," replied my mother; "I am not likely to forget my promise now; it is hard to part with him, but I leave him in the hands of—"

"You forget the boy is there," interrupted Captain Delmar; "take him away now; to-morrow morning I will send my coxswain for him, and you must go back to Chatham."

"God bless you, sir," replied my mother, weeping, as Captain Delmar shook her hand, and then we left the room. As we were walking back to our lodging, I inquired of my mother—"What's the secret between you and Captain Delmar, mother?"

"The secret, child! Oh, something which took place at the time I was living with his aunt, and which he does not wish to have known; so ask me no more questions about it."

After our return, my mother gave me a great deal of advice. She told me that, as I had lost my father Ben, I must now look upon Captain Delmar as a father to me; that Ben had been a faithful servant to the captain, and that she had been the same to Mrs Delmar, his aunt; and that was the reason why Captain Delmar was interested about me, and had promised to do so much for me; begging me to treat him with great respect and never venture to play him any tricks, or otherwise he would be highly offended, and send me home again; and then I should never rise to be an officer in his Majesty's service.

I cannot say the advice received the attention it deserved, for I felt more inclined to play tricks to my honourable captain than any person I ever met with; however, I appeared to consent, and, in return begged my mother to take care of my dog Bob, which she promised to do.

My mother cried a great deal during the night; the next morning she gave me five guineas as pocket-money, recommending me to be careful of it, and telling me I must look to Captain Delmar for my future supply. She tied up the little linen I had brought with me in a handkerchief, and shortly after the coxswain knocked at the door, and came upstairs to claim me for his Majesty's service.

"I'm come for the youngster, if you please, marm," said the coxswain, a fine, tall seaman, remarkably clean and neat in his dress.

My mother put her arms round me, and burst into tears.

"I beg your pardon, marm," said the coxswain, after standing silent about a minute, "but could not you *do the piping* after the youngster's gone? If I stay here long I shall be blowed up by the skipper, as sure as my name's Bob Cross."

"I will detain you but a few seconds longer," replied my mother; "I may never see him again."

"Well, that's a fact; my poor mother never did me," replied the coxswain.

This observation did not raise my mother's spirits. Another pause ensued, during which I was bedewed with her tears, when the coxswain approached again—

"I ax your pardon, marm; but if you know anything of Captain Delmar, you must know he's not a man to be played with, and you would not wish to get me into trouble. It's a hard thing to part with a child, I'm told, but it wouldn't help me if I said anything about your tears. If the captain were to go to the boat, and find me not there, he'd just say, 'What were my orders, sir?' and after that, you know, marm, there is not a word for me to say."

"Take him, then, my good man," replied my mother, pressing me convulsively to her heart—"take him; Heaven bless you, my dear child."

"Thanky, marm; that's kind of you," replied the coxswain. "Come, my little fellow, we'll soon make a man of you."

I once more pressed my lips to my poor mother's, and she resigned me to the coxswain, at the same time taking some silver off the table and putting it into his hand.

"Thanky, marm; that's kinder still, to think of another when you're in distress yourself; I shan't forget it. I'll look after the lad a bit for you, as sure as my name's Bob Cross."

My mother sank down on the sofa, with her handkerchief to her eyes.

Bob Cross caught up the bundle, and led me away. I was very melancholy, for I loved my mother, and could not bear to see her so distressed, and for some time we walked on without speaking.

The coxswain first broke the silence:— "What's your name, my little Trojan?" said he.

"Percival Keene."

"Well I'm blessed if I didn't think that you were one of the Delmar breed, by the cut of your jib; howsomever, it's a wise child that knows its own father."

"Father's dead," replied I.

"Dead! Well, fathers do die sometimes; you must get on how you can without one. I don't think fathers are of much use, for, you see, mothers take care of you till you're old enough to go to sea. My father did nothing for me, except to help mother to lick me, when I was obstropolous."

The reader, from what he has already been informed about Ben, the marine, may easily conceive that I was very much of Bob Cross's opinion.

"I suppose you don't know anybody on board—do you?"

"Yes, I know Tommy Dott—I knew him when the ship was at Chatham."

"Oh! Mr Tommy Dott; I dare say you're just like him, for you look full of mischief. He's a very nice young man for a small party, as the saying is; there is more devil in his little carcase than in two women's, and that's not a trifle; you'll hunt in couples, I dare say, and get well flogged at the same gun, if you don't take care. Now, here we are, and I must report my arrival with you under convoy."

Bob Cross sent a waiter for the captain's steward, who went up to Captain Delmar. I was ordered to go upstairs, and again found myself in the presence of the noble captain, and a very stout elderly man, with a flaxen wig.

"This is the lad," said Captain Delmar, when I came into the room and walked up to him; "you know exactly what he requires; oblige me by seeing him properly fitted out and the bill sent in to me."

"Your orders shall be strictly obeyed, Captain Delmar," said the old gentleman, with a profound bow.

"You had better not order too many things, as he is growing fast; it will be easy to make good any deficiencies as they may be required."

"Your orders shall be most strictly obeyed, Captain Delmar," replied the old gentleman, with another bow.

"I hardly know what to do with him for to-day and to-morrow, until his uniforms are made," continued the captain: "I suppose he must go on board."

"If you have no objection, Captain Delmar," said the old gentleman, with another low bow, "I am sure that Mrs Culpepper will be most proud to take charge of any *protégé* of yours; we have a spare bed, and the young gentleman can remain with us until he is ready to embark in the uniform of his rank."

"Be it so, Mr Culpepper; let your wife take care of him until all is complete, and his chest is ready. You'll oblige me by arranging about his mess."

"Your wishes shall be most strictly attended to, Captain Delmar," replied Mr Culpepper, with another profound inclination, which made me feel very much inclined to laugh.

"If you have no further orders, Captain Delmar, I will now take the young gentleman with me."

"Nothing more, Mr Culpepper—good morning," replied Captain Delmar, who neither said how d'ye do to me when I came in, or good bye when I went away in company with Mr Culpepper. I had yet to learn what a thing of no consequence was a "sucking Nelson."

I followed Mr Culpepper down stairs, who desired me to remain with the coxswain, who was standing under the archway, while he spoke to the captain's steward.

"Well," said Bob Cross, "what's the ticket, youngster,—are you to go abroad with me?"

"No," said I; "I am to stay on shore with that old chap, who does nothing but bob his head up and down. Who is he?"

"That's our nipcheese."

"Nipcheese!"

"Yes; nipcheese means purser of the ship—you'll find all that out by-and-by; you've got lots to larn, and, by way of a hint, make him your friend if you can, for he earwigs the captain in fine style."

Perceiving that I did not understand him, Bob Cross continued: "I mean that our captain's very fond of the officers paying him great respect, and he likes all that bowing and scraping; he don't like officers or men to touch their hats, but to take them right off their heads when they speak to him. You see, he's a sprig of nobility, as they call it, and what's more he's also a post-captain, and thinks no small beer of himself; so don't forget what I say—here comes the purser."

Mr Culpepper now came out, and, taking my hand, led me away to his own house, which was at Southsea. He did not speak a word during the walk, but appeared to be in deep cogitation: at last we arrived at his door.

Chapter Fourteen

Why is it that I detain the reader with Mr Culpepper and his family? I don't know, but I certainly have an inclination to linger over every little detail of events which occurred upon my first plunging into the sea of life, just as naked boys on the New River side stand shivering a while, before they can make up their minds to dash into the unnatural element; for men are not ducks, although they do show some affinity to geese by their venturing upon the treacherous fluid.

The door was opened, and I found myself in the presence of Mrs Culpepper and her daughter,—the heiress, as I afterwards discovered, to all Mr Culpepper's savings, which were asserted to be something considerable after thirty years' employment as purser of various vessels belonging to his Majesty.

Mrs Culpepper was in person enormous—she looked like a feather-bed standing on end; her cheeks were as large as a dinner-plate, eyes almost as imperceptible as a mole's, nose just visible, mouth like a round O. It was said that she was once a great Devonshire beauty. Time, who has been denominated *Edax rerum*, certainly had as yet left her untouched, reserving her for a *bonne bouche* on some future occasion.

She sat in a very large arm-chair—indeed, no common-sized chair could have received her capacious person. She did not get up when I entered; indeed, as I discovered, she made but two attempts to stand during the twenty-four hours; one was to come out of her bedroom, which was on the same floor as the parlour, and the other to go in again.

Miss Culpepper was somewhat of her mother's build. She might have been twenty years old, and was, for a girl of her age, exuberantly fat; yet as her skin and complexion were not coarse, many thought her handsome; but she promised to be as large as her mother, and certainly was not at all suited for a wife to a subaltern of a marching regiment.

"Who have we here?" said Mrs Culpepper to her husband, in a sort of low croak; for she was so smothered with fat that she could not get her voice out.

"Well, I hardly know," replied the gentleman, wiping his forehead; "but I've my own opinion."

"Mercy on me, how very like!" exclaimed Miss Culpepper, looking at me, and then at her father. "Would not you like to go into the garden, little boy?" continued she: "there, through the passage, out of the door,—you can't miss it."

As this was almost a command, I did not refuse to go; but as soon as I was in the garden, which was a small patch of ground behind the house, as the window to the parlour was open, and my curiosity was excited by their evidently wishing to say something which they did not wish me to hear, I stopped under the window and listened.

"The very picture of him," continued the young lady.

"Yes, yes, very like indeed," croaked the old one.

"All I know is," said Mr Culpepper, "Captain Delmar has desired me to fit him out, and that he pays all the expenses."

"Well, that's another proof," said the young lady; "he wouldn't pay for other people's children."

"He was brought down here by a very respectable-looking, I may say interesting, and rather pretty woman,—I should think about thirty."

"Then she must have been handsome when this boy was born," replied the young lady: "I consider that another proof. Where is she?"

"Went away this morning by the day-coach, leaving the boy with the captain, who sent his coxswain for him."

"There's mystery about that," rejoined the daughter, "and therefore I consider it another proof."

"Yes," said Mr Culpepper, "and a strong one too. Captain Delmar is so high and mighty, that he would not have it thought that he could ever condescend to have an intrigue with one beneath him in rank and station, and he has sent her away on that account, depend upon it."

"Just so; and if that boy is not a son of Captain Delmar, I'm not a woman."

"I am of that opinion," replied the father, "and therefore I offered to take charge of him, as the captain did not know what to do with him till his uniform was ready."

"Well," replied Miss Culpepper, "I'll soon find out more. I'll pump everything that he knows out of him before he leaves us; I know how to put that and that together."

"Yes," croaked the fat mother; "Medea knows how to put that and that together, as well as any one."

"You must be very civil and very kind to him," said Mr Culpepper; "for depend upon it, the very circumstance of the captain's being compelled to keep the boy at a distance will make him feel more fond of him."

"I've no patience with the men in that respect," observed the young lady: "how nobility can so demean themselves I can't think; no wonder they are ashamed of what they have done, and will not acknowledge their own offspring."

"No, indeed," croaked the old lady.

"If a woman has the misfortune to yield to her inclinations, they don't let her off so easily," exclaimed Miss Medea.

"No, indeed," croaked the mamma again.

"Men make the laws and break them," continued Miss Culpepper. "Mere brute strength, even in the most civilised society. If all women had only the spirit that I have, there would be a little alteration, and more justice."

"I can't pretend to argue with you, Medea," replied Mr Culpepper; "I take the world as I find it, and make the best of it. I must go now,—my steward is waiting for me at the victualling office. Just brush my hat a little, Medea, the wind has raised the nap, and then I'll be off."

I walked very softly from the window; a new light had burst upon me. Young as I was, I also could put that and that together. I called to mind the conduct of my mother towards her husband Ben; the dislike of my grandmother to Captain Delmar; the occasional conversations I had overheard; the question of my mother checked before it was finished— "If I knew who it was that I had been playing the trick to;" the visits my mother received from Captain Delmar, who was so haughty and distant to everybody; his promise to provide for me, and my mother's injunctions to me to be obedient and look up to him as a father, and the remarks of the coxswain, Bob Cross,—"If I were not of the Delmar breed:" all this, added to what I had just overheard, satisfied me that they were not wrong in their conjectures, and that I really was the son of the honourable captain.

My mother had gone; I would have given worlds to have gained this information before, that I might have questioned her, and obtained the truth from her; but that was now impossible, and I felt convinced that writing was of no use. I recollected the conversation between her and the Captain, in which she promised to keep the secret, and the answer she gave me when

I questioned her; nothing, then, but my tears and entreaties could have any effect, and those, I knew, were powerful over her; neither would it be of any use to ask Aunt Milly, for she would not tell her sister's secrets, so I resolved to say nothing about it for the present; and I did not forget that Mr Culpepper had said that Captain Delmar would be annoyed if it was supposed that I was his son; I resolved, therefore, that I would not let him imagine that I knew anything about it, or had any idea of it.

I remained more than an hour in deep thought, and it was strange what a tumult there was in my young heart at this discovery. I hardly comprehended the nature of my position, yet I felt pleased on the whole; I felt as if I were of more importance; nay, that I was more capable of thinking and acting than I was twenty-four hours before.

My reveries were, however, disturbed by Miss Medea, who came to the back-door and asked me if I was not tired of walking, and if I would not like to come in.

"Are you not hungry, Master Keene? Would you like to have a nice piece of cake and a glass of currant wine before dinner? We shall not dine till three o'clock."

"If you please," replied I: for I would not refuse the bribe, although I had a perfect knowledge why it was offered.

Miss Medea brought the cake and wine. As soon as I had despatched them, which did not take very long, she commenced her pumping, as I had anticipated, and which I was determined to thwart, merely out of opposition.

"You were sorry to leave your mamma, weren't you, Master Keene?"

"Yes; very sorry, miss."

"Where's your papa, dearest? He's a very pretty boy, mamma, ain't he?" continued the young lady, putting her fingers through my chestnut curls.

"Yes; handsome boy," croaked the old lady.

"Papa's dead."

"Dead! I thought so," observed Miss Medea, winking at her mother.

"Did you ever see your papa, dearest?"

"Oh yes; he went to sea about eighteen months ago, and he was killed in action."

After this came on a series of questions and cross-questions; I replied to her so as to make it appear that Ben was my father, and nobody else, although I had then a very different opinion. The fact was, I was determined that I would not be pumped, and I puzzled them, for I stated that my aunt Milly was married to Captain Bridgeman, of the marines; and not till then did Miss Medea ask me what my father was. My reply was that he had also been in the marines, and they consequently put him down as a marine officer, as well as Captain Bridgeman.

This added so much to the respectability of my family, that they were quite mystified, and found that it was not quite so easy to put that and that together as they had thought.

As soon as they were tired of questioning, they asked me if I would not like to take another turn in the garden, to which I consented; and, placing myself under the window as before, I heard Miss Medea say to her mother —

"Father's always finding out some mare's nest or another; and because there is some likeness to the captain, he has, in his great wit, made an important discovery. It's quite evident that he's wrong, as he generally is. It's not very likely that Captain Delmar should have had an intrigue with the wife of a marine officer, and her sister married also into the corps. The widow has brought him down herself, it is true, but that proves nothing; who else was to bring him down, if it was not his mother? and the very circumstance of her going away so soon proves that she felt it improper that she should remain; and, in my opinion, that she is a modest, interesting young woman, in whom Captain Delmar has taken an interest. I wish father would not come here with his nonsensical ideas, telling us to make much of the boy."

"Very true, Medea," replied the mother; "you might have saved that cake and wine."

Thinks I to myself, you have not pumped me, and I never felt more delighted than at having outwitted them. I thought it, however, prudent to walk away from the window.

Shortly afterwards, Mr Culpepper returned, accompanied by one of the numerous Portsmouth fitting-out tailors. I was summoned; the tailor presented a list of what he declared to be absolutely necessary for the outfit of a gentleman.

Mr Culpepper struck out two-thirds of the articles, and desired the remainder to be ready on the Friday morning, it being then Wednesday. The tailor promised faithfully, and Mr Culpepper also promised most faithfully, that if the articles were not ready, they would be left on his hands. As soon as the tailor had gone, Miss Medea asked me if I would not like to take another run in the garden. I knew that she wished to speak to her father, and therefore had a pleasure in disappointing her. I therefore replied, that I had been there nearly the whole day, and did not wish to go out any more.

"Never mind whether you wish it or not; I wish you to go," replied Miss Medea, tartly.

"Medea, how can you be so rude?" cried Mr Culpepper; "surely Mr Keene may do as he pleases. I'm surprised at you, Medea."

"And I'm surprised at you, papa, finding out a mystery when there is none," replied Miss Medea, very cross. "All you said this morning, and all your surmises, have turned out to be all moonshine. Yes, you may look, papa; I tell you—all moonshine."

"Why, Medea, what nonsense you are talking," replied Mr Culpepper.

"Medea's right," croaked Mrs Culpepper; "all moonshine."

"So you need not be so very particular, papa, I can tell you," rejoined Miss Medea, who then whispered in her father's ear, loud enough for me to hear, "No such thing, nothing but a regular marine."

"Pooh, nonsense," replied the purser, in a low voice; "the boy has been taught to say it—he's too clever for you, Medea."

At this very true remark of her father's, Miss Medea swelled into a towering passion, her whole face, neck, and shoulders—for she wore a low gown in the morning—turning to a fiery scarlet. I never saw such a fury as she appeared to be. She rushed by me so roughly, that I was thrown back a couple of paces, and then she bounced out of the room.

"Medea knows how to put that and that together, Mr Culpepper," croaked out Mrs Culpepper.

"Medea's wise in her own conceit, and you're a regular old fool," rejoined Mr Culpepper, with asperity; "one too knowing and the other not half knowing enough. Master Keene, I hope you are hungry, for we have a very nice dinner. Do you like ducks and green peas?"

"Yes, sir, very much," replied I.

"Were you born at Chatham, Master Keene?"

"No, sir, I was born at the Hall, near Southampton. My mother was brought up by old Mrs Delmar, the captain's aunt."

I gave this intelligence on purpose; as I knew it would puzzle Miss Medea, who had just returned from the kitchen.

Mr Culpepper nodded his head triumphantly to his daughter and wife, who both appeared dumb-founded at this new light thrown upon the affair.

Miss Medea paused a moment and then said to me, — "I wish to ask you one question, Master Keene."

"I will not answer any more of your questions, miss," replied I; "You have been questioning me all the morning, and just now, you were so rude as nearly to push me down. If you want to know anything more, ask Captain Delmar; or, if you wish it, I will ask Captain Delmar whether I am to answer you, and if he says I am, I will, but not without."

This was a decided blow on my part; mother and Medea both looked frightened, and Mr Culpepper was more alarmed than either of the females. It proved to them that I knew what they were inquiring for, which was to them also proof that I also knew who I was; and further, my reference to Captain Delmar satisfied them that I felt sure of his support, and they knew that he would be very much irritated if I told him on what score they had been pumping me.

"You are very right, Master Keene," said Mr Culpepper, turning very red, "to refuse to answer any questions you don't like; and, Medea, I'm surprised at your behaviour; I insist upon it you do not annoy Master Keene with any more of your impertinent curiosity."

"No, no," croaked the old lady; "hold your tongue, Medea, hold your tongue."

Miss Medea, who looked as if she could tear my eyes out if she dared, swallowed down her rage as well as she could. She was mortified at finding she had made a mistake, annoyed at my answering her so boldly, and frightened at her father's anger; for the old gentleman was very apt to vent it in the *argumentum ad feminam*, and box her ears soundly.

Fortunately dinner was served just at this moment, and this gave a turn to the conversation, and also to their thoughts. Mr Culpepper was all attention, and Miss Medea, gradually recovering her temper, also became affable and condescending.

The evening passed away very agreeably; but I went to bed early, as I wished to be left to my own reflections, and it was not till daylight that I could compose my troubled mind so as to fall asleep.

Chapter Fifteen

Although the aversion which I had taken to the whole Culpepper family was so great, that I could have done anything to annoy them, my mind was now so fully occupied with the information which I had collected relative to my supposed birth and parentage, that I could not think of mischief.

I walked on the common or in the little garden during the whole of the following day, plunged in deep thought, and at night, when I went to bed, I remained awake till the dawn. During these last two days I had thought and reflected more than I had perhaps done from the hour of my birth.

That I was better off than I should have been if I had been the son of a private in the marines, I felt convinced; but still I had a feeling that I was in a position in which I might be subjected to much insult, and that, unless I was acknowledged by my aristocratic parent, my connection with his family would be of no use to me;—and Captain Delmar, how was I to behave to him? I did not like him much, that was certain, nor did this new light which had burst forth make me feel any more love for him than I did before. Still my mother's words at Chatham rung in my ears, "Do you know who it is that you have been?" etcetera. I felt sure that he was my father, and I felt a sort of duty towards him; perhaps an increase of respect.

These were anxious thoughts for a boy not fourteen; and the Culpeppers remarked, that I had not only looked very pale, but had actually grown thin in the face during my short stay.

As I was very quiet and reserved after the first day, they were very glad when my clothes were brought home, and I was reported ready to embark; so was I, for I wanted to go on board and see my friend Tommy Dott, with whom I intended, if the subject was brought up, to consult as to my proceedings, or perhaps I thought it would be better to consult Bob Cross, the captain's coxswain; I was not sure that I should not advise with them both.

I had made up my mind how to behave to my mother. I knew that she would never acknowledge the truth, after what had passed between the captain and her when I was present; but I was resolved that I would let her know that I was in the secret; and I thought that the reply to me would be a guide as to the correctness of the fact, which, with all the hastiness of boyhood, I considered as incontrovertible, although I had not the least positive proof.

The day that I was to go on board, I requested Miss Culpepper to give me a sheet of paper, that I might write to my mother; she supplied me very readily, saying, "You had better let me see if you make any mistake in your spelling before the letter goes; your mamma will be so pleased if you write your letter properly." She then went down into the kitchen to give some orders.

As I had not the slightest intention that she should read what I wrote, and resolved to have it in the post before she came up again, I was very concise in my epistle, which was as follows:—

> "Dear Mother:— I have found it all out—I am the son of
> Captain Delmar, and everyone here knows what you have
> kept a secret from me. I go on board to-day.
> "Yours truly, *P. Keene*."

This was very short, and, it must be admitted, direct to the point. I could not perhaps have written one which was so calculated to give my mother uneasiness.

As soon as it was finished, I folded it up, and lighted a taper to seal it. Old Mrs Culpepper, who was in the room, croaked out, "No, no; you must show it to Medea." But I paid no attention to her, and having sealed my letter, put on my hat, and walked out to the post-office. I dropped it into the box, and, on returning, found Mr Culpepper coming home, accompanied by Bob Cross, the captain's coxswain, and two of the boat's crew.

As I presumed, they were sent for me; I joined them immediately, and was kindly greeted by Bob Cross, who said:—

"Well, Mr Keene, are you all ready for shipping? We've come for your traps."

"All ready," replied I, "and very glad to go, for I'm tired of staying on shore doing nothing."

We were soon at the house; the seamen carried away my chest and bedding, while Bob Cross remained a little while, that I might pay my farewell to the ladies.

The ceremony was not attended with much regret on either side. Miss Culpepper could not help asking me why I did not show her my letter, and I replied, that there were secrets in it, which answer did not at all add to her good temper; our adieus were, therefore, anything but affectionate, and before the men with my effects were a hundred yards in advance, Bob Cross and I were at their heels.

"Well, Master Keene," said Bob, as we wended our way across South Sea Common, "how do you like the purser's ladies?"

"Not at all," replied I; "they have done nothing but try to pump me the whole time I have been there; but they did not make much of it."

"Women will be curious, Master Keene—pray what did they try to pump about?"

I hardly knew how to reply, and I hesitated. I felt a strong inclination towards Bob Cross, and I had before reflected whether I should make him my confidant; still, I was undecided and made no reply, when Bob Cross answered for me:—

"Look ye, child—for although you're going on the quarter-deck, and I am before the mast, you are a child compared to me—I can tell you what they tried to pump about, as well as you can tell me, if you choose. According to my thinking, there's no lad on board the frigate that will require good advice as you will; and I tell you candidly, you will have your cards to play. Bob Cross is no fool, and can see as far through a fog as most chaps; I like you for yourself as far as I see of you, and I have not forgotten your mother's kindness to me, when she had her own misery to occupy her thoughts; not that I wanted the money—it wasn't the money, but the way and the circumstances under which it was given. I told you I'd look after you a bit—a bit means a great deal with me—and so I will, if you choose that I shall; if not, I shall touch my hat to you, as my officer, which won't help you very much. So, now you have to settle, my lad, whether you will have me as your friend, or not."

The appeal quite decided me. "Bob Cross," replied I. "I do wish to make you my friend; I thought of it before, but I did not know whether to go to you or to Tommy Dott."

"Tommy Dott! Well, Master Keene, that's not very flattering, to put me in one scale, and Tommy Dott in the other; I'm not surprised at its weighing down in my favour. If you wish to get into mischief you can't apply to a better hand than Tommy Dott; but Tommy Dott is not half so fit to advise you, as you are, I expect, to advise him; so make him your playmate and companion, if you please, but as to his advice, it's not worth asking. However, as you have given me the preference, I will now tell you that the Culpepper people have been trying to find out who is your father. Ain't I right?"

"Yes, you are," replied I.

"Well, then, this is no time to talk about such things; we shall be down to the boat in another minute, so we'll say no more at present; only recollect, when you are on board, if they talk about appointing a man to take charge of your hammock, say that Bob Cross, the captain's coxswain, is, you understand, to be the person; say that and no more. I will tell you why by-and-by, when we have time to talk together and if any of your messmates say anything to you on the same point which the Culpeppers have been working at, make no reply and hold yourself very stiff. Now, here we are at the sally port, so there's an end to our palaver for the present."

My chest and bedding were already in the boat, and as soon as Cross and I had stepped in he ordered the bowman to shove off; in half an hour we arrived alongside the frigate, which lay at Spithead, bright with new paint, and with her pennant proudly flying to the breeze.

"You'd better follow me, sir, and mind you touch your hat when the officers speak to you," said Bob Cross, ascending the accommodation ladder. I did so, and found myself on the quarter deck, in the presence of the first lieutenant and several of the officers.

"Well, Cross," said the first lieutenant.

"I've brought a young gentleman on board to join the ship. Captain Delmar has, I believe, given his orders about him."

"Mr Keene, I presume?" said the first lieutenant, eyeing me from head to foot.

"Yes, sir," replied I, touching my hat.

"How long have you been at Portsmouth?"

"Three days, sir; I have been staying at Mr Culpepper's."

"Well, did you fall in love with Miss Culpepper?"

"No, sir," replied I; "I hate her."

At this answer the first lieutenant and the officers near him burst out a-laughing.

"Well, youngster, you must dine with us in the gun-room to-day; and where's Mr Dott?"

"Here, sir," said Tommy Dott, coming from the other side of the quarter-deck.

"Mr Dott, take this young gentleman down below, and show him the midshipmen's berth. Let me see, who is to take care of his hammock?"

"I believe that Bob Cross is to take care of it, sir," said I.

"The captain's coxswain—humph. Well, that's settled at all events; very good—we shall have the pleasure of your company to dinner, Mr Keene. Why, Mr Dott and you look as if you knew each other."

"Don't we, Tommy?" said I to the midshipman, grinning.

"I suspect that there is a pair of you," said the first lieutenant, turning aft and walking away; after which Tommy and I went down the companion ladder as fast as we could, and in a few seconds afterwards were sitting together on the same chest, in most intimate conversation.

My extreme resemblance to our honourable captain was not unobserved by the officers who were on the quarter-deck at the time of my making my appearance; and, as I afterwards heard from Bob Cross, he was sent for by the surgeon, on some pretence or another, to obtain any information relative to me. What were Bob Cross's reasons for answering as he did I could not at that time comprehend, but he explained them to me afterwards.

"Who brought him down, Cross?" said the surgeon, carelessly.

"His own mother, sir; he has no father, sir, I hear."

"Did you see her? What sort of a person was she?"

"Well, sir," replied Bob Cross, "I've seen many ladies of quality, but such a real lady I don't think I ever set my eyes upon before; and such a beauty—I'd marry to-morrow if I could take in tow a craft like her."

"How did they come down to Portsmouth?"

"Why, sir, she came down to Portsmouth in a coach and four; but she walked to the George Hotel, as if she was nobody."

This was not a fib on the part of the coxswain, for we came down by the Portsmouth coach; it did, however, deceive the surgeon, as was intended.

"Did you see anything of her, Cross?"

"Not when she was with the captain, sir, but at her own lodgings I did; such a generous lady I never met with."

A few more questions were put, all of which were replied to in much the same strain by the coxswain, so as to make out my mother to be a very important and mysterious personage. It is true that Tommy Dott could have contradicted all this; but, in the first place, it was not very likely that there would be any communication upon the point between him and the officers; and in the next I cautioned him to say nothing about what he knew, which, as he was strongly attached to me, he strictly complied with: so Bob Cross completely mystified the surgeon, who, of course, made his report to his messmates.

Mr Culpepper's report certainly differed somewhat from that of Bob Cross. There was my statement of my aunt being married to a marine officer—but it was my statement; there was also my statement of my mother residing with Captain Delmar's aunt; altogether there was doubt and mystery; and it ended in my mother being supposed to be a much greater person than she really was—everything tending to prove her a lady of rank being willingly received, and all counter-statements looked upon as apocryphal and false.

But whoever my mother might be, on one point every one agreed, which was, that I was the son of the Honourable Captain Delmar, and on this point I was equally convinced myself. I waited with some anxiety for my mother's reply to my letter, which arrived two days after I had joined the frigate. It was as follows:—

"My dear Percival:—

"You little know the pain and astonishment which I felt upon receipt of your very unkind and insulting letter; surely you could not have reflected at the time you wrote it, but must have penned it in a moment of irritation arising from some ungenerous remark which has been made in your hearing.

"Alas, my dear child, you will find, now that you have commenced your career in life, that there are too many whose only pleasure is to inflict pain upon their fellow-creatures. I only can imagine that some remark has been made in your presence, arising from there being a similarity of features between you and the Honourable Captain Delmar; that there is so has been before observed by others. Indeed your uncle and aunt Bridgeman were both struck with the resemblance, when Captain Delmar arrived at Chatham; but this proves nothing, my dear child—people are very often alike, who have never seen each other, or heard each other mentioned, till they have by accident been thrown together so as to be compared.

"It may certainly be, as your father was in the service of Captain Delmar, and constantly attended upon him, and indeed I may add as I was occasionally seeing him, that the impression of his countenance might be constantly in our memory, and—but you don't understand such questions, and therefore I will say no more, except that you will immediately dismiss from your thoughts any such idea.

"You forget, my dearest boy, that you are insulting me by supposing any such thing, and that your mother's honour is called in question; I am sure you never thought of that when you wrote those hasty and inconsiderate lines. I must add, my dear boy, that knowing Captain Delmar, and how proud and sensitive he is, if it should ever come to his knowledge that you had suspected or asserted what you have, his favour and protection would be lost to you for ever: at present he is doing a kind and charitable action in bringing forward the son of a faithful servant; but if he imagined for a moment that you were considered related to him he would cast you off for ever, and all your prospects in life would be ruined.

"Even allowing it possible that you were what you so madly stated yourself in your letter to be, I am convinced he would do so. If such a report came to his ears, he would immediately disavow you, and leave you to find your own way in the world.

"You see, therefore, my dear boy, how injurious to you in every way such a ridiculous surmise must prove, and I trust that, not only for your own sake, but for your mother's character, you will, so far from giving credence, indignantly disavow what must be a source of mischief and annoyance to all parties.

"Captain Bridgeman desires me to say, that he is of my opinion, so is your aunt Milly: as for your grandmother, of course, I dare not show her your letter. Write to me, my dear boy, and tell me how this unfortunate mistake happened, and believe me to be your affectionate mother, *Arabella Keene* ."

I read this letter over ten times before I came to any conclusion; at last I said to myself, there is not in any one part of it any positive denial of the fact, and resolved some future day, when I had had some conversation with Bob Cross, to show it to him, and ask his opinion.

Chapter Sixteen

The next morning, at daylight, the blue Peter was hoisted at the foremast, and the gun fired as a signal for sailing; all was bustle—hoisting in, clearing boats of stock, and clearing the ship of women and strangers.

At ten o'clock Captain Delmar made his appearance, the hands were piped up anchor, and in half an hour we were standing out for St. Helen's. Before night it blew very fresh, and we went rolling down the Channel before an easterly wind. I went to my hammock very sick, and did not recover for several days, during which nobody asked for me, or any questions about me, except Bob Cross and Tommy Dott.

As soon as I was well enough, I made my appearance on deck, and was ordered by the first lieutenant to do my duty under the signal midshipman: this was day duty, and not very irksome; I learnt the flags, and how to use a spy-glass.

We were charged with despatches for the fleet, then off Cadiz, and on the tenth day we fell in with it, remained a week in company, and then were ordered to Gibraltar and Malta. From Malta we went home again with despatches, having been out three months.

During this short and pleasant run, I certainly did not learn much of my profession, but I did learn a little of the ways of the world. First, as to Captain Delmar, his conduct to me was anything but satisfactory; he never inquired for me during the time that I was unwell, and took no notice of me on my reappearance.

The officers and young gentlemen, as midshipmen are called, were asked to dine in the cabin in rotation, and I did in consequence dine two or three times in the cabin; but it appeared to me, as if the captain purposely took no notice of me, although he generally did say a word or two to the others; moreover as the signal mids were up in the morning watch, he would occasionally send to invite one of the others to breakfast with him, but he never paid me that compliment.

This annoyed me, and I spoke of it to Bob Cross, with whom I had had some long conversations. I had told him all I knew relative to myself, what my suspicions were, and I had shown him my mother's reply. His opinion on the subject may be given in what follows:—

"You see, Master Keene, you are in an awkward position; the captain is a very proud man, and too proud to acknowledge that you are any way related to him. It's my opinion, from what you have told me, and from other reasons, particularly from your likeness to the captain, that your suspicions are correct; but, what then? Your mother is sworn to secrecy—that's clear; and the captain won't own you—that's also very clear. I had some talk with the captain's steward on the subject when I was taking a glass of grog with him the other night in this berth. It was he that brought up the subject, not me, and he said, that the captain not asking you to breakfast, and avoiding you, as it were, was another proof that you belonged to him; and the wishing to hide the secret only makes him behave as he does. You have a difficult game to play, Master Keene; but you are a clever lad, and you ask advice—mind you follow it, or it's little use asking it. You must always be very respectful to Captain Delmar, and keep yourself at as great a distance from him as he does from you."

"That I'm sure I will," replied I, "for I dislike him very much."

"No, you must not do that, but you must bend to circumstances; by-and-by things will go on better; but mind you keep on good terms with the officers, and never be saucy, or they may say to you what may not be pleasant; recollect this, and things will go on better, as I said before. If Captain Delmar protects you with his interest, you will be a captain over the heads of many who are now your superiors on board of this frigate. One thing be careful of, which is, to keep your own counsel, and don't be persuaded in a moment of confidence to trust anything to Tommy Dott, or any other midshipman; and if any one hints at what you suppose, deny it immediately; nay, if necessary, fight for it—that will be the way to please the captain, for you will be of his side then, and not against him."

That this advice of Bob Cross was the best that could be given to one in my position there could not be a doubt; and that I did resolve to follow it, is most certain. I generally passed away a portion of my leisure hours in Bob's company, and became warmly attached to him; and certainly my time was not thrown away, for I learnt a great deal from him.

One evening, as I was leaning against one of the guns on the main deck, waiting for Cross to come out of the cabin, I was amused with the following conversation between a boatswain's mate and a fore-top man. I shall give it verbatim. They were talking of one that was dead; and after the boatswain's mate had said—

"Well, he's in heaven, poor fellow."

After a pause, the fore-top man said—

"I wonder, Bill, whether I shall ever go to heaven?"

"Why not?" replied the boatswain's mate.

"Why, the parson says it's good works; now, I certainly have been a pretty many times in action, and I have killed plenty of Frenchmen in my time."

"Well, that's sufficient, I should think; I hold my hopes upon just the same claims. I've cut down fifty Frenchmen in my life, and if that ain't good works, I don't know what is."

"I suppose Nelson's in heaven?"

"Of course; if so be he wishes to be there, I should like to know who would keep him out, if he was determined on it; no, no; depend upon it he walked *slap* in."

On our return to Portsmouth, the captain went up to the Admiralty with the despatches, the frigate remaining at Spithead, ready to sail at a moment's notice.

I was now quite accustomed to the ship and officers; the conviction I had of my peculiar position, together with the advice of Bob Cross, had very much subdued my spirit; perhaps the respect created by discipline, and the example of others, which produced in me a degree of awe of the captain and the lieutenants, assisted a little—certain it is, that I gained the goodwill of my messmates, and had not been in any scrape during the whole cruise.

The first lieutenant was a stern, but not unkind man; he would blow you up, as we termed it, when he scolded for half an hour without ceasing. I never knew a man with such a flow of words; but if permitted to go on without interruption, he was content, without proceeding to further punishment. Any want of respect, however, was peculiarly offensive to him, and any attempt to excuse yourself was immediately cut short with, "No reply, sir."

The second day after our return to Spithead, I was sent on shore in the cutter to bring off a youngster who was to join the ship; he had never been to sea before; his name was Green, and he was as green as a gooseberry. I took a dislike to him the moment that I saw him, because he had a hooked nose and very small ferrety eyes. As we were pulling on board he asked me a great many questions of all kinds, particularly about the captain and officers, and to amuse myself and the boat's crew, who were on the full titter, I exercised my peculiar genius for invention.

At last, after I had given a character of the first lieutenant, which made him appear a sort of marine ogre, he asked how it was I got on with him:—

"O, very well," replied I; "but I'm a freemason, and so is he, and he's never severe with a brother mason."

"But how did he know you were a mason?"

"I made the sign to him the very first time that he began to scold me, and he left off almost immediately; that is, when I made the second sign; he did not when I made the first."

"I should like to know these signs. Won't you tell them to me?"

"Tell them to you! oh no, that won't do," replied I. "I don't know you. Here we are on board—in bow,—rowed of all, men. Now, Mr Green, I'll show you the way up."

Mr Green was presented, and ushered into the service much in the same way as I was; but he had not forgotten what I said to him relative to the first lieutenant; and it so happened that, on the third day he witnessed a jobation, delivered by the first lieutenant to one of the midshipmen, who, venturing to reply, was ordered to the mast-head for the remainder of the day; added to which, a few minutes afterwards, the first lieutenant ordered two men to be put both legs in irons. Mr Green trembled as he saw the men led away by the master-at-arms, and he came to me:

"I do wish, Keene, you would tell me those signs," said he; "can't you be persuaded to part with them? I'll give you any thing that I have which you may like."

"Well," said I, "I should like to have that long spy-glass of yours, for it's a very good one; and, as signal-midshipman, will be useful to me."

"I will give it you with all my heart," replied he, "if you will tell me the signs."

"Well, then, come down below, give me the glass, and I will tell them to you."

Mr Green and I went down to the berth, and I received the spy-glass as a present in due form. I then led him to my chest in the steerage, and in a low, confidential tone, told him as follows:—

"You see, Green, you must be very particular about making those signs, for if you make a mistake, you will be worse off than if you never made them at all, for the first lieutenant will suppose that you are trying to persuade him that you are a mason, when you are not. Now, observe, you must not attempt to make the first sign until he has scolded you well; then, at any pause, you must make it; thus, you see, you must put your thumb to the tip of your nose, and extend your hand straight out from it, with all the fingers separated, as wide as you can. Now, do it as I did it. Stop—wait a little, till that marine passes. Yes, that is it. Well, that is considered the first proof of your being a mason, but it requires a second. The first lieutenant will, I tell you frankly, be or rather pretend to be, in a terrible rage, and will continue to rail at you; you must, therefore, wait a little till he pauses; and then, you observe, put up your thumb to your nose, with the fingers of your hands spread out as before, and then add to it your other hand, by joining your other thumb to the little finger of the hand already up, and stretch your other hand and fingers out like the first. Then you will see the effects of the second sign. Do you think you can recollect all this? for, as I said before, you must make no mistake."

Green put his hands up as I told him, and after three or four essays declared himself perfect, and I left him.

It was about three days afterwards that Mr Green upset a kid of dirty water upon the lower deck which had been dry holystoned, and the mate of the lower deck, when the first lieutenant went his round, reported the circumstance to exculpate himself. Mr Green was consequently summoned on the quarter-deck; and the first lieutenant, who was very angry, commenced, as usual, a volley of abuse on the unfortunate youngster.

Green, recollecting my instructions, waited till the first lieutenant had paused, and then made the first freemason sign, looking up very boldly at the first lieutenant, who actually drew back with astonishment at this contemptuous conduct, hitherto unwitnessed on board of a man-at-war.

"What! sir," cried the first lieutenant. "Why, sir, are you mad?—you, just come into the service, treating me in this manner! I can tell you, sir, that you will not be three days longer in the service—no, sir, not three days; for either you leave the service or I do. Of all the impudence, of all the insolence, of all the contempt I have heard of, this beats all—and from such a little animal as you. Consider yourself as under an arrest, sir, till the captain comes on board, and your conduct is reported; go down below, sir, immediately."

The lieutenant paused, and now Green gave him sign the second, as a reply, thinking that they would then come to a right understanding—but to his astonishment, the first lieutenant was more curious than ever; and calling the sergeant of marines, ordered him to take Mr Green down, and put him in irons, under the half-deck.

Poor Green was handed down, all astonishment, at the want of success of his mason's signs. I, who stood abaft, was delighted at the success of my joke, while the first lieutenant walked hastily up and down the deck, as much astonished as enraged at such insulting and insolent conduct from a lad who had not been a week in the service.

After a time the first lieutenant went down below, when Bob Cross, who was on deck, and who had perceived my delight at the scene, which was to him and all others so inexplicable, came up to me and said:—

"Master Keene, I'm sure, by your looks, you knew something about this. That foolish lad never had dared do so, if he knew what it was he had done. Now, don't look so demure, but tell me how it is."

I walked aft with Bob Cross, and confided my secret to him; he laughed heartily, and said:—

"Well, Tommy Dott did say that you were up to any thing, and so I think you are; but you see this is a very serious affair for poor Green, and, like the fable of the frogs, what is sport to you is death to others. The poor lad will be turned out of the service, and lose his chance of being a post captain; so you must allow me to explain the matter so that it gets to the ears of the first lieutenant as soon as possible."

"Well," replied I, "do as you like, Bob; if any one's to be turned out of the service for such nonsense, it ought to be me, and not Green, poor snob."

"No fear of your being turned out; the first lieutenant won't like you the worse, and the other officers will like you better especially as I shall say that it is by your wish that I explain all to get Mr Green out of the scrape. I'll go to the surgeon and tell him—but, Master Keene, don't you call such matters *nonsense*, or you'll find yourself mistaken one of these days. I never saw such disrespect on a quarter-deck in all my life—worse than mutiny a thousand times." Here Bob Cross burst out into a fit of laughter, as he recalled Green's extended fingers to his memory, and then he turned away and went down below to speak to the surgeon.

As soon as Cross had quitted the deck, I could not restrain my curiosity as to the situation of my friend Green; I therefore went down the ladder to the half-deck, and there, on the starboard side between the guns, I perceived the poor fellow, with his legs in irons, his hands firmly clasped together, looking so woeful and woe-begone, every now and then raising his eyes up to the beam of the upper deck, as if he would appeal to heaven, that I scarcely could refrain from laughing. I went up to him and said:—

"Why, Green, how is all this?—what has happened?"

"Happened?" said the poor fellow; "happened? see what has happened; here I am."

"Did you make the freemason's signs?" replied I.

"Didn't I? Yes—I did: Oh, what will become of me?"

"You could not have made them right; you must have forgotten them."

"I'm sure I made them as you told me; I'm quite sure of that."

"Then perhaps I did not recollect them exactly myself: however, be of good heart; I will have the whole matter explained to the first lieutenant."

"Pray do; only get me out of this. I don't want the glass back."

"I'll have it done directly," replied I.

As I went away, Bob Cross came up, and said I was wanted by the first lieutenant in the gun-room. "Don't be afraid," said he: "they've been laughing at it already, and the first lieutenant is it a capital humour; still he'll serve you out well; you must expect that."

"Shall I make him the sign, Cross?" replied I, laughing.

"No, no; you've gone far enough, and too far already; mind what I say to you."

I went down into the gun-room, when a tittering ceased as the sentry opened the door, and I walked in.

"Did you want me, sir?" said I to the first lieutenant, touching my hat, and looking very demure.

"So, Mr Keene, I understand it was you who have been practising upon Mr Green, and teaching him insult and disrespect to his superior officers on the quarter-deck. Well, sir?"

I made no reply, but appeared very penitent.

"Because a boy has just come to sea, and is ignorant of his profession, it appears to be a custom—which I shall take care shall not be followed up—to play him all manner of tricks, and tell him all manner of falsehoods. Now, sir, what have you to say for yourself?"

"Mr Green and I have both just come to sea, sir, and the midshipmen all play us so many tricks," replied I, humbly, "that I hardly know whether what I do is right or wrong."

"But, sir, it was you who played this trick to Mr Green."

"Yes, sir, I told him so for fun, but I didn't think he was such a fool as to believe me. I only said that you were a freemason, and that freemasons were kind to each other, and that you gave one another signs to know one another by; I heard you say you were a freemason, sir, when I dined in the gun-room."

"Well, sir, I did say so; but that is no reason for your teaching him to be impudent."

"He asked me for the signs, sir, and I didn't know them exactly; so I gave him the signs that Mr Dott and I always make between us."

"Mr Dott and you—a pretty pair, as I said before. I've a great mind to put you in Mr Green's place—at all events, I shall report your conduct when the captain comes from London. There, sir, you may go."

I put on a penitent face as I went out wiping my eyes with the back of my hands. After I went out, I waited a few seconds at the gun-room door, and then the officers, supposing that I was out of hearing, gave vent to their mirth, the first lieutenant laughing the loudest.

"Cross is right," thought I, as I went up the ladder; a minute afterwards, Mr Green was set free, and, after a severe reprimand, was allowed to return to his duty.

"You are well out of that trick, my hearty," said Bob Cross; "the first lieutenant won't say a word to the captain, never fear; but don't try it again."

But an event occurred a few hours afterwards which might have been attended with more serious consequences. The ship was, during the day, surrounded by shore boats of all descriptions, containing Jews, sailors' wives, and many other parties, who wished to have admittance on board. It was almost dusk, the tide was running strong flood, and the wind was very fresh, so that there was a good deal of sea. All the boats had been ordered to keep off by the first lieutenant, but they still lingered, in hope of getting on board.

I was looking over the stern, and perceived that the boat belonging to the bumboat woman, who was on board of the ship, was lying with her painter fast to the stern ladder; the waterman was in her, as well as one of the sailors' wives, who had left her own wherry in hopes of getting on board when the waterman went alongside to take in the articles not sold, when the bumboat woman left the ship, which would be in a few minutes, as it was nearly gun-fire for sunset. The waterman, who thought it time to haul alongside, and wished to communicate with his employer on board, was climbing up by the stern ladder.

"That's against orders, you know," cried I to the man.

"Yes, sir; but it is so rough, that the boat would be swamped if it were to remain alongside long, and I hope you won't order me down again; there's some nice cakes in the boat, sir, just under the stern sheets, if you would like to have them, and think it worth while to go down for them."

This was a bribe, and I replied, "No, I don't want your cakes, but you may come up."

The man thanked me, and walked forward as soon as he had gained the deck. On second thoughts, I determined that I would have the cakes; so I descended by the stern ladder, and desiring the woman who was left in the boat to haul upon the rope, contrived to get into the boat.

"What is it you want, my dear?" said the woman.

"I come for some of those cakes under the stern sheets," replied I.

"Well, I'll soon rummage them out," said she, "and I hope you will let me slip on board when the boat is alongside. Mind, sir, how you step, you'll smash all the pipes. Give me your hand. I'm an old sailor."

"I should not think so," replied I, looking at her. I could hardly make out her face, but her form was small, and, if an old sailor, she certainly was a very young woman.

We had a good many articles to remove before we could get at the cakes, which were under the stern sheets; and the boat rocked and tossed so violently with the sea which was running, that we were both on our knees for some little while before we obtained the basket: when we did, to our surprise, we found that the boat's painter, somehow or another, had loosened, and that during our search we had drifted nearly one hundred yards from the ship.

"Mercy on me!—why, we are adrift," exclaimed the woman. "What shall we do? It's no use hailing, they'll never hear us; look well round for any boat you may see."

"It is getting so dark that we shall not see far," replied I, not much liking our position. "Where shall we go to?"

"Go to!—clean out to St. Helen's, if the boat does not fill before we get there; and further than that too, if I mistake not, with this gale of wind. We may as well say our prayers, youngster, I can tell you."

"Can't we make sail upon her?" replied I. "Can't we try and pull on shore somewhere? Had we not better do that, and say our prayers afterwards?"

"Well said, my little bantam," replied the woman: "you would have made a good officer if you had been spared; but the fact is, boy, that we can do nothing with the oars in this heavy sea; and as for the sail, how can you and I step the mast, rolling and tossing about in this way? If the mast were stepped, and the sail set, I think I could manage to steer, if the weather was smoother, but not in this bubble and this gale; it requires older hands than either you or I."

"Well, then, what must we do?"

"Why, we must sit still and trust to our luck, bale out the boat, and keep her from swamping as long as we can, and between times we may cry, or we may pray, or we may eat the cakes and red herrings, or the soft bread and other articles in the boat."

"Let's bale the boat out first," said I, "for she's half full of water; then we'll have something to eat, for I feel hungry and cold already, and then we may as well say our prayers."

"Well, and I tell you what, we'll have something to drink, too, for I have a drop for Jem, if I could have got on board. I promised it to him, poor fellow, but it's no use keeping it now, for I expect we'll both be in Davy's locker before morning."

The woman took out from where it was secreted in her dress, a bladder containing spirits; she opened the mouth of it, and poured out a portion into one of the milk-cans; having drunk herself, she handed it to me, but not feeling inclined, and being averse to spirits, I rejected it, "Not just now," said I, "by-and-by perhaps."

During the time of this conversation we were swept by a strong tide and strong wind right out of the anchorage at Spithead; the sea was very high, and dashed into the boat, so that I was continually baling to keep it free; the night was as dark as pitch; we could see nothing except the lights of the vessels which we had left far away from us, and they were now but as little twinkles as we rose upon the waves. The wind roared, and there was every appearance of a heavy gale.

"Little hopes of our weathering this storm," said the woman; "we shall soon be swamped if we do not put her before the wind. I'll see if I cannot find the lines."

She did so after a time, and by means of a rudder put the boat before the wind; the boat then took in much less water, but ran at a swift rate through the heavy sea.

"There, we shall do better now; out to sea we go, that's clear," said the woman; "and before daylight we shall be in the Channel, if we do not fill and go down; and then, the Lord have mercy upon us, that's all! Won't you take a drop?" continued she, pouring out some spirits into the can.

As I felt very cold, I did not this time refuse. I drank a small quantity of the spirits; the woman took off the remainder, which, with what she had previously drunk, began to have an effect upon her.

"That's right, my little Trojan," said she, and she commenced singing. "A long pull, a strong pull, and a pull altogether; in spite of wind and weather, boys, in spite of wind and weather. Poor Jem," continued she, "he'll be disappointed; he made sure of being glorious to-night, and I made sure to sleep by his side—now he'll be quite sober—and I'll be food for fishes; it's a cold bed that I shall turn into before morning, that's certain. Hand me the cakes, boy, if you can fumble them out; the more we fill ourselves, the less room for salt water. Well, then, wind and waves are great bullies; they fly slap back in a fright when they bang against a great ship; but when they get hold of a little boat like this, how they leap and topple in, as if they made sure of us (here a wave dashed into the boat). Yes, that's your sort. Come along, swamp a little boat you washy cowards, it's only a woman and a boy. Poor Jim, he'll miss me something, but he'll miss the liquor more; who cares? Let's have another drop."

"Give me the lines, then," said I, as I perceived she was letting them go, "or we shall be broadside to the waves again."

I took the rudder lines from her, and steered the boat, while she again resorted to the bladder of spirits.

"Take another sip," said she, after she had filled the milk-can; "it won't harm you."

I thought the same, for I was wet through, and the wind, as it howled, pierced me to the bones; I took a small quantity as before, and then continued to keep the boat before the wind. The sea was increasing very much and although no sailor, I felt fully convinced that the boat could not live much longer.

In the meantime the woman was becoming intoxicated very fast. I knew the consequence of this, and requested her to bale out the boat: she did so, and sang a mournful sort of song as she baled, but the howling of the wind prevented me from distinguishing the words.

I cannot well analyse my feelings at this time—they were confused; but this I know, self-preservation and hope were the most predominant. I thought of my mother, of my aunt, of Captain Bridgeman, Captain Delmar, and Bob Cross; but my thoughts were as rapid as the gale which bore us along, and I was too much employed in steering the boat, and preventing the seas from filling it, to have a moment to collect my ideas.

Again the woman applied to the bladder of spirits, and offered some to me; I refused. I had had enough, and by this time she had had too much, and after an attempt to bale she dropped down in the stern sheets, smashing pipes and everything beneath her, and spoke no more.

We had now been more than four hours adrift; the wind was as strong as ever, and, I thought, the sea much higher; but I kept the boat steady before the wind, and by degrees, as I became more accustomed to steer, she did not take in so much water; still the boat appeared to be sinking deeper down, and after a time I considered it necessary to bale her out. I did so with my hat, for I found it was half full of water; and then I execrated the woman for having intoxicated herself, so as to be useless in such an emergency.

I succeeded in clearing the boat of the major portion of the water, which was no easy task, as the boat, having remained broadside to the wind, had taken in the sea continually as I baled it out. I then once more resumed the helm, and put the boat before the wind, and thus did I continue for two hours more, when the rain came down in torrents, and the storm was wilder than ever, but a Portsmouth wherry is one of the best boats ever built, and so it proved in this instance. Still I was now in a situation most trying for a lad between fourteen and fifteen; my teeth chattered with the cold, and I was drenched through and through; the darkness was opaque, and I could see nothing but the white foam of the waves, which curled and broke close to the gunwale of the boat.

At one moment I despaired, and looked for immediate death; but my buoyant spirit raised me up again, and I hoped. It would be daylight in a few hours, and oh! how I looked and longed for daylight. I knew I must keep the boat before the wind; I did so, but the seas were worse than ever; they now continually broke into the boat, for the tide had turned, which had increased the swell.

Again I left the helm and bailed out; I was cold and faint, and I felt recovered with the exertion; I also tried to rouse the woman, but it was useless. I felt for her bladder of liquor, and found it in her bosom, more than half empty. I drank more freely, and my spirits and my courage revived. After that, I ate, and steered the boat, awaiting the coming daylight.

It came at last slowly—so slowly; but it did come, and I felt almost happy. There is such a horror in darkness when added to danger; I felt as if I could have worshipped the sun as it rose slowly, and with a watery appearance, above the horizon. I looked around me: there was something like land astern of us, such as I had seen pointed out as land by Bob Cross, when off the coast of Portugal; and so it was—it was the Isle of Wight: for the wind had changed when the rain came down, and I had altered the course of the boat so that for the last four hours I had been steering for the coast of France.

But, although I was cold and shivering, and worn out with watching, and tired with holding the lines by which the wherry was steered, I felt almost happy at the return of day. I looked down upon my companion in the boat; she lay sound asleep, with her head upon the basket of tobacco pipes, her bonnet wet and dripping, with its faded ribbons hanging in the water which washed to and fro at the bottom of the boat, as it rolled and rocked to the motion of the waves; her hair had fallen over her face, so as almost to conceal her features; I thought that she had died during the night, so silent and so breathless did she lie. The waves were not so rough now as they had been, for the flood tide had again made; and as the beams of the morning sun glanced on the water, the same billows which appeared so dreadful in the darkness appeared to dance merrily.

I felt hungry; I took up a red herring from one of the baskets, and tore it to pieces with my teeth. I looked around me in every quarter to see if there was any vessel in sight, but there was nothing to be seen but now and then a screaming sea-gull. I tried to rouse my companion by kicking her with my foot; I did not succeed in waking her up, but she turned round on her back, and, her hair falling from her face, discovered the features of a young and pretty person, apparently not more than nineteen or twenty years old; her figure was slight and well formed.

Young as I was, I thought it a pity that such a nice-looking person—for she still was so, although in a state of disorder, and very dirty—should be so debased by intoxication; and as I looked at the bladder, still half full of spirits I seized it with an intention to throw it overboard, when I paused at the recollection that it had probably saved my life during the night, and might yet be required.

I did not like to alter the course of the boat, although I perceived that we were running fast from the land; for although the sea had gone down considerably, there was still too much for the boat to be put broadside to it. I cannot say that I was unhappy; I found my situation so very much improved to what it was during the darkness of the night. The sun shone bright, and I felt its warmth. I had no idea of being lost—death did not enter my thoughts. There was plenty to eat, and some vessel would certainly pick us up. Nevertheless, I said my prayers, more devoutly than I usually did.

About noon, as near as I could guess, the tide changed again, and as the wind had lulled very much, there was little or no swell. I thought that, now that the motion was not so great, we might possibly ship the foremast and make some little sail upon the boat; and I tried again more earnestly to rouse up my companion; after a few not very polite attempts, I succeeded in ascertaining that she was alive.

"Be quiet, Jim," said she, with her eyes still closed; "it's not five bells yet."

Another kick or two, and she turned herself round and stared wildly.

"Jim," said she, rubbing her eyes, and then she looked about her, and at once she appeared to remember what had passed; she shrieked, and covered her face up with her hands.

"I thought it was a dream, and was going to tell Jim all about it, at breakfast," said she, sorrowfully, "but it's all true—true as gospel. What will become of me? We are lost, lost, lost!"

"We are not lost, but we should have been lost this night if I had been as drunk as you have been," replied I; "I've had work enough to keep the boat above water, I can tell you."

"That's truth," replied she, rising up and taking a seat upon the thwart of the boat. "God, forgive me, poor wretch that I am: what will Jim think, and what will he say, when he sees my best bonnet in such a pickle?"

"Are you quite sure that you'll ever see Jim again, or that you'll ever want your best bonnet?" replied I.

"That's true. If one's body is to be tossed about by green waves, it's little matter whether there's a bonnet or shawl on. Where are we, do you know?"

"I can just see the land out there," replied I, pointing astern. "The sea is smooth; I think we could ship the foremast, and get sail upon her."

The young woman stood up in the boat.

"Yes," said she, "I'm pretty steady; I think we could. Last night in the dark and the tossing sea I could do nothing, but now I can. What a blessing is daylight to cowards like me—I am only afraid in the dark. We must put some sail upon the boat, or nobody will see us. What did you do with the bladder of liquor?"

"Threw it overboard," replied I.

"Had you courage to do that?—and watching through the the night so wet and cold. Well you did right—I could not have done it. Oh! that liquor—that liquor; I wish there wasn't such a thing in the world, but it's too late now. When I first married James Pearson, and the garland was hung to the main-stay of the frigate, nobody could persuade me to touch it, not even James himself, whom I loved so much. Instead of quarrelling with me for not drinking it, as he used to do, he now quarrels with me for drinking the most. If you'll come forward, sir, and help me, we'll soon get up the foremast. This is it, you see, with the jib passed round it. Jim often says that I'd make a capital sailor, if I'd only enter in man's clothes—but as I tell him, I should be put up at the gangway, for not being sober, before I'd been on board a week."

We contrived to ship the mast, and set the jib and foresail. As soon as the sheets were hauled aft, my companion took the steering lines, saying, "I know how to manage her well enough, now it's daylight, and I'm quite sober. You must be very tired, sir; so sit down on the thwart, or lie down if you please, and take a nap; all's safe enough now—see, we lie up well for the land;" and such was the case, for she had brought the boat to the wind, and we skimmed over the waves at the rate of three or four miles an hour. I had no inclination to sleep; I baled the boat out thoroughly, and put the baskets and boxes into some kind of order. I then sat down on the thwarts, first looking round for a vessel in sight; but seeing none, I entered into conversation with my companion.

"What is your name?" said I.

"Peggy Pearson; I have my marriage lines to show: they can throw nothing in my face, except that I'm fond of liquor, God forgive me."

"And what makes you so fond of it now, since you say that, when you were married, you did not care for it?"

"You may well say that: it all came of *sipping*. James would have me on his knee, and would insist on my taking a sip; and to please him I did, although it made me almost sick at first, and then after a while I did not mind it; and then, you see, when I was waiting at the sallyport with the other women, the wind blowing fresh, and the spray wetting us as we stood on the shingle with our arms wrapped up in our aprons, looking out for a boat from the ship to come on shore, they would have a quartern, and make me take a drop; and so it went on. Then James made me bring him liquor on board, and I drank some with him; but what finished me was, that I heard something about James when he was at Plymouth, which made me jealous, and then for the first time I got tipsy. After that, it was all over with me; but, as I said before, it began with sipping—worse luck, but it's done now. Tell me what has passed during the night. Has the weather been very bad?"

I told her what had occurred, and how I had kicked her to wake her up.

"Well, I deserved more than kicking, and you're a fine, brave fellow; and if we get on board the Calliope again—and I trust to God we shall—I'll take care to blow the trumpet for you as you deserve."

"I don't want any one to blow the trumpet for me," replied I.

"Don't you be proud; a good word from me may be of use to you and it's what you deserve. The ship's company will think highly of you, I can tell you. A good name is of no small value—a captain has found out that before now; you're only a lad, but you're a regular trump, and the seamen shall all know it, and the officers too."

"We must get on board the ship first," replied I, "and we are a long way from it just now."

"We're all right, and I have no fear. If we don't see a vessel we shall fetch the land somewhere before to-morrow morning, and it don't look as if there would be any more bad weather. I wonder if they have sent anything out to look after us?"

"What's that?" said I, pointing astern, "it's a sail of some kind."

"Yes," said Peggy, "so it is; it's a square-rigged vessel coming up the Channel—we had better get on the other tack, and steer for her."

We wore the boat round and ran in the direction of the vessel; in three hours we were close to her; I hailed her as she came down upon us but no one appeared to hear us or see us, for she had lower studding-sails set, and there was no one forward. We hailed again, and the vessel was now within twenty yards, and we were right across her bows; a man came forward, and cried out, "Starboard your helm," but not in sufficient time to prevent the vessel from striking the wherry, and to stave her quarter in; we dropped alongside as the wherry filled with water, and we were hauled in by the seamen over the gunwale, just as she turned over and floated away astern.

"Touch and go, my lad," said one of the seamen who had hauled me on board.

"Why don't you keep a better look out?" said Peggy Pearson, shaking her petticoats, which were wet up to the knees. "Paint eyes in the bows of your brig, if you haven't any yourself. Now you've lost a boatful of red-herrings, eggs, and soft tommy—no bad things after a long cruise; we meant to have paid our passage with them—now you must take us for nothing."

The master of the vessel, who was on deck, observed that I was in the uniform of an officer. He asked me how it was we were found in such a situation? I narrated what had passed in few words. He said that he was from Cadiz bound to London, and that he would put us on shore at any place up the river I would like, but that he could not lose the chance of the fair wind to land me anywhere else.

I was too thankful to be landed anywhere; and telling him that I should be very glad if he could put me on shore at Sheerness, which was the nearest place to Chatham, I asked leave to turn into one of the cabin bed-places, and was soon fast asleep.

I may as well here observe, that I had been seen by the sentry abaft to go down by the stern ladder into the boat, and when the waterman came back shortly afterwards to haul his boat up, and perceived that it had gone adrift, there was much alarm on my account. It was too dark to send a boat after us that night, but the next morning the case was reported to the admiral of the port, who directed a cutter to get under weigh and look for us.

The cutter had kept close in shore for the first day, and it was on the morning after I was picked up by the brig, that, in standing more out, she had fallen in with the wherry, bottom up. This satisfied them that we had perished in the rough night, and it was so reported to the port-admiral and to Captain Delmar, who had just come down from London.

I slept soundly till the next morning, when I found that the wind had fallen and that it was nearly calm. Peggy Pearson was on deck; she had washed herself and smoothed out with an iron the ribbons of her bonnet, and was really a very handsome young woman.

"Mr Keene," said she, "I didn't know your name before you told it to the skipper here; you're in a pretty scrape. I don't know what Jim Pearson will say when you go back, running away with his wife as you have done. Don't you think I had better go back first, and smooth things over."

"Oh! you laugh now," replied I; "but you didn't laugh the night we went adrift."

"Because it was no laughing matter. I owe my life to you, and if I had been adrift by myself, I should never have put my foot on shore again. Do you know," said she to me, very solemnly, "I've made a vow—yes, a vow to Heaven, that I'll leave off drinking; and I only hope I may have strength given me to keep it."

"Can you keep it?" said I.

"I think I can; for when I reflect that I might have gone to my account in that state, I really feel a horror of liquor. If James would only give it up, I'm sure I could. I swear that I never will bring him any more on board—that's settled. He may scold me, he may beat me (I don't think he would do that, for he never has yet); but let him do what he pleases, I never will; and if he keeps sober because he hasn't the means of getting tipsy, I am sure that I shall keep my vow. You don't know how I hate myself; and although I'm merry, it's only to prevent my sitting down and crying like a child at my folly and wickedness in yielding to temptation."

"I little thought to hear this from you. When I was with you in the boat, I thought you a very different person."

"A woman who drinks, Mr Keene, is lost to everything. I've often thought of it, after I've become sober again. Five years ago I was the best girl in the school. I was the monitor and wore a medal for good conduct. I thought that I should be so happy with James; I loved him so, and do so still. I knew that he was fond of liquor, but I never thought that he would make me drink. I thought then that I should cure him, and with the help of God I will now; not only him, but myself too."

And I will here state that Peggy Pearson, whose only fault was the passion she had imbibed for drinking, did keep her vow; the difficulty of which few can understand who have not been intemperate themselves; and she not only continued sober herself, but by degrees broke her husband of his similar propensity to liquor.

It was not till the evening of the fourth that we arrived at the Nore. I had four pounds in my pocket at the time that I went adrift, which was more than sufficient, even if I had not intended to go and see my mother. A wherry came alongside, and Peggy Pearson and I stepped into it, after I had thanked the captain, and given a sovereign to the seamen to drink my health.

As soon as we landed at Sheerness I gave another of my sovereigns to Peggy, and left her to find her way back to Portsmouth, while I walked up to Chatham to my mother's house.

It was past eight o'clock and quite dark when I arrived; the shop was closed, and the shutters up at the front door; so I went round to the back to obtain admittance. The door was not fast, and I walked into the little parlour without meeting with anybody. I heard somebody upstairs, and I thought I heard sobbing; it then struck me that my supposed loss might have been communicated to my mother. There was a light on the parlour table, and I perceived an open letter lying near to it. I looked at it; it was the handwriting of Captain Delmar. The candle required snuffing; I raised the letter to the light that I might read it, and read as follows:—

" *My dear Arabella* :—
"You must prepare yourself for very melancholy tidings, and it is most painful to me to be compelled to be the

party who communicates them. A dreadful accident has occurred, and indeed I feel most sincerely for you. On the night of the 10th, Percival was in a boat which broke adrift from the ship in a gale of wind; it was dark, and the fact not known until too late to render any assistance.

"The next day a cutter was despatched by the admiral to look for the boat, which must have been driven out to sea; there was a woman in the boat as well as *our* poor boy. Alas! I regret to say that the boat was found bottom up, and there is no doubt but that *our* dear child has perished.

"You will believe me when I say that I deeply lament his loss; not only on your account, but because I had become most partial to him for his many good qualities, and often have I regretted that his peculiar position prevented me from showing him openly that regard which, as *his father*, I really felt for him.

"I know that I can say nothing that will alleviate your sufferings, and yet I fain would, for you have been so true, and anxious to please me in every point since our first acquaintance and intimacy, that there is nothing that you do not deserve at my hands.

"Comfort yourself, dear Arabella, as well as you can with the reflection that it has been the will of Heaven, to whose decrees we must submit with resignation. I am deeply suffering myself; for, had he lived, I swear to you that I intended to do much more for him than ever I had promised you. He would have made a good and gallant sailor had it pleased Heaven to spare him, and you would have been proud of him; but it has been decided otherwise, and we must bow in obedience to His will. God bless you, and support you in your afflictions, and believe me still,

"Yours, most sincerely and faithfully,

" *Percival Delmar* ."

"Then it is so," thought I; "here I have it under his own hand." I immediately folded up the letter, and put it into my bosom. "You and I never part, that is certain," murmured I. I had almost lost my breath from emotion, and I sat down to recover myself. After a minute or two I pulled the letter out and read it over again. "And he is my father, and he loves me, but dare not show it, and he intended to do more for me than even he had promised my mother."

I folded up the letter, kissed it fervently, and replaced it in my bosom. "Now," thought I, "what shall I do? This letter will be required of me by my mother, but never shall she get it; not tears, nor threats, nor entreaties shall ever induce me to part with it. What shall I do? Nobody has seen me—nobody knows that I have been here. I will go directly and join my ship; yes, that will be my best plan."

I was so occupied with my own reverie, that I did not perceive a footstep on the stairs, until the party was so far down that I could not retreat. I thought to hide myself. I knew by the list shoes that it must be my grandmother. A moment of reflection. I blew out the light on the table, and put myself in an attitude: one arm raised aloft, the other extended from my body, and with my mouth wide open and my eyes fixed, I awaited her approach. She came in—saw me—uttered a fearful shriek, and fell senseless on the floor; the candle in her hand was extinguished in the fall: I stepped over her body; and darting out into the back-yard, gained the door, and was in the street in a minute.

Chapter Seventeen

I was soon in the high road, and clear of the town of Chatham. As my object was that it should not be supposed that I had been there, I made all the haste I could to increase my distance; I therefore walked on in the direction of Gravesend, where I arrived about ten o'clock. A return chaise offered to take me to Greenwich for a few shillings, and before morning dawned I had gained the metropolis.

I lost no time in inquiring when the coaches started for Portsmouth, and found that I was in plenty of time, as one set off at nine o'clock.

Much as I wished to see London, my curiosity gave way to what I considered the necessity of my immediate return to the frigate. At seven o'clock in the evening I arrived at Portsmouth; I hastened down, jumped into a wherry, and was on board of the frigate again by eight.

It may be imagined that my sudden and unexpected appearance caused no little surprise. Indeed, the first lieutenant considered it right to send the gig on shore at that late hour to apprise the captain of my return, and Bob Cross had just time to give me a wring of the hand before he jumped into the boat, and went away to make the report.

I gave a history of my adventures to the officers, leaving them, however, to suppose that I had never been to Chatham, but had gone up to London in the merchant vessel.

Pearson, the boatswain's mate, came to make inquiries about his wife; and, soon after, Bob Cross came on board with the captain's orders, that I should go on shore to him in the gig on the following morning.

I wished very much to consult Bob Cross previous to my seeing the captain. I told him so, and he agreed to meet me on the gangway about ten o'clock, as by that time the officers would be almost all in bed, and there would be less chance of interruption.

It was a fine, clear night, and as soon as we found ourselves alone I narrated to him, in a low voice, all that had taken place, and gave him the contents of the letter which I had taken possession of. I then asked him what he thought I ought to do, now that I was certain of being the son of the captain.

"Why, Master Keene, you have done it very cleverly, that's the truth; and that letter, which is as good as a certificate from Captain Delmar, must be taken great care of. I hardly know where it ought to be put, but I think the best thing will be for me to sew it in a seal-skin pouch that I have, and then you can wear it round your neck, and next your skin; for, as you say, you and that must never part company. But, Master Keene, you must be silent as death about it. You have told me, and I hope I may be trusted, but trust nobody else. As to saying or hinting anything to the captain, you mustn't think of it; you must go on as before, as if you knew nothing, for if he thought you had the letter in your possession he would forget you were his son, and perhaps hate you. He never would have been induced to acknowledge you under his own hand as his son had he not thought that you were dead and gone, as everybody else did; so behave just as respectful and distant as before. It's only in some great emergency that that letter will do you any good, and you must reserve it in case of need. If your mother is suspicious, why, you must blind her. Your granny will swear that it was your ghost; your mother may think otherwise, but cannot prove it; she dare not tell the captain that she suspects you have the letter, and it will all blow over after a cruise or two."

I agreed to follow the advice of Bob Cross, as I saw it was good, and we parted for the night.

The next morning I went on shore to the captain, who received me, very stiffly, with, "Mr Keene, you have had a narrow escape. How did you get back?"

I replied, that the vessel which picked me up was bound to London and that I had taken the coach down.

"Well, I never had an idea that we should have seen you again and I have written to your mother, acquainting her with your loss."

"Have you, sir?" replied I; "it will make her very unhappy."

"Of course it will; but I shall write by this post, stating that you have been so fortunately preserved."

"Thanky, sir," replied I; "have you any further orders, sir?"

"No, Mr Keene; you may go on board and return to your duty."

I made my bow, and quitted the room; went down below, and found Bob Cross waiting for me.

"Well?" said he, as we walked away.

"Stiff as ever," replied I: "told me to go on board and 'tend to my duty."

"Well, I knew it would be so," replied Bob; "it's hard to say what stuff them great nobs are made of. Never mind that; you've your own game to play, and your own secret to keep."

"His secret," replied I, biting my lips, "to keep or to tell, as may happen."

"Don't let your vexation get the better of you, Master Keene; you've the best of it, if you only keep your temper; let him play his cards, and you play yours. As you know his cards and he don't know yours, you must win the game in the end—that is, if you are commonly prudent."

"You are right, Cross," replied I; "but you forget that I am but a boy."

"You are but a boy, Master Keene, but you've no fool's head on your shoulders."

"I hope not," replied I; "but here we are at the boat."

"Yes; and, as I live, here's Peggy Pearson. Well, Peggy, how did you like your cruise with Master Keene?"

"If I ever go on another, I hope he will be my companion. Master Keene, will you allow me to go on board with you to see my husband?"

"Oh, yes, Peggy," replied Cross; "the first lieutenant would not refuse you after what has happened, nor Captain Delmar either, stiff as he is: for, although he never shows it, he don't want feeling. Jim will be glad to see you, Peggy; you haven't an idea how he took on, when he heard of your loss. He borrowed a pocket-handkerchief from the corporal of marines."

"I suspect he'd rather borrow a bottle of rum from the purser," replied Peggy.

"Recollect, Peggy," said I, holding up my finger.

"Mr Keene, I do recollect; I pledge you my word that I have not tasted a drop of spirits since we parted—and that with a sovereign in my pocket."

"Well, only keep to it—that's all."

"I will, indeed, Mr Keene; and, what's more, I shall love you as long as I live."

We pulled on board in the gig, and Peggy was soon in the arms of her husband. As Pearson embraced her at the gangway—for he could not help it—the first lieutenant very kindly said, "Pearson, I shan't want you on deck till after dinner: you may go below with your wife."

"Now, may God bless you, for a cross-looking, kind-hearted gentleman," said Peggy to the first lieutenant.

Peggy was as good as her word to me; she gave such an account of my courage and presence of mind, of her fears and at last of her getting tipsy—of my remaining at the helm and managing the boat all night by myself, that I obtained great reputation among the ship's company, and it was all reported to the officers, and worked its way until it came from the first lieutenant to the captain, and from the captain to the port admiral. This is certain, that Peggy Pearson did do me a good service, for I was no longer looked upon as a mere youngster, who had just come to sea, and who had not been tried.

"Well, sir," said Bob Cross, a day or two afterwards, "it seems, by Peggy Pearson's report, that you're not frightened at a trifle."

"Peg Pearson's report won't do me much good."

"You ought to know better, Master Keene, than to say that; a mouse may help a lion, as the fable says."

"Where did you learn all your fables, Cross?"

"I'll tell you; there's a nice little girl that used to sit on my knee and read her fables to me, and I listened to her because I loved her."

"And does she do so now?"

"Oh, no; she's too big for that—she'd blush up to the temples; but never mind the girl or the fables. I told you that Peggy had reported your conduct, as we say in the service. Now do you know, that this very day I heard the first lieutenant speaking of it to the captain, and you've no idea how proud the captain looked, although he pretended to care nothing about it; I watched him, and he looked as much as to say, 'that's my boy.'"

"Well, if that pleases him, I'll make him prouder yet of me, if I have the opportunity," replied I.

"That you will, Master Keene, if I'm any judge of fizonomy; and that's the way to go to a parent's heart: make him feel proud of you."

I did not forget this, as the reader will eventually discover.

I had written to my mother, giving her a long account of my adventures, but not saying a word of my having been at Chatham. I made her suppose, as I did the captain, that I had been carried up to London. My letter reached her the day after the one announcing my safety, written to her by Captain Delmar.

She answered me by return of post, thanking Heaven for my preservation, and stating how great had been her anguish and misery at my supposed loss. In the latter part of the letter was this paragraph:—

"Strange to say, on the night of the 16th, when I was on
my bed in tears, having but just received the news of your
loss, your grandmother went downstairs, and declares that
she saw you or your ghost in the little back parlour. At
all events, I found her insensible on the floor, so that she
must have seen something. She might have been frightened
at nothing; and yet I know not what to think, for there
are circumstances which almost make *me* believe that
somebody was in the house. I presume you can prove an
alibi."

That my mother had been suspicious, perhaps more than suspicious,
from the disappearance of the letter, I was convinced. When I replied to her,
I said:—

"My *alibi* is easily proved by applying to the master and
seamen of the vessel on board of which I was. Old granny
must have been frightened at her own shadow: the idea of
my coming to your house, and having left it without seeing
you is rather too absurd; granny must have invented the
story, because she hates me, and thought to make you do
the same."

Whatever my mother may have thought, she did not again mention the
subject. I had, however, a few days afterwards, a letter from my aunt Milly,
in which she laughingly told the same story of granny swearing that she
had seen me or my ghost. "At first we thought it was your ghost, but since
a letter from Captain Delmar to your mother has been missing, it is now
imagined that you have been here, and have taken possession of it. You will
tell me, my dearest Percival, I'm sure, if you did play this trick to granny, or
not; you know you may trust me with any of your tricks."

But I was not in this instance to be wheedled by my aunt. I wrote in
return, saying how much I was amazed at my grandmother telling such fibs,
and proved to her most satisfactorily that I was in London at the time they
supposed I might have been at Chatham.

That my aunt had been requested by my mother to try to find out the
truth, I was well convinced: but I felt my secret of too much importance to
trust either of them and from that time the subject was never mentioned; and
I believe it was at last surmised that the letter might have been destroyed
accidentally or purposely by the maid-servant, and that my grandmother
had been frightened at nothing at all—an opinion more supported, as the
maid, who had taken advantage of my mother's retiring to her room, and
had been out gossiping, declared that she had not left the premises three

minutes, and not a soul could have come in. Moreover, it was so unlikely that I could have been in Chatham without being recognised by somebody.

My grandmother shook her head, and said nothing during all this canvassing of the question; but my aunt Milly declared that I never would have been at Chatham without coming to see her. And it was her opinion that the servant girl had read the letter when left on the table, and had taken it out to show to her associates; and somebody who wished to have a hold upon my mother by the possession of the letter had retained it.

I think my mother came to that opinion at last, and it was the source of much uneasiness to her. She dared not say a word to Captain Delmar, and every day expected to have an offer made of returning the letter, upon a certain sum being paid down. But the offer was never made, as the letter had been sewed up by Bob Cross in the piece of seal-skin, and was worn round my neck with a ribbon, with as much care as if it had been a supposed bit of the wood of the true cross, possessed by some old female Catholic devotee.

But long before all these discussions were over, H.M. ship Calliope had been ordered to sail, and was steering down the Channel before a smart breeze.

Chapter Eighteen

Although I have so much to say as to oblige me to pass over without notice the majority of my companions, I think I ought to dedicate one chapter to a more particular description of those with whom I was now principally in contact on board of the Calliope.

I have already spoken much of the Honourable Captain Delmar, but I must describe him more particularly. When young, he must have been a very handsome man; even now, although nearly fifty years of age, and his hair and whiskers a little mixed with grey, he was a fine-looking personage, of florid complexion, large blue eyes, nose and mouth very perfect: in height he was full six feet; and he walked so erect that he looked even taller.

There was precision, I may say dignity, in all his motions. If he turned to you, it was slowly and deliberately; there was nothing like rapidity in his movement. On the most trifling occasions, he wrapped himself up in etiquette with all the consequence of a Spanish Hidalgo; and showed in almost every action and every word that he never forgot his superiority of birth.

No one, except myself, perhaps, would ever have thought of taking a liberty with him; for although there was a pomposity about him, at the same time it was the pomposity of a high-bred gentleman, who respected himself, and expected every one to do the same.

That sometimes a little mirth was occasioned by his extreme precision is true; but it was whispered, not boldly indulged in. As to his qualities as an officer and seaman, I shall only say, that they were considered more than respectable. Long habit of command had given him a fair knowledge of the duties in the first instance, and he never condescended (indeed, it would have been contrary to his character) to let the officers or seamen know whether he did or did not know anything about the second.

As to his moral character, I can only say, that it was very difficult to ascertain it. That he would never do that which was in the slightest degree derogatory to the character of a gentleman was most certain: but he was so wrapped up in exclusiveness, that it was almost impossible to estimate his feelings. Occasionally, I may say very rarely, he might express them; but if he did, it was but for a moment, and he was again reserved as before.

That he was selfish is true; but who is not? and those in high rank are still more so than others, not so much by nature, but because their self is encouraged by those around them. You could easily offend his pride but he was above being flattered in a gross way. I really believe that the person in the ship for whom he had the least respect was the obsequious Mr Culpepper. Such was the Honourable Captain Delmar.

Mr Hippesley, the first lieutenant, was a broad-shouldered, ungainly-looking personage. He had more the appearance of a master in the service than a first lieutenant. He was a thorough seaman; and really, for a first lieutenant, a very good-natured man. All that was requisite, was to allow his momentary anger to have free escape by the safety-valve of his mouth: if you did not, an explosion was sure to be the result.

He was, as we use the term at sea, a regular ship husband—that is to say, he seldom put his foot on shore; and if he did, he always appeared anxious to get on board again. He was on good terms, but not familiar, with his messmates, and very respectful to the captain. There was no other officer in the service who would have suited Captain Delmar so well as Mr Hippesley, who, although he might occasionally grumble at not being promoted, appeared on the whole to be very indifferent about the matter.

The men were partial to him, as they always are to one who, whatever may be his peculiarities, is consistent. Nothing is more unpleasant to men than to sail under a person whom, to use their own expression, "they never knew where to find."

The second and third lieutenants, Mr Percival and Mr Weymss, were young men of good family, and were admitted to a very slight degree of familiarity with Captain Delmar: they were of gentlemanly manners, both good seamen, and kind to their inferiors.

Mr Culpepper, the purser, was my abomination—a nasty, earwigging, flattering, bowing old rogue. The master, Mr Smith, was a very quiet man, plain and unoffending, but perfectly master of, and always attentive to, his duty.

The marine officer, Mr Tusk, was a nonentity put into a red jacket. The surgeon was a tall, and very finicking sort of gentleman as to dress; but well informed, friendly in disposition, and perfectly acquainted with his profession.

My messmates were most of them young men of good birth, with the exception of Tommy Dott, who was the son of a warrant officer, and Mr

Green, whose father was a boot-maker in London. I shall not, however, waste my reader's time upon them; they will appear when required. I shall, therefore, now proceed with my narrative.

It is usually the custom for the midshipmen to take up provisions and spirits beyond their allowance, and pay the purser an extra sum for the same; but this Mr Culpepper would not permit—indeed, he was the most stingy and disagreeable old fellow that I ever met with in the service. We never had dinner or grog enough, or even lights sufficient for our wants.

We complained to the first lieutenant, but he was not inclined to assist us: he said we had our allowance, and it was all we could demand; that too much grog was bad for us, and as for candles, they only made us sit up late when we ought to be in bed: he was, moreover, very strict about the lights being put out. This, however, was the occasion of war to the knife between the midshipmen and Mr Culpepper.

But it was of no avail; he would seldom trust his own steward or the mate of the main deck; whenever he could, he superintended the serving out of all provisions and mixing of the grog: no wonder that he was said to be a rich man. The only party to whom he was civil was Mr Hippesley, the first lieutenant, and the captain; both of whom had the power of annoying him, and reducing his profits.

To the captain he was all humility; every expense that he required was, with his proffered bow, cheerfully submitted to; but he gained on the whole by this apparent liberality, as the captain was rather inclined to protect him in all other points of service, except those connected with his own comforts and luxuries; and many a good job did Mr Culpepper get done for him, by humbly requesting and obsequiously bowing.

We had been at sea for about a week, and were running down towards the island of Madeira, which we expected to reach the next morning. Our destination was a secret, as our captain sailed with sealed orders, to be opened when off that island.

The weather was very fine and warm, and the wind had fallen, when at sundown high land was reported from the mast-head, at about forty miles distant. I was, as on the former cruise, signal midshipman, and did day duty—that is, I went down with the sun, and kept no night watch.

I had been cogitating how I could play some trick to Mr Culpepper: the midshipmen had often proposed that we should do so, but I had made up my mind that, whenever I did, I would make no confidant. Tommy Dott often suggested an idea, but I invariably refused, as a secret is only a secret when it is known to one person: for that reason I never consulted Bob Cross, because I knew that he would have persuaded me not to do so; but after anything was happily executed, I then used to confide in him.

I observed before that Mr Culpepper wore a flaxen wig, and I felt sure, from his penuriousness, that he was not likely to have more than one on board. I, therefore, fixed upon his wig as the object of my vengeance, and having made up my mind on the night that we made the island of Madeira, I determined to put my project in execution.

For convenience, the first lieutenant had a small ladder which went down through the skylight of the gun-room so that they could descend direct, instead of going round by the after-hatchway, and entering by the gun-room doors, where the sentry was placed.

I went to my hammock and slept till the middle watch was called; I then got up and dressed myself without being perceived.

As soon as the lieutenant of the middle watch had been called by the mate, who lighted his candle and left him to dress himself, I came up by the after-ladder, and, watching an opportunity when the sentry at the captain's cabin door had walked forward, I softly descended by the skylight ladder into the gun-room.

The light in the cabin of the lieutenant, who was dressing, was quite sufficient, and the heat of the weather was so great, that all the officers slept with their cabin doors fastened back, for ventilation; I had, therefore, no difficulty in putting my hand on the purser's wig, with which I escaped unperceived, and immediately turned in again to my hammock, to consider what I should do with my prize.

Should I throw it overboard; should I stuff it down the pump-well, or slip it into the ship's coppers, that it might re-appear when the pea-soup was baled out or dinner; or should I put it into the manger forward, where the pigs were?

In the meantime, while I was considering the matter, the midshipman of the first watch came down and turned in, and all was again quiet, except an occasional nasal melody from some heavy sleeper.

At last, quite undecided, I peeped through the clews of my hammock to see what the sentry at the gun-room door was about, and found that he had sat down on a chest, and was fast asleep. I knew immediately that the man was in my power, and I did not fear him; and then it was that the idea came into my head, that I would singe the purser's wig. I went softly to the sentry's light, took it from the hook, and went down with it into the cockpit, as being the best place for carrying on my operations. The wig was very greasy, and every curl, as I held it in the candle, flared up, and burned beautifully to within a quarter of an inch of the caul.

It was soon done, and I replaced the sentry's light; and finding that the gun-room door was a-jar, I went in softly, and replaced the wig where I had taken it from, repassed the sentry, who was still fast asleep, and regained my hammock, intending to undress myself in it; but I had quite forgotten one thing (I was soon reminded of it) — I heard the voice of the officer of the watch I calling out to the sentry at the cabin door—

"Sentry, what's that smell of burning?"

"I don't know, sir," replied the sentry; "I was just thinking of going forward for the ship's corporal."

The smell, which had gradually ascended from the cockpit, now spread from deck to deck, and became stronger and stronger. The gun-room-door sentry jumped up at the voice of the lieutenant, and called out that there was a very strong smell in the cockpit. The lieutenant and mate of the watch came down, and it was immediately supposed that the spirit-room had caught fire, for the smell was really very powerful.

The first lieutenant, who had wakened up at the voices, was out in a minute; he put his head over the cockpit, and ordering the officer of the watch to call the drummer, and beat to quarters, ran up to inform the captain.

The drummer was out in a moment, and, seizing his drum, which hung up by the mainmast, ran up in his shirt and beat the tattoo.

The whole ship's company rose up at the sound, which they knew was the signal for something important; and the beat of the drum was followed up by the shrill piping of the boatswain's mates at each hatchway.

At that moment, some frightened man belonging to the watch cried out that the ship was on fire, and the lower decks were immediately a scene of bustle and confusion.

Perhaps there is nothing more awful than the alarm of fire at sea; the feeling that there is no escape — the only choice being by which element, fire or water, you choose to perish. But if it is awful in daylight, how much more so is it to be summoned up to await such peril when you have been sleeping in fancied bounty.

The captain had hurried on his clothes, and stood on the quarter-deck. He was apparently calm and collected; but, as usual, the first lieutenant carried on the duty, and well he did it.

"Where's the gunner? Mr Hutt, bring up the keys from my cabin, and have all ready for clearing the magazines if required. Firemen, get your buckets to bear; carpenters, rig the pumps. Silence there, fore and aft."

But the confusion became very great, and there evidently was a panic. The captain then interposed, calling out to the boatswain and his mates to send every man aft on the quarter-deck.

This order was obeyed; the men came thronging like a flock of sheep, huddling together and breathless.

"Silence there, my men," cried Captain Delmar—"silence. I say; is this the conduct of men-of-war's-men? Every man of you sit down on deck— pass the word there for every man to sit down."

The order was mechanically obeyed, and as soon as the ship's company were all seated, the captain said—

"I tell you what, my lads, I'm ashamed of you: the way to put out a fire is to be cool and calm, obeying orders and keeping silence. Now collect yourselves, all of you, for until you are all quiet and cool, you will sit where you are."

After a pause of a few seconds—

"Now, my men, are you more steady? Recollect, be cool, and keep silence. Carpenter, are the pumps rigged?"

"Yes, sir," replied the carpenter.

"Now, firemen, go for your buckets; let nobody else move. Silence—not a word: three foremast guns main-deck, to your quarters. Silence and quiet, if you please. Now, are you all steady?—then, to your quarters, my men, and wait for orders."

It was astonishing how collected the ship's company became by the judicious conduct of the captain, who now continued to command. When the men had gone down to their stations, he directed the two junior lieutenants to go and examine where the fire was, and to be careful not to lift the hatches if they discovered that it was in the spirit-room.

I had been on the quarter-deck some time, and, being aware of the cause, of course was not at all alarmed: and I had exerted myself very assiduously in keeping the men cool and quiet, shoving the men down who were unwilling to sit down on the deck, and even using them very roughly; showing a great deal more *sang froid* than any other of the officers, which of course was not to be wondered at.

Mr Culpepper, who was most terribly alarmed, had come up on deck, and stood trembling close to the side of the captain and first lieutenant; he had pulled on his wig without discovering that it had been burnt, and as I passed him, the burnt smell was very strong indeed; so thought the captain and the first lieutenant, who were waiting the return of the officers.

"I smell the fire very strong just now," said the captain to the first lieutenant.

"Yes, sir, every now and then it is very strong," replied the first lieutenant.

The purser's wig was just between them,—no wonder that they smelt it. After two or three minutes the officers came up, and reported that they could discover no fire, and that there was very little smell of fire down below.

"And yet I smell it now," said Captain Delmar.

"So do I, sir," said the second lieutenant; "and it really smells stronger on deck than it does down below."

"It's very odd; let them continue the search."

The search was continued; the first lieutenant now going down, and after a time they said that the strongest smell was from the purser's cabin.

"Mr Culpepper, they say the smell is in your cabin," said Captain Delmar; "go down, if you please; they may want to open your lockers."

Mr Culpepper, who still trembled like an aspen, went down the ladder, and I followed him; but in descending the second ladder his foot slipped, and he fell down the hatchway to the lower deck.

I hastened down after him; he was stunned, and I thought this a good opportunity to pull off his wig, which I did very dexterously, and concealed it. He was taken into the gun-room, and the surgeon called, while I walked up on deck, and quietly dropped the wig overboard at the gangway.

My reason for doing this was, that having no idea that my trick would have created so much confusion, and have turned up the officers and men as it did, I thought that the purser's wig would, the next morning, account for the smell of fire, and an investigation take place, which, although it might not lead to discovery, would certainly lead to suspicion; so the wig was now floating away, and with the wig went away all evidence.

After a search of nearly half an hour, nothing was discovered; the drummer was ordered to beat the retreat, and all was quiet again.

I went to bed quite satisfied with the events of the night, and slept the sleep of innocence—at least I slept just as soundly.

This mysterious affair ever remained a mystery: the only loss was the purser's wig, but that was nothing, as Mr Culpepper acknowledged that he did not know himself what he was about, and, for all he knew to the contrary, he might have thrown it overboard.

My conduct on this occasion again gained me great credit. It had been remarked by the captain and officers, and I rose in estimation. How I might have behaved had I really supposed that the ship was on fire, is quite another affair—I presume not quite so fearlessly. As it was, I was resolved to take all the credit given to me and for that reason it was not till a long while afterwards, that I hinted the secret even to Bob Cross.

Chapter Nineteen

The next morning, when we arrived at Funchal, we found that our orders were for the West Indies: we stayed one day to take in wine and then hove up the anchor, and went on to our destination. We soon got into the trades, and run them fast down till we arrived at Carlisle Bay, Barbadoes, where we found the admiral and delivered our despatches. We were ordered to water and complete as soon as possible, as we were to be sent on a cruise.

Tommy Dott, my quondam ally, was in disgrace. He had several times during the cruise proposed that I should join him in several plots of mischief, but I refused, as I did not consider them quite safe.

"You are not the keen fellow I thought you were," said he; "you are up to nothing now; there's no fun in you, as there used to be."

He was mistaken; there was fun in me, but there was also prudence, and from what I had latterly seen of Tommy Dott, I did not think he was to be trusted.

The day after we anchored at Carlisle Bay, Tommy came to me and said, "Old Culpepper serves out plums and suet this afternoon; I heard him tell steward. Now, I think we may manage to get some—I never saw better plums on board of a ship."

"Well," said I, "I like raisins as well as you do, Tommy—but what is your plan?"

"Why, I've got my squirt: and old Culpepper never lights more than one of his purser's dips (small candles) in the steward's room. I'll get down in the cockpit in the dark, and squirt at the candle—the water will put it out, and he'll send the steward for another light, and then I'll try and get some."

It was not a bad plan, but still I refused to join in it, as it was only the work of one person, and not two. I pointed that out to him and he agreed with me, saying that he would do it himself.

When Mr Culpepper went down into the steward's room, Tommy reconnoitred, and then came into the berth and filled his squirt.

Although I would not join him, I thought I might as well see what was going on and therefore descended the cockpit ladder soon after Tommy, keeping out of the way in the foremost part of the cockpit, where it was quite dark.

Tommy directed his squirt very dexterously, hit the lighted wick of the solitary candle, which fizzed, sputtered, and finally gave up the ghost.

"Bless me!" said Mr Culpepper, "what can that be?"

"A leak from the seams above I suppose," said the steward:

"I will go to the gallery for another light."

"Yes, yes, be quick," said Mr Culpepper, who remained in the steward's room in the dark, until the return of the steward.

Tommy Dott then slipped in softly, and commenced filling all his pockets with the raisins; he had nearly taken in his full cargo, when, somehow or another, Mr Culpepper stepped forward from where he stood, and he touched Tommy, whom he immediately seized crying out, "Thieves! thieves!—call the sentry!—sentry, come here."

The sentry of the gun-room door went down the ladder as Mr Culpepper dragged out Tommy, holding him fast by both hands.

"Take him, sentry—take him in charge. Call the master-at-arms—little thief. Mr Dott! Hah—well, we'll see."

The consequence was, that Mr Tommy Dott was handed from the sentry to the master-at-arms, and taken up on the quarterdeck, followed by Mr Culpepper and his steward.

There was no defence or excuse to be made: the pockets of his jacket and of his trowsers were stuffed with raisins; and at the bottom of his pocket, when they were emptied by the master-at-arms, was found the squirt.

As soon as the hue and cry was over, and all the parties were on the quarter-deck, as the coast was clear, I thought I might as well take advantage of it; and therefore I came out from my hiding-place, went into the steward's room, filled my handkerchief with raisins, and escaped to the berth unperceived; so that while Tommy Dott was disgorging on the quarter-deck, I was gorging below.

Mr Dott was reported to the captain for this heinous offence; and, in consequence, was ordered below under arrest, his place in the captain's gig being filled up by me; so that in every point of view Tommy suffered, and I reaped the harvest. What pleased me most was, that, being midshipman of the captain's boat, I was of course continually in the company of the coxswain, Bob Cross.

But I must not delay at present, as I have to record a very serious adventure which occurred, and by which I, for a long while, was separated from my companions and shipmates.

In ten days we sailed in search of a pirate vessel, which was reported to have committed many dreadful excesses, and had become the terror of the mercantile navy. Our orders were to proceed northward, and to cruise off the Virgin Islands, near which she was said to have been last seen.

About three weeks after we had left Carlisle Bay, the look-out man reported two strange sail from the mast-head. I was sent up, as signal mid, to examine them, and found that they were both schooners, hove to close together; one of them very rakish in their appearance. All sail in chase was made immediately, and we came up within three miles of them, when one, evidently the pirate we were in search of, made sail, while the other remained hove to.

As we passed the vessel hove to, which we took it for granted was a merchantman, which the pirate had been plundering, the captain ordered one of the cutters to be lowered down with a midshipman and boat's crew to take possession of her. The men were all in the boat, but the midshipman had gone down for his spy-glass, or something else, and as it was merely with a view of ascertaining what the vessel was, and the chief object was to overtake the pirate vessel, to prevent the delay which was caused by the other midshipman not being ready, Mr Hippesley ordered me to go into the boat instead of him, and, as soon as I was on board of the schooner, to make sail and follow the frigate.

The captain did say, "He is too young, Mr Hippesley; is he not?"

"I'd sooner trust him than many older, sir," was the reply of the first lieutenant. "Jump in, Mr Keene." I did so, with my telescope in my hand. "Lower away, my lads—unhook, and sheer off;" and away went the frigate in pursuit of the pirate vessel, leaving me in the boat, to go on board of the schooner.

We were soon alongside, and found that there was not a soul on board of the vessel; what had become of the crew, whether they had been murdered, or not, it was impossible to say, but there were a few drops of blood on the deck.

The vessel was an American, bound to one of the islands, with shingle and fir planks; not only was her hold full, but the fir planks were piled up on each side of the deck, between the masts, to the height of five or six feet. The pirate had, apparently, been taking some of the planks on board for her own use.

We dropped the boat astern, let draw the foresheet, and made sail after the frigate, which was now more than a mile from us, and leaving us very fast.

The schooner was so over-loaded that she sailed very badly, and before the evening closed in, we could just perceive the top-gallant sails of the Calliope above the horizon: but this we thought little of, as we knew that as soon as she had captured the pirate she would run back again, and take us out.

There were some hams and other articles on board, for the pirates had not taken everything, although the lockers had been all broken open, and the articles were strewed about in every direction in the cabin and on the deck.

Just before dark, we took the bearings of the frigate, and stood the same course as she was doing, and then we sat down to a plentiful meal to which we did justice. I then divided the boat's crew into watches, went down into the cabin, and threw myself on the standing bed-place, of which there was but one, with all my clothes on; the men who had not the watch went down, and turned in in the cuddy forward, where the seamen usually sleep.

It was not till past midnight that I could obtain any sleep; the heat was excessive, and I was teased by the cockroaches, which appeared to swarm in the cabin to an incredible degree, and were constantly running over my face and body. I little thought then why they swarmed. I recollect that I dreamt of murder, and tossing men overboard; and then of the vessel being on fire and after that, I felt very cool and comfortable, and I dreamed no more; I thought that I heard a voice calling my name: it appeared that I did hear it in my sleep, but I slept on.

At last I turned round, and felt a splashing as of water, and some water coming into my mouth: I awoke. All was dark and quiet; I put my hand out, and I put it into the water—where was I—was I overboard? I jumped up in my fright; I found that was still on the standing bed-place, but the water was above the mattress.

I immediately comprehended that the vessel was sinking, and I called out, but there was no reply.

I turned out of the bed-place, and found myself up to my neck in water, with my feet on the cabin-deck. Half swimming, and half floundering, I gained the ladder, and went up the hatchway.

It was still quite dark, and I could not perceive nor hear anybody. I called out but there was no reply. I then was certain that the men had left the vessel when they round her sinking, and had left me to sink with her. I may as well here observe, that when the men had found the water rising upon them forward they had rushed on deck in a panic, telling the man at the wheel that the vessel was sinking, and had immediately hauled up the boat to save their lives; but they did recollect me, and the coxswain of the boat had come down in the cabin by the ladder, and called me: but the cabin was full of water, and he, receiving no answer, considered that I was drowned, and returned on deck.

The boat had then shoved off, and I was left to my fate; still I hoped that such was not the case, and I hallooed again and again, but in vain, and I thought it was all over with me. It was a dreadful position to be in. I said my prayers and prepared to die, and yet I thought it was hard to die at fifteen years old.

Although I do not consider that my prayers were of much efficacy, for there was but little resignation in them, praying had one good effect—it composed me, and I began to think whether there was any chance of being saved.

Yes, there were plenty of planks on the deck, and if it were daylight I could tie them together and make a raft, which would bear me up. How I longed for daylight, for I was afraid that the vessel would sink before I could see to do what was requisite. The wind had become much fresher during the night, and the waves now dashed against the sides of the water-logged vessel.

As I watched for daylight, I began to reflect how this could have happened; and it occurred to me that the pirates had scuttled the bottom of the vessel to sink her; and in this conjecture I was right.

At last a faint light appeared in the east, which soon broke into broad day, and I lost no time in setting about my work.

Before I began, however, I thought it advisable to ascertain how much more water there was in the vessel since I had quitted the cabin which it appeared to me must have been about two hours. I therefore went down in the cabin to measure it. I know how high it was when I waded through it. I found, to my surprise, and, I may say, to my joy, that it was not higher than it was before.

I thought that perhaps I might be mistaken, so I marked the height of the water at the cabin ladder, and I sat down on deck to watch it; it appeared to me not to rise any higher.

This made me reflect, and it then struck me that, as the vessel was laden with timber, she would not probably sink any lower, so I deferred my work till I had ascertained the fact.

Three hours did I watch, and found that the water did not rise higher, and I was satisfied; but the wind increased, and the vessel's sails, instead of flapping to the wind as she drove without any one at the helm, were now bellied out, and the vessel careened to leeward.

I was afraid that she would turn over; and finding an axe on the deck, I mounted the rigging with it, and commenced cutting away the lacing of the sails from the mast. I then lowered the gaffs, and cleared away the canvass in the same way, so that the sails fell on the deck. This was a work of at least one hour; but when the canvass was off, the vessel was steady.

It was well that I had taken this precaution; for very soon afterwards the wind was much fresher, and the weather appeared very threatening; the sea also rose considerably. I was very tired, and sat down for some time on the deck abaft.

It then occurred to me that the weight of the planks upon the deck must not only keep the vessel deeper in the water, but make her more top-heavy, and I determined to throw them overboard; but first I looked for something to eat, and found plenty of victuals in the iron pot in which the men had cooked their supper the night before.

As soon as I had obtained from the cask lashed on the deck a drink of water, to wash down the cold fried ham which I had eaten, I set work to throw overboard the planks on deck.

When I had thrown over a portion from one side I went to the other, and threw over as many more, that I might, as much as possible, keep the vessel on an even keel.

This job occupied me the whole of the day; and when I had completed my task I examined the height of the water at the cabin ladder, and found that the vessel had risen more than six inches. This was a source of great comfort to me, and what pleased me more was, that the wind had gone down again, and the water was much smoother.

I made a supper off some raw ham, for the fire had been extinguished, and committing myself to the protection of Heaven, lay down as the sun set, and from the fatigue of the day was soon in a sound sleep.

I awoke about the middle of the night. The stars shone brightly, and there was but a slight ripple on the water.

I thought of my mother, of my aunt Milly, of Captain Delmar, and I felt for the seal-skin pouch which was fastened round my neck. It was all safe.

I calculated chances, and I made up my mind that I should be picked up by some vessel or another before long.

I said to myself—"Why, I am better off now than I was when in the wherry, with Peggy Pearson; I was saved then, why should I not be now?"

I felt no desponding, and lay down, and was soon fast asleep.

It was broad daylight when I awoke; I took my spy-glass, and looking round the horizon, discovered a vessel several miles off, standing towards me. This gave me fresh spirits.

I made a raw breakfast, and drank plenty of water as before. The wind, which was very light, increased a little. The vessel came nearer, and I made her out to be a schooner. In two hours she was close to me, and I waved my hat, and hallooed as loud as I could.

The schooner was full of men, and steered close to me—she was a beautiful craft, and, although the wind was so light, glided very fast through the water, and I could not help thinking that she was the pirate vessel which the frigate had been in chase of.

It appeared as if they intended to pass me, and I hallooed, "Schooner, ahoy! Why don't you send a boat on board?"

I must say, that when the idea struck me that she was a pirate vessel, my heart almost failed me.

Shortly afterwards the schooner rounded to and lowered a boat, which pulled to the vessel. The boat's crew were all negroes.

One of them said, "Jump in, you white boy; next jump he take be into the shark's mouth," continued the man, grinning, as he addressed himself to the others in the boat.

I got into the boat, and they rowed on board the schooner. I did then think that I was done for; for what mercy could I expect, being a king's officer, from pirates, which the words of the negro convinced me they were?

As soon as I was alongside of the schooner, they ordered me to go up the side, which I did, with my spy-glass in my hand. I leaped from the gunwale down on the deck, and found myself on board of an armed vessel, with a crew wholly composed of blacks.

I was rudely seized by two of them, who led me aft to where a negro stood apart from the rest. A more fierce, severe, determined-looking countenance, I never beheld. He was gigantic in stature and limbed like the Farnesian Hercules.

"Well, boy, who are you?" said he, "and how came you on board of that vessel?"

I told him in very few words.

"Then you belong to that frigate that chased us the day before yesterday?"

"Yes," replied I.

"What is her name?"

"The Calliope."

"She sails well," said he.

"Yes," replied I; "she is the fastest sailer on this station."

"That's all the information I want of you, boy: now you may go."

"Go where?" replied I.

"Go where?—go overboard, to be sure," replied he, with a grin.

My heart died within me; but I mustered courage enough to say, "Much obliged to you, sir; but I'd rather stay where I am, if it's all the same to you."

The other negroes laughed at this reply, and I felt a little confidence; at all events, their good-humour gave me courage, and I felt that being bold was my only chance.

The negro captain looked at me for a time, as if considering, and at last said to the men, "Overboard with him."

"Good-bye, sir, you're very kind," said I; "but this is a capital spy-glass, and I leave it to you as a legacy." And I went up to him and offered him my spy-glass. Merciful Heaven! bow my heart beat against my ribs when I did this!

The negro captain took the glass, and looked through it.

"It is a good glass," said he, as he removed it from his eyes. It was poor Green's spy-glass, which he had given me for showing him the mason's signs.

"Well, white boy, I accept your present; and now, good bye."

"Good-bye, sir. Do me one kindness in return," said I, very gravely, for I felt my hour was come.

"And what is that?" replied the negro.

"Tie a shot to my heels, that I may sink quickly; it won't take them long."

"You don't ask me to spare your life, then?" replied the negro.

"He de very first white dat not ask it," said one of the negroes.

"Dat really for true," said another.

"Yes, by gum," replied a third.

Oh, how I wished to know what to say at that moment! The observations of the negroes made me imagine that I had better not *ask* for it and yet how I clung to life! It was an awful moment—I felt as if I had lived a year in a few minutes. For a second or two I felt faint and giddy—I drew a long breath and revived.

"You don't answer me, boy," said the negro captain.

"Why should I ask when I feel certain to be refused? If you will give me my life, I will thank you: I don't particularly wish to die, I can assure you."

"I have taken an oath never to spare a white man. For once I am sorry that I cannot break my oath."

"If that is all, I am a boy, and not a man," replied I. "Keep me till I grow bigger."

"By golly, captain, that very well said. Keep him, captain," said one of the negroes.

"Yes, captain," replied another; "keep him to tend your cabin. Proper you have white slave boy."

The negro captain for some time made no reply; he appeared to be in deep thought. At last he said—

"Boy, you have saved your life: you may thank yourself and not me. Prossa, let him be taken below; give him a frock and trousers and throw that infernal dress overboard, or I may change my resolution."

The negro who was addressed, and who wore a sort of uniform as an officer—which he was, being second mate—led me below,—nothing loth, I can assure my readers.

When I was between decks. I sat down upon a chest, my head swam, and I fainted. The shock had been too powerful for a lad of my age. They brought water, and recovered me. When I revived, I felt that I might have lost in their good opinion by thus knowing my weakness; and I had sufficient presence of mind to ask for something to eat. This deceived them; they said to one another that I must have been on board that vessel for two days without food, and of course I did not deny it.

They brought me some meat and some grog. I ate and drank a little. They then took off my uniform, and put on me a check frock and white trousers; after which, I said I wished to lie down a little, and they left me to sleep on the chest where I had been seated.

I pretended to sleep, although I could not; and I found out by their conversation that I gained the goodwill not only of the crew, but of the captain, by my behaviour.

I considered that I had gained my life, at least for the present; but what security could I have in such company?

After an hour or two I felt quite recovered, and I thought it advisable to go on deck. I did so, and went right aft to the negro captain, and stood before him.

"Well, boy," said he, "why do you come to me?"

"You gave me my life; you're the greatest friend I have here, so I come to you. Can I do anything?"

"Yes; you may assist in the cabin, if your white blood does not curdle at the idea of attending on a black man."

"Not at all. I will do anything for them who are kind to me, as you have been."

"And think it no disgrace?"

"Not the least. Is it a disgrace to be grateful?"

The reader will observe how particularly judicious my replies were, although but fifteen years old. My dangerous position had called forth the reflection and caution of manhood.

"Go down into the cabin; you may amuse yourself till I come."

I obeyed this order. The cabin was fitted up equal to most yachts, with Spanish mahogany and gold mouldings; a beaufet full of silver (there was no glass) occupied nearly one-half of it; even the plates and dishes were of the same material. Silver candelabras hung down from the middle of the beams; a variety of swords, pistols, and other weapons were fixed up against the bulkhead; a small bookcase, chiefly of Spanish books, occupied the after-bulkhead, and the portraits of several white females filled up the intervals; a large table in the centre, a stand full of charts, half a dozen boxes of cigars, and two most luxurious sofas, completed the furniture.

A door from the starboard side led, I presumed, to the stateroom, where the captain slept; but I did not venture to open it.

I surveyed all this magnificence, wondering who this personage could be; and more still, how it was that the whole of the crew were, as well as the captain, of the negro race.

We had heard that the pirate we were in search of was a well-known character—a Spaniard—who went by the name of Chico, and that his crew consisted of Americans, English, and Spaniards. That this was the vessel, I knew, from the conversation of the men when I was below for they called her the Stella.

Now, it appeared that the vessel had changed masters; the crew were chiefly Spanish negroes, or other negroes who spoke Spanish, but some of them spoke English, and a few words of Spanish; these, I presumed, were American or English runaways. But the captain—his language was as correct as my own; Spanish he spoke fluently, for I heard him giving orders in that language while I was in the cabin; neither was he flat-nosed, like the majority. Had he been white, his features would have been considered regular, although there was a fierceness about them at times which was terrible to look at.

"Well," thought I, "if I live and do well, I shall know more about it; yes, if I live, I wish I was on the quarterdeck of the Calliope, even as Tommy was with his pockets stuffed full of the purser's raisins, and looking like a fool and a rogue at the same time."

I had been down in the cabin about half an hour, when the negro captain made his appearance.

"Well," said he, "I suppose you would as soon see the devil as me—eh, boy?"

"No: indeed," replied I, laughing—for I had quite recovered my confidence—"for you were about to send me to the devil, and I feel most happy that I still remain with you."

"You're exactly the cut of boy I like," replied he, smiling. "How I wish that you were black!—I detest your colour."

"I have no objection to black my face, if you wish it," replied I: "it's all the same to me what colour I am."

"How old are you?"

"I was fifteen a few months back."

"How long have you been to sea?"

"About eighteen months."

He then asked me a great many more questions, about the captain, the officers, the ship, and myself; to all of which I answered in a guarded way.

A negro brought down his supper; it was hot, and very savoury; without any order on his part, I immediately attended upon him during his meal. He told the negro not to wait and conversed with me during the time that he was eating: at last, he told me how he had doubled the frigate during the night. I then remarked that we had been informed that the vessel was called the Stella, that the captain's name was Chico, and the crew were composed of white men of different nations.

"A month or two ago, it was the case," replied the captain. "Now I have done, and you may clear away," continued he, rising from his chair and throwing himself down on one of the sofas. "Stop; you are hungry, I don't doubt; you can sit down and eat your supper, and remove the things afterwards."

I did as he told me: it was the first time in my life I had supped off massive plate—but I was in strange company; however, it did not spoil my appetite, and I did not forget to drink a goblet of wine by way of washing down my repast.

"Thank you, sir," said I, rising, and then performing my office of attendant.

At his order, I rang the bell for the negro, who assisted me in clearing away, and then went out with the remains of the supper.

"Am I to stay or go?" said I, respectfully.

"You may go now. Find the man who came in just now—José he is called; tell him to give you something to sleep upon."

"Good-night, sir," said I.

"Good-night, boy."

As I went forward looking for the negro servant, I was accosted more than once very kindly by the negro seamen. At last I went up on the forecastle, and they asked me to tell them how I was left on board the schooner. I did so to those who spoke English, and one of them, who could speak both languages, translated into Spanish for the benefit of the others.

"You be first white he hab spared, I tell you," said the American negro, who had translated into Spanish what I had told them, after the other had left me with him.

"The captain says he wishes I were black," said I to the negro; "I wish I was, too, while I am on board of this vessel—my colour makes him angry, I see that. Could not I be stained black?"

"Well, I do think it will be a very safe thing for you, if it could be; for you have not seen him sometimes in his moods; and if to-morrow morning he was chased and hard pressed by the frigate, you would stand a poor chance, suppose his eyes light upon you. I can't tink what make him to let you off, only but cause you give him de spy-glass in dat hold way. I tink I know a chap on board who understand dat—I go see—you wait here till I come back."

The negro left me, and in a few minutes returned, with a sort of half-Indian, half-negro-looking cut of fellow, with whom he conversed in Spanish.

"He say he know how to make brown like himself but not dark same as me. Suppose you wish he do it to-night—begin now?"

"Yes, I do wish it," replied I; and so I did sincerely, for I felt that it might be the saving of my life; and I had a great aversion to be torn to pieces by the sharks which followed the vessel, that being anything but an agreeable mode of going out of the world.

The American black remained with me, and we conversed for about half an hour, by which time we were joined by the Spanish Main negro, who brought up with him some decoction or another, boiling hot. They stripped me and rubbed me all over with a bit of sponge, not only the face and hands, but every part of my body and then I was left standing quite naked to dry; the crew had gathered round us, and were very merry at the idea of changing my colour.

As soon as the warm air had dried me, the application was created; and when I was again dry, the American told me to put on my clothes, and that he would call me early to have two more applications of the stuff, and that then I should be quite dark enough.

I asked for José, and told him what the captain had said; he gave me a bundle of matting for a bed, and I was soon fast asleep. About three o'clock in the morning I was called up, and the staining repeated twice, and I then lay down again.

When the hands were turned up at five bells (for everything was very regular on board), José brought me a glass to look at myself, and I was quite satisfied that my colour would no longer annoy the captain. I was not as black as a negro, but I was as dark as a mulatto.

I asked the Spanish negro, through José, who could speak both languages, whether I might wash myself? He replied, all day long if I pleased; that I should not get the colour off; it would wear off in time, and the stuff must be applied once a month, and that would be sufficient.

I went to the forecastle, and washed myself; the negro crew were much amused, and said that I now was a "bel muchaco"—a handsome boy. I dare say they thought so—at all events, they appeared to be very friendly with me, and my staining myself gave them great satisfaction. I was sitting with José between decks when the cabin bell rang.

"You go," said he, showing his white teeth as he grinned; "I go after, see what captain tink."

I went into the cabin, and knocked at the state-room door.

"Come in," said the captain.

I went in, and met him face to face.

"What!" said he, looking earnestly at me—"yet it must be—it is you, is it not?"

"Yes, sir," replied I, "it is me. I've turned dark to please you, and I hope it does please you."

"It does, boy, I can look at you now, and forget that you are white. I can. I feel that I can love you now—you've got rid of your only fault in my eyes, and I'm not sorry. I'm only glad that I did not—"

"Give me to the sharks," said I, finishing his sentence.

"Exactly so; say no more about it."

I immediately turned the conversation, by asking him what he required; and I attended him while dressing. From that time he became very friendly towards me, constantly conversing with me. I did my duty as his servant for more than a fortnight, during which time we became very intimate, and (I may as well confess it) I grew very fond of my new master, and thought less about the ship and my shipmates. We were going into a port, I knew, but what port I did not know.

I often had conversations with José and the American black, and gained a great deal of information from them; but I could not discover much of the history of the captain. On that point they refused to be communicative; occasionally hints were given, and then, as if recollecting themselves, they stopped speaking.

It was about three weeks before we made the land of Cuba, and as soon as we did so, the schooner was hove to till night, when sail was again made, and before ten o'clock we saw the lights of the Havannah. When about three miles off we again hove to, and about midnight we perceived under the land the white sails of a schooner, which was standing out. Sail was made, and we ran down to her, and before she was aware that we were an enemy, she was laid by the board and in the possession of our crew. The people belonging to the vessel were handed up, and she was examined. She proved to be a vessel fitted out for the slave trade, with the manacles, etcetera, on board of her, and was just sailing for the coast.

I was on the deck when the white men, belonging to the slaver, were brought on board, and never shall I forget the rage and fury of the captain.

All sail was made upon both schooners, standing right off from the land, and at daylight we had left it a long way astern.

José said to me, "You better not go to captain dis day. Keep out of his way—perhaps he recollect dat you white."

From what I had seen the night before, I thought this good advice; and I not only did not go into the cabin, but I did not show myself on deck.

About eight o'clock in the morning I heard the boat lowered down and orders given to scuttle the vessel, as soon as she had been well searched. This was done, and the boat returned, having found several thousand dollars on board of her, which they handed upon deck.

I remained below: I heard the angry voice of the negro captain—the pleadings and beggings for mercy of the prisoners—busy preparations making on deck; and several men came down and handed up buckets of sand; an iron grating was handed up. The countenances of the negroes who were thus employed appeared inflamed, as if their wrath was excited; now and then they laughed at each other, and looked more like demons than men. That some dreadful punishment was about to be inflicted I was certain and I remained crouched behind the foremast on the lower-deck.

At last the men were all on deck again, and I was left alone; and then I heard more noise, begging for mercy, weeping and wailing, and occasionally a few words from the mouth of the negro captain; then rose shrieks and screams, and appeals to Heaven, and a strong smell, which I could not comprehend, came down the hatchways.

The shrieks grew fainter, and at last ceased, and something was thrown overboard. Then the same tragedy, whatever it was, was acted over again—more attempts to obtain mercy—more shrieks—again the same overpowering smell. What could it be? I would have given much to know, but something told me that I must remain where I was. Ten times was this repeated, and then, as evening came on, there was a bustle on deck, and after a time the crew descended the hatchways.

I caught the eye of the American, with whom I was intimate, and as he passed me, I beckoned to him. He came to me.

"What has been done?" said I in a whisper.

"Captain punish slave traders," replied he; "always punish them so."

"Why, what did he do to them?"

"Do?—roast 'em alive. Dis third slave vessel he take, and he always serve 'em so. Serve 'em right; captain very savage; no go to him till morrow morning—you keep close." So saying, the American negro left me.

As I afterwards found out, the long boat on the booms had been cleared out, the sand laid at the bottom to prevent the fire from burning the boat, the captain and crew of the slave vessel laid on one after the other upon the iron grating, and burnt alive. This accounted for the horrible smell that had come down the hatchways.

It may be considered strange that I really did not feel so much horror as perhaps I ought to have done. Had this dreadful punishment been inflicted upon any *other* persons than slave dealers, and *by* any other parties than negroes, I should not have been able to look at the captain without abhorrence expressed in my countenance; but I know well the horrors of the slave trade from conversation I had had with Bob Cross; and I had imbibed such a hatred against the parties who had carried it on, that it appeared to me to be an act of retaliation almost allied to justice. Had the negro captain only warred against slave dealers, I do not think I should have cared about remaining in the vessel; but he had told me and fully proved to me, that he detested all white men, and had never spared them except in my own instance.

I must acknowledge that I felt very much like going into the lion's den, when the next morning, on his ringing the cabin bell, I presented myself to the captain; but so far from being in an ill-humour, he was very kind to me.

After breakfast, as I was going out, he said to me, "You must have a name: I shall call you Cato—recollect that; and now I have a question to ask you—What is that which you carry round your neck on a ribbon?"

"A letter, sir," replied I.

"A letter! and why do you carry a letter?"

"Because it is of the greatest importance to me."

"Indeed! Now, Cato, sit down on the other sofa, and let me know your history."

I felt that I could not do better than to make this man at once my confidant. He might take a strong interest in me, and it was not likely to go farther. I therefore told him everything connected with my birth and parentage, what my suspicions had been, and how the letter had confirmed them. I unsewed the seal-skin, and gave him the letter to read—without being aware that he could read: he took it and read it aloud.

"Yes," said he, "that's proof under his own hand; and now, Cato, never be afraid of me, for, however I may wreak my vengeance upon others, I swear *by my colour* that I never will hurt you, or permit others to do so. I am a tiger—I know it; but you have often seen a little spaniel caressed by the tiger, whose fangs are turned against every other living thing. You are quite safe."

"I feel I am, since you say so," replied I; "and since I am to be your pet, I shall take liberties, and ask you, in return, to tell me your history."

"I am glad that you have asked it, as I wish you to know it. I will begin at once—

"I was born in America, in the state of Pennsylvania, of free parents. My father was a sail-maker, and was worth money; bet a free black in America is even worse treated and more despised than a slave. I had two brothers, who went to school with me.

"My father intended to bring me up for the Church. You look astonished; but in the States we have clergymen of our colour, as well as white ones; looked down upon and despised, I grant, although they do teach the Word of God; but I was very unfit for that profession, as you may suppose. I was very proud and haughty; I felt that I was as good as a white man, and I very often got into scrapes from my resenting injuries.

"However, my education went on successfully, much more so than that of my brothers, who could not learn. I could, and learnt rapidly but I learnt to hate and detest white men, and more especially Americans; I brooded over the injuries of people of colour, as we were called, and all my father's advice and entreaty could not persuade me to keep my thoughts to myself. As I grew up to manhood, I spoke boldly, and more than once nearly lost my life for so doing; for most Americans think no more of taking the life of one like me than of a dog in the street. More than one knife has been directed to my heart, and more than once was I then up before the judge, and sentenced to imprisonment for no fault; my evidence, and the evidence of those of my colour, not being permitted to be received in a court of justice. Any white villain had only to swear falsely—and there is no want of that class in America—and there was no appeal. At last I was sentenced to be whipped; then my blood boiled, and I vowed a vengeance which I have fearfully adhered to."

"I do not wonder at that," said I; "I would have done the same."

"The man who had sworn falsely against me in this last instance had come up from the South; I obtained what money I could from my father, and went away in pursuit of him. I found him—dogged him, and one evening I accosted him, and plunged my bowie-knife into his heart. I fled that State, and crossed the Mississippi.

"I had not been long in Arkansas before a man—a cotton-grower, who owned about a hundred and fifty slaves—inquired who I was, and whether I had a pass; I replied that I was a free man, born in Pennsylvania, and was there on my own affairs. The next day I was taken up, brought before the magistrate, and this scoundrel swore that I was his slave, and had absconded from him ten years before.

"My defence—the proof which I offered to bring, was not listened to. I was made over to him, and the rascal grinned as the constables brought me away with him. His plantation was at the Red River. It was difficult to escape and indeed, almost useless to attempt it: but the fact was, that I did not wish to do so; I remained to have my revenge. I tried to make the other slaves rise against him, but they were too cowed; they even informed against me, and I was tied down, and flogged by the drivers until the flesh fell from my shoulders.

"As soon as I recovered, I determined to do—or die. I heard that there were some pirate vessels in the Barataria lagoons on the other side of New Orleans; I resolved to join the crews, but first to have my revenge. I did so: I set fire to the plantation house—struck the scoundrel who had made me a slave senseless as he attempted to escape, and threw his body into the flames; I then made the door fast, and fled. I was met by one of the overseers, who was armed, and who would have stopped me: I beat his brains out with his own musket, and then gained the woods. You see that I am powerful; you hardly know how much so. After several days' travelling, I arrived at the lagoons. I found this very vessel at anchor. I offered myself, and they accepted me immediately.

"There were several of my colour on board—runaway slaves—and all good determined men. These were the people I required, for they understood me. Even on board of a pirate vessel, the same contempt was shown towards us—still considered as inferior beings. All the heavy work all the dirty work, was for the negro race; and we often worked like slaves, while the captain and the rest of the crew caroused. I was three years on board of this vessel. Our rendezvous where we are going to now, is a small land-locked bay on the island of Cuba. No vessel in it can be seen from seaward, and there is but one narrow pass by which it communicates with the interior, and it is far from any habitation. A better retreat for a pirate vessel could not well be found. We used very often to go in to refit, and take in provisions and water; for in a cave there, we keep the provisions which we take from other vessels.

"In a desperate fight which we had with an English man-of-war brig, we lost nearly forty of our men. The captain, Chico, as he was called, was obliged to fill up with black men, until he could procure others. The consequence was, that with the ten before on board, there were fifty blacks to seventy whites. It was then that I made up my mind that I would retaliate for all that my race had suffered. I was sure of the ten with whom I had sailed so long; I sounded the others, and found them all willing.

"We sailed from the Mexican Gulf, and made for the Rendezvous Bay, in Cuba. As soon as we arrived, of course, as with all pirate vessels, the first day was dedicated to revelling and intoxication—that is, by the white portion of the crew. We negroes were employed in getting the casks ashore for water. That very night, when they all lay asleep and drunk, we put every soul of them to death, and the Stella belonged to me and my brave black who chose me for their captain, and swore by their wrongs eternal enmity to the European race.

"As you may suppose, I was short-manned; but we soon found plenty of men, and have now as fine a crew as ever trod a deck."

"How long is it since you took possession of the vessel?"

"About eight or nine months, during which time I have spared none except you. The usual death is drowning; but if I fall in with a slaver, then—you know what took place yesterday."

I was silent for a time. "I do not wonder," said I, at last, "at your hatred of the whites, especially of the Americans. As for your wreaking your vengeance upon those employed in the slave trade, dreadful as it is, I scarcely pity them; but in your general warfare against the whites, recollect that you may murder those who are your friends, and who have done all they can to put an end to slavery. Even in America, there are many who are opposed to it."

"It is impossible to make a distinction," replied the negro.

"What is your name?" said I, musing.

"Why do you ask? You may as well know; I wish it to be known: it is James Vincent."

"But tell me, if you were to meet with a very superior force, what would you do?"

"Run if I could; if not, fight."

"But you might be captured, and then—"

"Never, boy; never."

"Well," said I, "as you have begun by sparing me, I hope you will spare others now."

"I don't know why I spared you. Had you shown any fear of death I should not have done so; but I felt that you would not care about it. I believe it was that."

About ten days after, we made the east end of the island of Cuba, and ran into the Bay of Rendezvous, as it was named by the pirate. It was very small, but completely land-locked, and the land so high on every side that the masts of the vessel could not be seen from the seaward. The bay on the land side was met by a deep, narrow ravine, between mountains which were almost perpendicular, the ravine itself being accessible from the main land by only one narrow path known to the pirates, and which they seldom made use of, except when a spy was sent to the Havannah to ascertain what vessels were about to sail.

On the high land which shut in the bay from the sea, the pirates had a man constantly on the look-out, to report any vessel which might be in the offing, and Vincent himself passed much of his time there, as the breeze was fresh and the air cool to what it was down in the land-locked bay. I was, for the same reason, very fond of being on the look-out hill, and generally followed up the captain when he went out there. He certainly now showed a strong affection for me, and I liked him better than I ever thought I could have done. He was constantly telling me of the treatment he and the other poor blacks had received in America, and I could not help feeling my blood boil, and a conviction that, had I been so treated, I should probably have been equally under the influence of revenge. It is the world, and the treatment we receive from it, which makes us chiefly what we are.

One day the captain told me he was going that evening to obtain information, as the spy he had sent had returned unsuccessful, and that he should be absent for three or four days.

Although I was not discontented with my position, still, as the reader may well suppose, I had a strong wish to be out of it as soon as possible, and I had determined to escape if I could; it immediately occurred to me, that his absence would give me the opportunity.

I replied with a laugh, "Had you not better take me with you?"

"Very likely, indeed, you would be so very useful; I shall have quite enough to do to take care of myself; besides, you might betray me," added he, with a fierce and penetrating look.

"Thank you, for your good opinion," replied I, indignantly. "So you think, because you have saved my life, that I would take yours. I am not yet such a rascal, whatever I may become by keeping bad company."

"Well, well," replied the negro captain, "I believe I am wrong, so don't get into a passion; but, at all events, you must see that it is impossible I can take you with me."

"If you don't choose, I can't help it," said I; "but I don't like remaining here without you; I shall run away if I can, so I give you fair warning."

"You won't find that quite so easy," replied he, laughing; "and I recommend you not to attempt it."

Here the conversation dropped. About midnight the captain commenced his ascent of the ravine, and I resolved that I would not lose the opportunity, if it offered, of following him. I watched him as long as I could see him, that I might know the direction of the secret path, and then I joined the crew, who were lying down by the tents which they had pitched on the shore. Shortly afterwards, the Spanish Indian, who had coloured me, passed by me, and, as I intended to make the attempt before it was quite dark, I thought that I would remove any suspicion, and I therefore requested him to stain me again. This he consented to do, and in half an hour I was again naked among the negroes and undergoing the operation. Having received the two applications, as before, I then quitted them.

As soon as it was quite dark, I armed myself with a pair of pistols, and crawled underneath the back of the captain's tent, in which I always slept, and, without being perceived, gained the narrow path in the brushwood by which the captain had left.

I continued in the path for some time, by feeling the brushwood on either side; but before I had crawled half way up the ravine, I found that the brushwood had not been cut away any farther and I was at a loss how to proceed. All traces were gone, and all I had to do was to climb up to the summit, and to take my chance of finding any egress. I toiled on with difficulty, sometimes stopped by a rock which would take me minutes to climb over at others, holding on by the brushwood for my life. By twelve o'clock I had gained more than two-thirds of the ascent, and then the moon rose, and assisted me with her light. I must say, that when I looked up and saw the rocks towering above me, and overhanging my path, I felt that escape was nearly impossible: however, I recommenced my labour, and gained some ground, when, as I was clinging to the side of a rock by a small shrub, it gave way, and I rolled and fell down many feet, between that rock and another opposite to it.

I was not much hurt, and I regained my legs. Looking up and about me, I found that I was in a narrow passage, between the rocks, leading both up and down—in fact, I had tumbled into the secret path that I had been in search of. Delighted with this discovery, I now set off with great spirit, and in half an hour found myself on the other side of the lull which formed the ravine, and looking down upon an expanse of country in the interior. Being very tired, I sat down, that I might recover my strength before I continued my journey.

"I am free at last," thought I, and my memory wandered back to my mother my ship, and my captain—old Culpepper, Tommy Dott, and Bob Cross. "I shall see them all," I thought, "and what a story I shall have to tell." As soon as I had rested myself and recovered my breath, I thought I might as well start.

I had not proceeded more than a hundred yards before I thought heard a noise, as if some one was approaching. I listened—I felt sure that such was the case, and I also heard the deep baying of a hound. The noise increased rapidly—it was that of one forcing his way through the brushwood, which covered the side of the hill.

In a minute afterwards I perceived a man coming up the hill at a swift pace, directly towards me. As he approached I could almost swear that it was Vincent, the negro captain; but when within ten yards of me, I perceived, him turn round and flourish his sabre in the air, while, at the same time, three large bloodhounds sprang at him. One fell by the blow of his sabre, but the other two flew at his throat, and fastened on him, tearing him to the around, and holding him in spite of all his struggling and his immense strength.

I recollected my pistols: I cocked them, ran up, and putting one to the head of the nearest dog, blew out its brains. I was equally successful with the other—they both lay dead by his side, and Vincent was released. He started up.

"It is me, Cato," said I.

"Cato!" replied he; "but there is not a moment to be lost. I understand it all."

He seized me by the arm, and dragged me with him to the narrow entrance of the pass, and as soon as we came in he rolled three large rocks, which had evidently been used for such purpose before, so as completely to block up the entrance.

"There," said he, leaning back quite exhausted; "be quiet, Cato. We are safe now; they will be on the top of the hill directly."

We remained where we were about ten minutes, when we heard voices not very far from us. They were the pursuers of the negro captain who were evidently baffled. After a time the sounds receded from us, and we heard them no more. Vincent then spoke:—

"You were escaping, Cato."

"I had escaped," replied I: "I told you that I would."

"Strange that you should have discovered the path; did any one betray it to you?"

"No one," replied I: and I then told him how I had fallen into it.

"Well you have returned all obligations, and more than ever you owed me," said he: "you have saved my life this time, and that when all chance was over."

"Then," replied I, "although I shall be very sorry to part with you, give me that liberty which I had gained, and which I lost in defending you from the dogs."

"I would have let you go then, Cato," replied he, "but your life would have been sacrificed. My pursuers would have hurried you to prison before you could have explained who you were. You forget your colour is changed; they were not seeking me, but a runaway slave, and the bloodhounds came upon my track. Those white men show no mercy; they have more pleasure in seeing a runaway slave torn to pieces by those dogs than in recovering possession of him. It is a sort of fox-chase to them," continued he, grating his teeth after he had said so. "Cato, I will give you your liberty, if you wish it, and I know you do wish it, as soon as I can with any prudence; that I promise you, and you know that I will keep my word."

"I am quite satisfied," replied I.

"And do you promise me that you will not attempt to escape a second time?"

"I promise you that I will not," replied I.

"Enough," said Vincent. "Now let us go down the hill, for I am very much torn by those infernal brutes, and must have the wounds washed and attended to."

We descended the hill, in silence, and in a quarter of an hour had gained the tent. Vincent was severely bitten and torn: as soon as his wounds had been dressed he lay down on his mat, and I did the same.

It was some days before Vincent recovered from the severe injuries which he had received from the bloodhounds; and he did not appear to be inclined to run any more risks of that sort. Although he said little, I could perceive that he was brooding over future vengeance and he was now nearly the whole of the day with his glass on the look-out hill.

One morning a schooner hove in sight, steering from the Havannah to the southward and eastward, either for the islands of the Spanish Main. The Stella had for many days been ready for instant sailing, and having watched her till near sunset, Vincent sent down orders for every soul to be on board, and the anchor hove up. Just as it was dark we towed out of the bay, and made all sail.

At daylight the schooner was but a few miles ahead of us and not being a fast sailer, in little more than an flour we were alongside of her. She proved to be bound to the island of Curaçao, being the property of an old Dutch gentleman, who was on board with his daughter, a little girl about seven years old. The crew consisted chiefly of negroes, slaves to the owner; the master of the vessel and the mate being, with the exception of the old gentleman and the little girl, the only white people on board.

As usual, the crew were brought on board by the pirates, who reported to the captain that the vessel was in ballast, and of no value. As the crew of the Stella were already more than requisite, Vincent did not require the negroes; he told them that they might go on board the schooner again, and take her into any port they pleased; with the white people, however it was another affair.

I had remained below, not wishing to witness a scene of butchery; but I was induced to look up the ladder, in consequence of José telling me that there was a little white girl come on board. At the time that I did so, Vincent had just done speaking with the negroes belonging to the captured vessel; they had fallen back, and there was then standing before Vincent, the master and mate of the vessel, the old Dutch gentleman, and the little girl.

A more interesting child I never had seen, and my heart bled at the idea of her being sacrificed. I could not help hoping that Vincent would have a similar feeling, but I was mistaken. The master and mate were pointed at, and immediately seized by negroes and tossed over into the sea. The old gentleman bowed his head over the beautiful child, and she knelt to him, as if for his blessing before she died. At that very moment Vincent gave the sign—I could remain quiet to longer—I sprang on the deck.

"Stop!" cried I to the men who were about to seize the old gentleman— "stop!" The negroes did fall back at my voice.

"What is this?" cried Vincent.

"Captain Vincent," cried I, "do you call yourself a man, to war with children and old grey-headed men? You must not, shall not, touch these two. You have wreaked your vengeance upon the white men; be content—let these go."

"Cato," replied Vincent, fiercely, "it is well that it is you that have dared to snatch the prey from the fangs of the wild beast. Had it been another, this pistol should have sent a ball whizzing through his brain; as it is, go down below immediately."

"I do not fear your pistol, Captain Vincent, nor will I go below; that very pistol, in my hand, saved you from the fangs of the blood-hound. I tell you, therefore, that you must not destroy that innocent child—if you love me, you must not; for I will hate, detest, and scorn you ever afterwards. I entreat you—I implore you to let them go: they are not fit objects for your vengeance; and if you destroy them, I tell you, you are a coward."

"What!" roared the tiger, "a coward!" and, no longer able to contain himself he levelled his pistol at me and drew the trigger. It missed fire; Vincent looked very confused—he tossed the pistol on deck, folded his arms and turned his face away.

There was a dead silence. The negro crew looked first at me and then at the captain, as if awaiting orders, and uncertain of the issue. The Dutch gentleman seemed to be so lost in surprise, as to almost forget his impending fate; while the little girl clung to him and stared at me with her deep blue eyes. It was what on the theatres they would call a tableau.

I followed up my advantage. Stepping forward, and placing myself before the old man and the child, I first broke the silence.

"Captain Vincent," said I, "you did once promise me that you would never injure me or attempt my life; that promise you have broken. Since that, you have made me another promise—you may recollect it—which was, that you would allow me to leave you on the first favourable opportunity; there cannot be any opportunity more favourable than the present. The negroes whom you are to send back to the schooner do not know how to navigate her. I request, therefore, to know whether you intend to keep this second promise, or to break it as you have the first? I ask my liberty."

"If I broke my promise just now, it was your fault," replied Vincent, coolly. "I am sorry for it, and I can say no more; I intended to keep it, and, to prove so, I now keep my second—you may go."

"I thank you for that. I only wish that, now I leave you, I could leave you with feelings of good-will and not of—I must say it—of horror and disgust. Captain Vincent, once more let me beg, as a last favour, that you will spare these poor people."

"Since you are so particularly interested about this useless old man and still more useless child," replied Vincent, sarcastically, "I will now make a proposal to you. You have your liberty. Do you choose to give it up and remain here, provided I let them go away in the schooner? Come now—take your choice; for I swear by my colour, that if you go away in the schooner, the moment you shove off, they shall go over the gunwale."

"My choice is then made," replied I; for I knew that when he swore by his colour he was in earnest: "release them, and I will remain here." I little knew what I was to undergo in consequence of this decision.

"Be it so," said Vincent: then turning to one of the mates, "let them go back with the negroes; hoist the boat up when she returns, and sail for the Rendezvous." So saying, he went down into the cabin.

"You are saved," said I, going up to the old Dutch gentleman; "lose no time; get into the boat as fast as possible, and make sail on your vessel as soon as you get on board. Good bye, little girl," said I, taking her hand.

"I thank you," replied the gentleman in good English—"I cannot say how much; I am so surprised at what I have seen but recollect the name of Vanderwelt, of Curaçao; and if ever we meet again, you will find me grateful."

"I will; but ask no more questions now—into the boat—quick," said I, shaking his proffered hand. They were handed down into the boat by the negroes.

I remained on deck until they were put on board; the boat returned, was hoisted up, the schooner made sail again, and then I went down into the cabin. I found the negro captain stretched upon the sofa, his face covered up with both his hands; he remained in the same position, taking no notice of my coming down. Although my confidence in him was destroyed after his snapping the pistol at me, yet when I reflected how I had bearded him in his rage, I did make some excuse for him; moreover, I knew that it was my interest to be on the best terms with him, and, if possible, make him forget what had passed, for I felt that his proud spirit would make it difficult for him to forgive himself for having been induced by his passion to break an oath which he had sworn to by his colour; I therefore, after a little reflection, went up to him and said—

"I am sorry that I made you so angry, Captain Vincent; you must forgive me, but I thought that deed beneath you, and I could not bear to have a bad opinion of you."

"Do you mean to assert that you have not a bad opinion of me now?" replied he, fixing his eyes upon me.

"No, certainly not; you have released those I pleaded for, and I am very grateful to you for having done so."

"You have made me do what I never did before," replied he, raising himself and sitting with his feet on the deck.

"I know I have; I have made you spare those of my colour."

"I did not mean that; you have irritated me so as to make me break my oath."

"That was my own doing—my fault rather than yours. I had no right to speak as I did; but I was in a great rage, and that is the truth. I do believe that, if I had had a pistol in my hand, I should have fired it at you; so we may cry quits on that score."

"I am angry with myself—the more so, that I little imagined that you would have remained with me after my breaking my oath. Either you must have felt great interest about those people, or you must have great confidence in me, a confidence winch I have proved that I do not deserve."

"That you did forget yourself, I grant; but I have that confidence that it will be a warning to you, and you will not forget yourself again; I therefore remain with you with perfect confidence, feeling I am quite safe, until you think proper to give me my liberty."

"You will wish to leave me then?"

"I have relations and friends—a profession to follow. What can I gain by remaining here, except your friendship? I never will be a pirate, you may be assured, I wish from my heart that you were not one."

"And who should be pirates if the blacks are not?" replied Vincent. "Have they not the curse of Cain? Are they not branded? Ought not their hands to be against every one but their own race? What is the Arab but the pirate of the desert—the sea of sand? Black is the colour for pirates. Even the white pirates feel the truth of this, or why do they hoist the *black* flag?"

"At all events, it's a profession that seldom ends well."

"And what matter does that make? We can die but once—I care not how soon. I have not found life so very sweet as to care for it, I assure you. Cato, there is but one thing sweet in existence—one feeling that never clogs and never tires, and that is revenge."

"Are not love and friendship sweet? I certainly know nothing about the first."

"I know no more than you do of it. They say friendship is the more lasting; and as a proof of how lasting that is I snapped my pistol at you, and, had it not missed fire, should have killed the only one for whom I ever felt friendship in this world."

"That's a bad habit you have of carrying your pistols at all times; they are too handy, and give no time or reflection. Only suppose, now, you had blown out my brains, you would have been very sorry."

"Cato, I have many lives on my hands, and hope to have many more before I die. I never have repented one act of my life—a murder, as you may call it—and I never shall. But I tell you frankly, that had I destroyed you in my passion I should have been a miserable man. I know it; I feel it."

"Let's say no more about it: that I'm just as glad as you are that you did not kill me, I assure you most positively. Here's José coming with the dinner."

Here ended our conversation, which I have given just to show the peculiar disposition of this extraordinary man, with whom I had become domesticated. Verily and truly was I, as he said, "like a little dog in the cage of a tiger," and, from familiarity: just as bold as dogs become under such peculiar circumstances.

Before morning we were again at anchor in the Rendezvous Bay, and the tents were pitched as before. We remained there for more than a fortnight, during which my intimacy with the captain was even greater than before. He appeared to endeavour to do all in his power to restore my confidence in him, and he succeeded. Still, I must say, that I began to be weary of this sort of life. My dreams were ever of murder and bloodshed; and more than once I felt inclined to make my escape: but I had promised, and the remembrance of my promise prevented me.

One afternoon the man on the look-out made the usual signal for a vessel in sight. Vincent went up immediately, and I followed him. It was a schooner, very long, with very taut, raking masts. Vincent examined her for some time, and then gave me the glass, and asked me what I thought of her. I replied, that I thought she was a man-of-war schooner.

"You are right," said he, "I know her well; it is the Arrow, and she has come out to cruise for me. This is the third time that she has been sent after me. Once we exchanged a few broadsides, but another man-of-war hove in sight, and I was compelled to leave her. She shall not accuse me of running from her, now that she is alone, and by to-morrow morning I will give her the opportunity of making the report of my capture if she can; but if I capture her, you may guess the rest."

We remained till nearly sunset watching the motions of the schooner. Vincent then went down the hill to give orders for sailing, leaving me with the glass. I again directed it to the schooner, and perceived that she was making signals.

Then she is not alone, thought I; and Vincent may not capture her quite so easily as he expects. I looked in vain for the other vessel; I could not see her; I therefore concluded that she must be somewhere under the land, and hidden by it from my sight.

The signals were repeated till dusk when I went down the hill, and found that all was bustle and activity, Vincent superintending himself the preparations for sailing. I did not interrupt him to tell him that I had perceived the schooner making signals. I had an idea, somehow or another, that I should regain my liberty, and was as anxious as Vincent that the Stella should be under weigh.

Before ten o'clock everything was ready. Vincent had told his men that the English man-of-war schooner was outside, and that he intended to fight her; the men appeared delighted at the proposal, and as resolute and determined as men should be.

As soon as the Stella was clear of the bay, everything was got ready for action, and I must say that nothing could be more rapid or more quiet than their movements. We stood out until we had gained an offing of five miles, and then made a reach along the shore towards the Havannah.

As soon as the Stella had laid her head towards the Havannah, Vincent came down below. I had latterly slept on one of the cabin sofas, but had this night remained with my clothes on, for I was not sure that we might not be in action before the morning.

The Arrow had gained the knowledge that our Rendezvous Bay was somewhere about the east end of the island, and had cruised accordingly, but could not discover it.

Vincent threw himself on the other sofa, and I pretended to asleep; as I did not wish to enter into conversation with him was too much occupied with my own thoughts, and felt that there would be nothing in common between us at such a moment. He was very soon asleep, and he talked in his sleep. He was evidently in action, and gave his orders, every now and then speaking a few words aloud, and then it appeared as if he had taken the English schooner, and that he was fulfilling his vows of retaliation. I shuddered as I heard the half-broken menaces—the exulting laugh which occasionally burst from his lips. I arose and watched him as he slept; his hands were continually in motion, and his fists clenched, and he smiled.

Merciful Heaven! what a tale of savage cruelty that smile foretold if he were successful! I knelt down and prayed that he might be foiled in his endeavours. As I rose I heard a noise and talking on deck, and one of the mates came down in the cabin.

"How does she bear?" cried Vincent, starting up from his couch, as if he instinctively knew what was to be told.

"Two points on the weather bow, captain," replied the negro. "I think she has her foresheet to windward."

"What's the time?"

"One bell in the morning watch; it will be daylight in an hour."

"Very good. How far is she off?"

"About four miles."

"Pipe to quarters; I will be up directly."

Vincent took down his sword and buckled on his belt; then his pistols, which after having examined the primings, he fixed in his girdle. I still remained as if asleep, and as he was going out of the cabin, he turned to me. "He sleeps, poor boy; well, why should I wake him?—the guns will rouse him up soon enough." So saying, he went on deck.

I considered what I should do. To be on deck was hardly safe for me as a white person; and, indeed, what business had I there? Why should I expose myself to the shot of my countrymen, or run the risk of losing my life from the rage of the negroes? I therefore resolved on remaining where I was—at all events, for the present.

The negroes now came into the cabin, for the after-magazine was under the forepart of it. The hatch was taken up, the screens let down, and all was dark. I had nothing to do but to catch now and then the commands given by the negro captain, and draw my inference as to what was taking place.

Although for the first half-hour I gained little information, after that time had elapsed I knew what was going on. I heard a voice hailing us from another vessel, and the reply of the Stella was a broadside. There could be no mistake in that. The Stella was then put about, and the other broadside given without a return from her opponent. At last it came, and as the shot whizzed over or tore up the planking of the gunwales, I certainly did feel very strangely. I had never been in action before, and the sensation was, I confess, that of alarm; but it was so mingled with curiosity as to what was going on, that it was impossible to say what my feelings were. I longed to be on deck, and certainly would have been, if I had thought that I was safe with the pirate crew: that alone prevented me; I remained, therefore, in a most unpleasant state of ignorance and suspense.

The broadsides were now exchanged rapidly and the wounded, brought down between decks every minute, told me that the action was severe. The orders of the negro captain were occasionally heard—they were cool and determined. Every minute some fresh manoeuvre was executed, and the guns still worked as if there was nothing else to attend to. At last, the daylight came down the hatchway, and I left the cabin and walked forward between decks; I found the deck strewed with wounded and dying men, calling for water. I was glad to be able to do something which I could consistently do, and I brought water from the cask and gave it to them, one after another, as fast as I could; I think there were at least thirty men lying about the lower deck, some in pools of their own blood, and sinking fast, for there was no surgeon on board of the Stella.

Some more wounded men were brought down, and a conversation took place between one of the mates of the schooner, who was hurt, and the men who brought down the wounded, and listening to them, I found that at daylight they had discovered that an English frigate was under all sail, beating up to them, and about five miles to leeward; that in consequence, the Stella was now carrying on a running fight with the schooner (who was to windward of her), and trying to escape. This accounted for the signals which I had perceived that the English schooner was making the evening before. My anxiety at this intelligence was naturally much increased. The Stella was trying to escape, and her sailing powers were so remarkable, that I was afraid she would succeed.

The action was still continued between the two schooners, but now the shot no longer hit the Stella, nor were there any more wounded men brought down; it was evident that the two vessels were now firing at each other's masts and rigging, the one to prevent, and the other to effect her escape, by dismantling her antagonist. I felt as if I could have given my left hand to have gone on deck. I waited half an hour more, and then, curiosity conquering my fear, I crept gradually up the fore ladder. The men were working the guns to windward, the lee-side of the deck was clear, and I stepped forward, and got into the head, where I could see both to windward and to leeward. To leeward I perceived the frigate about four miles distant with every stretch of canvass that she could set on a wind; I knew her directly to be the Calliope, my own ship, and my heart beat quick at the chance of being once more on board of her.

To windward, as the smoke occasionally cleared away, I saw the Arrow schooner close hauled on the same tack as the Stella, and distant about a mile, every ten seconds the smoke from her guns booming along the water's surface, and the shot whizzing through our rigging; she had not suffered much from our fire: her sails were full of shot-holes, it is true, but her spars were not injured. I then turned my eyes upon the masts and rigging of the Stella: apparently, the damage done was about equal to that received by the Arrow; our sails were torn, but our spars were unscathed.

The water was smooth, although the breeze was fresh, and both schooners were running at the rate of six or seven miles an hour; but the Stella had evidently the advantage of sailing, and fore-reached upon her opponent. I perceived that everything depended upon a lucky hit and having satisfied myself with what I had seen, I hastened down below.

For more than half an hour the firing continued without advantage on either side, when a yell was given by the negro crew, and I heard them cry on the deck that the Arrow's foretop-mast was shot away. I heard the voice of Vincent cheering his men, and telling them to be steady in their aim. My heart sunk at the intelligence, and I sat down on a chest.

The firing now slackened, for the Stella had shot ahead of the English schooner, and the negroes on deck were laughing and in high good-humour. For a few minutes the firing ceased altogether, and I took it for granted that the Stella had left her pursuers far behind; when of a sudden, a whole broadside of guns were poured into us, and there was a terrible crashing and confusion on the deck.

I ran up the ladder to see what had happened. It appeared that as the Stella was crossing the bows of the Arrow, the latter had, as a last chance thrown up in the wind, and discharged her whole broadside into us: two shots had struck our mainmast, which had fallen by the board. I perceived at once that the Stella's chance was over—nothing could save her; she might resist the schooner but could not escape the frigate.

I ran down below, and went into the cabin; I was afraid that the negroes might perceive the joy in my countenance. I heard the angry voice of the negro captain—I heard him stamping with rage, and I thanked God that I was not by his side. The wreck of the mast was soon cleared away; I heard him address his negroes, point out to them that it was better to die like men at the guns, than swing at the yard-arm like dogs. Some of them came down and took on deck a quarter-cask of spirits, which was plentifully supplied to all.

The English schooner had borne down upon us, and the action now commenced at pistol-shot. Never shall I forget what took place for nearly three-quarters of an hour; the negroes, most of them intoxicated, fought with rage and fury indescribable—their shouts—their screams—their cursing and blasphemy, mingled with the loud report of the guns, the crashing of the spars and bulwarks, the occasional cry of the wounded, and the powerful voice of Vincent. It was terrific between decks; the smoke was so thick, that those who came down for the powder could not see, but felt their way to the screen. Every two seconds, I heard the men come aft, toss off the can of liquor, and throw it on the deck, hen they went to resume their labour at their guns.

At the end of the time I have mentioned, the shot flew from to leeward, as well as from to windward: the frigate had got within range, and was pouring in her broadside; still the firing and the shouting on the deck of the Stella continued, but the voices were fewer; and as the firing of the frigate became more severe, they became fainter and fainter; and at last but an occasional gun was fired from our decks.

I became so uneasy, that I could remain where I was no longer; I went forward on the lower deck again, and tumbling over the wounded and the dead, I crept up the fore-ladder. I looked over the coamings of the hatchway; the decks were clear of smoke, for not a gun was being fired. Merciful Heaven! what a scene of slaughter! Many of the guns were dismantled, and the decks were strewed with the splinters and plankings of the gunwale, broken spars, and negroes lying dead, or drunk, in all directions—some cut and torn to pieces, others whole, but mixed up with the fragments of other bodies: such a scene of blood I have never since witnessed. Out of the whole crew, I do not think there were twenty men left unhurt, and these were leaning or lying down, exhausted with fatigue or overcome with liquor, on various parts of the deck.

The fighting was over; there was not one man at his gun—and of those who remained still alive, one or two fell, while I was looking up from the shot, which continued every minute to pierce the bulwarks. Where was Vincent? I dare not go aft to see. I dare not venture to meet his eye. I dived down below again, and I returned aft to the cabin; there was no more demand for powder; not a soul was to be seen abaft. Suddenly the after-hatchway grating was thrown off; I heard some one descend; I knew it was the hurried tread of the negro captain. It was so dark, and the cabin so full of smoke, that, coming from the light, he did not perceive me, although I could distinguish him. He was evidently badly wounded, and tottered in his walk: he came into the cabin, put his hand to his girdle, and felt for his pistol, and then he commenced pulling down the screen, which was between him and the magazine. His intentions were evident; which were to blow up the vessel.

I felt that I had not a moment to lose. I dashed past him, ran up the ladder, sprung aft to the taffrail, and dashed over the stern into the sea. I was still beneath the surface, having not yet risen from my plunge, when I heard and felt the explosion—felt it, indeed, so powerfully, that it almost took away my senses; so great was the shock, even when I was under the water, that I was almost insensible. I have a faint recollection of being drawn down by the vortex of the sinking vessel, and scrambling my way to the surface of the water, amidst fragments of timbers and whirling bodies. When I recovered myself, I found that I was clinging to a portion of the wreck, in a sort of patch, as it were, upon the deep blue water, dark as ink, and strewed with splintered fragments.

There I remained some minutes, during which time I gained my recollection: I looked around and perceived the Arrow schooner, lying about one hundred yards off, totally dismantled, and my own frigate about a quarter of a mile to leeward, as bright and as fresh as if she had just been refitted. I observed a signal, made by the Calliope to the schooner, which was answered. I looked in vain towards the schooner, expecting her to lower down a boat. The fact was, that the Calliope had made the signal for her to do so, and the schooner had replied that she had no boat that could swim. I then perceived that the frigate had lowered down a boat which was pulling towards me, and I considered myself as safe.

In a few minutes, during which I had quite recovered myself, the boat pulled into the mass of floating fragments, and then the sailors ceased rowing to look about them. They perceived and pulled towards me—hoisted me in over the gunwale, and laid me at the bottom of the boat. I scrambled on my feet, and would have gone *aft*, when the midshipman of the boat said to the men, "Pass that cursed young pirate forward—don't let him come aft here."

"Oh, oh, Mr Lascelles," thinks I—"so you don't know me; you shall know me by-and-by." I quite forgot that I was stained black, till one of the men who seized me by the collar to pass me forward, said, "Hand along the nigger. He's a young one for the gallows, any how."

They handed me forward, and I did not choose to say who I was. My love of fun returned the moment that I was again with my shipmates. After looking well round and ascertaining that I was the only one left alive, they pulled back to the frigate; and the midshipman went up to report. I was handed up the side and remained at the break of the gangway, while the captain and first lieutenant were talking with Mr Lascelles: during which Mr Tommy Dott came up to me, and, putting his finger to his left ear, gave a cluck with his tongue, as much as to say, "You'll be hanged, my good fellow."

I could not help giving the first mason's sign which I taught to Mr Green in return for Tommy's communication; to wit, putting my thumb to my nose, and extending my finger out towards him; at which Tommy Dott expressed much indignation, and called me a precious impudent varmin. The men who were near us laughed, and said that I was game at all events. No one knew me; for not only was my face well stained, but I was covered from head to foot with a solution of salt water and gunpowder, which made me still more indistinguishable.

I had remained at the gangway about two minutes, when the first lieutenant said, "Bring the prisoner here."

I immediately went aft; and as soon as I was standing before Captain Delmar and the first lieutenant—(and behind were all the officers, anxious to hear what I had to disclose)—I put my hand to my head, having no hat, as may be supposed, and said, "*Come on board, sir*," reporting myself, as is usually the custom of officers when they return from leave or duty.

"Good Heavens! that voice!—why, who are you?" cried Captain Delmar, starting back a pace.

"Mr Keene, sir," replied I, again putting my hand to my head.

Bob Cross, who was, with many of the seamen, close to me, quite forgetting etiquette, ran up and caught me round the waist, looking me full in the face: "It is him, sir—it is him! Huzzah! huzzah!" and all the seamen joined in the huzzahs, which were, however, mingled with a great deal of laughter.

"Merciful Heaven! and so you have been blown up in that vessel," said the first lieutenant, coming to me, with great kindness. "Are you much burnt? Why, he's quite black—where's the surgeon?"

"Aren't hurt at all, sir," replied I.

"Let him be taken down and examined," said the captain with some emotion; "if not hurt, let him come into the cabin to me."

The captain went down the ladder, and then I shook hands with Tommy Dott and all the other officers and midshipmen; and I will say that my re-appearance appeared to give unusual satisfaction. I went down into the gun-room and was stripped. They were much surprised to find that I was not hurt, and even more when they discovered that I was black all over, and that washing would not restore my colour.

"Why, Keene," said the first lieutenant, "how is it that you have changed your colour?"

"Oh, sir, I've been playing the nigger for these last three months. It is a long story, but I will go with you to the captain, and I will tell it there."

As soon as I had put on my uniform, I went up with Mr Hippesley to the cabin, and having, at the captain's request, taken a chair, I entered into a full explanation, which lasted more than an hour.

As soon as I had finished, Mr Hippesley who had plenty to do on deck, but who could not leave until he had heard my story, quitted the cabin, and I found myself alone with the captain.

"I must say that I gave you up for lost," said Captain Delmar; "the boat's crew were picked up the next morning, and reported that you were drowned in the cabin of the vessel. Scoundrels, to desert you in that way."

"I do not think they were to blame, sir; the water being so high in the cabin, and my not answering to their call."

"But did they call you?"

"Yes, sir; I heard them call when I was half asleep, and I did not answer."

"Well, I am glad to hear you say so; but so convinced have we been of your loss, that I have written to your mother on the subject. Strange, this is the second time that she has been distressed in this way. You appear to have a charmed life, Mr Keene."

"I hope I shall long live to do credit to your protection, sir," replied I.

"I hope so too, Mr Keene," replied the captain, very kindly; "I sincerely hope so too. In all this business you have conducted yourself very manfully. It does you great credit, and your mother ought to be proud of you."

"Thanky, sir," replied I, for I was overjoyed at such language from Captain Delmar, and I thought to myself, if he says my mother ought be proud of me, he feels so himself.

"Of course, you cannot do duty under such a masquerade as you are at present," continued the captain, who referred to my stained skin. "I presume it will wear off by-and-by. You will dine with me to-day; now you may go to your messmates."

I left the cabin, bowing very respectfully, and pleased with what had occurred. I hastened to join my messmates, not, however, until I had shaken hands with Bob Cross, who appeared as delighted to see me as if he was my father.

I leave the reader to imagine the sort of levee which I held both on the quarter-deck and below. Mr Hippesley could not get any of the officers to mind their duty. I certainly was for two or three days the greatest personage in the ship. After that, I had time to tell the whole of my history quietly to Bob Cross.

Bob Cross, when he had heard me without interruption, said, "Well, Master Keene, there's no telling what a man's born to till after he's dead, and then it's all known: but it does appear to me that you are born to something out of the common. Here you are, not sixteen, not only playing a man's part, but playing it manfully. You have been put in most difficult situations, and always have fallen upon your feet in the end. You appear to have an old head upon very young shoulders; at one moment to be a scampish boy full of mischief, and at another a resolute, cool, and clever man. Sarcumstances, they say, make men, and so it appears in you; but it does seem strange for one and the same lad to be stealing the purser's plums at one moment, and twisting a devil of a nigger pirate round his finger the very next; and then you have had such escapes—twice reported dead at head-quarters, and twice come to life again. Now Master Keene, I've very good news to tell you: you don't know how high you stand with the captain and officers: there's a feeling of envy against a lad who goes ahead (as well as a man) which blinds people to his real merits; but when he is supposed to be dead and gone, and no longer in the way of others, then every one tells the real truth; and I do assure you that not only the officers, but the captain himself, grieved most sorely at your loss. I saw the captain's eyes wink more than once when speaking of you, and the first lieutenant was always telling the other mids that he had not one worth his salt, now that you were gone. And now that you have come back and gained so much credit for what has passed, I do really think that the captain is proud of you. I overheard a little conversation between the captain and first lieutenant the day you came on board, after you had been in the cabin telling your adventures, and all that I can say is, that the game is in your own hands, if you only play your cards well, and never let Captain Delmar have the least idea that you know that you have such claims upon him."

"That I certainly will not," replied I, "as it might check his feeling towards me."

"Exactly: I've often thought about you, and now that I like you so much, I watch the captain for your sake, and listen particularly to what he says after dinner especially, when I've the opportunity; for you see, when gentlemen drink wine, they speak more freely as to what they really think, just as we foremast-men do when we get our grog on board. The greatest misfortune which could happen to you in your position would be, the captain marrying and having children on the right side of the blanket as they call it. Now I've often heard the captain express a dislike to matrimony, and laugh at people's getting married, which has pleased me very much for your sake,

Master Percival. You see, a man don't think much of marrying after forty, and the captain must be fifty, if not more."

"Yes: but if his brother dies—and he is a very infirm man—the captain will then be Viscount de Versely, and inherit very large estates, and then he will marry to have an heir to the title and estates even if there is no love in the case."

"So he may," replied Cross—"there's no saying; but still, even if he does, it ain't certain that he has a family; chickens must not be counted before they are hatched. All you have to pray for then is, that the brother may prove as tough as our old admirals, whose senses get tired of staying any longer in their bodies, and leave them long before their hulks are worn out."

"Why do admirals live so long?"

"Well, I suppose it is for the same reason that salt meat keeps so much longer than fresh; they have been forty or fifty years with the salt spray washing in their faces and wetting their jackets, and so in time, d'ye see, they become as it were pickled with brine. Talking about that, how long will it be before you get that tanning off you?"

"I don't know; but as the captain says I'm to do no duty while it lasts, I hope it won't wear off too soon."

"Spoken like a midshipman: now take my advice, although not ordered to your duty, come up on deck and take your spy-glass."

"I've lost it, unfortunately. That was a good glass, for it saved my life."

"Yes, it turned out as good for you as a Freemason's sign, which is more than Mr Green can say. I don't think he'll ever make a sailor—he'd better bear up for clerk, and then he might do very well for a purser by-and-by. There's eight bells, Master Keene, so I think we had better say good night."

Chapter Twenty

The Arrow schooner had suffered very severely in the contest, having lost her commanding officer and thirteen men killed and wounded: indeed, had not the Calliope been at hand, it was the general opinion that the Stella would have overpowered her, notwithstanding that the latter had lost her mainmast, for the Arrow was completely dismantled, and would not have been able to have made sail.

The Calliope sent her carpenters and best seamen on board to repair her damages, and the next day we stood away for Port Royal, Jamaica, to announce the destruction of the pirate vessel.

In the morning Captain Delmar sent for me.

"Mr Keene, as you cannot do duty for the present, and as I do not wish you to be idle, I think you had better pay a little attention to navigation. You send in your day's work, I perceive, but I suppose you have never regularly gone through a course of study."

"No, sir," replied I; "I fudge my day's work, and I should be very glad to learn navigation properly."

"So I presume. Well, then, I have spoken with Mr Smith, the master, who has promised me to give you the necessary instruction. You will commence to-morrow; you can sit at the table in the fore-cabin, where you will have nothing to distract your attention. You may go now."

I bowed and left the cabin, and meeting Bob Cross on the main deck, I told him what the captain had said.

"I'm glad of it, Master Keene; it shows that the captain does now take a strong interest in you. He has never taken any trouble of that kind with any midshipman before. It will be of great service to you, so pay attention; it will please the captain if the master gives a good report of you. Who knows but you may be sent away in a prize, and I sent with you to take care of you? Wouldn't that be a capital spree?"

The next day I commenced accordingly, under the tuition of the master, and as I had not Tommy Dott to play with, I gave satisfaction, and continued to do so until our arrival at Port Royal, when the captain went up to the admiral's, stating all the particulars of the action, and, by way of sequel, my adventures on board of the pirate vessel. The admiral was so much interested that he requested Captain Delmar to bring me on shore to dine with me the next day.

I was still very black; but that made me, I presume more interesting. I told my story over again, and it afforded great amusement to the company; particularly to the ladies; and I have reason to believe that many compliments were paid me behind my back, by the admiral and officers who dined there; at all events, Captain Delmar was much pleased.

My strange history soon got wind. The governor heard of it, and asked Captain Delmar about it. The consequence was, that I received another invitation from the governor, and Captain Delmar again informed me that I might tell my own story, which I did, modestly as before. I say modestly, for I never was a boaster at any time; and I really believe that I thought much less of the circumstances than those did to whom I narrated them. I had at that time but one wish, which was to find favour in the sight of Captain Delmar. I felt that all my prospects in life depended upon that; and aware of his disposition, and the deference that he expected, humility had become, as it were, habitual.

During the time that we remained at Port Royal I continued my studies in the cabin and as the captain remained almost altogether on shore, I found the run of the cabin very pleasant; but as I had no inclination to study the whole of the day, I was not sorry that Tommy Dott was very often my companion in the cabin, an entrance to which, as he could not pass the sentry at the door, he obtained by climbing down the mizen chains, and creeping into the port windows. As soon as the captain's boat was seen coming off Tommy was out again by the port as quick as a monkey, and I was very studiously poring over right-angled triangles. I rose, of course, as the captain entered the cabin. "Sit down, Mr Keene," he would say—"sit down; the master has reported favourably of you, and I am glad to hear of it."

One morning, when, as usual, Tommy Dott had come through the port, we were so busily employed with a caricature which we were making of old Culpepper, that the captain's boat came alongside without our being aware of it, and the captain's voice speaking to the first lieutenant as he was descending the after-ladder was the first intimation we received of his being on board.

It was impossible for Tommy Dott to escape without being seen as he climbed out. The table which was in the centre of the cabin was covered with a blue cloth, large enough for the table when all the additional leaves were put to it, and in its present reduced size the cloth fell down to the deck; I pointed it out to Tommy, as the sentry's hand upon the handle of the door announced the immediate entrance of the captain, and he darted underneath the table, that he might escape detection intending as soon as the captain went into the after-cabin to make his retreat by the cabin-door or windows. The captain entered, and I rose, as usual, from my chair.

"Mr Keene," said he, "I have occasion to speak to the first lieutenant on important private business; oblige me by leaving the cabin till that is done. You may as well tell Mr Hippesley that I wish to see him."

"Yes, sir," replied I making a bow, and leaving the cabin. I felt very much alarmed lest Tommy should be discovered in his hiding-place; and after the captain had stated that he had particular business with the first lieutenant, it was my duty, knowing that Mr Dott was there, to have said so. I hardly knew what to do, or how to act. After all, it was no great crime as it stood. Tommy Dott had come into the cabin without leave, and had concealed himself; but if I was to allow Tommy to remain there and listen to important and particular business, evidently of a secret nature, I should forfeit the good opinion and confidence of the captain: nevertheless, I was very unwilling to betray him; I was dreadfully puzzled, and when I went to the first lieutenant he perceived my confusion.

"Why, what is the matter with you, Mr Keene?—you look quite frightened," said he.

"Well, sir, I am," replied I; "and I think it my duty to tell you why I am so."

I then informed him that Tommy Dott was under the cabin-table, and would, of course, hear the secret communications of the captain.

"You have done very right, Mr Keene, and I know how unpleasant it is to you to inform against your messmate; but at present there is no harm done."

He then laughed, and said, "However, Mr Dott shall never know that you have said anything about it, and I will frighten him out of the cabin for the future."

He then went down the ladder, and into the fore-cabin. I expected that he would have discovered Tommy as if by accident, but such was not the case. The captain had just gone into the after-cabin, and Mr Hippesley immediately followed him, and shutting the door, informed him of Mr Dott's position, and why I had made it known. The captain could not help laughing, as, after all, it was no great offence.

He then gave the necessary information to the first lieutenant, and they both walked into the fore-cabin; the first lieutenant saying, "If you please, then, Captain Delmar, I will send a boat immediately with the letter."

"Certainly," replied the captain, sitting down, and who evidently was inclined to join in the joke with Mr Hippesley. "Sentry, send the officer on deck to man the jolly-boat, and tell Mr Dott to come here immediately."

I was on deck when the sentry put his head up the ladder and gave the order, and I immediately perceived the plan of the first lieutenant and the state of alarm in which Tommy Dott must have been put.

The jolly-boat was manned, and Mr Dott called for in every quarter of the ship, but he did not make his appearance. After a delay of several minutes, the officer on deck went down into the cabin, reporting that the jolly-boat had been manned some time but that Mr Dott was not to be found.

"Not to be found!" replied the captain; "why, he can't have fallen overboard."

"Not he, sir," replied the first lieutenant; "he has gone to sleep somewhere: either in the tops or the fore-topmast staysail netting."

"He appears to be a very troublesome boy," replied the captain.

"Very useless, indeed, sir," replied the first lieutenant. "Sentry, have they found Mr Dott?"

"No, sir; quarter-masters have been everywhere. He's not in the ship."

"Very odd!" observed the captain.

"Oh! he'll turn up soon, sir; but really, Captain Delmar, if you were to give him two or three dozen at the cabin gun, it would bring him to his senses."

"That I most certainly will do," replied Captain Delmar; "and I authorise you to do it, Mr Hippesley, as soon as he makes his appearance; it will be of some service to him; but I hope no accident has happened to him."

"I have no fear of that, sir," replied the first lieutenant: "if the purser's steward's room had been open to-day, I should have sent to see if he was not locked up in another attempt to steal raisins, but that has not been the case. By-the-by, the spirit-room was open this morning, and he may have been down there, and may have had the hatches put over him."

"Well, we must send another midshipman; call Mr Keene," said Captain Delmar.

The sentry called me, and I made my appearance.

"Mr Keene, you'll go on shore to the dockyard in the jolly-boat: give that letter to the master attendant, and wait for an answer."

"Yes, sir," replied I.

"Have you seen anything of Mr Dott?" said the first lieutenant; "you are constantly together."

"I saw him just before Captain Delmar came on board, sir, but I have not seen him since."

"Well, well, we will settle accounts with the young gentleman as soon as he turns up," replied the captain: "you may go, Mr Keene."

I perceived that the captain and first lieutenant both smiled as I left the cabin. It appeared that soon after they left it and the captain went on shore; but Tommy was so frightened that he remained in his hiding-place, as he made sure he would be flogged if he made his appearance, and he resolved to remain where he was until my return, that he might consult me.

As soon as I had reported myself, and given the answer to the first lieutenant, I hastened to the cabin, and then poor Tommy crawled from under the table; the tears were still wet on his cheeks.

"I shall be flogged, Keene, as sure as I stand here. Tell me, what can I do—what can I say?"

"Tell the truth; that's the best way," replied I.

"Tell the captain that I was hid under the table! that would never do."

"Depend upon it, it's the best plan," replied I; "and it is the only advice I can give you: you may be flogged if you tell the truth, but you are *sure* to be flogged if you tell a lie. It will only add to your offence."

"Well, I've been thinking about it—I'm sure that Mr Hippesley will flog me if he catches me to-day or to-morrow; but if I remain hid for a day or two, they will really think that I have fallen overboard, and then they will say, 'poor Tommy Dott,' and perhaps be so glad when I do make my appearance, that they will forgive me."

"Yes," replied I, delighted at the idea; "I'm sure they will, if you do tell the truth when you appear again."

"Then, that is what I'll do. The first lieutenant said that I might be in the spirit-room. Where shall I go to?"

"Why," said I, "you must remain under the table till dark, and then you may easily slip down into the coal-hole, where it is so dark that they never will see you, even if they go down for coals. It is the only place I know of;

stay there all to-morrow and next day, and come up in the evening; or the next morning perhaps will be better."

"Well, it's a very good place," replied Tommy; "anything better than being flogged; but will you bring me something to eat and drink?"

"Depend upon me, Tommy," replied I; "I'll contrive to bring you something every night."

"Well, then, I'll do that," replied he.

"Yes; and tell the truth when you come out," said I.

"Yes, upon my honour I will;" and so saying, Tommy, hearing a noise, again dived under the cabin table.

Soon afterwards I went out of the cabin. The first lieutenant beckoned me to him, and asked me where Mr Dott was, and I told him what had been arranged between us. He laughed very much, and said—

"Well, if Master Tommy punishes himself by two days' confinement in the coal-hole, and tells the truth when he comes out, I think I may promise he will get off his flogging; but don't you say that I have spoken to you about it, and let him do as he proposes."

When it was dark, I supplied Tommy with provisions, and he gained the coal-hole without being discovered.

The next day the speculations at his disappearance were general, and it was now believed that poor Tommy had fallen overboard, and, as the sharks are thick enough in Port Royal, that he was safely stowed away in one of their maws. I will say that the whole of the ship's company were very sorry for him, with the exception of Mr Culpepper, who observed that no good ever came of a boy who stole raisins.

"So you think, that because a lad steals a few of your confounded plums," observed the second lieutenant, "he deserves to be eaten by the sharks. If I were Tommy Dott, I would haunt you if I could."

"I'm not afraid of dead men," replied Mr Culpepper; "they are quiet enough."

"Perhaps so; but recollect, you make them chew tobacco, and therefore they ought to rise up in judgment against you, if they do against any one."

As this conversation passed on the quarter-deck, it put an idea in my head. That night I went to Tommy, whom I found terribly tired of sitting on the coals. I brought him a bottle of mixed grog, and some boiled beef and biscuit. I consoled him by telling him that every one was sorry at his disappearance, and that I was convinced that he would not be punished if he told the truth.

Tommy was for leaving the coal-hole immediately, but I pointed out to him that the captain had not been on board that a and that it was necessary that the captain should believe that he had fallen overboard as well as the officers, or his compassion would not be roused. Tommy saw the propriety of this, and consented to remain another day. I then told him what Mr Culpepper had said, and I added, "Now, Tommy, if Mr Culpepper should see you by any chance, pretend to be your ghost."

"That I will," replied Tommy, "if I get six dozen for it." I then left him.

On my return on deck, I saw Bob Cross; he was on shore during the major portion of the day, attending upon the captain, and as I was no longer in the captain's gig, I saw but little of him.

"Well, Mr Keene," said he, "I think you have quite recovered your colour by this time, and I hope to see you in the gig again."

"I do not think I shall yet awhile—I have not yet learnt navigation enough; but the master says he will be done with me in a fortnight, if I go on as well as I do now."

"Yes; I heard him tell the captain that you were very quick, and would be a good navigator but I can't get over the loss of poor Tommy Dott; he was a little scampish, that's sartin, but still he was a merry, kind-hearted boy— too good for the sharks, at all events. You must feel his loss, Mr Keene, for you were always together."

"No, I don't, Bob," replied I.

"Well, I'm sorry to hear you say that, Mr Keene; I thought you had a kinder heart."

"So I have, Bob; but I'll tell you a secret, known only to the first lieutenant and me; and that is, Tommy's in the coal-hole, very dirty, but quite safe."

Bob Cross burst into a fit of laughing, which lasted some time.

"Well, Mr Keene, you have really taken a weight off my mind; now tell me all about it. You know I'm safe."

I then told Bob what had happened, and of Tommy's intention to make his appearance on the following evening or the next morning.

"Well," said Bob, "you're mischief itself, Master Keene, and that's a fact; however, it's all right this time, and you have the captain and first lieutenant as your confidants and partners in the joke. You did perfectly right and I'm sure the captain and first lieutenant must be pleased with you; but recollect, Master Keene, keep your distance as before; don't presume."

"Never fear, Bob," replied I: "but now I have told you that, I want you to assist me." I then repeated the conversation of Mr Culpepper with the second lieutenant.

"Now," continued I; "you see, Cross, I can't do anything myself; Mr Culpepper hates me, and would suspect me; but if we could only frighten him: you might, for he would not think you were playing him a trick."

"I see," replied Bob; "it will be a good thing for Tommy Dott, and a nice wind-up of this affair. Let me alone. When I come on board to-morrow evening I'll manage it if I can."

After a little more conversation, we separated for the night.

The next morning the captain came on board. He remained on deck with the first lieutenant for some minutes, during which of course, he was made acquainted with Tommy Dott's position. When he came down into the cabin, I moved from my seat, as respectful and serious as before; and when ordered to sit down again, resumed my studies with great apparent diligence. He did not say a word to me about Tommy Dott; and as he was going out of the cabin, Mr Culpepper was announced by the sentry.

"If you please, Captain Delmar," said Mr Culpepper, with his usual profound bow, "what are we to do with the effects of Mr Dott, who has fallen overboard? By the regulations of the service, they should be sold before the mast. And I also wish to know whether he is to be continued to be victualled, or whether it is your pleasure that he is discharged as dead?"

The captain smiled, and turned his face towards me; but I continued with my eyes down on my book.

"Perhaps we had better wait till to-morrow, Mr Culpepper," replied the captain, "and then you may sell his effects, and put DD to his name, poor fellow." And having made this reply, the captain went out of his cabin. Mr Culpepper followed; and shortly afterwards the captain went on shore again.

Before dusk, the captain's gig, as usual, returned on board, and I was at the gangway to meet Bob Cross; the boat was hoisted up, and then Bob came to me.

"I must first go down and see Mr Dott, that I may be able to swear to the fact." Bob did so, and then returned on deck. Mr Culpepper was abaft, walking by himself, when Bob went up and accosted him.

"If you please, sir," said Bob, touching his hat, "did the captain say anything to you about coals, for I expect we shall not stay here much longer?"

"No," replied Mr Culpepper.

"Then he must have forgot it, I suppose sir."

"Well, there's plenty of coals," replied Mr Culpepper.

"Well, sir, I don't know; but I think I heard the cook's mate say as how they were getting rather low."

"Getting rather low! then there must have been great waste," exclaimed Mr C, who was very careful of his expenses.

"I don't know how far it may be so; but I think it might be as well to know how matters stand; and if so be there's plenty, why I can tell Captain Delmar when I go on shore to-morrow."

"I'll see; I'll go down myself to-night," replied Mr Culpepper. "The midshipmen are allowed a stove to themselves—very unusual—and they are cooking all day."

"Talking about midshipmen, sir," replied Cross, "you may think it's very odd but as I stand here—and you know, Mr Culpepper, I am not easily scared—I saw that young Tommy Dott, or his ghost, this very evening."

It was now quite dark; and Mr Culpepper stared at the coxswain, and then replied, "Pooh, nonsense!"

"It's no nonsense, I do assure you. I saw him with these eyes, sure as I stand here."

"Where?" exclaimed Mr C.

"Right forward, sir. I only mention it to you, but don't say a word about it, for I should only be laughed at; but I do assure you that I would kiss the Bible to it, if it was required. I never did before believe in anything of that sort, that's sartain; but it's no use talking about it, sir. I think I had better get a lantern, and get over this coal business at once."

"Yes, yes," replied Mr Culpepper; "but you won't know how much coals there are: I must go myself and see."

Bob Cross was soon ready with the lantern, and went forward with Mr Culpepper. The hammocks had been piped down, and they were obliged to bend double under them to get along the lower deck. I followed unperceived.

The descent into the coal-hole was by battens, and not very easy for an old man like Mr C But Cross went down first, holding the light for the purser to follow, which he did very slowly, and with great caution. As soon as they both stood on the coals below, the purser took the light to make his survey.

"Why, there's plenty of coals for three months, coxswain," said he. "I thought there was; you see they are nearly up to the beams abaft."

"Look! sir—look!" exclaimed Cross, starting back; "what's that?"

"Where?" exclaimed Mr C, alarmed.

"There, sir—there he is: I told you so."

The purser's eyes were directed to where Bob pointed, and then he beheld Tommy Dott standing immovable, with his arms extended, as if denouncing him—his eyes staring, and his mouth wide open.

"Mercy!—murder!" cried the purser, dropping the lantern, which went out and left them in the dark; and he tumbled down on the coals.

Bob Cross stepped over him, and hastened up to the lower deck, followed by Tommy Dott, who first, by way of revenge, jumped several times upon the purser's face and body before he climbed up.

The cry of the purser had given the alarm. The master-at-arms hastened forward with his lantern just as Tommy had made his appearance above the coamings. Seeing Tommy as black as a sweep, he too was frightened; the men had put their heads out of their hammocks and some of them had seen Tommy.

Bob Cross, as he crawled aft, cried out, "Tommy Dott's ghost!" I had pretended to be terrified out of my wits as I ran aft, and all was confusion on the lower deck. The first lieutenant had come out of the wardroom, and seeing me, he inquired what was the matter. I replied that Mr Culpepper had gone down into the coal-hole, and had seen Mr Dott's ghost. He laughed heartily, and went back.

Tommy had in the mean time made his appearance in the mids' berth, at which they had all rushed from him in dismay, just as I entered; when I caught him by the hand saying, "Tommy, my boy, how are you?" They then perceived that it was Tommy himself, and order was restored.

Mr Culpepper was hoisted up out of the coal-hole; Master Tommy having jumped upon his face, he looked a very miserable object, as he was well blackened, as well as much bruised from the soles of Tommy's shoes, and his nose had bled profusely. He was very incoherent for some time; but the doctor gave him an opiate, and put him to bed.

The next morning the whole affair was explained on the quarterdeck, Master Tommy well reprimanded, and desired to return to his duty. The captain was very much amused at the winding up of this affair, as it was a capital story to tell at the governor's. Tommy never had an idea that I had blown upon him, nor did Mr Culpepper imagine that their meeting was premeditated.

I had now completed the usual course of navigation under the master, and had no longer any cause for remaining in the cabin; I therefore returned to my berth; but as I had taken a liking to navigation, I now was employed daily in working sights and rating the chronometer.

We remained three weeks longer in Port Royal, and then were ordered out on a cruise, on the South American coast. There we continued for nearly six months without anything occurring worth relating, except our having captured four good prizes. We were returning to Jamaica, when we fell in with a schooner, which gave us the intelligence of the capture of the island of Curaçao by four English frigates.

As we were near to the island and short of water, Captain Delmar resolved to touch at it, and remained two or three days.

The reader will perhaps recollect that the old Dutch gentleman, whose life I had saved in the pirate vessel, had stated that his name was Vanderwelt, and that he lived at Curaçao. The next evening we entered the harbour, and it was astonishing to every one how so strong a place could have been taken by so small a force. The commodore, who had plenty of work on hand, requested, or rather ordered, our captain to remain with him for ten days or a fortnight, to assist him.

On the third day after our arrival I obtained leave to go on shore, as I wished to find out the old Dutch gentleman. As I was again in the captain's gig, I had very often landed, but had not had an opportunity of making inquiries, as I could not leave my boat and boat's crew.

This afternoon I landed in the gig, and went up through the gate into the town, but I could not find anyone who spoke English. At last, by asking for the house of Mynheer Vanderwelt, it was pointed out to me, and I went up to the door; it was a very large house, with a verandah all round it, painted bright green and while alternately. There were several slaves sitting down at the entrance, and I asked for Mynheer Vanderwelt; they stared at me, and wondered what I wanted, but as I was in midshipman's uniform, they were of course very civil, and one of them beckoned me to follow him, which I did, and was introduced to the old gentleman, who was sitting in a cane arm-chair with his pipe in his mouth, and fanned by two slave girls, about twelve years old.

As he had spoken to me in English on board of the pirate, I immediately went up to him, and said, "How do you do, sir?"

"I am very well, sir," replied he, taking the pipe out of his mouth. "What do you want? do you come from the English commodore? What is his pleasure?"

"No, sir," replied I; "I do not come from the commodore; but I came up to see you."

"Oh, that is all," replied the old gentleman, putting his pipe in his mouth again, and resuming his smoking. I felt rather nettled at his treatment, and then said —

"Don't you know me, sir?"

"No, sir," replied he, "I have not that honour. I have never seen you in my life before, and I do not know you."

My blood was up at this cool declaration.

"Then I wish you a good morning, sir," replied I; and turning on my heel, I was strutting out with all the dignity of an offended midshipman, when I was met face to face by the little girl, his daughter. She stared at me very much, and I passed her in sovereign contempt; she followed me timidly, and looked into my face, then panting for breath, seized me by the arm. I turned to her at being stopped in this manner, and was about to shake her off with anything but politeness, when she screamed out, and in a moment had sprung up, and was hanging with both arms round my neck.

"Fader, fader," she cried out as I struggled to disengage myself.

The old gentleman came out at the summons.

"Stop him! fader; don't let him go away," cried she in Dutch; "it is he! it is he!"

"Who, my child?" asked the old gentleman.

"The pirate-boy," replied the little girl, bursting into a paroxysm of tears, on my shoulders.

"Mein Gott! it cannot be; he was *black*, my child; yet," continued the old gentleman, looking at me, "he is like him. Tell me, sir, are you our preserver?"

"Yes," replied I, "I was; but that is of little consequence now. Will you oblige me by removing this young lady?" continued I, for I was highly offended.

"Sir, I ask your pardon," replied the old gentleman; "but I am not to blame. How could I recognise you in a white person when you were so dark-coloured at our meeting on board of that vessel? I am not to blame; indeed I am not, my dear young friend. I would have given ten thousand rix dollars to have met you, that I might prove my gratitude for your noble defence of us, and our preservation at such a risk. Come, sir, you must forgive the mistake of an old man, who was certainly not inclined to be civil to an officer who belonged to the squadron, who had within these few days so humiliated us by their astonishing bravery and success. Let my little girl, whose life you saved, persuade you, if I cannot."

In the mean time the little girl had dropped from my shoulder, and was on the floor, embracing my knees, and still sobbing. I felt convinced that what the old gentleman said was true, and that he had not recognised me. I had forgotten that I had been stained dark at the time that I had met them on board of the Stella.

I therefore held out my hand to the old gentleman, and raising the little girl, we all three went in together to where we had found the old gentleman on my first introduction to him.

"If you knew how delighted I am to see you, and be able to express my thanks," said Mynheer Vanderwelt, "and poor Minnie too. How often have we talked over that dreadful day, and wondered if ever we should see you again. I assure you, on my honour, that now I no longer regret the capture of the island."

Minnie stood by me during the time her father was speaking, her large blue eyes beaming through the tears with which they brimmed; and as I turned to her, our eyes met, and she smiled. I drew her towards me. She appeared as if she only required some encouragement, for she immediately kissed me several times on the cheek nearest to her, every now and then saying a word or two in Dutch to her father, which I could not understand.

I hardly need say, that after this, intimacy was soon brought about. If I thought that at first I had been treated with ingratitude, ample amends was made afterwards.

The old gentleman said during the evening, "Good heaven! if my daughter's eyes had not been sharper than mine; if you had gone away, thinking that I did not choose to recognise you—had I found it out afterwards, it would have broken my heart, and poor Minnie's too. Oh! I am grateful—very grateful to God that it was not so."

That I passed a very pleasant evening the reader may imagine. The household who had been told who I was, appeared to almost worship me.

The old gentleman asked me a hundred questions as to my parentage, etcetera, about Captain Delmar and the service, and begged of me to remain with him altogether while the frigate was in port. I told him that was impossible, but that I would come as often as I could obtain leave. At nine o'clock I bade them good night, and was escorted to the boat by six of the slaves carrying lanterns.

Captain Delmar, as well as all the other captains of the frigates, had taken up his quarters on shore for the harbour was so narrow and landlocked, that the heat on board was excessive. I found that the next day old Mr Vanderwelt had paid his respects to Captain Delmar, giving him an account of what had occurred on board of the pirate much more flattering to me than what I had stated myself. The steward was present at the time, and he had told Bob Cross, who communicated it to me. Mynheer Vanderwelt had also begged as a favour that I might be permitted to stay on shore with him during the time that the frigate was in harbour, but to this Captain Delmar had not consented, promising, however, that I should have occasional leave when the service would permit of it.

The reader may recollect that the island of Curaçao had been surrendered to the English in 1800, and restored to the Dutch in 1802. During that interval several English merchants had settled there and remained after the restoration, and now at the second capture we found them still on the island. From these we received the information that Mr Vanderwelt was the richest man on the island, and that the Dutch government was indebted to him in very large sums; that he had long retired from business, although he had large property in the Havannah, which he received with his wife, who had been a Spanish lady, and that it was his intention to have gone back to Holland by the first man-of-war which should have arrived.

We remained three weeks at Curaçao, during which time the first lieutenant gave me leave to go on shore almost every evening after the captain had dismissed his gig, and to remain at Mr Vanderwelt's till half-past eight the following morning, when I joined my boat, and attended on the captain. By this plan my duty was not interfered with, and I had many pleasant meetings with my new friends, and became, as may be imagined, very intimate with little Minnie.

I may as well describe her. She was about ten years old, tall for her age; she was very fair, with deep blue eyes, and very dark hair; her countenance was very animated and expressive, and she promised to be a very handsome woman. Her father doted upon her, for he had no other child; he had married late in life, and his wife had died a few days after Minnie was born. She was very affectionate in disposition, and very sweet-tempered; up to the present she had received but little education, and that was one principal reason for Mr Vanderwelt's wishing to return to Holland. I soon became as one of the family, and certainly was treated as such.

Minnie was very curious to know what it was that I carried about my neck in the seal-skin pouch, but I never could tell either her or her father what it really was. Mr Vanderwelt very often asked me if I liked being at sea, and I invariably replied in the affirmative.

At last the frigate was to sail, and I had but one more evening to pass with them. Mr Vanderwelt appeared very grave, and little Minnie would every now and then during the evening burst into tears at the idea of our separation.

At last the hour of parting arrived—it was very painful. I promised to write to them, and Mr Vanderwelt told me that his house was always ready to receive me, and begged that if I wanted anything I would let him know.

I cried, myself, when I left the house—the first time that I ever cried, I believe, on such an occasion. The next morning we were again under weigh, to rejoin the admiral at Jamaica.

Bob Cross had told me that he wished to have a little talk with me in the first watch, and I met him on the gangway, our usual rendezvous.

"Master Keene, I have some news for you, which I gained from the steward last night. I will say, that his ears are always open; not that I think he is generally what is called an eavesdropper but he likes you, and when you are concerned, he does care to find out what is going on. Now you see, sir, that Dutch gentleman whom you saved from the nigger pirate came to call on Captain Delmar yesterday morning, and, after some palaver, he told the captain that he wished you to remain with him altogether, and leave his majesty's service; and he begged the captain to allow you to be discharged, and then he would be a father to you, as you had no father. There was a great deal more which the steward could not make out, but it was all to that effect. Well, the captain said that it was very true that you had lost your father but that he considered you as *his own* son, and could not part with you on any account; and he stated that you were so promising an officer, that it be very wrong that you should leave the service, and that it must not be thought of. The old gentleman said a great deal, and tried very hard to persuade the captain, but it was of no use. The captain said he would never let you go till you were a post-captain and commanded a fine frigate, and then you would of course be your own master, and act as you please."

"I am very glad to hear all this, Bob, I can assure you."

"Yes, sir, it is very good news: but, Master Keene, I only hope, knowing Captain Delmar as you do, that you will act towards him as if you had never heard it."

"I will, depend upon it, Cross. As for leaving the service, that I would not have done even if Captain Delmar had agreed to it. I'm an Englishman, and I don't want to be under Dutch protection."

"That's right, sir—that's right—just as I wished you to feel. How time flies away. Why, Master Keene, you have been afloat nearly three years."

"Within a month, Bob."

"And you're growing such a tall fellow, they won't keep you much longer in the captain's gig, I expect: I shall be sorry for that. So Master Tommy Dott is in another scrape."

"How?—I heard nothing of it."

"No, because it's only within this half-hour that he's got in it."

"Tell me."

"Why, sir, Mr Culpepper had fallen fast asleep on the gunroom table, under the skylight, which, as you know, is always open, and his head had fallen back, and his mouth was wide open: there was no other officer in the gun-room except Mr Culpepper: and Tommy Dott, who perceived him, asked Timothy Jenkins, the maintop-man, to give him a quid of tobacco; well, Jenkins takes it out of his cheek, red-hot, as you may suppose, and hands it to Master Tommy, who takes his perpendicular very accurately, and drops the quid into the purser's open mouth.

"Mr Culpepper was almost choked, but after a terrible coughing, the quid comes up again; notwithstanding, he turns as sick as a dog, and is obliged to run to the basin in his cabin. Well, sir, as soon as he comes out again, he goes up under the half deck, and inquires of the sentry who it was that did it; and the sentry, who is that sulky fellow, Martin, instead of knowing nothing about it, says directly, it was Master Tommy; and now there's a formal complaint made by Mr Culpepper on the quarter-deck, and Master Tommy will get it as sure as a gun."

"He don't know how to play a trick," replied I; "he is always found out and punished: the great point is, not to be discovered—that's the real pleasure in playing a trick."

"Well, you certainly do manage well, Master Keene; but I think it's almost time you left them off now, you're getting an oldster. Why, you must be seventeen, sir?"

"Yes, Bob, not very far from it."

"Well, I suppose I must say Mister Keene for the future."

"You may call be what you like, Bob; you have been a good friend to me."

"Well, sir, I only hope that Captain Delmar will make you a post-captain, as he says, and that you'll get a fine frigate, and I'll be your coxswain; but that's a long way to look to, and we shan't have any more councils of war on the gangway then."

"No; but we may in the cabin, Cross."

"A large sail on the starboard bow," cried the look-out man forward.

"A large sail on the starboard bow," reported the mate of the watch.

My glass was on the capstern, and I ran for it, and went forward to examine the vessel, although my duty as signal midshipman was ended at sunset.

"What do you make of it, Mr Keene?" said the officer of the watch.

"I think she is a man-of-war; but it is so dark, that I cannot make her out very clearly."

"Is she standing this way?"

"Yes, sir, under top-sails and top-gallant-sails, I think."

The officer of the watch went down to report to the captain, who had not yet turned into his cot. Captain Delmar had been informed that a Dutch frigate was expected at the island, but not until the following month; still we had no reason to suppose that there were any of our frigates down in these latitudes, except those lying in the harbour at Curaçao. The wind was light, about a three knot breeze, and there being no moon till after twelve o'clock, it was very difficult to make out what she was. Some said she was a two-decked vessel. The captain went down to look at his private signals for the night, and before he came up I was all ready with the lanterns.

"Two lights over one in a triangle; be quick, Mr Keene."

"Aye, aye, sir," replied I.

The lights were soon hoisted at the peak, but as they could not well be seen by the other vessel, as we were standing towards her, we went about and hove to across her hawse. For a quarter of an hour she continued to stand towards us without noticing the signals; at last the captain said, "They must be all asleep on board of the vessel."

"No, Captain Delmar," replied I, keeping my telescope on the vessel, "they are not all asleep, for I saw lights on the main-deck through the bow-ports. I see them again now."

"So do I," said the first lieutenant.

"Then we'll beat to quarters, Mr Hippesley," rejoined the captain.

The men were summoned to quarters, and hammocks piped up and stowed in a very short time, the guns cast loose, and every man at his post (but the ports not opened), waiting the coming down of the stranger, now about a mile distant, when suddenly she rounded to the wind on the same tack that we were, and set her royals and flying-jib.

"She does not answer our signals," observed the captain: "I suspect by that and her present manoeuvre she must be an enemy."

"I have no doubt of it, sir," observed the first lieutenant; "an English frigate would not behave in that way."

"Open the ports and get up the fighting lanterns, then," said the captain; for, up to the present, we had been careful not to show any lights.

It was now plain to see that her men were at their quarters and that she was prepared for action. When everything was ready on deck, the royals and flying-jib were set, and we gave chase. The strange vessel was about three-quarters of a mile on our weather-beam; in half an hour we had gained upon her considerably, and our sailing was so superior that we were satisfied, should she prove an enemy, that in an hour more we should be engaged.

Of course, we might have engaged her at the distance we were from her, but you cannot be too careful in a night action, and ought never to engage without first hailing the vessel to make sure that she is an enemy, as circumstances may, and have occurred by which an English vessel may not be able to answer the private signal, and, of course, a vessel belonging to a neutral power would be in the same position.

The incertitude which existed as to whether the strange vessel was an enemy or not created great excitement. My duty, as signal midshipman, placed me abaft on the quarter-deck, and Bob Cross, who was really a quarter-master, although doing duty as captain's coxswain, was at the wheel.

At last we had brought the chase well on our weather quarter, and when we tacked we found that we lay well up, she being about a point on our lee bow. Another half-hour brought us within two cables' length of her, when we kept away, so as to pass her to leeward, close enough to have thrown a biscuit on board. The stranger still remaining on the opposite tack, Captain Delmar then hailed from the gangway—

"Ship, a-hoy!"

There was a death-like silence on board of both vessels, and his voice pierced sonorously through the night wind.

"Ah! yaw!" was the reply.

"What ship is that?" continued Captain Delmar.

During this time every man was at his gun; the captains, with the lanyards of the locks in their hands, ready to pour in a broadside.

The reply from the other vessel was—"Vat chip is dat?"

"His Britannic Majesty's ship Calliope," replied Captain Delmar; and then he repeated—"What ship is that? Let every man lie down at his quarters," said Captain Delmar. The order was hardly obeyed, when the stranger frigate poured in her broadside, and as we were then very close, with great execution to our hull and rigging: but as the men had been lying down, very few of them were hurt.

As soon as the crash was over, Captain Delmar cried out—"Up, men, and fire, as I round to under her stern."

In a few seconds we had passed through the volumes of smoke, and luffed up under her stern: we poured in our whole broadside.

"Let her go off again—flatten in there forward. Reedy about," was the next order given.

We ran away from her about three cables' length, until we had sufficient way to tack, and then we went about and stood towards her, steering for her weather quarter, as if we were going to engage her to windward.

"Over to the larboard guns, my lads. Hands by, after bracings and howlings, Mr Hippesley."

"Aye, aye, sir, all ready."

As soon as we were near enough, the after-yards were shivered, the jib sheet to windward, and the helm put up. The Calliope worked beautifully; she paid sharp off, and we again passed under her stern, and gave another raking broadside; very unexpected on the part of the Dutchman, who presumed that we were going to engage him to windward, and had his men all ready at his larboard guns in consequence.

The Dutch captain was evidently much annoyed: he stood at the taffrail, and, much to our amusement, cried out, in bad English, "You coward—not fight fair."

As we shot ahead of her, to leeward, she gave us a portion of her starboard broadside: but the men, having been over at the guns on the other side, were not quick enough, and they did us no injury; whereas, her mizzen-mast fell over the side a few minutes after we passed her.

She then raid off, and so did we, so that she might not rake us, and broadsides were exchanged on equal terms; but before we had exchanged these broadsides, both ships running with the wind on the quarter, we found that our superiority in sailing free was so great, that we shot ahead of him out of his fire, and we were enabled to luff up and rake him again.

The last raking broadside brought down his main-topmast and then she was all our own, as Bob Cross said; as she could not round to with no after sail, and we could from our superiority in sailing, take our position as we pleased, which we did, constantly keeping ahead of him, and raking him, broadside after broadside, and receiving but one broadside in return, until his foremast went by the board, and he had nothing but his main-mast standing.

This bettered his condition on the whole; as, although hardly manageable with so little wind, he had more power over his vessel, as far as rounding to the wind, which he did, and the action continued; but our fighting under sail gave us great advantage, and although an occasional shot would come in, and we had to carry some men into the cockpit, for one shot we received, we certainly returned ten. The action had continued about an hour, when, by the continual cannonading, the light wind was beaten down, and it fell dead calm. This put us again upon a more equal footing, as the Calliope had not steerage way.

We were then about a quarter of a mile apart, lying head and stern; but both ships had fallen off during the calm, so that only the quarter guns of each could be brought to bear. The major portion of the ship's company being, therefore, not able to use their guns, were employed in repairing the damages we had received, which were very considerable, especially in the sails and rigging.

I was standing by Bob Cross, who was looking out for cats' paws, as we call slight breaths of wind, when he said in a low voice:—

"Master Keene, I never had an idea that the captain could handle his ship so well: he really knows what he's about as well as any man in the service."

"I thought so, too," replied I. "Whew! there's a nasty shot," cried I, as one came in and upset half a dozen of the marines, who were hauling upon the mizzen-topsail sheet, which had just been spliced.

"Yes, sir, that chap is made of good stuff, depend upon it—all the Dutchmen are: if they could only keep their hands out of their breeches pockets, they would be rummer customers than they are now; as it is, they are not to be played with; and, depend upon it, we're a long way off having him yet: we must pray for wind to come up and he must pray for the calm to continue."

"Where's Mr Keene?" said the captain, who was on the other side of the deck.

"Here, sir," said I, running up and touching my hat.

"Mr Keene, go down quietly and ascertain how many men we have hurt: the doctor will be able to tell you pretty nearly."

"Aye, aye, sir," replied I, and I dived down below; just as I did so, a shot came in and cut away the lower rail of the copper stanchions which were round the hatchway, about a foot beyond my hat: had I not gone down so quickly, it would have taken my head off.

I went down into the gun-room, for the doctor preferred being there to the cockpit, as there was so much more room to operate, and I gave him the captain's message.

He was very busy taking off a poor fellow's leg. It was a horrible sight and made me sick and faint. As soon us the bone had been sawed off, he said—

"You will find all the wounded I have dressed in the steerage; those they have brought me down dead are in the cockpit. There have been five amputations already the master is badly wounded, and Mr Williams the mate, is killed: those whom I have not been able to attend to yet, are here in the gun-room. You must ascertain what the captain wishes to know yourself, Mr Keene. I cannot, leave a leg with the arteries not taken up, to count heads. Mr Rivers, the tenaculum—ease the tourniquet, now."

As I felt what the doctor said to be true, I got a lantern and commenced my examinations. I found fourteen wounded men waiting the doctor's care in the gun-room, which was almost a pool of blood. In the steerage there were nine who had been dressed, and four in their hammocks, who had undergone amputation of the arm or leg. I then went down into the cockpit, where I counted eleven of our best men lying dead. Having obtained the information required, I was proceeding up the cockpit ladder, when I turned towards the purser's steward's room, and saw Mr Culpepper, the purser, on his knees before a lantern; he looked very pale—he turned round and saw me.

"What's the matter?" cried he.

"Nothing, sir; only the captain wishes to know how many men are killed and wounded."

"Tell him I do not know: surely he does not want me on deck?"

"He wants to know how many men are hurt, sir," replied I, for I perceived that he thought that the message was sent to him.

"Mercy on me! Stop a minute, Mr Keene, and I'll send up word by you."

"I can't stop, sir," replied I, going up the ladder.

Mr Culpepper would have called me back, but I preferred leaving him in his error, as I wished to see which he most dreaded, the captain's displeasure or the shot of the enemy.

I returned on deck and made my report. The captain looked very grave, but made no reply.

I found that the two frigates were now lying stern to stern, and firing occasional guns, which raked fore and aft. Except the men who worked the guns aft, our people were lying down at their quarters, by the order of the captain.

"If we only had but a capful of wind," said the captain to the first lieutenant, "but I see no appearance of it."

I touched my hat and said, "The moon will rise in about ten minutes, sir, and she often brings the wind up with her."

"That's true, Mr Keene, but it's not always the case. I only hope she will; if not, I fear we shall lose more of our men."

The firing continued, and our main-mast had received so many shots, that we were obliged to hold it for its support. While so employed, the moon rose, and the two vessels had now a good view of each other. I directed my glass to the horizon under the moon, and was delighted to perceive a black line, which promised wind; I reported it to the master, and the promise was kept good, for in a quarter of an hour our sails flapped, and then gradually filled.

"She has steerage way, sir," reported Bob Cross.

"Thank Heaven for that," replied Captain Delmar. "Jump up, men. Brace round the yards, Mr Hippesley."

"The enemy's main yard is cut in two in the slings, sir," reported I, after I had my glass upon her.

"Then her last hope is gone," replied Mr Hippesley. "Haul over the starboard jib-sheet forward—let her come to, quartermaster. Larboard guns, my lads."

"Now, my men," cried Captain Delmar, "make short work of her."

This injunction was obeyed. We had now a good sight of the enemy, and brought our whole broadside to bear upon her stern; and after a quarter of an hour more firing I perceived that her ensign was no longer on the staff, where it had been hoisted after the fall of the mizenmast; neither had she for the last five minutes given us a gun in return.

"She has struck, sir, I think," said I to Captain Delmar; "her ensign is down."

"Pass the word 'Cease firing,' Mr Hippesley; but let the guns be all reloaded in case of accidents. Have we a boat that can swim? Examine the cutters, Mr Keene."

I found the cutter on the larboard quarter, with her bottom out: she could not swim, that was clear. The starboard one was in better condition.

"The starboard cutter will float, sir; her gunwale is all torn away, but there are rollocks enough to pull."

"Let her be cleared away and lowered down, Mr Hippesley. Send for the second lieutenant."

"I believe he's not on deck sir," replied the first lieutenant.

"Not much hurt, I hope?"

"A splinter, I was told, sir."

"Where's Mr Weymss, the third lieutenant? Mr Weymss, jump into the boat, and take possession of the prize: take as many men as you can; and, Mr Keene, with Mr Weymss, and as soon as you have gained the necessary information, come back with the boat and two hands."

I followed the third lieutenant info the boat, and we pulled on board of our antagonist. A junior officer received us on the deck, and presented his sword. His left arm was bound up, and he was very pale from loss of blood. He spoke pretty good English; and we found that we had captured the Dort, Dutch frigate, of thirty-eight guns, bound to Curaçao, with a detachment of troops for the garrison, and a considerable quantity of ammunition and specie on board for the use of the colony.

We inquired whether the captain was much hurt, as he did not appear on deck.

"He is dead, gentlemen," replied the young officer: "he was my father. Our loss has been very great. I am only a cadet, yet I am commanding officer."

A tear rolled down his cheek as he said that the captain was his father, and I felt for him. Shortly afterwards he staggered to a carronade slide, and dropped down on it, and very soon was in a state of insensibility.

The carnage had been dreadful, and the bulwarks of the vessel had been shattered to pieces. The scene was almost as had as the Stella's decks before she was blown up by the negro captain. Several of the guns were dismounted and two of them had burst. I had only time to go round the gun-deck, and then I ordered two hands into the boat, that I might make my report to Captain Delmar.

I asked the third lieutenant to allow me to take on board the young officer, who still remained lifeless on the carronade slide, and, as it was proper for me to bring back with me the commanding officer, he consented. We lowered him with a rope into the boat, and then I returned on board of the Calliope, and went up to the captain to make my report, and present him with the sword of the officer commanding the prize.

Just as I was commencing my story, Mr Culpepper came up without his wig, and in a state of great disorder, with a piece of dirty paper in his hand. He trembled very much from the effects of his alarm, but made a very profound bow, and said to Captain Delmar—

"Here is the state of killed and wounded, Captain Delmar, as far as I have been able to collect them. I could not possibly get them ascertained before, although I have been an hour or two employed—ever since Mr Keene came down."

The captain, who did not like the interruption, replied very haughtily, "Mr Culpepper, it's the duty of the surgeon to send in the report of killed and wounded. You had better go down below, get your dress in a little better order. Now, Mr Keene."

Old Culpepper slunk away as I proceeded to give the information, and the captain now asked the carpenter if the pinnace was sufficiently repaired.

"In a few minutes, sir," was the reply.

"Mr Hippesley, you must, then, send forty hands on board the prize to repair her damages, as far as we can. Mr Weymss must remain on board."

In the meantime the young officer had been taken down below to the surgeon, who had now some leisure to attend to him. He was soon restored, and the surgeon expressed his opinion that it would be possible to save his arm. I went down to see him, and I gave him my hammock to sleep in for the present, and as soon as he was comfortably arranged under the half-deck I returned to the quarter-deck, and made myself as useful as I could, for we had plenty to do on board of our own frigate, knotting and splicing, having only made temporary repairs.

It was now dawn of day, and very soon afterwards broad daylight. The men were ordered aft with the buckets, and the decks, which were smeared and black with powder and the blood of the wounded, were washed down. That we were all very tired I hardly need say, but it was not yet time for repose; the magazines had been secured and the fires lighted.

Another boat, with the carpenter and assistant-surgeon, had been sent on board the prize to remedy any serious damage and to assist in dressing the wounded. I was sent with the boat. Mr Weymss, the third lieutenant, had not been idle: jury-masts were in preparation, the decks had been cleared, the dead thrown overboard, and the wounded taken below.

On mustering the remainder of the Dort's ship's company, and calling over the muster-roll of the troops on board, we found that she had lost the captain, 2 lieutenants and 10 officers, 73 seamen and 61 soldiers, killed; and the first-lieutenant, 13 officers, and 137 wounded—147 killed and 151 wounded: total 298. She had received several shot between wind and water, and had a good deal of water in the hold: this was, however, soon remedied by the carpenter and his crew, and the frigate pumped out by the prisoners.

I returned on board of the Calliope with this intelligence to the captain, and found that the surgeon had just sent in the report of our own loss, which was, 1 officer and 17 men killed—master, 2 lieutenants, 2 midshipmen, and 47 wounded.

"Do you know who are the midshipmen wounded?" said the captain to me.

"I heard that Mr James was killed, sir, but not the names of those who are wounded; but I think one of them must be Mr Dott, or we certainly should have seen him about."

"I should not be surprised," replied the captain. "Sentry, ask who are the young gentlemen wounded."

The sentry replied, "Mr Castles and Mr Dott."

"Well," replied the captain, "he'll be in no more mischief for some time; I heard of his trick to the purser."

As the captain was saying this, I perceived the piece of paper which the purser had brought up as his report of killed and wounded lying on the table with the other reports. It had, apparently, not been examined by the captain, but my eye caught it, and I observed, written in a shaking hand, "Pieces of beef, 10; ditto pork, 19; raisins, 17; marines, 10." I could not help smiling.

"What are you amused with, Mr Keene, may I ask?" said the captain, rather gravely.

"I beg your pardon, sir, for venturing so in your presence," replied I; "but it is Mr Culpepper's report of killed and wounded;" which I then took up, and handed to the captain.

This proof of Mr Culpepper's state of mind during the conflict was too much for even Captain Delmar, who laughed outright.

"The old fool," muttered he.

"You may go now, Mr Keene. If breakfast is ready, tell Mr Hippesley to let the men have it as soon as possible."

"Aye, aye, sir," replied I, and bowing respectfully, I quitted the cabin; for I felt that Captain Delmar thought that he had not been quite so reserved towards me as he always wished to be.

As soon as I had given the captain's orders, I went down to find out Tommy Dott. He was in his hammock, next to mine, in which I had put the young Dutch officer. Dott was wide awake, and, apparently, very feverish.

"Where are you hurt, Tommy?"

"I am sure I don't know," said he. "Get me some water, Keene."

I got a pannikin of water, and he drank it.

"Don't you know where you are hurt?"

"I believe it's my side—somewhere about the body, I know; but I'm so stiff all over, that I can't tell exactly where. Something hit me, and I fell right down the hatchway; that's all I know about it until I found myself in my hammock."

"Well, at all events, you won't be punished now for dropping the quid into Mr Culpepper's mouth."

"No," replied Tommy, with a smile, in spite of his pain; "but I would have played him a better trick than that if I had had any idea that we should have been so soon in action. I wish I could turn round, Keene—I think I should be easier."

I turned poor Tommy in his hammock, and then left him. I looked at the son of the Dutch captain—he was slumbering; he was a very slight youth, with very beautiful, but very feminine features. I felt a kindness towards him, poor fellow; for he had lost his father, and he was about to pass his best years in prison. But the boatswain's mates piped to breakfast, and I hastened down into the berth to get my share of the cocoa.

As soon as the men had finished their breakfast, the hands were again turned up, the lower deck cleared and washed, new sails bent and the guns properly secured; screens were put up round the half-deck where the wounded were in their beds. The dead were brought up and sewed up in their hammocks, laid out on gratings, and covered with the ensign and union jack, preparatory to their being committed to the deep. Another party was sent to assist on board of the prize, and the prisoners were brought on board, and put down in the fore-hold, which had been cleared for their reception.

By noon everything was so far ready that we were enabled to take the prize in tow, and make sail on the Calliope, after which the men, who were exhausted, went to dinner, and were permitted to sleep during the remainder of the day until the evening, when the ship's company was ordered up, and the dead were committed to the deep blue sea with the usual ceremonies.

The breeze was steady but the water was smooth during the night, and glad I was to throw myself on one of the lockers in the midshipmen's berth, after so many hours of excitement. I slept till four in the morning, and finding the planks not quite so soft as they might be, I then turned into the hammock of the midshipman of the morning watch, and remained till six bells, when Bob Cross came down and told me that the captain would soon be on deck.

"Well, Cross," said I, as I came on deck and went aft to look at the prize in tow, "this is a nice business, and our captain will gain a great deal of credit."

"And he deserves it, Master Keene," replied Cross: "as I said before, I never had an idea that he could handle his ship so well—no, nor none of the ship's company. We all thought Mr Hippesley the best officer of the two, but we have found out our mistake. The fact is, Mr Keene, Captain Delmar wraps himself an in his dignity like a cloak, and there's no making him out, till circumstances oblige him to take it off."

"That's very true, Bob," replied I: "it is only this very morning that he laughed himself, and I laughed also, and he pulled up immediately afterwards, twice as stiff to me as before."

I then told Bob of Mr Culpepper's report, which amused him very much.

"I am sure that he is pleased with you, Mr Keene, and I must say that you were very useful and very active."

"Do you know that the carpenter says that we have received injuries that cannot be well repaired without the ship going into dock, and I should not be surprised if we were to be sent home, if the survey confirms his report. I hope we shall; I am tired of the West Indies, and I should like to see my mother; we have a nice breeze now, and we are two points free. If it lasts, we shall be at Jamaica in a fortnight or less."

The captain coming on deck put an end to our conversation.

Before night the prize had got up jury-masts, and sail set upon them, and we went through the water more rapidly. In ten days we arrived at Port Royal with our prize. The captain went on shore, and what was still more agreeable, we got rid of all our prisoners and wounded men. A survey, in consequence of the carpenter's report was held upon the Calliope, and the result was, she was ordered home to be repaired. The Dort was commissioned by the admiral, and Mr Hippesley received an acting order to the sloop of war, which had become vacant by the commander of her being promoted into the Dort, which was now christened the Curaçao.

In ten days after our arrival we were ready, and made sail for Old England. Tommy Dott and the second lieutenant remained on board, and were both convalescent before we entered the Channel. Tommy Dott's wound, by the bye, was a splinter in the back, added to severe bruises from tumbling down the hatchway.

Captain Delmar had shown great kindness to the son of the Dutch captain and he did not send him on shore with the rest of the prisoners, but permitted him to remain, and come home in the Calliope. He recovered slowly, but was soon out of danger, and was walking about with his arm in a sling long before we arrived in England. It appeared to me that, during the passage home, old Culpepper was not so much in the good graces of Captain Delmar as he used to be; he was, however, more obsequious than ever. We had a fine run home, and in seven weeks from our leaving Port Royal, we dropped our anchor at Spithead.

I may have been wrung, but it certainly did appear to me that as we neared the coast of England, the behaviour of Captain Delmar was more reserved to me (I may say it was harsher) than ever it had been before. Hurt at treatment which I felt I did not deserve, I tried to analyse the cause as I walked up and down the deck, and at last I decided that his pride was again alarmed. On the one hand he was returning to his own country, to meet with his aristocratical connections, and on the other he was reminded of my mother, and his *mésalliance* with her—if such a term can be used to a woman who had sacrificed herself to one above her in rank. At all events, I was the result of that connection, and I presumed that he was ashamed of it, and consequently kept me at a distance, and checked his feelings towards me. Perhaps he thought that my mother might be induced to disclose to me that which I had under his own hand-writing, and wore next my heart; or he might consider I was no longer a boy, but a tall young man, and one who might be induced to claim his protection. Such were my reflections, and my resolutions were taken accordingly—I wanted no Bob Cross to counsel me now.

When the captain left the ship, I made no request, as did the other midshipmen, for leave to see my friends; nor even when he returned on board, which he did several times after the ship had gone into harbour, and was stripping, preparatory to being docked. One thing, however, gave me great satisfaction, which was, that when the despatch which we brought home was published, I found my name honourably mentioned in conjunction with other officers, and but three midshipmen were named.

When the Calliope went into dock the report of the dockyard was very unfavourable. She required a thorough repair which would take some months. She was therefore ordered to be paid off. In the mean time the captain had gone to London. During his sojourn at Portsmouth I had never spoken to him, except on duty, and he had left me without a word of explanation as to his intentions towards me. As soon, however, as the order came down for paying off the ship, I received a letter from him, very cold and stiff, stating that I might, if I pleased, join any other ship, and he would recommend me to the captain; or I might remain on the books of the guard-ship, and wait until he commissioned another vessel, when he would be happy to take me with him.

My reply was immediate. I thanked him for his kindness, and hoped I might remain on board the guard-ship until he took the command of another vessel, as I did not wish to sail with any other captain. I had been brought forward by him in the service, and preferred waiting for months rather than lose his kind protection.

The only reply to my letter was an order from the Admiralty, for me to be discharged into the guard-ship when the Calliope was paid off.

I hardly need say that I had written and received letters from my mother, who was delighted at my name being mentioned in the despatches; but I will defer family news till the proper opportunity, as I must first tell all that occurred in the Calliope before she was paid off.

The reader will recollect that the son of the Dutch captain, whose name was Vangilt, had been permitted to come home in the ship, instead of being sent to prison. He and I were very intimate and when I discovered that he was the cousin of Minnie Vanderwelt, I became more partial to him. He was very melancholy during the passage home; how, indeed, could he be otherwise, with the prospect of being a prisoner during the remainder of the war? and he often expressed his feelings on the subject.

"Could you not escape?" said I, one evening.

"I fear not," replied he. "If once out of prison, I have no doubt but that I could get a conveyance over the Channel by means of the smugglers; indeed, I have connections in England who would assist me."

When Captain Delmar went away to town, he had quite forgotten the poor fellow, and Mr Weymss, who was the commanding officer, did not make any special report of him as he thought he might defer it till the last moment, as every day out of prison would be so much gained by young Vangilt, who was a general favourite.

In this instance, my regard for the young man made me quite forget my duty as an officer, and the Articles of War. I knew that I was about to do wrong; but I considered that, with so many thousand prisoners which we had in England, one more or less could be of no consequence, and I set to work to see if I could not effect his escape.

After much cogitation, I found I could do nothing without Bob Cross and I consulted with him. Bob shook his head, and said it was, he believed, hanging matter; but, after all, it was a pity that such a nice lad should be peeping between iron bars. "Besides," continued he, "he lost his father in the action, and he ought not to lose his liberty also. Well, Mr Keene, show me how I can help you."

"Why, Bob there's a very pretty little girl, who very often comes alongside with the old woman, and you go down into the boat and talk with her."

"Yes, sir," replied Bob, "that's the little girl I told you of, that used to repeat her fables on my knee. The fact is, I hope to splice her some of these days. It's her mother who is with her, and she will not let her come on board to mix with the other women, because she is good and modest; too good for me, I'm afraid, in one sense of the word."

"How do you mean Bob?"

"Why, sir, when I first knew her, she and her mother were living upon what they could earn, for the father was killed in action many years ago, and I used to help them as far as I could; but now I find that, although they are not changed, things are, most confoundedly. Her uncle lost his wife; he is considered a rich man, and being stone blind, and having no one to take care of him after his wife's death, he sent for this girl and her mother to keep his house and he is very fond of the girl, and declares that he will leave her all his money, and that she shall marry well. Now, sir, if she was to marry me, a petty officer only, it would not be considered that she married well; so you see, sir, there's a hitch."

"Who and what was he?"

"He was a smuggler, sir, and a very successful one; he has six or seven houses, all his own property besides the one he lives in himself. He lives about a quarter of a mile out of Gosport. I know all about him, although I have never seen him. Soon after he left off smuggling, he lost his eyesight, and, somehow or another, he considered it was a judgment upon him—at least his wife, who had joined the Ranters, persuaded him so—and so he took a religious turn, and now he does nothing but pray, and call himself a poor blind sinner."

"Well, Bob, but I do not see why you should give up the girl."

"No, sir; nor will she or her mother give me up. I could marry her to-morrow without his consent, but I do not like to do her that injury."

"He is stone-blind, you say?"

"Yes, sir."

"We'll talk your affair over another time. What I want at present is, to help this poor young Vangilt to escape. He says, that if once clear, the smugglers would put him on the other side of the water. Now, it appears to me that it would be very easy for him to get out of the ship unperceived, if he were dressed in woman's clothes, so many women are going and coming all day long."

"Very true, sir, especially on pay-day, when nobody keeps any look-out at all. I see now, you want some of Mary's clothes for him; they would fit very well."

"Exactly; and I think that, as her uncle had been a smuggler, we might go and consult him as to his escape over the water. Vangilt will pay 100 pounds with pleasure—he told me so. That will be an introduction for you as well as for me to the old fellow."

"I think we had better let the old fellow suppose it's a woman—don't you, sir? But what shall we call ourselves?"

"Why, I will be a sort of agent for ships, an you shall be a captain."

"A captain! Mr Keene."

"Yes; a captain, who has had a ship, and expects another. Why, you were a captain of the fore-top before you were rated coxswain."

"Well, sir, I must consult Mary and her mother, and then I'll let you know: they will come this afternoon. Perhaps in helping Mr Vangilt, I may help myself."

That night Bob Cross told me that Mary and her mother were quite willing to assist, and that they thought it would be a very good introduction to old Waghorn: that we must expect some religious scruples at first, but we must persevere, and they had no doubt that the old man would contrive to get the young man over to Cherbourg, or some other place on the other side; that we had better call on him in the evening, and they would be out of the way.

As soon as the work was over for the day, Bob Cross and I obtained leave, and set off for Mr Waghorn's house. We were met by Mary and her mother, who pointed it out to us, and then continued their walk. We went to the door, and found the old man smoking his pipe.

"Who's there?" cried he, as we lifted the latch of the gate.

"Friends, sir," replied Cross; "two persons who come to talk on business."

"Business! I've no business—I've done with business long ago: I think of nothing but my perishing soul—poor blind worm that I am."

He was a very fine-looking old man, although weather-beaten, and his silver locks hung down on his collar; his beard was not shaved, but clipped with scissors: his want of sight gave him a mournful look.

"Nevertheless, sir, I must introduce myself and my friend, the captain," replied I, "for we want your assistance."

"My assistance! poor blind beetle—how can I assist you?"

"The fact is, sir, that a young woman is very anxious to return to her friends, on the other side of the water; and knowing that you have acquaintance with those who run to and fro, we thought you might help the poor young woman to a passage."

"That's to say, you've heard that I was a smuggler. People do say so; but, gentlemen, I now pay customs and excise—my tea has paid duty, and so has my tobacco; so does everything—the king has his own. The Bible says, 'Render under Caesar the things which are Caesar's.' Gentlemen, I stand by the Bible. I am a poor, sinful old wretch—God forgive me."

"We ask nothing against the Bible, Mr Waghorn; it's our duty to assist those who are in distress; it's only a poor young woman."

"A poor young woman. If she's poor, people don't do such work for nothing; besides, it's wrong, gentlemen—I've given up all that,—I've a precious soul to look after, and I can't divert my attention from it. I wish you good-bye, gentlemen."

At this moment Mary and her mother returned, and we rose up. "Mrs James, is that you and Mary? Here's a captain and his friend come to me; but it's a fool's errand, and so I've told them."

I then stated to Mrs James what we had come for, and begged that she would persuade Mr Waghorn.

"Well, Mr Waghorn, why won't you?—it's a good action, and will have its reward in heaven."

"Yes; but she's a poor young woman, and can't pay her passage, so it's no use."

"On the contrary," replied I, "the captain here will become security, that 100 pounds shall be paid down as soon as she arrives in any part of France or Holland."

"Will he? But who's the captain?"

"I haven't a ship just now, but I expect one soon," replied Bob; "the money shall be paid at once, if you will only receive the young woman until she can be sent off."

"Well let me see—there's James Martin; no he won't do. There's Will Simpson; yes, that's the man. Well, it's a good act; and, captain, when will you bring the money?"

Now the ship was to be paid off on Wednesday and as we had each three years' pay due, there was no difficulty about that; so I replied, "On Wednesday, the captain will give the money to this lady, or whoever comes with us to receive the young woman; will you not, Captain Cross?"

"Oh! certainly; the money is ready at an hour's notice," replied Bob. "I'm sure that she'll pay me back, if she can; and if she can't, it's of no consequence."

"Well, well, it's a bargain," replied the old man. "I'm a poor blind beetle, a sinful old soul; I've nothing to do but to make my peace with Heaven. It's charity—'Charity covereth a multitude of sins,' saith St. Paul. Recollect 100 pounds—that's the bargain. I'll send Mrs James to you; you must not call again till she's on the other side of the water."

"Many thanks, sir," replied Bob. "I won't call till I hear she is safe, and then I'll bring you some tobacco to smoke, such as you don't often pick up nowadays."

"Happy to see you, Captain Cross, and your friend there," replied the old man.

We then took our leave. Mrs James, after we were gone, praised the appearance of Captain Cross, as such a nice-looking man, and old Waghorn evidently thought well of him by the answer he made. Mary, however, pretended to prefer me.

As soon as I returned on board, I told young Vangilt what I had been about. He wrung my hand, and the tears started in his eyes. "You, as an officer, are indeed risking much for me. As to the money, you know me, I trust, too well, not to be sure of receiving it as soon as I can send it; but I never can repay your kindness."

"Perhaps you may be able to help me one of these days," I replied. "Who knows? It's fortune of war, my good fellow; but it's as well not to be seen too much together." So saying, I left him.

The next day, Mrs James came off with the necessary garments and bonnet for his escape, and they were given me by Bob Cross. The day after was pay-day; and the ship was in such a state of confusion, and there were so many people on board, that there was no difficulty whatever. Vangilt changed his clothes in the midshipmen's berth, which was empty, and Bob Cross handed him down the side into the boat, where Mrs James waited to receive him. Bob and I had both been paid, and we gave her the 100 pounds for old Waghorn. The boat shoved off; Vangilt arrived safe at Waghorn's house, where he was kept concealed for eight days, when, for the sum of 20 pounds, he was safely landed on the French coast, old Waghorn having pocketed 80 pounds by the transaction which, considering he acted out of pure charity, was a pretty good reward.

Having thus successfully managed, by being guilty of high treason, in aiding and abetting the enemy, I bade farewell to Bob Cross, leaving him to follow up his amour, while I went to Chatham to pay my respects to my mother. I had made up my mind how to act. I was no longer a child, but a man in reflection as well as appearance.

I arrived, and hastened to the house from which I had escaped so mysteriously the last time I was in it. My mother threw herself in my arms, embracing me, and then looking at me with surprise and pleasure. Three years and a half had changed me; she hardly knew me, for her association of ideas had still pictured me as the smart stripling whom she had, with so much anguish, consigned into the hands of Bob Cross. She was proud of me—my adventures, my dangers, my conduct, and my honourable mention in the Gazette, were all known to her, and she had been evidently congratulated by many upon my successful career. My grandmother, who had grown much older in appearance, seemed to be softened towards me, and I had sense enough to receive her advances with great apparent cordiality. My aunt and the captain were delighted to see me, and I found that my two cousins, of whose appearance I had been duly apprised, were very pretty children. I found that my mother had two assistants in her business and everything appeared to be on a grander scale, and more flourishing than ever.

The first two or three days were devoted to narratives, communications, explanations, and admirations, as is usually the case after so long an absence; after which we quietly settled down in the relative positions of mother and son, and she assumed, or rather would have assumed, her control over me; but this was not my wish; I had made up my mind that, although a clever woman, I must in future control her, and I took the first opportunity of a long *tête-à-tête* to let her know that such was my intention.

Speaking of Captain Delmar, I at once told her that I knew he was my father, and that I had his own handwriting to prove it. She denied it at first; but I told her that all denial was useless, that I had possession of the letter he had written to her upon my supposed death, and that it was no ghost, but I, who had frightened my grandmother.

This was my first blow, and a heavy one, to my poor mother; for what woman can bear to be humiliated by her offspring being acquainted with her indiscretion? I loved my mother, and would fain have spared her this pang, had it not been that all my future plans were based upon this one point, and it was necessary she should aid and abet me in them.

My poor mother was bowed to the earth when she found that it was in vain to deny my parentage; she covered her face with her hands in deep shame before her child, but I consoled, and caressed, and told her (what I really felt), that I was indebted to her for not being the son of a private marine; that, at all events, I had noble blood in my veins, and would prove myself worthy of my descent, whether it were acknowledged or not; but from that hour I took the command over her—from that hour it was I that dictated, and her authority as a parent was gone for ever. Let it not be imagined that I treated her harshly; on the contrary, I was more kind, and, before other people, more dutiful than ever I was before. She was my only confidant, and to her only did I explain the reasons of my actions: she was my adviser, but her advice was not that of a parent, but that of an humble, devoted, and attached friend; and during the remainder of her days this position was never altered.

As soon as my mother had acknowledged the fact there was no longer any reservation on my part. I told her what was the conduct of Captain Delmar towards me. I pointed out his checking any display of paternal feelings towards me, and also the certainty that I had that he was partial to and proud of me. I explained to her the line of conduct which I had pursued, and was determined still to pursue, towards him.

"Percival," said my mother, "I see the judiciousness of what you say and of your behaviour towards him; but allow me to ask you: What is the object you are aiming at—I mean particularly aiming at? Of course you hope to obtain advancement from his interest, and perhaps, if he becomes more attached to you, he may not forget you when he dies; but it appears to me that you have something nearer to your heart than all this—tell me, am I right?"

"You are, my dear mother; my great end is, that Captain Delmar should acknowledge me as his son."

"I fear that he will never do that, Percival; nor, indeed, do I think you would gain by it. When you are more advanced in the world, your parentage may be considered as obscure, but still, being born in wedlock, it will be more respectable than the acknowledgment you would seek from Captain Delmar. You are not aware of the affronts you may meet with by obtaining what you evidently wish; and once known as the son of Captain Delmar, you may wish that it was never promulgated."

"I was born in wedlock, mother, as you say, and as many others are, who now are peers of the realm, and in virtue of their being born in wedlock, succeed to property to which they would otherwise not be entitled. Your shame (excuse me for using the word) and my disgrace are equally covered by that wedlock, which is an answer to any accusations of illegitimacy. As to affronts, I do not fear them, or ever shall, from those who know me. I can defend and protect myself; but it is a great difference to me to let the world suppose that I am the son of Ben the marine, when I know myself to be the son of the future Lord de Versely. I wish to be acknowledged by Captain Delmar in such a way as to convince the world that such is the fact, without the world being able to throw it up in my face. That is easily done if Captain Delmar chooses to do it; and if done as it ought to be done, will lead to my benefit. At all events, it will satisfy my pride; for I feel that I am not the son of your husband, but have blood boiling in my veins which would satisfy the proudest aristocrat. I prefer the half relation to that class, such as it is, with all its penalties to being supposed to be the son of the man whom, from prudential motives alone, you took to be your husband."

"Well, Percival, I cannot blame you; and do not you, therefore, blame your mother too much, when you consider that the same feeling was the cause of her becoming your mother."

"Far from it my dear mother," replied I; "only let us now act in concert. I require your assistance. Allow me to ask you one question—Have you not realised a sufficient sum of money to enable you to retire from our business?"

"I certainly have, my dear Percival, much more than is necessary for me to live in comfort, and I may say, some little luxury; but I have thought of you, and for your sake, every year, have continued to add to my profits."

"Then, my dear mother, for my sake give up your business as soon as possible; money is not my object."

"Tell me what your reasons are for this demand."

"My dear mother, I will be candid with you. I wish you to retire from business, and leave this place for any distant part of England; I wish you to change your name, and, in one word, I wish Captain Delmar should believe that you are dead."

"An why so, Percival? I cannot see how that will benefit you; it was on my account that he took charge of you. You are not sure that he may not be severed from you, and who knows but that my supposed death may occasion him to desert you altogether?"

"You assist my cause, my dear mother, by what you say, if it is on your account that Captain Delmar is my friend; and if as you say, he might desert me when you are dead, or supposed to be so, it is evident that his motive of action must be fear. You have the secret of my birth, which he supposes to be known only to you and to him. I am convinced that if you were supposed dead, and that the secret was his own, if he thought that there was no proof whatever against him, he would then not care showing towards me that regard which he is inclined to feel as a father, and which is now checked by his pride. Captain Delmar is naturally of a kind and affectionate disposition—that I am sure of. Your memory would do more for me than your existence ever can, and as for the rest, leave that to me. At all events, if he should, as I do not believe he will, be inclined to throw me off, I have still his written acknowledgment that I am his son, to make use of in case of necessity. Now, my dear mother, you must consent to do as I wish. Give up your business as soon as possible, and retire to another part of the country. When I consider it a proper time to do so, your death shall be made known to him. I have no doubt that he will be afloat again in a few months, and when we are out of England I will bide the proper time."

"But your grandmother, Percival—must I tell her?"

"No; tell her only that you intend to retire from business and go away from Chatham; say that you will in future reside in Devonshire, and ask her to accompany you. Depend upon it she will be pleased with your intentions. As to what we arrange relative to Captain Delmar, say nothing to her—she hates his very name, and is not likely to talk about him."

"Well, Percival you will allow me till to-morrow to think about it before I give a decided answer."

"Certainly, my dear mother; I wish you so to do, as I am convinced that you will agree with me; and I infinitely prefer that you should decide on conviction, than be induced by maternal regard."

As I was well assured, my mother's decision was favourable to my wishes. She consulted with my grandmother, who approved of her intentions, and then it was made public that Mrs Keene intended to retire from business, and that the good-will was to be disposed of along with the stock. My aunt Milly and Captain Bridgeman appeared well content that my mother should take the step which she proposed. In short, all the family approved of the measure, which is not a very usual circumstance in this world. I now employed myself in assisting my mother in her affairs. In a month we found a purchaser of the stock and good-will, and when the sum paid was added to my mother's former accumulations, she found herself possessed of 12,000 pounds in the Three per Cents, the interest of which, 360 pounds, was more than sufficient for her living comfortably in Devonshire, especially as my grandmother had still remaining an income very nearly amounting to 200 pounds per annum.

In another month everything was arranged, and my mother bade farewell to her sister and all her friends, and left Chatham, after having resided there more than seventeen years.

Long before my mother had removed from Chatham I received a letter from young Vangilt, announcing his safe arrival in Amsterdam, and enclosing an order to receive the money advanced, from a house in London. His letter was very grateful, but, as I had cautioned him, not one word was in it which could implicate me, had it fallen into other hands.

I may as well here observe, that in the hurry of paying off the ship, Vangilt was never missed, and although it did occur to the commanding officer after he had gone on shore that Mr Vangilt had not been sent to prison, he thought it just as well not to raise a question which might get himself into a scrape; in short, nothing was thought or said about it by anybody.

A few days before my mother quitted Chatham I went up to London to receive the money, and then went to Portsmouth to repay the portion belonging to Bob Cross. I found that Bob had made good use of his time, and that the old smuggler now received him as a suitor to his niece.

As however, Mary was still very young—not yet seventeen—and Bob had acknowledged that he had not laid by much money as yet, the old man had insisted that Bob Cross should get another ship, and try a voyage or two more before he was spliced; and to this arrangement both the mother and Mary persuaded him to consent. I went to call upon them with Bob, and did all I could, without stating what was not true, to give the old man a favourable opinion of Cross. I even went so far as to say that if he could not procure another vessel, I was ready to put down a sum of money to assist him; and so I was; and had it been requisite, I have no doubt but that my mother would have advanced it; but Bob, a fine seaman, not yet thirty years old, was always sure of a ship—that is, a man-of-war. To save himself from impressment, Cross had dressed himself in long toggery as a captain of a merchant vessel, and was believed to be such.

Having satisfied myself that everything went on favourably in that quarter, I again returned to Chatham, that I might escort my mother and grandmother into Devonshire. We bade farewell to my aunt and Captain Bridgeman, and set off for London, where we remained a few days at an hotel, and then took the day coach down to Ilfracombe, where my mother had decided upon taking up her future residence, changing her name to Ogilvie, which had been my grandmother's maiden name.

Ilfracombe was then a beautiful retired spot, and well suited to my mother from its cheapness: with their joint incomes, my grandmother and she could command anything they wished. We soon hired a very pretty little cottage *ornée*, ready furnished, as my mother would not furnish a house until she had ascertained whether there were no drawbacks to the locality. I ought to observe, that my grandmother now appeared quite as partial to me as she had before been otherwise. I treated her with great respect.

Although it was not difficult to obtain a renewal of leave from a guard-ship, after I had remained six weeks with my mother, it was necessary that I should make my appearance at Portsmouth. It was arranged that I should take my departure for Portsmouth in three days, when, on reading the Plymouth newspaper, I learnt that the newly-launched frigate Manilla, of 44 guns, was put in commission, and that the Honourable Captain Delmar had come down and hoisted his pennant. This, of course, changed my plans. I resolved to set off for Plymouth, and wait upon Captain Delmar. I wrote to Bob Cross, enclosing an order for my chest and bedding on board of the guard-ship at Portsmouth, acquainting him with my intention, but requesting him not to act until he heard from me again.

I had a long conversation with my mother, from whom I obtained a renewal of her promise to abide and act by my instructions. I took a respectful farewell of my grandmother, who gave me 100 pounds, which I did not want, as my mother had given me a similar sum, and then set off for Plymouth.

The reader may perhaps inquire how it was that Captain Delmar—as he had promised to pay my expenses—had not made any offer of the kind, or communicated with me on the subject? But the fact was, that he knew I had three years' pay due, besides the prize-money for the Dutch frigate, which, however, I had not yet received, although it was payable. In pecuniary matters I was certainly well off, as my mother desired that I would draw for any money that I required, feeling convinced that, being aware of her circumstances, I should not distress her by any extravagancies in that she did me justice.

I was now eighteen years old, and just starting again on my career. As I grew up, my likeness to Captain Delmar became more remarkable every day. My mother could not help observing it even to me. "I almost wish that it was not so, my dear mother. I fear it will be the cause of annoyance to Captain Delmar; but it cannot be helped. At all events, it must satisfy him, allowing that he has any doubt (which I am sure he has not), that I am his own child."

"That I believe to be quite unnecessary," replied my mother with a deep sigh.

"I should think so too, my dear mother," replied I, caressing her kindly. "At all events, I will prove, whether I ever obtain it or not, that I am not unworthy of the name of Delmar: but I must wait no longer—the coach is about to start. Adieu, and may God bless you."

On my arrival at Plymouth—or Plymouth Dock, as Devonport was then called—I inquired at which hotel Captain Delmar had taken up his quarters. It was the one to which I had intended to have gone myself; but I immediately had my luggage taken to another, for I really believe that Delmar would have considered it a great liberty for any one of his officers to presume, to lie down in the same caravanserai as himself. The next morning I sent up my name and was admitted.

"Good morning, Mr Keene," said the captain. "I presume that you have come down to request to join my ship, and I therefore consent before you make the request. I trust you will always show the same zeal and deference to your officers that you did in the Calliope. You have grown very much, and are now a young man. I shall give you the rating of mate, and I trust you will not do discredit to my patronage."

"I trust not, Captain Delmar," replied I. "I have but one wish in the world, which is to please you, who have so befriended me from my boyhood. I should be very ungrateful if I did not do my duty with zeal and fidelity; I am indebted to you for everything, and I am aware I must look to you for every future prospect. I have to thank you, sir, for your great kindness in publishing my name in the public Gazette."

"You deserved it, Mr Keene, and it certainly will be of great advantage to you when you have served your time. Has your time gone on since the Calliope was paid off?"

"Yes, sir; I am still on the books of the Salvadore?"

"How much time have you served?"

"Nearly four years and a half, sir."

"Well, the rest will soon be over; and if you do your duty, my patronage shall not be wanting."

Here there was a bow on my part, and a pause, and I was backing out with another bow, when the captain said, "How is your mother, Mr Keene?"

"She has been advised to retire from business, and to settle in the country," replied I, mournfully; "her health is such, that—" Here I stopped, as I preferred deceiving him by implication, or rather allowing him to deceive himself.

"I am sorry to hear that," replied he; "but she never was strong as a young woman." Here the captain stopped, as if he had said too much.

"No, sir," replied I; "when in the service of Mrs Delmar she could not be put to anything that required fatigue."

"Very true," replied the captain. "You may go on board, Mr Keene, and desire my clerk to make out a letter, requesting your discharge from the Salvadore into the Manilla. Do you require anything?"

"No, sir, I thank you. I need not trespass on your generosity just now. Good morning, sir."

"Good morning, Mr Keene."

"I beg your pardon Captain Delmar," said I, as I held the door ajar; "but should you like Robert Cross, your former coxswain, should join you in the same capacity? I know where he is."

"Yes, Mr Keene, I should like to have him: he was a steady, good man. You will oblige me by writing to him, and requesting him to join immediately. Where is he?"

"At Portsmouth, Captain Delmar."

"Very well; tell him to come round as fast as he can. By the bye, you will have two of your old messmates—Mr Smith, the master, and Mr Dott. I hope the latter is a little more steady than he was. I was in hopes to have had your old acquaintance, Mr Culpepper, with us; but he died about six weeks back—a fit, or something of that kind."

"Thank heaven for that," thought I. Again I made my most respectful bow, and quitted the room.

I returned to my own hotel, and sitting down, I began to reflect upon the interview. I recalled all that had passed, and I made up my mind that I was right in preparing him for the report of my mother's death: his reception of me was all that I could have expected from him—it was cordial; but my blood boiled when I called to mind that he had only made a casual inquiry after my mother, as I was leaving the room; and then his checking himself because he had inadvertently said that she was not strong when she was a young woman. "Yes," thought I; "he cannot bear the remembrance of the connection; and it is only for myself, and not from any natural affection of a parent, that he cares for me; or if he does care for me as his son, it is because I have his blood in my veins; and he despises and looks down upon the mother. I am sure that he will be anything but sorry to hear that my mother is dead, and he shall be gratified. I will now write to her."

I could not help observing that there was some change in the appearance of Captain Delmar. Strange to say, he looked more youthful; and as I compared our two faces in the mirror on the mantel-piece behind him, when I stood up, he appeared more like me in appearance than ever. What was it? "Oh!" thought I, "I have it. His hair is no longer mixed with grey: he must wear a wig." This was the fact, as I afterwards ascertained; the colour of his wig was, however, much darker than my own hair.

By the same post I wrote to Bob Cross, acquainting him with what had passed, and begging him to come round by the first water conveyance, and bring my chest and bedding with him. I then walked down to the dockyard to have a look at the Manilla, which was, as I had heard, a splendid vessel; went up again to order a mate's uniform, and returned to the hotel. It was useless going to the ship at that time, as the marines and boys had only been drafted into her that morning; and there was nothing to do until she was clear of the shipwrights, who were still on board of her, and employed in every part of her. The first lieutenant had not yet come down. The master was the only officer who had joined, and he had hoisted the pennant. I was delighted to find that he was to sail with us; and we passed that evening together.

During the evening the master said, "I hear there are plenty of good men stowed away by the crimps at different places. I wish we could only find out where they are, and get hold of them. I fear, if we do not, we shall either be badly manned in haste from the Tower tender, or have to wait a long while before we sail. Now, Keene, don't you think you could manage so as to get us some men?"

"I've got one already," replied I: "Bob Cross, the captain's coxswain."

"And a real good one too," replied the master; "the best helmsman we had in the Calliope. You and he were very thick together."

"Yes," replied I: "when I came on board, a mere lad, he was very kind to me, and I am very partial to him in consequence."

That night after the master and I had parted, I thought over the question he had put to me, as to obtaining good seamen for the ship, and I made up my mind that I would wait till Cross arrived, and consult with him as to a project which I had in my head. In the mean time I went to a slop-shop by the dockyard wall, and provided myself with a common sailor's toggery, of the real cut, with a banyan covered hat, and all complete. Three days afterwards Cross joined me, having found a passage round in a cutter; and as soon as I had talked over his affairs, I proposed my plan to him, in which he heartily coincided.

That I did this to please the captain is certain: I had no other view. It was necessary, however, that I obtained the captain's permission, and I went to him and explained my ideas. The captain was too willing to let me try it, and thanked me for my zeal.

"Go on board, Mr Keene, and tell them I have given you six weeks' leave of absence, and then you can do as you propose."

I did so, for it was absolutely necessary that as few as possible should be acquainted with what I was about, as I ran a great risk. I have no hesitation in saying that I should have been made away with by the crimps, had they discovered me.

I dressed myself as a common seaman, darkened my face, and dirtied myself a little, especially on the hands, and Bob Cross and I then went at night into one of the low public houses, with which the town is filled; there we pretended to be much alarmed lest we should be pressed, and asked for a back-room to smoke and drink in. We called in the landlord, telling him we were second mates of vessels, and not secure from the impress; that we never were at Plymouth before, our ships having put in damaged, and that the crew were discharged; and asked if there was no safe place where we could be stowed until we could find another vessel ready to start.

He replied, that there was a house at Stonehouse where we could be quite safe; but that, of course, we must pay the crimps well for our board and lodging and that they would find us a ship when we wished to go; and further, that we must give him something handsome for taking us there. To this we agreed, and at midnight we set off in company with our landlord, each of us carrying our bundles, and in less than an hour arrived at a sort of farm-house detached from the road.

After a short parley we obtained entrance, and were taken into a small room where the crimp inquired of us what money we had, and then told us what his charges were. The reason of his doing this was, because if we had no money, or very little, he would have disposed of us very soon by sending us on board of some ship, and obtaining an advance of our wages from the captain as his indemnification; but if we had plenty of money, he would then keep us as long as he could that he might make his profit of us; his charges were monstrous, as may be supposed, and we had replied that we had very little money. We contrived to look as careless and indifferent as we could, agreed to everything, paid the landlord of the pothouse a guinea each for taking us to the house, and were then ushered into a large room, where we found about twenty seamen sitting at a long table, drinking, and playing cards and dominoes.

They did not appear to notice us, they were so busy either playing or looking on. Cross called for a pot of ale, and we sat down at the farther end of the table.

"What a dislike the men must have to the press," said Cross to me, "when they submit to be mured up here in prison."

"Yes, and cheated by such a scoundrel as the crimp appears to be."

"Don't talk so loud, Jack," replied Cross; for I had insisted upon his calling me Jack, "lest we should be overheard."

We then asked to go to bed, and were shown by the crimp into a room which had about fourteen beds in it.

"You may take your choice of those five," said he, pointing to five nearest the door: "I always come up and take away the candle."

As we found some of the other beds occupied, we did not resume our conversation, but went to sleep.

The next morning we found that we mustered about thirty-five, many of the more steady men having gone to bed before we arrived. After breakfast, Cross and I each entered into conversation with a man, and pumped them very cleverly. Our chief object was, to ascertain the houses of the other crimps, and, as the men knew most of them, having invariably resorted to them at the end of their voyages, we obtained the locality of five or six, all apparently public-houses, but having back premises for the concealment of seamen: all these were carefully noted down.

As we became more intimate, the seamen, who were glad to talk, from weariness of confinement, asked us many questions. We said that we had deserted from a man-of-war, and then a hundred questions were asked us as to our treatment. I allowed Bob Cross to be spokesman, and his replies were very sensible. He told them that all depended upon what sort of captains and first lieutenants were on board; that he had been pressed twice: the first time he was comfortable enough, and made 200 pounds prize-money in eight months; but in the last man-of-war he was very uncomfortable, and had therefore cut and run. Altogether, he made the service appear much more favourable than they supposed, although the crimp, who had stood by, did all he could to persuade the men to the contrary.

We remained in this house for more than a week, and then declared that we had no more money, and must find a ship. The crimp said that he had a berth for one of us as second mate of a brig, and I agreed to take it, leaving Bob Cross to get a berth for himself as soon as he could. As I raid up, there was no demand upon the owners of the vessel, and it was arranged that I should be down at a certain wharf at three o'clock in the morning, when I should find a boat waiting for me. I waited up with Bob Cross until the clock had struck two, and then the crimp let me out. He did not offer to go down with me, as he had no money to receive; and, as it was pitch-dark, there was little chance of my being picked up by a press-gang at that hour. I wished Cross good-bye, and set off for Plymouth Dock with my bundle on my stick.

Not knowing where to go at such an hour, I walked about to see if I could perceive a light in any house: I did so at last through the chinks of the shutters of a small ale-house, and tapped at the door; it was opened, I was ushered in, and the door closed immediately upon me. I found myself in the presence of several marines with their side-arms, and seamen with cutlasses. An officer started up from his seat, and collaring me said, "You're just the fellow we want. We're in luck to-night." In fact, I was in the hands of a press-gang, and I was pressed myself.

"Yes, he'll do: he'll make a capital maintop-man," said a midshipman, getting up and surveying me.

I looked at him, and perceived my old acquaintance Mr Tommy Dott, grown a great deal taller; I perceived that he did not recognise me. "But, sir," said I to the officer of the party, who was so disguised that I could not tell his rank, "suppose I belong to a man-of-war already?"

"That you do not; or if you do, you must be a deserter, my good fellow; that is evident by your stick and bundle. Now sit down and drink some beer, if you like; you are going to serve in a fine frigate—you may as well make yourself comfortable, for we shall not go on board yet, for this hour."

I determined to keep up my *incognito*, as it amused me. I sat down, and it then occurred to me that my not going on board of the vessel might lead to an explanation with the crimp, and that an alarm might be created and the men dispersed in consequence. There were still two hours to daylight, and if I could take up the press-gang, we might secure all the men in the house before the dawn of day.

As I had just made up my mind to act, there was a stamping of feet outside and a knock at the door. When it was opened, another portion of the press-gang, headed by another officer, entered. I counted heads, and found that they mustered thirty hands—quite sufficient, as they were armed, to secure all my late companions. I therefore went up to the officer, and begged to speak with him aside.

I then told him that I had just come from a crimp's house near Stonehouse, where I left in their beds thirty-five as fine men as ever walked a plank, and that, as I was pressed myself, I did not mind telling him where they were, and he could take them all.

The officer curled up his lip, as if to say, "You're a pretty scoundrel to betray your companions," but immediately resolved to act upon it. Without stating his intentions, he ordered all the men out, and putting me between two marines, so as to prevent my escaping, I was desired to lead on. I did so, and we proceeded in silence until we arrived near to the house. I then pointed out to the officer that it must be surrounded, or the men would escape, and that it must be done very carefully, as there was a large dog which would be sure to give the alarm. My advice was attended to, and when all the men were at their stations, the whole advanced slowly towards the house. The dog commenced baying, as I had foreseen, and shortly afterwards the crimp put his head out of a window, and perceived that the press-gang were below. But all attempts to force an entrance were in vain, every window below, and the doors, being secured with iron bars.

"Is there no way of getting into this den?" said the officer to me.

"Why sir, I'll try."

As Bob Cross had given another name, I knew that I risked nothing in calling out his, and I therefore requested the officer to impose silence, and when it was obtained, I cried out, "Bob Cross! Bob Cross!! Where's Bob Cross?"

After that, I went to the small door at the side of the house, which led to the homestead, and again cried out, "Bob Cross!—where's Bob Cross?"

I then told the officer that we must wait patiently, and that if it was daylight before we got in, all the better.

About ten minutes after that, as I remained at the small door, I heard the bars quietly removed; I then requested the officer to attempt to force the small door, and it yielded almost immediately to their efforts.

"Now, sir, leave a guard at the other door, that they may not open it,' and escape by it, also five or six hands to catch any who may jump out of the upper windows, and then enter with the rest of your party."

"You know what you are about, at all events," said he, giving the directions which I had pointed out, and then entering with the remainder of his party, with the exception of one marine that held me by the arm, with his bayonet drawn.

The scuffle within was very severe, and lasted for many minutes: at last, the armed force, although not so numerous, prevailed, and one by one, the men were brought out, and taken charge of by the marines, until the whole of them were discovered in their retreats, and secured.

Day now dawned, and it was time to be off. To make more secure, the pressed men were lashed two and two, with small rope, which had been provided on purpose. Bob Cross, who, of course, had not mixed in the affray, gave me a nod of recognition, and we set off as fast as the men could be persuaded to move; certainly not a very gay procession, for although the wounds were not dangerous, there was scarcely one of the party, amounting in all to upwards of sixty men, who was not bleeding. Hardly a word was exchanged. We were all put into the boats, and rowed off to the hulk appropriated to the crew of the frigate, until she was rigged, and as soon as we were on board, we were put below under the charge of sentries.

"What! you here?" said some of the pressed men.

"Yes," replied I: "they picked me up as I went to ship myself last night." The crimp, who had been brought on board with the others, then started forward. "It is he who has blown upon us; I'll swear to it."

"You may swear if you please," replied I; "that will do you no good, and me no harm."

The crimp talked with the other men, and then indignation was levelled against me. Most of them swore they would be even with me, and have my life if they could; indeed, they could hardly be prevented laying hands upon me; but Bob Cross told the sentry, and he interfered with his bayonet; notwithstanding which, fists continued to be shook in my face, and vengeance threatened every minute.

"I told you, my lads," said Bob Cross, "that I have been on board of a man-of-war before this, and you'd better mind what you're about, or you'll repent it; at all events, if one of you touches him, you'll have five dozen lashes at the gangway before to-morrow morning."

This made the poor fellows more quiet; most of them lay down, and tried to sleep off their misery.

"Why don't you make yourself known, Mr Keene?" said Cross to me, in a whisper: "I saw the master go on the quarterdeck just now."

"I think I had better not: there are more houses to examine, and if my trick was known, it would soon get wind from the women, and I should be waylaid, and perhaps murdered by the crimps. The captain will be on board by ten o'clock, I have no doubt, and then I will contrive to see him, somehow or another."

"But you could trust the master—why not see him?"

"I'll think of it—but there's no hurry."

I was afraid that Tommy Dott would have discovered me, and I kept out of his way as much as I could.

"I'll tell you what, sir—as I've not joined the ship, why not let it be supposed that I am impressed with the other men, and then I can send for Mr Dott and make myself known? The commanding officer will, of course, send for me, and I will enter, and then I shall be allowed to go about, and can speak to the captain when he comes on board."

"Well, that is not a bad idea. Talk to the sentry."

"Who's the captain of this ship, sentry?" said Bob Cross.

"Captain Delmar."

"Delmar!—why, he's my old captain. Did not I see a Mr Dott, a midshipman?"

"Yes there is a Mr Dott on board."

"Well, I wish you would just pass the word to Mr Dott, to say that one of the pressed men wishes to speak to him."

The sentry did so, and Mr Dott came down.

"How d'ye do, Mr Dott?" said Bob Cross, while I turned away.

"What Cross, is that you? Are you dressed?"

"Yes, sir, can't be helped. I'm glad I'm to sail with you, sir. What's become of Mr Keene?"

"Oh, I don't know; but if he's not hanged by this time, I believe that he's to join the ship."

"Won't I pull your ears for that?" thought I.

"What other officers have we of the Calliope, sir?"

"There's the master, Mr Smith, and the surgeon."

"Well, Mr Dott, one must always make a virtue of necessity. Tell Mr Smith that I shall enter for the ship; and I'll put my name down at once, instead of being penned up here."

"That's right, Cross; and I say, you chaps, you'd better follow a good example. Sentry, let this man go with me."

Bob Cross then went with Tommy Dott, and entered for the service. The master was very glad to see him again and said, "Why, Cross, Mr Keene said that you had promised him to join us."

"Why, sir, so I had; but it's a long story. However, it's all the same in the end: here I am, and I hope I shall get my old rating."

Soon after, Bob Cross came down and said, "Well, my lads, I'm free now, and I advise you all to do the same. Come, Jack," said he to me, "what d'ye say?"

"No, no," replied I. "I won't unless all the rest do."

Bob then took me on one side, and told me what had taken place, and asked me what he should say to the captain. I told him, and then he left us.

At ten o'clock the captain came on board. Bob Cross went up to him and said he wished to say something to him in the cabin. He followed the captain down, and then explained to him that I was among the pressed men but as a means of obtaining plenty more men, I had remained among them, and had not made myself known, for fear my trick should get wind; also that I thought the crimp should be kept on board, although he was of no use as a seaman.

"Mr Keene has behaved very prudently," replied Captain Delmar. "I understand his motives—leave the rest to me."

A few minutes after Bob had communicated to me what the captain had said, the pressed men were ordered up, and ranged along the quarter-deck. A finer set of men I never saw together: and they all appeared to be, as they afterwards proved to be prime seamen. The captain called them one by one and questioned them. He asked them to enter, but they refused. The crimp begged hard to be released. Their names were all put down on the ship's book together.

The captain, turning to me—for I had stood up the last of the row—said, "I understand the officer of the impress agreed to release you if you would tell him where your comrades were. I don't like losing a good man, but still I shall let you go in consequence of the promise being made. There, you may take a boat and go on shore."

"Thank your honour," replied I. I went to the gangway immediately; but I never shall forget the faces of the pressed men when I passed them: they looked as if I had a thousand lives, and they had stomach enough to take them all.

I went on shore immediately, and going to my hotel, washed the colour and dirt off my face, dressed myself in my mate's uniform, and went to the hotel where the captain lived. I found that he had just come on shore, and I sent up my name, and I was admitted. I then told the captain the information which we had received with regard to nine or ten more houses, and that I thought I might now go on board, and never be recognised.

"You have managed extremely well," replied Captain Delmar; "we have made a glorious haul: but I think it will be better that you do not go on board; the press-gang shall meet you every night, and obey your orders." I bowed, and walked out of the room.

The next night, and several subsequent ones, the press-gang came on shore, and, from the information I had received, we procured in the course of a fortnight more than two hundred good seamen. Some of the defences were most desperate: fort as one crimp's house after another was forced, they could not imagine how they could have been discovered; but it put them all on their guard; and on the last three occasions the merchant seamen were armed and gave us obstinate fights; however, although the wounds were occasionally severe, there was no loss of life.

Having expended all my knowledge, I had nothing more to do than go on board, which I did, and was kindly received by the master and the other officers, who had been prepossessed in my favour. Such was the successful result of my plan. The crimp we did not allow to go on shore, but discharged him into a gun-brig, the captain of which was a notorious martinet; and I have no doubt, being aware of his character and occupation, that he kept his word, when he told Captain Delmar that he would make the ship a hell to him—"and sarve him right too," said Bob Cross, when he heard of it; "the money that these rascals obtain from the seamen, Mr Keene, is quite terrible; and the poor fellows, after having earned it by two or three years' hard work, go to prison in a crimp-house to spend it, or rather to be swindled out of it. It is these fellows that raise such reports against the English navy, that frighten the poor fellows so; they hear of men being flogged until they die under the lash, and all the lies that can be invented. Not that the masters of the merchant vessels are at all backward in disparaging the service, but threaten to send a man on board a man-of-war for a punishment, if he behaves ill—that itself is enough to raise a prejudice against the service. Now, sir, I can safely swear that there is more cruelty and oppression—more ill-treatment and more hard work—on board of a merchantman, than on board any man-of-war. Why so? Because there is no control over the master of a merchant vessel, while the captain of a man-of-war is bound down by strict regulations, which he dare not disobey. We see many reports in the newspapers of the ill-treatment on of merchant vessels; but for one that is made known, ninety-nine are passed over; for a seaman has something else to do than to be kicking his heels at a magistrate's office; and when he gets clear of his vessel, with his pay in his pocket, he prefers to make merry and forget his treatment, to seeking revenge. I say again, sarve that crimp right, and I hope that he'll get a lash for every pound which he has robbed from the poor seamen."

I may as well inform the reader that, as it is mostly the case after the men have been impressed, nearly the whole of them entered the service; and when, some time afterwards, they ascertained that it was I that had tricked them, so far from feeling the ill-will towards me that they had on their first coming on board, they laughed very much at my successful plan, and were more partial to me than to any other of the officers.

Our frigate was now well manned, and nearly ready for sea. I wrote to my mother, enclosing the heads of a letter to her which she should send to Captain Delmar, and in a day or two I received an answer, with a copy of what she had sent. It was to the effect that I was now going away for the second time, and that it was possible she might never see me or Captain Delmar again; that she wished him success and happiness, and begged him, in case she should be called away, not to forget his promises to her, or what she had undergone for his sake; but she trusted entirely to him, and that he would watch over me and my interests, even more out of regard to her memory, than if she were alive to support my claims upon him.

The letter was given to Captain Delmar when he was on the quarter-deck, and he went with it down below. He came on deck shortly afterwards. I looked at him but did not perceive that he was in any way put out or moved by its reception. Claims for past services, whether upon the country or upon individuals, are seldom well received; like the payment of a tavern bill, after we have done with the enjoyments, we seem inclined to cavil at each separate item—*ainsi va le monde*.

It was reported down at Mutton Cove, that our ship, which sailed with sealed orders was to be sent to the West Indies. This the captain did not expect or wish, as he had had enough of the tropics already. When he, however, opened his orders, it was found that Mutton Cove was correct, and the captain's instructions were, to seek the admiral of the station with all possible dispatch.

We carried sail day and night, and as the Manilla proved a remarkably fast sailer, we were very soon in Carlisle Bay, Barbadoes, where we found the admiral and six sail of the line, and a few smaller vessels. As soon as the despatches were opened by the admiral, our signal, as well as that of all the smaller vessels, was made, and before the evening we had spread our canvas in every direction, being sent to recall the whole of the disposable force to rendezvous at Carlisle Bay. We knew that something was in the wind, but what, we had no idea of. Our orders were to proceed to Halifax, and we had a quick passage. We found two frigates there, and we gave them their instructions; and then, having remained only twenty-four hours, we all made sail together for Barbadoes.

On our arrival there, we round the bay crowded with vessels: twenty-eight sail of pennants and a fleet of transports, containing ten thousand troops. Three days afterwards the signal was made to weigh, and the whole fleet stood out from Carlisle Bay, it being now well known that the capture of the island of Martinique was the object of the expedition. On the third day we arrived off the island, and our troops were disembarked at two points, expecting to meet with strong opposition. Such, however, to our surprise, was not the case. It appeared that the militia of the island, being composed of slaves, and who were sent to oppose us, did not consider that slavery was worth fighting for quite as well as liberty, and therefore very quietly walked home again, leaving the governor and regular troops to decide the question as to whether the island was for the future to belong to the French or English. But the two following days there was some hard fighting, and our troops, although they advanced, had a severe loss. The French retired from the advanced posts to Fort Dessaix, and we obtained possession of the fort on Point Salamon.

The next point to be attacked was Pigeon Island, and there the navy were called into action; we had to get the carronades and mortars up a hill almost inaccessible; we did it, much to the surprise of the troops, who could hardly believe it when the battery opened fire. After a brisk cannonading of ten hours, Pigeon Island surrendered, and then the admiral stood into, and anchored the fleet in Fort Royal Bay; not, however, in time to prevent the French from setting fire to the frigates which were in the harbour. A few days after, the town of St. Pierre and the town of Fort Royal surrendered, and Fort Dessaix only held out. For more than a week we were very busy constructing batteries and landing cannon and mortars; and when all was ready, the bombardment of Fort Dessaix commenced, and five days afterwards the French capitulated, and the island was formally surrendered to the English.

I have hurried over the capture, as it has oftentimes been described in detail. All I can say is, that it was very hard work for the seamen, and that they had their full share of the fatigue; but, from the peculiar nature of the service, an affair took place which was of much importance to me. I said before that the sailors were employed in the hard duty of getting the guns, etcetera, on shore, and up to where the batteries were to be erected—in short, working like slaves in the heat of the sun, while the troops remained quiet investing the fort. There was no objection raised to this, and the seamen worked very willingly; but the staff and mounted officers of the army, who rode to and fro giving orders, were not quite as civil as they might be—that is, some of them; and a certain feeling of dissension and ill-will was created in consequence.

The junior officers of the navy, and the lieutenants who could be spared to direct the labour of the seamen on shore, received occasionally very harsh language from some of the military officers, and did not fail to give very prompt replies to those who they did not consider had any right to control them. Complaints were made to the captains of the men-of-war, and, on being investigated, the result generally was, that the captains defended their officers, and the military gentlemen obtained no redress. The active service, however, did not admit of any notice being taken of it at the time; but after the island had surrendered, these unfortunate animosities were resumed.

A few days after the capture of the island, the prisoners and troops were embarked an the fleet sailed, a sufficient garrison being left upon the island for its defence. The admiral also thought proper to leave two or three men-of-war in the harbour, and our frigate was one. For the first few days everything went on smoothly. The French inhabitants were soon on good terms with us, and balls and parties had commenced; but the seamen and soldiers, when they met at the liquor-stores, began to quarrel as to which branch of the service had done most towards the taking the island. This will always be the case with people so addicted to intoxication. Several severe wounds were received in the various skirmishes which took place, and at last the seamen were interdicted from going on shore. Indeed, as they were not armed, and the soldiers carried their bayonets, it was too unequal a contest when an affray took place; but the ill-will spread, and at last arrived to the superior officers.

The consequence was, that a challenge was given to one of the captains of the frigates by an adjutant. It was accepted; but not an hour after it was accepted, the captain was taken with a fever, and on the morning of the following day, when the duel was to have taken place, he was not able to quit his bed; and the military gentlemen, on arriving at the ground, found an excuse instead of an antagonist. Whether it was really supposed that the fever was a mere excuse to avoid the duel, or that the animosity prevailing gave rise to the report, certain it is, that there were many sneers on the part of the military men, and great indignation on the tart of the naval officers; who, if they could have so done, would have gone on shore on purpose to insult every officer they could meet who wore a red coat; but in consequence of this excitement being known all leave was prohibited.

Captain Delmar, who was the naval commanding officer, had taken up his quarters on shore; he had done all he possibly could to prevent the unpleasant feeling from continuing, and had shown great forbearance and good sense: but it so happened that, being in company with some of the military staff, observations were made in his presence, relative to the conduct of the naval captain ill with the fever, that he could not permit. He gave a flat denial to them, and the consequence was, that language was used which left no alternative but a duel.

This was the Monday night, and as it was too late then, it was agreed that the meeting should take place on the following evening at sunset. I believe this was proposed by Captain Delmar, in preference to the morning, as he knew his antagonist was a regular duellist and he wished to have the next day to put his affairs in order, previous to the meeting. I should here observe that the captain had not been on anything like intimate terms with his lieutenants. The surgeon and master were old shipmates, and with them he was sociable: whether it was that he did not choose to ask the favour of the commissioned officers, certain it is, that he sent for the master to be his second on the occasion, and on the master returning on board, he desired me to go on shore with the boat and take the captain's pistols with me, but not to allow them to be seen by any one; a message was also sent for the surgeon to go on shore to the captain.

When the surgeon and I arrived at the house where the captain resided, and were ushered up, the sitting-room was empty. I had put the case of pistols in a piece of canvas, so as to look like despatches about to be sent to England, and I uncovered them and placed them on one of the tables. A few minutes afterwards the captain came out, and I was very much surprised at his appearance; he was very flushed and heated in the face, and appeared to tremble as he walked. The surgeon also looked at him with surprise. We knew him to be incapable of fear, and yet he gave us the appearance of a person very much troubled.

"Doctor," said he, "I am glad that you are come. I feel very unwell—feel my pulse."

"Yes, sir," said the doctor, "that you certainly are; you have the same fever on you as Captain W. Singular."

"Yes, but it will be rather too singular, doctor. Poor W had obloquy enough on account of his illness; and if a second captain in the navy were to be obliged to send a similar excuse, we should be at a pretty discount with the red-coats. If you can do any thing for me, do; but it must be perfectly understood that fight to-morrow evening I will, even if I am carried to the ground."

"Certainly, Captain Delmar, if it is possible. I think that a little blood must be taken from you immediately, and probably the fever may subside."

But before his arm could be bound up, the captain became incoherent in his discourse; and after the bleeding had been performed, when he attempted to look at his papers, he was so confused that he found it impossible, and was obliged to be put to bed immediately. When the surgeon came out of his bed-room, he said to us, "He'll never get up to fight that duel, depend upon it; the fever increases—it may be that he may never rise again—I fear it is the yellow fever."

"A bad job," replied the master—"a very bad job indeed; two captains in the navy receiving challenges, and both sending excuses on account of illness. The service will be disgraced. I'll fight the soldier myself."

"That will never do," replied the surgeon; "it will not help the captain that he has sent one of his officers in his stead. Steward, make a bed up here in this room; I shall not leave the house to-night."

"It's of no use my staying here," observed the master: "nor you either, Keene: let's go on board, and we will be here early to-morrow morning. Confounded bad job this. Good-bye."

The master and I returned to the boat. I had been reflecting a good deal on the disgrace which would, at all events for a certain period, be thrown upon the service and Captain Delmar by this unfortunate circumstance, and before I had gone up the ship's side I had made up my mind. As soon as we were on board, I requested the master to allow me to speak to him in his cabin; and when we were there, after canvassing the question, and pointing out to him what discredit would ensue, and working him up into a great state of irritation, I then proposed to him what I considered to be the best course to pursue. "Every one says how like I am to Captain Delmar, Mr Smith," said I.

"If you were his own son, you could not be more so," replied the master.

"Well, sir, I am now as tall as he is: the colour of my hair is lighter, certainly; but the captain wears a wig. Now, sir, I am perfectly sure that if I were to put on the captain's uniform and wig, as the duel is to take place in the evening, they never could find out that it was not the captain; and as for a good shot, I think I can hit a button as well as the best duellist in existence."

The master bit his lips, and was silent for a short time. At last he said, "What you propose is certainly very easy; but why should you risk your life for Captain Delmar?"

"Why, did you not offer to do it just now for the honour of the service? I have that feeling, and moreover wish to serve Captain Delmar, who has been my patron. What's the life of a midshipman worth, even if I were to fall?—nothing."

"That's true enough," replied the master bluntly; and then correcting himself, he added, "that is, midshipmen in general; but I think you may be worth something by-and-by. However, Keene, I do think, on the whole, it's a very good plan; and if the Captain is not better to-morrow, we will then consider it more seriously. I have an idea that you are more likely to pin the fellow than the captain, who, although as brave a man as can be, he has not, I believe, fired twenty pistols in his life. Good night; and I hardly need say we must keep our secret."

"Never fear, sir. Good night."

I went to my hammock, quite overjoyed at the half-consent given by the master to my proposition. It would give me such a claim on Captain Delmar, if I survived; and if I fell, at all events he would cherish my memory; but as for falling, I felt sure that I should not. I had a presentiment (probably no more than the buoyant hope of youth) that I should be the victor. At all events, I went to sleep very soundly, and did not wake until I was roused up by the quartermaster on the following morning.

After breakfast the master requested a boat to be manned, and we went on shore. On our arrival at the house, we found the surgeon in great anxiety: the captain was in a state of delirium, and the fever was at the highest.

"How is he?" demanded the master.

"More likely to go out of the world himself than to send another out of it," replied the surgeon. "He cannot well be worse, and that is all that I can say. He has been raving all night, and I have been obliged to take nearly two pounds of blood from him; and, Mr Keene," continued the surgeon, "he talks a great deal of you and other persons. You may go in to him, if you please; for I have as much as possible kept the servants away—they will talk."

"Bob Cross is down below, sir," replied I: "he is the safest man to wait upon him."

"I agree with you, Keene—send for him, and he shall remain at his bedside."

The master then spoke with the surgeon, and communicated my proposition; and the surgeon replied, "Well, from what I have learned this night, there is no person who has so great a right to take his place; and perhaps it will be as well, both for the captain's sake and his own; at all events, I will go with you, and, in case of accident, do my best."

The matter was, therefore, considered as arranged, and I went into the captain's room. He was delirious, and constantly crying out about his honour and disgrace; indeed, there is no doubt but that his anxiety to meet his antagonist was one very great cause of the fever having run so high; but at times he changed the subject, and then he spoke of me and my mother. "Where is my boy—my own boy, Percival?" said he—"my pride—where is he? Arabella, you must not be angry with me—no, Arabella; consider the consequence;" and then he would burst out in such fond expressions towards me, that the tears ran down my cheeks as I planted a kiss upon his forehead; for he was insensible, and I could do so without offence.

Bob Cross, who had for some time been at his bedside, wiped the tears from his eyes, and said, "Master Keene, how this man must have suffered to have cloaked his feelings towards you in the way which he has done. However, I am glad to hear all this, and, if necessary, I will tell him of it—ay, if I get seven dozen for it the next minute."

I remained with Bob Cross at his bedside for the whole day, during which he more than twenty times acknowledged me as his son. As the evening closed in, I prepared in silence for the duty I had to perform. To the surprise of Cross, who was ignorant of what I intended, I stripped off my own clothes and put on those of the captain, and then put his wig over my own hair. I then examined myself in the glass, and was satisfied.

"Well," said Cross, looking at me, "you do look like the captain himself, and might almost go on board and read the articles of war; but, surely, Master Keene," added he, looking at the captain as he lay senseless in bed, "this is no time for foolery of this sort."

"It is no foolery, Bob," replied I, taking his hand; "I am going to represent the captain and fight a duel for him, or the service will be disgraced."

"I didn't know that the captain had a duel to fight," replied Bob, "although I heard that there had been words."

I then explained the whole to him. "You are right, Master Keene—right in everything. May God bless you, and send you good luck. I wish I might go with you."

"No, Bob, that must not be."

"Then, God bless you, and may you floor the soldier. Lord, what a state I shall be in till I know what has taken place!"

"It will soon be known, Bob; so good-bye, and I trust we shall meet again." I then went out of the bed-room.

The surgeon actually started when I made my appearance, and acknowledged that the personation was exact. Taking the arm of the surgeon and the master, we set off, the master carrying the pistols, which had been prepared; and in a quarter of an hour we arrived at the place of meeting. My disguise was so complete that we had not hesitated to walk out sooner than we had intended; and we found ourselves the first on the field of action, which I was glad of.

About dusk, which was the time agreed upon and about five minutes after our arrival, our antagonists made their appearance. There was no time to be lost, as there is little or no twilight in the West Indies; so a polite bow was exchanged, and the ground marked out at eight paces by the master and the second of my opponent. A very short parley then took place between Mr Smith and the other gentleman, who officiated for the adjutant, in which it was decided that we should turn back to back, with our pistols ready, and that on the words, "Make ready—present—fire" given in succession, we were to turn round to each other, level, and fire. This made it more difficult to hit; indeed it was almost impossible to take aim, as the words were given so quick after each other; and the great point was, to fire as soon as the word was given.

The first discharge was not lucky for me. I missed my antagonist, and received his bullet in my left shoulder; this did not, however, disable me, and I said nothing about it. The pistols were again loaded and handed to us; and on the signal being given, my adversary's pistol went off a little before the word "fire" was given, and I felt myself again hit; but I returned the fire with fatal success. The ball went through his body, and he fell. The surgeon, master, and his second, immediately went up, and raised him in a sitting position; but in a few minutes he was senseless.

In the meantime I remained where I was, having dropped my pistol on the ground. That I had an unpleasant pang at the idea of a fellow-creature having fallen by my hand in a duel, I acknowledge; but when I called to mind why I had fought the duel, and that if had saved the honour of the captain (may I not say at once my father's honour? for that was my feeling), I could not, and did not, repent the deed. But I had not time given me to analyse my feelings; a sensation of faintness rapidly crept over me. The fact was that I had been bleeding profusely; and while the surgeon and the others were still hanging over the expiring adjutant, I dropped and fell fainting on the ground. When I recovered I found myself in bed, and attended on by the surgeon, the master, and Bob Cross.

"Keep quiet, Keene," said the surgeon, "and all will be well; but keep quiet, that we may have no fever. Here, drink this, and try if you cannot go to sleep." They raised me up, and I swallowed the mixture; my head was so confused, and I was so weak, that I felt as if I hardly dared breathe, lest my breath should leave my body, and I was glad to find myself again on the pillow. I was soon in a sound seep, from which I did not arouse for many hours, and, as I afterwards was told, had had a very narrow escape, from the exhaustion arising from the excessive haemorrhage.

When I opened my eyes the next morning, I could scarcely recall my senses. I saw Bob Cross sometimes, and I heard moaning and talking. I thought the latter was my own voice, but it was Captain Delmar, whose fever still continued, and who was in an alarming state. It was not till the evening, twenty-four hours after the duel, that I could completely recall my senses; then I did, and motioned to Cross that I wanted drink. He gave me some lemonade—it was nectar; he then went out for the surgeon, who came to the bedside, and felt my pulse.

"You'll do now, my boy," said he; "get another good sleep to-night, and to-morrow morning you will have nothing to do but to get well."

"Where am I hit?" said I.

"You had a ball in your shoulder and another in your hip, but they are both extracted; the one in the hip cut through a large vein, and the haemorrhage was so great before you could be brought here, that at one time I thought you were gone. Your life hung upon a thread for hours; but we may thank God that all is right now. You have no fever, and your pulse is getting strong again."

"How's the captain, sir?"

"As bad as bad can be just now; but I have hopes of a change for the better."

"And Captain W, sir?"

"Poor fellow! he is dead; and has so decidedly proved that his fever was not a sham, the soldiers are a little ashamed of themselves—and so they ought to be; but too often good feelings come too late. Now, Keene, you have talked quite enough for to-night; take your sedative mixture, and go to sleep again; to-morrow, I have no doubt, you will be able to ask as many questions as you like."

"Only one more, sir:— is the adjutant dead?"

"I have not heard," replied the surgeon; "but we shall know to-morrow: now go to sleep, and good-night."

When the surgeon left the room, "Bob?" said I.

"Not an answer will I give to-night, Mr Keene," said Bob Cross; "to-morrow morning we'll have the rights and wrongs of the whole story. You must obey orders, sir, and go to sleep."

As I knew Bob would do as he said, I laid my head down, and was soon once more in forgetfulness. It was not daylight. When I again awoke, and found Cross snoring in the chair by the bedside; poor fellow, he had never lain down since he came on shore, when the captain was first taken ill. I felt much better, although my wounds tingled a little, and I was very anxious to know if Captain Delmar was out of danger; but that could not be ascertained till I saw the surgeon. I remained thinking over the events which had passed. I called to mind that the captain, in his delirium, had called me his own boy, his Percival and I felt more happy.

About an hour after I had awoke, the surgeon came into the room. "How is Captain Delmar, sir?" said I.

"I am glad to say that he is much better; but I must wake up poor Cross, who is tired out."

Cross, who was awake the moment that we spoke, was now on his legs.

"You must go to the captain, and keep the bed-clothes on him, Cross. He is now in a perspiration, and it must not be checked—do you understand?"

"Yes," replied Bob, walking away into the other room.

"You are all right again, Keene," said the surgeon, feeling my pulse; "we will look at your wounds by-and-by, and change the dressing."

"Tell me, sir," said I, "how have you managed? Nobody has found it out?"

"Oh, no; it is supposed that Captain Delmar is badly wounded, and that you have the yellow fever, and we must keep it up—that is the reason why Bob Cross is the only one allowed to come into the sick rooms. I have no doubt that Captain Delmar will be sensible in a few hours, and then we shall be puzzled what to say to him. Must we tell him the truth?"

"Not at present, sir, at all events: tell him that he has fought the duel, and killed his man; he will think that he did it when he was out of his senses, or else that the fever has driven it from his memory."

"Well, perhaps that will be the best way just now; it will relieve his mind, for with his return to sensibility will also revive his feelings of disgrace and dishonour; and if they are not checked, the fever may come on again."

The surgeon gave me some breakfast this morning, and then dressed my wounds, which he pronounced were doing quite well; and about twelve o'clock the master came on shore with the first lieutenant. The master came into my room after the first lieutenant went away, who had been told by the surgeon that he could not see Captain Delmar—and he, of course, did not wish to come into contact with me, who he supposed had the yellow fever. In the afternoon Captain Delmar woke up from his stupor—the fever had left him, and he had nothing to combat with but extreme debility. "Where am I?" said he, after a pause; and, recollecting himself, he continued to Cross, who was the only person in the room, and who had received his instructions from the surgeon, "How long have I lain here?"

"Ever since the duel, sir."

"The duel—how do you mean?"

"I mean ever since your honour fought the duel, and killed the soldger officer."

"Killed—duel—I can't recollect having fought the duel."

"Dare say not, your honour," replied Bob; "you were in a roaring fever at the time; but you would not stay in bed, all the surgeon could do—go you would; but when you had fought, we were obliged to carry you back again."

"And so I really have fought—I have not the least recollection—I must have been in a high fever indeed. Where's the surgeon?"

"He's in the verandah below, sir, speaking to some soldger officers who have come to inquire after your health. Here he comes."

The surgeon came in, and Captain Delmar then said to him, "Is this all true that Cross has been telling me? Have I really fought a duel and killed my adversary?"

"I regret to say, sir, that he is dead, and was buried yesterday; but, if you please, you must not talk any more at present—you must be quiet for a few hours."

"Well, doctor, so that my honour is saved, I am content to obey you—it's very odd—" Here the captain was exhausted, and was silent, and in a few minutes he was again asleep, and remained slumbering till the next morning, when he was much better. He then entered into conversation with the surgeon, making him describe the duel; and the latter did so, so as to satisfy the captain; and he also informed him that I had been taken ill with the fever, and was in the next room.

"Next room!" replied the captain: "why was he not sent on board? Are all the midshipmen who are taken ill to be brought to my house to be cured?"

I overheard this reply of the captain, and it cut me to the heart. I felt what an invincible pride had to be conquered before I could obtain my wishes.

The surgeon answered Captain Delmar,—"As only you and Mr Keene were taken with the fever, I thought it better that he should remain here, than that the ship's company should take it by his being sent on board. I trust, Captain Delmar, I have done right?"

"Yes, I see," replied the captain; "you did perfectly right—I did not think of that. I hope Mr Keene is doing well?"

"I trust that we shall get him through it, sir," replied the surgeon.

"Pray let him have anything that he requires, Mr —; let him want for nothing during his illness and convalescence. He would be a heavy loss to the service," added the captain.

"He would, indeed, sir," replied the surgeon.

"Here are the journals of St. Pierre, in which there are several accounts of the duel, most of them incorrect. Some say that you were twice wounded, others once."

"I dare say they thought so," replied the captain, "for Cross tells me that I was carried home. It's very singular that I should have fought in such a condition. Thank you, Mr —; I will read them when I have lain down a little, for I am tired again already."

The surgeon then informed the captain of the death of Captain W.

"Poor fellow!" replied Captain Delmar. "Well, I will not make any appointments until I am better." The captain then lay down again, leaving the newspapers on the coverlet.

A week now passed, during which both the captain and I became nearly convalescent: we had both been out of bed, and had remained for a few hours on the sofas in our respective rooms. The surgeon told me that it would be necessary to tell him the truth very soon, and that he thought he would do so on the following day. It did, however, happen that the discovery was not made to him by the surgeon. In the afternoon, when the latter was on board, Captain Delmar felt so strong that he resolved to put on his clothes, and go into the sitting-room. He desired Cross to give them to him, and the first articles handed to him were his trowsers, and Bob quite forgot that I had worn them.

"Why, how's this?" said the captain—"here's a hole through the waistband, and they are bloody."

Bob was so frightened, that he walked out of the room as if he had not heard what the captain had said. It appears that the captain took up his coat, and discovered another hole in the shoulder, with the same marks of blood.

"This is quite a dream," said the captain, talking to himself—"I've no wound, and yet the newspapers say that I was wounded twice. Cross! Cross!—Where is Cross?"

Bob, who had taken refuge in my room, where we overheard everything he said, whispered, "It's no use now, Mr Keene,—I must tell it all; never fear me, I know how to do it." And then he obeyed the captain's summons, leaving me in a state of great nervous anxiety.

"Cross," said the captain sternly, "I insist upon knowing the truth: I have been deceived by my officers. Did I, or did I not, fight this duel?"

"Well, sir," replied Cross, "the truth was only kept back from you till you were quite well again, and I suppose I must tell it to you now. You were too ill, and you raved about our honour, and that you were disgraced, and that—"

"Well, go on, sir."

"I will, Captain Delmar; but I hope you'll not be angry, sir. Mr Keene could not bear to see you in that way, and he said he would lay down his life for you at any time, and he begged Mr Smith, the master, to allow him to fight the duel, because he said that he was so like you in person (which, somehow or other he is, that's certain), that no one would know it was him if he put on your honour's wig and uniform: that's how it was, sir."

"Go on," said the captain.

"Well, sir, the master could not bear the sneering of the sogers on shore, and he consented that Mr Keene should take your place, which he did, sir; and I hope you will not be angry with Mr Keene, for it's your old coat, sir, and I think it may have a piece let in, that it won't be seen."

Cross then went on describing the whole affair—of course praising me—and told the captain that everybody on board, as well as on shore, thought that he was wounded and that I had been taken with the yellow fever, and that nobody knew the real truth except the master, the surgeon, and himself.

"Is Mr Keene seriously hurt?" inquired the captain, after a pause.

"No, sir; the doctor says he will do very well. He was as near gone as ever a man was: at one time his breath would not move a feather—all the blood was out of his body."

For a minute the captain made no reply; at last he said, in a quiet tone, "You may leave the room, Cross."

What were the thoughts and feelings of Captain Delmar when he was left to reflect upon the information which he had received, I cannot tell but that he was not angry I inferred by the tone in which he desired Cross to leave the room. I was absorbed in my own feelings, when the surgeon entered the room, and gave me a letter. "Here's a schooner just come in with despatches from the admiral," said the surgeon: "the second lieutenant has brought them on shore for the captain, and among the letters from England I found this one for you. I have seen Cross," continued the surgeon, nodding his head significantly as he left the room.

"The second lieutenant, with despatches, sir," reported Bob Cross to the captain in the other room—"Shall I show him in?"

"No, I am not well; desire him to send them in by you," replied the captain.

While the captain was busy with his despatches, I read my letter, which was from my mother, enclosing a copy of one from my grandmother, announcing my mother's death. Of course there were a great many dying wishes; but that was a matter of course. I felt happy that this letter to the captain arrived at such a propitious time, as I knew that the announcement of my mother's death would be a great point in my favour. That it ought not to have been, I confess; but I knew whom I had to deal with: the captain was ashamed of his intimacy, and the claims of my mother upon him, but not so much ashamed of me; and, now that she was removed, probably he might not be at all ashamed. My mother was no relation, and below him—I was his own flesh and blood, and half ennobled by so being.

The captain sent on board orders for getting under weigh. It appeared that the admiral had written to him, desiring him to sail for the coast of South America, to look after a French frigate, and that, as there was no farther occasion for so large a force at Martinique, he was to leave the next senior officer in command; but this was Captain W, who had died of the fever.

As senior in command, Captain Delmar then filled up the vacancy; the captain of a corvette was appointed to Captain W's ship; our first lieutenant to the command of the corvette; but the lieutenant's vacancy was not filled up, much to the surprise of the officers of the squadron. This was the work of the afternoon; in the evening the master was sent for, and a consultation held with him and the surgeon, which ended in the captain's consenting to go on board with his arm in a sling, as if he had been wounded, and my being put into a cot, and removed on board to the captain's cabin, as if still too weak with the fever to quit my bed. Cross was enjoined silence, and I was made acquainted by the surgeon with the result of the conference.

The next morning we were all embarked, and we hove the anchor up, and made sail to the southward. It must be observed, that I had neither seen nor had any communications with the captain, during the whole of this time. He was informed by the surgeon that I was in great distress of mind at the news of my mother's death, and that my recovery would be retarded in consequence.

Chapter Twenty One

IT was not until three or four days after the ship had sailed from Martinique that the captain spoke to me. I had during that time remained in my cot, which was hung up in the fore-cabin, and when the surgeon dressed my wounds it was only in the presence of Bob Cross. On the fourth morning after our sailing, the captain came inside of the screen, which was hung round my cot:— "Well, Mr Keene," said he in a very kind voice, "how are you?"

"Much better, sir, I thank you; and hope you will look over the great liberty I ventured to take for the honour of the service."

"Why," replied the captain, smiling, "I think you have been sufficiently punished already for your temerity; I appreciate your motive of action and feel obliged to you for your great zeal towards the service and towards me. The only objection (I may say annoyance) I have on the subject is, the mystery and secrecy compelled to be observed in consequence of your taking my place; and still more, that one of the seamen of the ship should be a party to the secret."

"I certainly did not consider the consequences as I ought to have done, sir, when I ventured to act as I did," replied I.

"Say no more about it, Mr Keene. I am very sorry to hear of your mother's death; but it was not, I believe, unexpected."

"No, sir," replied I; "and therefore the shock has not been so great."

"Well, Mr Keene, of course it is from the interest I took in your mother that I was induced to take you under my protection, and her death will make no difference in that point, so long as you conduct yourself as you have hitherto done. You have now created a strong interest for yourself by your good conduct, and I shall not lose sight of you. How many months have you yet to serve before your time is out?"

"I have served five years and seven months, as far as I can recollect."

"So I thought. Now, Mr Keene, it was because I thought of you that I did not fill up the lieutenant's vacancy which was made by the death of Captain W and the promotion of the commander and my first lieutenant. As soon as you are well, I will give you an acting order as lieutenant of this ship; and, as we are now on a sort of roving commission, I have no doubt but that you will have served your time, and found the means of passing, before we join the admiral; your promotion will, under such circumstances, be, I have no doubt, confirmed; so all you have to do now is to get well as fast as you can. Good-bye."

The captain gave me a most gracious nod, and then went outside of the screen, giving me no time for thanks. I was, indeed, overjoyed; not so much at the promotion as at the change in the captain's manner towards me: a change so palpable that it filled me with the fondest anticipations. I remained for a long while reflecting upon my future prospects. As a lieutenant of the same ship I should be more in contact with him: he could now converse and take notice of me without its being considered remarkable; nay, he could be intimate with me. I resolved to be most careful of my conduct, so as not to alarm his pride by the least familiarity, and hoped, eventually, to play my cards so as to obtain my earnest wish; but I felt that there was a great deal of ground to go over first, and that the greatest circumspection was necessary. I felt that I had still to raise myself in his opinion and in the opinion of the world to a much higher position than I was in at present, before I could expect that Captain Delmar would, virtually, acknowledge me as his son. I felt that I had to wade through blood, and stand the chance of thousands of balls and bullets in my professional career, before I could do all this; a bright vista of futurity floated before me and, in the far distance, I felt myself in the possession of my ambition, and with my eyes still fixed upon it I dropped fast asleep, revelling still in the same dreams which I had indulged in when awake.

In a fortnight I was quite recovered; my wounds had healed up, and I now walked about. Having had my uniform altered by the ship's tailor, and procured an epaulet from one of the lieutenants, I took possession of my cabin in the gun-room, and was warmly received by my new messmates; but I did not return to my duty for nearly a month, on account of a little lameness still remaining, and which the surgeon declared was often the case after the yellow fever!!

I ought to have observed, that when my mother was so indulgent as to commit suicide for my sake, she had taken every precaution, and the letter of my grandmother informed Captain Delmar that my mother had bequeathed me 12,000 pounds in the three per cents, which she had laid by from her business, and that therefore there was no longer any occasion that I should be an expense to Captain Delmar. It must not, however, be supposed, from my grandmother stating this, that Captain Delmar was at all mercenary or stingy; on the contrary, considering that, as the second son of a nobleman, he had only 1,000 pounds per annum besides his pay, he was exceedingly liberal (although not extravagant) in all money matters.

At last I was well enough to return to my duty; and glad I was to be once more walking the quarter-deck, not as before, on the lee, but on the weather side, with an epaulet on my shoulder. Strange to say, there was not a midshipman in the ship (although there were so many) who had served so long as I had, and in consequence there was not any heart-burning or jealousy at my promotion, and I continued on the best terms with my old mess-mates, although gradually lessening the intimacy which existed between us. But that was not intentional on my part; it was the effect of my promotion, and removal from the berth of a set of lads to the company of the senior and older officers. I was now a man, and had the feelings and thoughts of a man. My frolics and tricks were discarded with the midshipman's coat; and in respecting my new rank I respected myself.

Now that I walked on the same side of the deck, Captain Delmar very often entered into conversation with me; and although at first it was with caution on his part, yet, when he found that I never presumed, and was, invariably, most respectful, he became on much more intimate terms with me.

During three months we continued cruising about without falling in with or having received any intelligence of the French frigate which we were sent in quest of; at last Captain Delmar resolved to change the cruising ground, and we ran up to ten degrees of latitude further north.

As we were running up, we fell in with an American brig, and brought her to; a boat was sent for the captain, who, when he came on board, was interrogated by Captain Delmar, as to his having seen or heard of any French vessel on that coast. As the conversation took place on the quarter-deck, and I was officer of the watch, I can repeat it.

"Well," replied the American through his nose, "I reckon there is a Frenchman in these parts?"

"Have you fallen in with her?" inquired Captain Delmar.

"Well, I may say I have; for I lay alongside of her in Cartagena when I was taking in my cargo of hides. You haven't such a thing as a spar as will make me a pole top-gallant mast, captain, have you?"

"Is she large or small?"

"Well, captain, I don't care whether the spar be large or small; I've two carpenters on board, and I'll soon dub it down into shape."

"I inquired about the vessel—I did not refer to the spar," replied Captain Delmar, haughtily.

"And I referred to the spar, which is my business, and not to the vessel, which is no consarn of mine," replied the American captain. "You see, master, we have both our wants; you want information, I want a spar: I have no objection to a fair swop."

"Well," replied Captain Delmar, rather amused, "give me the information and you shall have the spar."

"That's agreed."

"Send for the carpenter, and desire him to get out a small spar, Mr —," said Captain Delmar to the first lieutenant.

"Well, captain, that looks like business, and so now I'll go on. The Frenchman is as large as you; may be," said he, looking round the deck, "he may be a bit larger, but you won't mind that, I suppose."

"Did you leave her in port when you sailed?"

"I reckon she was off two days before me."

"And how many days is it since you sailed?"

"Just four days, I calculate."

"And did you hear where she was going to?"

"Yes, I did, and I've a notion I could put my finger upon her now, if I choosed. Captain, you haven't got a coil of two-inch which you could lend me—I ain't got a topsail brace to reeve and mine are very queer just now. I reckon they've been turned end for end so often, that there's an end of them."

"You say that you know where the vessel is—where is she?"

"Captain, that's telling—can't I have the two inch?"

"We have not a whole coil of two-inch left, sir," said the master, touching his hat. "We might spare him enough for a pair of new braces."

"Well, well, I'm reasonable altogether, and if so be you haven't got it, I don't expect it. It's very odd now, but I can't just now remember the place that the French vessel was going to; it's slipped clean out of my memory."

"Perhaps the two-inch might help your memory," replied the captain. "Mr Smith, let the rope be got up and put into the boat."

"Well," said the American captain, "as you say, mister, it may help my memory. It's not the first time that I've freshened a man's memory with a bit of two-inch myself," continued he, grinning at his own joke; "but I don't see it coming."

"I have ordered it to be put in the boat," replied Captain Delmar, haughtily: "my orders are not disobeyed, nor is my word doubted."

"Not by them as knows you, I dare say, captain, but you're a stranger to me; I don't think I ask much, after all—a bit of spar and a bit of rope—just to tell you where you may go and take a fine vessel, and pocket a nation lot of dollars as prize-money. Well, there's the rope, and now I'll tell you. She was going off Berbice or Surinam, to look after the West Indiamen, who were on the coast, or expected on it, I don't know which. There you'll find her, as sure as I stand here; but I think that she is a bit bigger than this vessel—you don't mind that, I dare say."

"You may go on board now, sir," said Captain Delmar.

"Well, thank ye, captain, and good luck to you."

The American captain went down the side; and as soon as our boat returned, and was hoisted up, we made all sail for the coast of Demerara.

"She must be a fine vessel," said Captain Delmar to me, as he was walking the deck,—"a very fine vessel, if she is bigger than we are."

"You will excuse me, Captain Delmar, if I venture to observe that there was an expression in the eye of the American, when he said a bit bigger, which made me take it into my head, that in saying so, he was only deceiving us. The Americans are not very partial to us, and would be glad of any revenge."

"That may be, Mr Keene; but I do not see that he can be deceiving us, by making her out to be larger, as it is putting us on our guard. Had he said that she was smaller, it would then have been deceiving us."

"I did not take it in that sense, sir," replied I. "He said a bit bigger; now, I can't help thinking that a bit bigger was meant to deceive us, and that it will prove that the Frenchman is a line-of-battle ship, and not a frigate: he wished to leave us under the impression that it was a larger frigate than our own and no more."

"It may be so," replied Captain Delmar, thoughtfully; "at all events, Mr Keene, I am obliged to you for the suggestion."

The captain took two or three more turns fore and aft in silence and then quitted the deck.

Chapter Twenty Two

In three days we had gained the latitude of Berbice, and on the fourth morning the men at the mast-head were keeping a sharp look-out for any strange sail. Our head was then towards the land, which, being very low, could not be seen; the breeze was light, the royals had been set, and the men piped down to breakfast, when the mast-head-man reported three sail right ahead. We soon made them out to be merchant vessels, and as they separated, and made all sail from us, we made sure that they had been captured; and so it proved when we took possession of them, which we did not do of the third before night-fall.

Upon interrogating the prisoners and the few English who had been left on board the prizes, we found out that I had been right in my conjecture; they had been captured by a French line-of-battle ship, which they had left in shore the evening before. The English reported her a very fast sailer, and believed her to be an eighty gun ship—indeed the French prisoners acknowledged that such was the case.

This was very important intelligence, and Captain Delmar walked up and down deck in deep thought: the fact was, he was puzzled how to act. To attempt to cope with such a force, unless under peculiarly favourable circumstances, would be madness: to leave the coast and our mercantile navy exposed to her depredations, was at the same time very repulsive to his feelings and sense of duty. The prizes had been manned, the prisoners were on board, the boats hoisted up, and the Manilla still remained hove to. The fact was, the captain did not know which way to put the ship's head; and he walked up and down in deep thought.

"Mr Keene, is it your watch?"

"No, sir."

"Oblige me by telling the master to work up the reckoning; I wish to know exactly where we are."

"It is done already, sir," replied I, "and pricked off on the chart—I have just left the gun-room."

"Then, Mr Keene, bring the chart into my cabin." I followed into the cabin with the chart, which I laid down on the table, and pointed out the position of the ship.

"You were right in your supposition, Mr Keene," said the captain; "and really this vessel turning out to be a line-of-battle ship has put me in a very awkward predicament—I really am puzzled. Fighting is of no use, and yet run away I will not, if I can possibly help it."

Now, I had been studying the chart, and had made up my own mind how I should have acted under the circumstances, had I been in Captain Delmar's position. The great point was, to give him my ideas without appearing to offer advice; I therefore replied, "We have one advantage, at all events sir; we have been cruising so long that we are flying light—I don't think we draw sixteen feet water."

"Yes, that may give us the heels of her in light winds, certainly," replied the captain.

"I think she cannot draw less than twenty-six or twenty-seven feet of water, sir," continued I, to put him on the right scent, "which, on this coast, will be a great advantage. I think, sir, when I was down below, I measured from soundings to soundings, and the water is so shallow, and deepens so gradually, that there is a distance of four miles between seventeen feet and twenty-eight feet water."

I took up the compass so as to take in the two soundings laid down in the chart, and then measuring the distance, showed that my assertion was true. The captain said nothing for a little while. At last I perceived a smile on his lips. "Tell the officer of the watch to lower down the cutter, Mr Keene. Go on board of the prizes, and tell them, in addition to their present orders, to follow us, that in case of an enemy, they are to run as close in shore as the water will allow them, and drop their anchors."

"Aye, aye, sir," replied I, leaving the cabin.

This order satisfied me that the captain perceived what I would suggest, which was, that if we once got in shore and in shallow water we might laugh at the line-of-battle ship, which, in all probability would not be able to get near enough to reach us with her guns; or, if she attempted it, she would run on shore, and then we should have the best of it.

As soon as I had given the orders to the prize-masters and returned on board, the boat was hoisted up, and all sail made for the land. At twelve o'clock we sounded, and found ourselves in nine-fathom water, by which we calculated we were about thirty miles from the land. I hardly need say that a most careful lookout was kept up, that we might not fall in with our formidable adversary.

At one o'clock the moon rose, and I, having the middle watch, surveyed the horizon on every side, but without discovering the enemy; but at half-past three the day dawned, and before my watch was over it was broad daylight; and then, just as I was going down, having been relieved by the second lieutenant, a strange sail was reported about eight miles to leeward, two points before the beam.

The second lieutenant hastened down to the cabin, to report to the captain, and I went up to the mast-head to make her out, and I soon discovered that she was a line-of-battle ship: I immediately descended, and reported to the captain, who had come on deck. As we could distinguish the masts and sails of the enemy very well from the deck, the glasses were fixed upon her at the gang-way, and she was seen to set her royals and flying jib in chase of us; but we felt that we were safe, as we should be in shallow water long before she could beat up to us. All we had to fear for was the merchant vessels which we had re-taken, and which were two or three miles astern of us, with all the sail that they could carry.

It was a five-knot breeze, and the water quite smooth, which was very favourable for the line-of-battle ship and ourselves, but not for the merchant vessels, which, with their cargoes, required more wind to propel them through the water. The state of affairs, when the hands were piped to breakfast, was as follows:—

The French line-of-battle ship had stood in for the land, under all sail, until half-past-seven, being then, as she was when we first saw her, exactly two points before the beam, when, probably being in shoal water, she had tacked, and was now a little abaft our beam, and lying pretty well up for the merchant vessel the furthest astern of us. Since she had tacked, she had risen her hull out of water, so as to show her upper tier of guns. Two of the merchant vessels were about three miles astern of us,—the other one, five, and stood a fair chance of being cut off; the more so, because when we discovered the enemy, we were standing about two points free, right for the coast; whereas, upon her hauling her wind in chase, we of course did the same, which made us approach the shallow water in a more slanting direction, and consequently not get in quite so soon. We were now in seven fathoms water, and, by our pricking off on the chart, about eleven miles from land, which was so low as to be barely visible from the mast-head. The men were allowed an hour to their breakfast, and then we beat to quarters. The captain did not, however, put out the fires, so as to prevent the ship's company's dinner being cooked, as everything was ready, and the magazines could be opened in a minute.

At ten o'clock we had drawn into six fathoms water; the Frenchman was now nearly astern of us, still on the opposite tack, and passing about three miles to leeward of the merchant vessel which lagged most behind. It was now considered certain that she would re-capture this vessel, which was at least seven miles astern of us, and not impossible that she might take one, if not both of the others, as it was evident she was a prime sailer, as fast almost as our own ship.

At a quarter-past ten, the French line-of-battle ship tacked, and stood right after us in our wake, being now hull down about twelve miles from us.

"He'll soon have the starnmost vessel, Mr Keene," said Bob Cross to me. "Mr Dott has charge of her; he is always in some scrape or other."

"Yes," replied I; "but he gets out of them, and I dare say he will out of this."

"Helm up there, quarter-master—flatten in forward."

"The wind's heading us, sir," said the master; "she's full again now. Thus, boy, and nothing off."

"She has broken off two points, sir."

"All the better," replied the captain; "it's a squeak for Mr Dott."

In a few minutes we perceived that the other vessel had met the change in the wind and had broken off as well as ourselves. The Frenchman did not now lay up for the merchant vessel as she did before, and the latter had some chance of escape. It was very exciting: for as the time drew nearer to noon, the wind became more light and more variable, and at one time all the vessels broke off another point; shortly afterwards, the wind flew back again to the point which it at first blew from, and the enemy lay once more right up for the merchant vessels. The French line-of-battle ship was still about four miles astern of the merchant vessel nearest to her.

"I think we shall have a calm soon," observed Captain Delmar. "Square the mainyard; we may as well be nearer to her, as not, now; for if it falls calm she will recapture them with her boats, and we shall be too far to give any assistance. Get the yard tackles up: all ready, Mr —?"

"Aye, aye, sir," replied the first lieutenant.

"Pipe the boat's crew away, and let them get their guns and ammunition on the gangway."

It was about a quarter to eleven when we hove to, the breeze still continuing variable and light, and the French line-of-battle ship did not come up so fast as before. We sounded after we hove to, and found that we were in five and a half fathoms water.

At twelve o'clock, in consequence of our having hove to, the relative positions of the vessels were as follows:— The two merchant vessels which had been about four miles astern of us were now alongside of us; the third was about three miles astern of us; and the Frenchman was about the same distance astern of her; so that our frigate was about six miles from the French line-of-battle ship.

Captain Delmar had given orders to pipe to dinner at seven bells (half-past eleven o'clock); that in case the boats were required, the men might have dined before the were sent away. A few minutes after twelve o'clock it fell a dead calm; the hands were turned up, the boats hoisted out and lowered down, the guns and ammunition put in them, and everything in readiness; we keeping our glasses upon the enemy, and watching her manoeuvring, which, at the distance we were, was now easily to be distinguished. Captain Delmar was aware that he ran some risk in sending his boats away, for it might so happen that a breeze might spring up from the seaward, and the enemy have the advantage of it long before us; if so, it might bring her up to the vessel astern, and the boats be captured: indeed it might bring her up nearly alongside of us before we caught the wind. It was necessary therefore, to be very cautious, and not send the boats away till the last moment—that is, before we saw the French ship hoisting out or lowering down her own. That the Frenchman knew that our boats had been hoisted out, could not be doubted, as their eyes were quite as sharp as ours. They, however, tried to double us; for all of a sudden, as I had my glass upon the French ship, I perceived three boats coming round her quarter, and pulling right for the merchant vessel: the fact was, that she had lowered down her stern and quarter boats to leeward, which we could not perceive. I reported this immediately to the captain, who ordered the boats' crews to be piped away.

"Who is to command the boats, sir?" said the first lieutenant.

"Mr Keene," said the captain.

"Mr Keene, I wish to speak with you before you go."

Captain Delmar then walked to the capstern, and, in few words, pointed out what I have just stated as the difficulty which might occur, and the chances of capture.

"You understand me, Mr Keene?"

"Perfectly, sir," replied I.

"Well, then, I trust to your discretion, Mr Keene, and hope I shall not be disappointed. Now you may go."

"The French ship is getting up her yard tackles," said the signal man.

"Then you have no time to lose, Mr Keene. As for the small boats, they are of no consequence."

I went down the side, and shoved off. Our men gave way cheerfully and manfully; and the three boats of the Frenchmen had but a little start of us. In half an hour we were both within less than a mile of the merchant vessel; but the French boats were the nearest of the two. The affair now became very exciting. In another ten minutes the French boats had gained the merchant vessel, and the men were clambering up her sides, while we were not more than three cables' length from them. That Tommy Dott was defending himself was to be presumed, as a good deal of firing took place; but before we could get alongside, it was evident that he and his men had been mastered, and the French were in possession of the vessel. But now our turn came. Dividing my boats, six in number, into two divisions, we boarded on both sides, and very soon had regained the vessel and mastered the French, who did not amount to more than thirty-five men, while we had more than seventy.

We found that the Frenchmen had not spared our people on board of the vessel, all of them being wounded or killed; but the fact was that Tommy Dott had fought most nobly, and resisted to the very last. He himself—poor fellow!—lay against the cap-stern, with his head cut open by a blow of a cutlass, and quite insensible. As soon as we had secured the prisoners, I turned my eyes to the line-of-battle ship, and saw that her large boats had shoved off; they were five in number, but much larger, and holding more men than we had.

A little reflection decided me that we should have a better chance of resisting them on board of the vessel than in the boats; and I determined that I would get my boats' guns up on board of the vessel, and arm her in that way. It was necessary, however, to secure our boats, that they might not cut them away from alongside; I therefore, as soon as the guns and ammunition were on board, lowered the iron chain cable down from the bows, and passed it from one boat to the other under the fixed thwarts of each boat, including those captured from the French, hauling the end of the cable on board again through the stern port. We had plenty of time to do this, and make any other preparation on board, before the French boats arrived.

It was a dead calm; the sea was like a mirror, and the advancing boats, as their oars rose and fell in the water, gave you the idea of creatures possessed of life and volition, as they rapidly forced their way through the yielding fluid. The vessel's stern was towards the line-of-battle ship, and the boats were pulling up a little on the starboard quarter. The guns which I had hoisted on board had, for want of any other means, been sufficiently secured by ropes to the slides and breechings to enable us to fire them with effect. When the boats were about a quarter of a mile from us, we opened our fire; not that we expected much from our guns, as we knew we could not obtain more than two good shots at the boats before they were alongside; still there was a chance of hitting and disabling them, and no chance was to be thrown away.

Our first shot was successful; it struck one of the pinnaces, and she swamped immediately. Our men cheered, while the other French boats pulled to it, and took up the men who were floating in the water. Before they could effect this, another gun was fired with grape and round, which apparently did some execution, as there appeared to be much confusion on board of the two boats that had gone to the assistance of their comrades. We now fully expected the boats to advance; on the contrary, they spread out on each quarter, and opened their fire upon us with their guns—a very foolish act on their part, as it gave us every advantage; for they were far superior to us in number of men, and should have boarded us at once, instead of risking the loss of more of their boats. So little did we expect this, that at one time I was debating whether I should not leave the guns in the boats alongside, instead of getting them on board, that there might be no delay in case wind sprang up, and it were necessary that we should be off; of course, as it was, I was very glad that I had decided otherwise.

The action, if it may be so termed, now continued for about half an hour without any great casualty on either side: we had five or six men wounded on board of the vessel, but none killed. I had occasionally looked round to see if there was any appearance of wind, and just about this time I perceived a black line in the offing, which promised not only wind, but wind from the very quarter which would be most disastrous to us, and I began to feel very anxious, when I heard a bugle sounded from the largest French boat. This was the signal to advance, and I was very glad, as the affair would now be soon decided.

As all our boats were secured on the starboard side of the vessel, the Frenchmen did not attempt to board on that side, as in so doing it would have been at a double disadvantage; they had therefore no alternative but to board all together on the larboard side. Two of the boats' guns had been fixed on that side—double shotted and depressed, so as to be fired at the moment one of the boats should pass beneath them; they were both fired at the leading boat, the launch, which was very large and full of men, and the shot went through her bottom. This did not prevent her coming alongside: but she filled and sank almost immediately afterwards, while the men were climbing up the sides of the vessel. The sinking of this boat prevented the men of the other boats outside of her from supporting their companions, and we had therefore only to meet the force of the launch and the two other boats which had come alongside ahead of her, and which was in number not equal to our own.

We always had an idea that the French would never do much in the way of boarding, and so it proved; they were beat down as fast as they made their appearance above the bulwarks. The French lieutenant was attempting to get over the gunwale; he was unsupported, as almost all his men had tumbled back into the sea. Instead of cutting him down, I caught him by the collar, and hauled him on board, and as soon as he was disarmed, gave him in charge of a marine. In ten minutes all was over: two of the French boats remained alongside, and the others shoved off, half manned, and dropped astern. We gave them three cheers as a parting salutation, but we had no time to lose—the wind was evidently springing up fast; already cat's paws were to be seen here and there rippling the water, and the line on the horizon was now dark and broad. I ordered our boats to be ready for starting, the guns to be got in, and the wounded men divided among them as fast as possible. The two large French boats which remained on the starboard side we cleared of the men who lay in them, and then had their bottoms beat out to sink them. The French lieutenant and two other officers I ordered into our own boats, to take on board as prisoners; the rest of the French who had been captured, with their wounded, we put into the three small French boats which had been captured in the first attack, taking away their oars, that, when I shoved off and left the vessel, they might drift about till they were picked up by the French ship.

Every thing being in readiness, I had now to decide what I should do with the merchant vessel. The wind coming up so fast from the seaward, gave her no chance of escape, and I decided that I would set her on fire. Having so done in three different parts, to ensure her destruction, I then shoved off with our boats, having first pushed off the Frenchmen in their boats without oars, and wished them good-bye; they certainly did look very foolish, and anything but pleased.

As we pulled for the frigate, I perceived that the line-of-battle ship's sails were filling, and that it was touch and go with us; but I also knew that she could not leave her boats and that it would take some time to pick them up; two were half-manned, and pulling towards her; the other three were without oars, and must be picked by the other boats; all of which would occasion delay. Notwithstanding, we pulled as hard as we could and were halfway back before the breeze was sufficiently steady to enable the line-of-battle ship to make much progress through the water. Of course we could not well see what was going on when we had pulled away in the boats, and were at a distance; all we could see was, that the French line-of-battle ship was not yet in chase, from which we presumed that she had not yet picked up her boats. In the meantime the merchant vessel burnt furiously, and the columns of smoke very often hid the enemy from our view.

Before we arrived on board the breeze had passed us and caught the sails of our frigate and the two merchant vessels, so that we were more easy on that score. Captain Delmar had been very anxious; the yards, tackles, and stays, and the tackles for hoisting up the quarter-boats, were already hanging down as we pulled alongside, and "all hands in boats" was piped before we could get up the gangway. There was no time to be lost: the French line-of-battle ship had picked up her boats, and was now in chase, with studding-sails below and abaft. The two merchant vessels had made all sail, and were running inshore ahead of us. I touched my hat to the captain, and said, "Come on board, sir—shall I see the quarter-boats hoisted up?"

"If you please, Mr Keene," replied he.

The fact was, it was very easy to tell my story after the boats were up and sail made upon the frigate, and I knew there was no time for talking.

I never witnessed such a rapidity as was shown on this occasion; in less than five minutes all the boats were on board, and all sail made. I looked at the French line-of-battle ship; she was within four miles of us, and bringing up a very steady breeze. But we were now drawing through the water, and as the re-captured vessels were three miles ahead of us, there was nothing to fear. Captain Delmar came aft to look at the Frenchman, who had already passed by the vessel which I had set on fire.

"Now, then, Mr Keene," said he, "we will know what has taken place. Of course we have seen most of it."

I narrated what the reader already knows.

"What do you suppose to have been the loss?"

"I should say three boats, and about forty men, sir. I forgot, sir, to tell you that we have a lieutenant and two officers prisoners, whom I brought on board with me."

"Desire them to be brought on deck," said the captain. "Mr Keene, you have done your work well—with great gallantry and great judgment."

I touched my hat, not a little pleased at such a compliment from. Captain Delmar.

"What's the last soundings, Mr Smith?" inquired the captain.

"And a quarter four, sir," said the master.

"This chase won't last long," observed the captain. "Take in the lower studding-sail."

The French lieutenant was then questioned; but with the exception of the name of the ship and captain, there was little to be expected from him, and he was dismissed and sent below.

This affair, however, was not without loss on our side (principally arising from Tommy Dott's stout defence). We had two men killed, and we had altogether fourteen men wounded—some of them very severely. My friend Tommy Dott came on board a miserable object, his face and hair matted with blood; but when it was washed away, he proved to be not so much hurt as was supposed: the cut was severe, but the bones were not injured. He was very soon out of his hammock again, and his chief pleasure was to put his tongue in his cheek and make faces at the French lieutenant, who at last became so annoyed, that he complained to Captain Delmar, who ordered Mr Tommy to leave off these expressions of national animosity, if he had any wish to obtain his promotion. But to return.

As the breeze freshened, and the French ship had the first of it; she rapidly gained upon us, and in an hour and a half was about three miles from us. We had now shoaled our water to three fathoms and a half, which was quite near enough to the ground, as it left but four feet between our keel and the bottom; the studding-sails were taken in, and we ranged the cable. A few minutes afterwards the French line-of-battle ship was seen to shorten sail, and haul to the wind; she had followed us into as shoal water as far as she dared to venture in, and as she rounded to, out of spite, I presume, she fired a gun. The evening was now closing in, and as there was every appearance of fine weather, we stood out till we were again in four fathoms, and then dropped our anchor.

The next morning, when the day broke, the French line-of-battle ship was in the offing about eight miles distant. It may easily be imagined that the French were very much annoyed at what had taken place; their prizes re-captured, three boats lost, and their ship's company weakened, and all by an inferior force close to them, and without any prospect of their having any revenge. But we, on the other hand, were not very pleasantly situated. It is true that we were safe, but, at the same time, we were in prison, and could not hope for escape, unless some vessel came down to our assistance;

and how long we might be compelled to remain where we were, or what the chapter of accidents might bring about, no one could foresee.

About eight o'clock the French ship again stood in, and when as close as she dare come to us, she ran up and down, trying for deeper water on one side or the other, but in vain. She was within gun-shot of us, it is true, as we had run out into four fathoms; but we could always trip our anchor when we pleased and stand further in. At last she tried a shot at us, and it fell very close. Captain Delmar did not, however, get under weigh and stand further in, although he ordered the capstern bars to be shipped, and the messenger passed. A second and a third shot were fired, and one went over us. At last the Frenchman anchored, and set to work in good earnest. He found that he was within range, and as we did not move, presumed that we were in as shallow water as we could run into.

As the wind was still to seaward, we laid head on to him, and one of his shot struck us in the forefoot; Captain Delmar then ordered the cable to be hove in and the anchor tripped, by which means we drifted in shore and increased our distance without his being aware of it, and his firing still continued, but without injury to us. The reason for Captain Delmar's doing this was evident; he wished the French ship to continue firing, as the report of her guns might be heard and bring down some vessel to our assistance. At all events, such was not our good fortune on the first day, and I began to be tired of our situation; so did Captain Delmar; for on the second day he sent a boat to the recaptured vessels, which were at anchor inshore of us, directing them to heave up as soon as it was dark, and make the best of their way to Barbadoes, keeping well in shore till they got more to the northward; this they did, and the following morning they were not in sight.

The French ship still remained at anchor, and it appeared that she had been lightening so as to get further in; for on that morning she weighed, and stood in to a mile and a half of us, and we were obliged to do the same, and run inshore out of his reach. To effect this we anchored in three and a quarter fathoms, so that we actually stirred up the mud. Towards the evening the wind fortunately shifted to off shore, and as soon as it was dark the captain ordered the anchor to be weighed, and we made all sail to the northward, trusting to our heels; the following morning we had run seventy miles, and as the French ship was not to be seen, it was to be presumed that she was not aware of our having so done.

Ten days afterwards we dropped our anchor in Carlisle Bay, Barbadoes. We found two men-of-war, both captains junior officers to our own, and I took this opportunity of passing my examination, which was a mere matter of form. Having watered and taken in provisions, we then sailed for

Jamaica, to join the admiral, who, upon Captain Delmar's representation, immediately confirmed the acting order of lieutenant given to me by him.

A few days afterwards a packet arrived from England, and letters were received by Captain Delmar, informing him of the death of his elder brother and his succeeding to the title of Lord de Versely; for his elder brother, although married, had no male issue. Upon this intelligence, Captain Delmar immediately resigned the command of the Manilla, and another Captain was appointed to her. I did not much like this, as I wished to remain with Captain Delmar, and gain his good-will. I was, however, consoled by his sending for me, previous to his sailing for England in a frigate ordered home, and saying, "Mr Keene, my duties in the House of Lords, and family affairs, require my presence in England, and I think it most probable that I now quit the service altogether; but I shall not lose sight of you. You have conducted yourself much to my satisfaction, and I will take care of your advancement in the service, if you only continue as you have begun. I shall be happy to hear from you, if you will write to me occasionally. I wish you every success. Is there anything that I can do for you?"

"I am most grateful, my lord," replied I, "for all your kindness. I had hoped to have been longer under your protection and guidance; but I am aware that your high station must now prevent it. If I might be so bold as to ask a favour, my lord?"

"Certainly, Keene," replied his lordship.

Keene! not *Mr* Keene, thought I.

"It is, sir, that I—think I should have a better chance of doing something if I were to obtain the command of the Firefly schooner; the lieutenant commanding her is about to invalid."

"I agree with you. I will speak to the admiral this very day. Is that all?"

"Yes, my lord; unless you think you could ask for Cross, your coxswain, to be appointed to her. I should like to have a man on board whom I knew, and could trust."

"I will see about it, and so good-bye."

His lordship held out his hand. I took it very respectfully; he had never done so before, and the tears ran down my cheeks as I was quitting him. His lordship observed it, and turned away. I left the cabin, quite overcome with his kindness, and so happy, that I would not have changed positions with the grand sultan himself.

Lord de Versely was faithful to his promise: the next day I received from the admiral my appointment to the Firefly, and, what was more unexpected, Bob Cross received a warrant as her boatswain. This was a very kind act of Lord de Versely, and I was as much delighted as Bob himself. I also received an invitation to dinner with the admiral on that day. On my arrival at the house, a few minutes before dinner, the admiral called me aside to the verandah, and said to me, "Mr Keene, I have not forgotten your cruise in the pirate schooner, and Lord de Versely has told me of your good behaviour in many instances since; particularly of your conduct in the boats off Berbice. In his despatches he has given you great praise, and I have added mine to back it; so that if you only keep steady, you will command a sloop of war very soon. You have now been seven months a lieutenant, for your commission will be confirmed to your first appointment; a few months more, and I hope to see you with a commander's commission in your pocket."

I replied, that I was very grateful, and only hoped that he would send me out in the schooner to where I might prove myself deserving of his patronage.

"Never fear. I'll find something for you to do, Mr Keene. By-the-bye, Lord de Versely told me last night, when we were alone, the history of the duel at Martinique. You did well, Mr Keene; I thank you in the name of our service—it won't do for the soldiers to crow over us, though they are fine fellows, it must be admitted. However, that secret had better be kept."

"Most certainly, sir," replied I.

"Now, then, there's that black fellow come up to tell us dinner is ready; so come along, or you'll be where the little boat was—a long way astern."

Chapter Twenty Three

The admiral was very kind to me, and shook hands with me when I left him. I returned on board of the Manilla, took leave of the surgeon, and master, and other officers, and then of all my mess-mates, and a boat was manned to take Bob Cross and me on board of the Firefly. After the boat shoved off and was a little distance from the frigate, the men suddenly tossed up their oars.

"What are you about, men?" said I.

"Look there, sir," said Bob Cross, pointing to the frigate.

I turned round, and perceived all the men in the rigging, who gave me three cheers from a pipe of the boatswain; a compliment which I had not dreamt of, and which moved me to tears. I rose, and took off my hat; the men in the boat returned the cheers, dropped their oars in the water, and rowed to the schooner. I stepped on board, ordered the hands aft and read my commission, and then Cross's warrant; after which I went down into the cabin, for I wished to be alone.

I was now in command of a vessel, and not more than twenty years old. I reflected what a career was before me, if I was fortunate, and never neglected an opportunity of distinguishing myself; and I vowed that I never would, and prayed to Heaven to assist my endeavours. Lord de Versely's kindness to me had struck deep into my heart, and my anxiety was, that he should be proud of me. And then I thought of the chances for and against me; he might marry and have children; that would be the worst thing that could happen to me: if he did not marry, his other brother had a large family, and the title would go to the eldest son; but that was nothing to me.

While I was summoning up all these contingencies in my mind, there was a knock at the cabin door. "Come in," said I. "Oh! is it you, Cross? I'm glad to see you. Sit down there. You see I command a vessel at last, Bob."

"Yes, sir; and you'll command a larger one before long, I hope; but as to your being in command of a vessel—there's nothing very surprising in that; what is surprising is, to find myself a warrant officer—the idea never came into my head. I must write, and tell my little girl of my good fortune; it will make her and her mother very happy."

"I must do the same, Cross. My mother will be very much pleased to hear all I have to tell her."

"I haven't heard it myself yet, Mr Keene, and that's why I came in," replied Bob. "I know you don't want advice now; but I can't help having a wish to know what took place between you and his lordship."

"No one has a better right to know than you, Cross, who have been such a sincere friend to me; so now I'll tell you."

I then entered into a detail of all that had passed between Lord de Versely and me, and also what the admiral had said to me.

"All's right, Mr Keene," replied Bob; "and let the admiral only give us something to do and I think you'll believe me when I say that the boatswain of the Firefly will back you as long as he has a pin to stand upon."

"That I'm sure of, Bob; you will ever be my right-hand man. There are two midshipmen on board, I perceive: what sort of lads may they be?"

"I haven't had time to find out; but you have a capital ship's company—that the gunner and carpenter both say."

"And a very fine vessel, Bob."

"Yes, sir, and a regular flyer, they say, if she is well managed. You have never been in a schooner, Mr Keene, but I have, and for nearly three years, and I know how to handle one as well as most people."

"So much the better, Cross, for I know nothing about it. Come, I will ring the bell; I suppose some one will answer it." A lad made his appearance.

"Were you Mr Williams's servant?"

"Yes, sir."

"Get me out a bottle of wine and some glasses—there, that will do."

"Now, Bob, let's drink success to the Firefly."

"Here's success to the Firefly, Mr Keene, and success to the captain. May you do well in her, and be soon out of her."

"Thank you, Bob: here's your health, and may we long sail together."

Bob and I finished the bottle, and then we parted.

The next day, I was very busy in examining my vessel and my ship's company. The schooner was a beautiful model, very broad in the beam, and very low in the water; she mounted one long brass thirty-two-pounder forward on a circular sweep, so that it could be trained in every direction; abaft, she had four brass nine-pound carronades. My ship's company consisted of sixty men and officers; that is, myself, two mids, boatswain, gunner, and carpenter. The mids were young lads of about sixteen years of age, a Mr Brown and a Mr Black, gawky tall boys, with their hands thrust too far though the sleeves of their jackets, and their legs pulled too far through their trowsers; in fact, they were growing lads, who had nothing but their pay to subsist upon, being both sons of warrant officers. They bore very good characters, and I resolved to patronise them, and the first thing which I did was, to present them each with a new suit of uniform and a few other necessaries, so as to make them look respectable; a most unheard-of piece of patronage, and which it is, therefore, my boast to record. The fact is, I was resolved that my schooner should look respectable; my ship's company were really a very fine body of men, most of them tall and stout, and I had received a very good character of them from the officer who had invalided. I had taken all his stores and furniture off his hands, for I had plenty of money, and to spare.

As soon as I had examined my ship's company, I made them a speech, the which, although they were bound to hear it, I shall not inflict upon the reader, and I then went down and examined every portion of the vessel, ascertained what there was in her and where everything was. Bob Cross accompanied me in this latter duty, which was not over till dinner-time.

The next morning my signal was made, and I went up to the admiral.

"Mr Keene," said the admiral, "here are despatches to take down to the governor of Curaçao. When can you be ready?"

"Now, sir," replied I; "and if you will make the signal for the Firefly to weigh anchor, there will be so much time gained."

"Very good, Keene; tell them to make the signal. You must make all the haste you can, as they are important. Here are your orders: after you have delivered your despatches, you will be allowed to cruise down in that quarter, as I understand there are some very mischievous vessels in that direction. I hope you will give me a good account of one or two of them, if you fall in with them."

"I will do my best, sir," replied I.

"Well, I sent you on purpose. I have ordered the senior officer at Curaçao to forward the return despatches by the Mosquito, that you may have a chance. I won't ask you to stay to dinner, as it is an affair that presses, so of course you will carry a press of sail. Good-bye, and I wish you success."

I took my leave of the admiral and hastened down to the town. In an hour afterwards the Firefly was driving along with a fine breeze on the quarter, and long before night the vessels in the harbour were not to be distinguished. The breeze freshened after the sun went down, and I remained on deck, carrying on to the last moment. Bob Cross once or twice ventured to say, that we had better reduce the sail; but I told Bob that the admiral was very anxious that I should make a quick passage.

"Yes, Mr Keene, but 'turning the turtle' is not making a quick passage, except to the other world, and the admiral does not wish his despatches to go there. She is a fine boat, sir, but there may be too much sail carried on a good vessel: the men say she never has been so pressed before."

"Well, you are right, Bob, and so we will take a little off her."

"Yes, sir; it's my watch coming on now, and I will carry all she can bear with safety, and I think she will go quite as fast as she does now. We shall have more wind yet, sir, depend upon it."

"Well, so long as it is fair, I don't mind how much," replied I. "Send the watch aft."

We reduced the sail, and then I went down to bed.

At daylight I awoke and went on deck. The carpenter had the watch, for the watches were entrusted to the warrant officers, who were all good seamen, and accustomed to the schooner. I found that the wind had freshened, but was steady from the same quarter, and the schooner was darting through the water at a tremendous rate.

"She sails well, Mr Hayter," said I.

"Yes, sir, that she does," replied he; "and never sailed better than she does now. I was a little alarmed for my sticks, last night, until you shortened sail."

"Admiral's order to carry a press of sail, Mr Hayter."

"Well, sir, then by Jove you obey orders; you half frightened the men, although they had been so long in the vessel."

I felt, by what the carpenter had said, that I had been rash. Neither he nor Bob Cross would have ventured so much if I had not been so; and they understood the vessel better than I did, so I resolved to be guided by them until I felt able to judge for myself. Notwithstanding that sail was afterwards carried more prudently, we had a most remarkably rapid passage; for we took the breeze with us down the whole way, not seeing a vessel during the run. I had another cause of impatience, which was, to ascertain if Mr Vanderwelt and Minnie had left the island.

On my arrival, I went first to the naval commanding officer, and then to the governor's, delivering my credentials. They complimented me on my having been so active. I accepted the governor's invitation to dinner, and then went to inquire after Mr Vanderwelt. I walked first to his house, but found it occupied by a Scotch merchant, who, however, was very polite. He stated that he was an old friend of Mr Vanderwelt, and could give me every information, as he had received letters from him very lately; and that, in those letters, Mr Vanderwelt had informed him that I had said, in my last letter to them, that I was again on the West India station, and requested him, if I came to the island, to show me every attention. "So, my dear sir," continued Mr Fraser, "I trust you will enable me to comply with my friend Mr Vanderwelt's injunctions, and consider this house as your home during your stay here."

I thanked Mr Fraser and accepted the offer. I sent for my portmanteau, and slept there that night after I had dined with the governor. At dinner I met Captain C—, who told me he had orders to send me on a cruise, and asked when I would be ready. I replied, that I should like a day or two to lift my rigging and overhaul it, as I had been very much strained in my passage down.

"No wonder," replied he; "you must have flown—indeed, your log proves it. Well, I will send you as soon as you are ready. The Naiad sloop is out, and so is the Driver brig, both in pursuit of three vessels, which have done a great deal of mischief. One is a French brig of fourteen guns, very fast and full of men. She has her consort, a large schooner, who is also a regular clipper. The other vessel is a brigantine, a very fine vessel, built at Baltimore—of course, under French colours: she cruises alone. I don't know how many guns she carries, but I suspect that both she and the brig will be too much for you; and unless you could catch the schooner away from her consort, you will not be able to do much with the Firefly."

"I will do my best, sir," replied I. "I have a very fine set of men on board, and I think, very good officers."

"Well, at all events, if you can't fight, you have a good pair of heels to run with," replied Captain C—; "but dinner's announced."

I left early, that I might have some conversation with Mr Fraser. On my return we sat down to some sangoree and cigars; and then he told me that Mr Vanderwelt had left Curaçao about nine months before, and that my last letter directed to him had been forwarded to Holland. He had often heard the history of my saving their lives on board of the pirate vessel from Mr Vanderwelt who made it a constant theme of his discourse; and, added Mr Fraser, "You do not know what a regard he has for you."

"And little Minnie, sir?" inquired I: "it is now nearly five years since I saw her."

"Little Minnie is no longer little Minnie, Mr Keene, I can assure you. She was *fifteen* when she left the island, and had grown a tall and very beautiful girl. All the young men here were mad about her and would have followed her not only to Holland, but to the end of the world, I believe, if they thought that they had the least chance—but from my intimacy with the family, I tell you candidly, that I think if you were to meet again, you would not have a bad one; for she talks incessantly of you when alone with her father: but I must not divulge family secrets."

"I fear there is little chance of my meeting again with her," replied I: "I have to carve my way up in my profession, and this war does not appear likely to be over soon. That I should like to see her and her father again, I grant; for I have made but few friendships during my life, and theirs was one of the most agreeable. Where is Mr Vanderwelt settled?"

"He is not in Holland—he is at Hamburg. Well there is no saying; accident may bring you together again, as it did on board of the pirate; and I hope it may."

Shortly afterwards we went to bed. I must say, his description of Minnie, which was even much more in detail than I have narrated to the reader, did prevent my going to sleep for a long while. Women, as the reader may have seen, never once troubled my thoughts! I had fed upon one sole and absorbing idea, that of being acknowledged by Captain Delmar; this was, and had been, the source and spring of every action, and was the only and daily object of reverie; it was my ambition, and ambition in any shape, in whatever direction it may be led, is so powerful as to swallow up every other passion of the human mind; but still I had a strong affection for Minnie—that is for little Minnie, as I saw her first, with her beautiful large eyes and Madonna countenance, clinging to her father. With the exception of my own relations, who were so much my seniors, I had had nothing to bestow my affections on—had not even made the acquaintance, I may say, of a woman, unless my casual intercourse with Bob Cross's Mary, indeed, might be so considered. A passion for the other sex was, therefore, new to me; but, although new, it was pleasing, and, perhaps, more pleasing, from being, in the present case, ideal; for I had only a description of Minnie as she was, and a recollection of what she had been. I could, therefore, between the two, fill up the image with what was, to my fancy, the ideal of perfection. I did so again and again, until the night wore away; and, tired out at last, I fell fast asleep.

The next day, after I had been on board of the schooner, and given my orders to Bob Cross, I returned to Mr Fraser, and sat down to write to Mr Vanderwelt; I also wrote to Minnie, which I had never done before. That my night reveries had an effect on me is certain, for I wrote her a long letter; whereas, had I commenced one before my arrival at Curaçao, I should have been puzzled to have made out ten lines. I told her I was sitting in the same chair, that I was sleeping in the same room, that I could not look around me without being reminded of her dear face, and the happy hours we passed together; that Mr Fraser had told me how tall she had grown, and was no longer the little Minnie that used to kiss me. In fact, I wrote quite romantically as well as affectionately, and when I read over my letter, wondered how it was that I had become so eloquent. I begged Mr Vanderwelt to write to me as soon as possible, and tell me all about their doings. I sealed my letter, and then threw myself back in my chair, and once more indulged in the reveries of the night before. I had a new feeling suddenly sprung up in my heart, which threatened to be a formidable rival to my ambition.

In two days the Firefly was ready, and I reported her as being so to Captain C—. He gave me my orders, which were to cruise for six weeks, and then to rejoin the admiral at Port Royal, unless circumstances should make me think it advisable to return to the island. The boats of the men-of-war were sent to tow me out of the harbour, and I was once more on the wide blue sea—the schooner darting along like a dolphin.

For a fortnight we cruised without seeing any vessel but the Naiad. I was very much afraid that the captain would have ordered me to keep company; but as he considered his vessel quite a match for the brig and schooner if he should fall in with them, and did not want the prize-money to be shared with the crew of the Firefly, he allowed me to go my own way, saying to me, laughingly, as I went over the side, "They will certainly take you if they meet you, and we shall have to recapture you."

"Well, I hope you will not forget your promise, sir," replied I; "I shall depend upon you."

During the fortnight that I had been out, I had taken great pains in exercising the men at their guns, the great gun particularly; and I had had an excellent sight put on it, which it had not, and very much required. During two or three days' calm, I had fired shot at a mark for three or four hours each day, and I found that the men, with this little practice, were very expert, and could hit a very small object, now that the sight was put on the gun. The two best shots, however, were the gunner and Bob Cross.

The night after we parted from the Naiad, I had run to the southward, having heard from the captain that the Driver was more to the northward than he was. There was nothing in sight on the next day, and when the evening set in, the wind being very light, and water smooth, I said to Cross,

"Suppose we furl sail at night—it is just as good as running about; we then shall see them if they come in our way, and they will not see us."

"A very good idea, Mr Keene; we must keep a good look-out, that's all."

I followed up my own suggestion; we furled the sails, and leaving two men with the officer of the watch to keep a sharp look-out, allowed the rest of the ship's company to remain in the hammocks during the whole of the night.

When day broke we had two look-out men at the mast-head, but remained with our sails furled as before, for the same reason, that we should discern a vessel by her sails long before she could discover us. The more I thought of it, the more convinced I was of the advantage to be gained by the following up of this plan. I was on the exact cruising ground I wished to be, and therefore could not do better while the weather remained so fine.

Chapter Twenty Four

Four nights and three days we remained in this way; during which my men had nothing to do but to exercise at the guns, and of that I took care they should have a good spell. On the fourth night the wind was a little fresher, but the water quite smooth. I had turned in about twelve o'clock, and had been asleep about an hour when Cross came and called me.

"Well, Cross," said I, "what is it?"

"Here they are, sir."

"What? — the privateers?"

"Yes, sir; the brig and schooner both coming down right before the wind; they are on our weather quarter, and will pass us within two miles, if not nearer."

I left my bed-place, and was dressed in a minute. I went on deck with my glass, and directed it to the vessels, which were quite plain to the naked eye.

"Put out the binnacle light, Cross," said I; "they might discover us."

The brig, which was the headmost of the two vessels, was now nearly crossing our stern. The schooner was about a mile astern of her.

"Turn the hands up, Cross; see all ready for action and making sail."

"Not yet, sir, surely!"

"No, not yet; we will let them run two or three miles dead to leeward, and then follow them till daylight, or till they see us, when, of course, they will be after us."

"It's very fortunate, sir, that we did furl the sails; for had they come down, and we under sail, they would have seen us, and we should have been to leeward of them, which would have given us a poor chance against such odds; now we shall have the weather-gage, and may choose, if our heels are as good as theirs, which I expect they are, if not better."

"I shall fight them in some shape or another, Bob, you may depend upon it."

"Of course you will, Mr Keene, or you'll disappoint us all. The ship's company have every confidence in you, I can tell you."

"Thanks to your long yarns, Bob, I presume."

"Thanks to my telling the truth, Mr Keene. The schooner is right astern of us now, so there's the weather-gage gone—thank God!"

We remained as we were till I considered the two vessels sufficiently to leeward, and the sails were then set upon the Firefly, and first running to the eastward, so as to get right in the wind's eye of them, I put the helm up, and followed them. We had continued our course in their wake for about an hour, when day dawned, and the schooner, who had discovered us, fired a gun as a signal to her concert.

"So you've found us out at last, have you?" said Bob Cross—"at all events, we keep a better look-out than you do, old fellow."

Shortly after the gun was fired, both vessels hauled to the wind on the larboard tack, and we did the same: being about four miles to windward of the schooner and five or five and a half of the brig, we could now examine our adversaries. The schooner was, apparently, about the same tonnage as the Firefly, a very beautiful vessel with her masts raking over her stern. She was painted black, and we could not ascertain, at first, how many guns she carried, as her ports were shut; but after a short time she knocked out her half ports to prepare for action, and then we discovered that she carried twelve guns, but not a long gun on a swivel like the one on board of the Firefly. I observed this to Cross, who replied, "Then, sir, all we have to do now is to try our rate of sailing with them, and if we are faster than they are we have not much to fear—unless we lose a spar, indeed; but luck's all, Mr Keene. The schooner has more sail on her than we have; shall we set exactly the same?"

"No, Cross, for I think we have fore-reached upon her already, and, if we can beat her with less sail set, it will do just as well. I think that the breeze is steady; if anything, we shall have more than less of it."

For an hour we continued running on the same tack with them, by which time we found that we had not only brought the schooner one point abaft our beam, but had weathered her at least half a mile. We therefore were fully satisfied that we had sailed better than the schooner. With the brig it was not so. Although we had brought the schooner two points abaft our beam, the brig was much in her former position, being still half a point abaft our beam, and moreover had come in much closer to the schooner, proving that we had neither weathered her, nor fore-reached upon her. As near as we could judge, our sailing with the brig was much upon a par.

Having ascertained this point more satisfactorily by allowing another hour of trial, I desired the men to get their breakfasts, while I and the officers did the same, and as soon as that was done, I ordered the Firefly to be kept away—edging down till within good range of our long brass thirty-two-pound gun—that is, about one mile and a half—when we again hauled our wind and hoisted the English colours.

The tri-colour was immediately thrown up by the two Frenchmen, and a shot was fired at us by the schooner: it fell exhausted into the water about half a cable's length from us.

"Now, Cross," said I, "see if we can't return the compliment with a little better success."

Cross, who had been training the gun, and had his eye on the sight, waited for a second or two, and fired: we saw the shot pass through the first reef of his main-sail, and dash into the water to leeward of him.

"Very good that, Cross; but hull him if you can."

The schooner now returned the fire with the whole broadside, apparently twelve pounders; but they did not throw so far as our long thirty-two-pounder, and no shot went over us, although one fell close under the stern. At the distance, therefore, that we were, we had everything in our favour and my object was to dismantle the schooner before any chance enabled the brig to assist her. We continued to fire at her, taking the greatest pains in our aim, for the next hour, during which we ascertained that we had hulled her more than once, and had very much cut up her spars and rigging. She continued to return the fire, but without effect. One or two shots hit us, but their force was so much spent by the distance they were propelled, that they did not enter the sides. At last a shot fired by the gunner did the job; it struck her foremast, which shortly afterwards went by the board. The Fireflies gave three cheers at the good fortune.

"She's done for, sir," said Cross. "Now for the brig—we must try what metal she carries."

"Stop a bit," said I, "Cross; we must give the schooner a little more before she gets away. They have lowered down the main-sail and I presume, intend getting up some head-sail, so as to pay off, and run under the lee of the brig for shelter. Put the helm up, and run down so as to keep the schooner about two points on our larboard bow. Get the gun round, and pitch it into her."

As we had supposed, the schooner got a stay up from her bowsprit and to her mainmast head, and hoisted a fore and aft sail upon it, that she might pay off, and run down to her consort for support; but as we ran three feet to her one, and now stood directly for her, we were enabled to get close to her, and put several shots into her from our long gun as we advanced. She did not attempt to round to, to give us her broadside, and our raking shot must have had great effect. When within half a mile of her we rounded to, and gave her our broadside; for had we followed her any further we should have been closer to the brig than might be agreeable. Indeed, we were nearer than we thought, for she had continued to hug the wind, and was so weatherly, that she was not more than a mile to leeward of us when we rounded to the wind again; but as she had fore-reached upon the schooner, she was distant from us about two miles. As we rounded to the brig tacked, and we immediately did the same; and we now had a fair trial of sailing with her.

"Cross, let the men go down and get what they can to eat," said I, "and get up the grog. We shall have plenty of work before the night is over, I expect."

"We must make a running fight of it, sir, I expect, for she is too heavy for us."

"I shall try her the same way as the schooner, Cross," replied I. "If I can only knock away some of her spars without losing my own, I shall then be able to do something; if, on the contrary, we lose our spars, and she gets alongside of us, why then we must fight to the last."

"I consider that schooner as our own," replied Bob; "she must haul down her colours when no longer protected by the brig."

"Yes; I was afraid that she would run away to leeward altogether; but I see she has rounded to, and is no doubt getting up a jury fore-mast."

I allowed the men to remain an hour at their dinner, and then they were summoned up. During the hour we found the rate of sailing between us and the brig so nearly balanced, that it was impossible to say which had the best of it.

"Now, my lads, we will wear round, and get a little closer to this fellow, and see what we can do with him."

The men were full of spirits and hope, and were as anxious to decide the question as I was. In ten minutes we passed the brig within a mile on opposite tacks, and had given her our long gun three times, and had received her broadside.

"He has long twelve-pounders, I think, sir," said Cross; "smart guns, at all events. There's a fore shroud and a back stay gone; but that's no great matter."

As soon as the brig was three points abaft the beam we tacked, and recommenced firing. Not a shot was thrown away by my men. I believe the brig was hulled every time; nor was her fire without effect upon us. Our rigging was much cut up; several of her shots had gone through our sails, and we had two men hurt. I was annoyed at this, as we had no surgeon on board. The assistant surgeon who had belonged to the schooner was at the hospital, and there was not one to replace him when we sailed. However, we had one of the men belonging to the hospital—a sort of dispenser—who knew very well how to manage anything that was not very serious.

The breeze had gradually died away, and we did not go more than three miles through the water; and as our sails were much torn, we did not hold so good a wind. The consequence was that the distance between us and our antagonist was, by two o'clock, decreased to half a mile, and the fight became very warm. Our broadside guns were now called into play, and assisted us very much, as we directed them chiefly at her sails and rigging, while our long thirty-two-pounder was fired at her hull, pointed below her water-line. She had the advantage in number of guns, certainly; but our large shots from the long gun were more destructive.

About three we knocked away her fore-topmast, which enabled us to shoot ahead about a quarter of a mile, and increase our distance, which was a boon to us, for we latterly had suffered very much. We had eight men wounded and one of my poor middies killed; and we had received several shots in the hull. Now that we had increased our distance, we had a better chance, as our long gun was more effective than those of the brig. At five o'clock it fell dead calm, and both vessels lay with their heads round the compass; this was also in our favour, as we could train our long gun on its circular bend in any direction we pleased; but the brig contrived, by getting sweeps out of her bow ports, to bring her broadside to bear upon us, and the action continued till night closed in.

Chapter Twenty Five

As it may be supposed, my men were completely worn out with the fatigue and excitement of the day; and Cross said, "There's no saying how this will end, Mr Keene; but, at all events, we have not the worst of it at present."

"No, Bob," replied I. "I wish the men were not so knocked up."

"Oh, as for that, sir, I'll answer for it, that if you serve out some more grog, make them eat half a biscuit at the tub before they drink it, and make them a little bit of a speech, that they'll go on for twenty-four hours more."

"If that will have the effect, I'm sure I'll try it," replied I. "Which shall they have first?"

"Oh, biscuit first, grog next, and then a speech afterwards."

"That fellow has not fired for this last five minutes; perhaps he wishes to put it off till to-morrow morning; but I'll not; so get up the grog—make it pretty strong: and I'll get something to eat myself, for I have had nothing to eat all day."

As soon as the ship's company had had their refreshment, I sent for them aft, and said, "My lads, you have behaved very well, and I am much obliged to you. We have had hard work, and I dare say you are tired enough; but I will tell you what my opinion is: I think that we have peppered that Frenchman very well; and I am convinced that you have put a good many shots into him between wind and water. Now, that he is anxious to leave off fighting till to-morrow morning, that he may stop his leaks and repair his damages, I have no doubt; indeed, he proves it by his having ceased to fire. For the very reason that he wants to leave off, I wish to go on; for he is much heavier armed than we are, and sails as well; and if we permit him to get all right and all ataunt by to-morrow morning, he may prove a very awkward customer yet. Now what I propose is this, that we should first get up fresh sails, and bend them, and then renew the action through the night. There will be no occasion for all of you to be on deck; we will fight the schooner watch and watch till daylight."

"That's my opinion, Mr Keene," said Bob Cross.

"And mine," replied the carpenter.

"And all of us, Mr Keene," replied the ship's company with one voice.

"Then, my lads, let's work hard; and when we have settled that fellow, we shall have plenty of time to sleep."

The men now set to with good-will; and the spare sails were got up, and those which were shattered by the enemy unbent and replaced. The new sails, which we had bent, we furled—it was a dead calm—and then we recommenced our fire, for we were nearer to her than when we ceased firing, and could distinguish her very well. We fired the long gun four times before she returned a shot; she then opened very briskly, but none of her shots did us any damage; our sails being furled, prevented her distinguishing us as well as we could her. After a time, we manned the small guns on our broadside, and worked them, for our large gun was so hot, that it was necessary to let it cool before we could reload it. At last one of their shots came in through the bulwarks; the splinters wounded me and the carpenter; but I was not so much hurt as to oblige me to leave the deck. I bound up my leg with my handkerchief; the carpenter, however, was taken down below.

"Are you much hurt, sir?" said Bob Cross.

"Oh, no; the flesh is lacerated a good deal, but it is not very deep."

"There's a little wind springing up, sir, from the right quarter," said Bob.

"I'm glad to hear it," replied I, "for it will soon be daylight now."

At this moment another shot struck the hammock rail and a piece of it about two feet long was sent with great force against Bob Cross's head; he was stunned, if not worse, and fell immediately. This was a severe blow to me, as well as to poor Bob. I desired two of the men who were abaft, to take him down into my cabin, and do all they could for him; and ordered the men to quit the broadside guns, and renew their fire with the long 32-pounder. In a quarter of an hour afterwards, the breeze came down very strong, and I resolved to shoot ahead, farther off from my antagonist, as I should have a better chance by using my long gun at a greater distance. The sails were set, and the schooner went fast through the water, leaving the brig, who had also the benefit of the breeze; and for a time the firing again ceased. On reflection, I determined that I would wait till daylight, which would appear in less than half an hour, before I renewed the action.

I contrived with some difficulty—for my leg was so numbed that I could scarcely feel that I had one—to go down into the cabin and see Bob Cross. He was recovering, but very wild and incoherent. As far as I could judge, his skull was not injured, although the splinter had torn off a large portion of the scalp, and he was drenched with his blood. At all events, he could be of no further assistance to me at present, nor could I be to him, so I regained the deck, and sat down abaft, for my leg had become so painful, that I could not stand but for a few minutes.

At last the day dawned, and I could distinctly make out both brig and schooner. I was about a mile and a half distant from the brig; she had, since the wind sprung up, driven a mile ahead of the schooner, who had contrived to get up a jury-mast during the night; but as she could not stir without reducing her after-sail, she had close-reefed her main-sail, so that she could make but little progress. The brig was very much cut up in her sails and rigging, and I saw at once that I had now the advantage in sailing; I therefore wore round and stood towards them; the brig did the same, and went down to the schooner that she might have her support. We immediately recommenced firing with our long gun, and as soon as we were within a mile, I hove to. The brig and schooner then both bore up and gave us their broadsides; they had just done so, when the midshipman who was on deck with me cried out, "A large sail coming down before the wind, Mr Keene."

I caught up my glass. It was a sloop of war; the cut of her sails and rigging evidently English. "It must be the Naiad," said I. "Well, I'm glad of it. We shall lose some prize-money; but at all events we require her surgeon, and that is of more consequence."

My men, who were quite tired out, were in great spirits at the appearance of a friend. The brig had set studding-sails; she had evidently seen the vessel to windward, and was now trying to escape, and the schooner was following her as well she could. I immediately kept away in pursuit, and when I fired into the schooner she hauled down her colours. I did not wait to take possession, but followed the brig, who appeared to sail as well off the wind as she did when close hauled. Once or twice she rounded to return my fire, but afterwards she continued running before the wind, having got two of her guns aft, with which she attempted to cut away my rigging. In the meantime, the strange vessel to windward had hoisted English colours, and was bringing down with her a spanking breeze: fortunately it was so, for my fore-topmast was knocked away by the fire of the brig, and I now dropped fast astern.

We had scarcely got up a new fore-topmast and set sail again, when the Naiad, who had exchanged numbers with me, passed the schooner without taking possession of her, and was very soon not a mile from us. In half an hour she was alongside and hailing me to haul my wind and take possession of the schooner, continued in chase of the brig. I obeyed my orders, and by the time I had put my men on board of the schooner, the brig had hove to and hauled down her colours to the Naiad.

We ran down to her in company with the prize, and then sent a boat requesting immediate surgical attendance. The Naiad's surgeon and his assistant were brought on board in one of the sloop-of-war's boats, and a lieutenant, to obtain from me the particulars of the action, which I gave to him. The lieutenant told me that they had heard the firing about one o'clock in the morning, and had in consequence bore up; but the brig had so many shot in her, and was making so much water, that they were almost afraid that they would not be able to get her into port. But I was now quite faint with the pain of my wound and exhaustion, and was carried below to have it dressed. All our men had been attended to, and I was glad to hear that Bob Cross was in no danger, although his wound was very severe. The surgeon's assistant was allowed to remain on board, and the captain of the Naiad sent all my men back and manned the prizes, giving me orders to keep company with him. As soon as my wound was dressed, and I was put into my bed, I felt much relieved, and soon afterwards fell fast asleep.

Chapter Twenty Six

The prizes proved to be the Diligente brig, of fourteen guns, and two hundred and ten men, and Caroline schooner, of eight guns, and one hundred and twenty men—they had done a great deal of mischief, and their capture was of importance. The captain of the Naiad's orders were to return to Curaçao, and we all made sail before sunset. Our loss had been severe: commanding officer, boatswain, carpenter, and twelve men wounded—one midshipman and two men killed.

The next morning our signal was made to pass within hail, and the captain of the Naiad inquired how I was. The surgeon's assistant replied that I and all the wounded were doing well, and there was no more communication till we arrived at Curaçao on the fourth day, by which time I was rapidly recovering.

Mr Fraser, as soon as he heard of my being hurt, immediately came on board and insisted upon my being taken on shore to his house, and I gladly consented. The next day I had a visit from Captain C, the commanding officer, and the captain of the Naiad. Captain C asked me if I was well enough to write the account of the action. I replied that I was, and that I would send it the next day. He and the captain of the Naiad both paid me many compliments for having fought a superior force for so long a time, and Captain C said that as soon as I was well enough he would send me up to Jamaica, as bearer of my own despatches to the admiral.

I requested, as a particular favour of Mr Fraser, that he would allow Bob Cross to be sent ashore to his house, and Mr Fraser immediately consented. My friend Bob was therefore brought up that evening, and was soon established in very comfortable quarters.

We had been a fortnight at the island, during which my wound was healing rapidly, and I was able to hop about with a crutch. Cross also was out of bed, and able to sit up for an hour or two on the verandah, in the cool of which I spent the best part of the day, with my wounded limb resting upon a sofa. From the veranda we had a view of the harbour, and one morning I perceived that there were two additional vessels which had anchored during the night; they proved to be the Driver and the brigantine privateer, which she had captured after a chase and running fight of forty-eight hours. I was glad of this, as I knew what pleasure it would give to the admiral.

I now again indulged in my dreams of Minnie, who had been forgotten as soon as I had left the harbour and been engaged in active service. Stretched upon a sofa, with my wounded leg, I had nothing else to do, or rather nothing else which was so agreeable to me. I wrote to her again, and also to my mother; neither did I forget that Lord de Versely had requested at parting that I should write to him. I did so in a very respectful manner, detailing what had occurred.

When we had been three weeks at Curaçao, all our wounded, as well as myself, had so far recovered, that there was no reason for the Firefly not proceeding to Jamaica. The commanding officer lent an assistant-surgeon to the schooner. I received my despatches, took a grateful leave of Mr Fraser, and the Firefly was once more skimming over the water. In three weeks we arrived at Port Royal, and I took up my despatches.

"Happy to see you, Keene," said the admiral. "Hollo! what makes you limp in that way? Have you hurt your leg?"

"Yes, sir," replied I; "I'm not quite well yet, but the despatches of Captain C will explain all."

As no vessel had sailed from Curaçao, the admiral had no idea of what had happened.

"Well, then," said he, "sit down on that sofa, Mr Keene, while I read the despatches."

I watched the admiral's countenance, and was delighted to witness the evident signs of satisfaction which he expressed as he read on.

"Excellent!" said he, as he closed them. "Keene, you have done me a great favour. The remonstrances of the merchants, the badgering I have received from the Admiralty by every packet, relative to the depredations on our commerce by these vessels, have been enough to make a saint swear. Now they are happily disposed of, and I have chiefly to thank you for it. Captain C informs me that the brig is well adapted for his Majesty's service, but that the schooner is an old vessel." The admiral then left the room. In a few minutes he returned with a paper in his hand, which he laid upon the table, and, taking up a pen, he signed it and presented it to me, saying— "*Captain* Keene, I trust you will give me the pleasure of your company to dinner; and, as you are still very lame, I think you had better make a signal for your servant and traps, and take up your quarters at the Penn till you are quite recovered."

Perceiving that I was too much agitated to reply, he continued, "I must leave you now;" then extending his hand, he said, "Allow me to be the first to wish you joy on your promotion, which you have so well deserved." He then went out of the room. It really was so unexpected—so little dreamt of, this sudden promotion, that I was confused. I had hoped that, by a continuance of good conduct, I might in a year or two obtain it; but that I should receive it after only one cruise in the schooner was beyond all my imagination. I felt grateful, and as soon as I was more composed, I returned thanks to Heaven, and vowed eternal gratitude to the admiral. I felt that I was a step nearer to Lord de Versely, and I thought of the pleasure it would give my mother and Minnie. I had been alone about half an hour, when the admiral returned.

"I have just sent for an old messmate of yours, Captain Keene, who was severely wounded in your action with the Dutch frigate; he has now passed, and Lord de Versely recommended him to me as a deserving young officer—a Mr Dott."

"Oh, yes, admiral; he was my first acquaintance when I went to sea. He has been to sea longer than I have, but he lost a good deal of his time."

"Well I am going to give him an acting order for your brig. I hope he is a good, smart officer."

"Yes, admiral, he is a very good officer indeed," replied I, laughing. "Will you oblige me by not telling him that I am to be his captain, till after we have met?"

"Ah, some mischief, I suppose; but if we make captains of such boys as you we must expect that. Are your wounded men all going on well?"

"All, sir,—even Bob Cross, the boatswain, whose head was half knocked off, is quite well again. He was Lord de Versely's coxswain, sir, and you were kind enough to give him his warrant."

"I recollect—a good man, is he not?"

"So good, sir, that the only regret I have in leaving the schooner is, that I cannot take him with me. He is my right-hand man and I owe much to him, and it will be a sore blow to him as well as to me."

"I see, you want him made boatswain of your brig—that's it."

"I assure you, admiral, I should be most grateful if you would have that kindness."

"I am always ready to promote a good man; your recommending him, and his severe wound, are sufficient. He shall be your boatswain, Keene."

"You are very kind, sir," replied I. "I hope I shall do justice to your patronage."

"I've no fear of that, Keene, and I know that a man, to work well, should, as far as he can, choose his own tools. Mr Dott is waiting now, and as soon as he has his acting order, I will send him in to you."

About ten minutes afterwards Mr Tommy Dott made his appearance; he extended his hand to me, saying, in a haw-haw way, "Keene, my dear fellow, I'm glad to see you." He certainly did look two or three inches taller, for he walked almost on tiptoe.

"Glad to see you, Tommy," said I; "well, what's the news?"

"Nothing, I believe, except what you have brought. I hear you had a bit of a brush, and got winged."

"Even so, Tommy," replied I, pointing to my wounded leg. "The admiral has kindly asked me to stay here until I'm better."

"I dine with him to-day," replied Tommy; "but as for staying here, I should think that rather a bore. By the bye, Keene, what sort of a craft is that Diligente brig which the Naiad and you took?"

"A very fine craft, Tommy: sails as well as the Firefly."

"Oh, you, of course, swear by your own vessel; and there's nothing like the schooner—that's natural enough; now, I must say, I prefer something a little larger, and, therefore, I'm not sorry that I have my commission for the new brig."

"Indeed! Tommy; I wish you joy," replied I.

"Thank ye, Keene," replied Tommy, very dignified. "I wonder," said he, "what sort of a skipper we shall have. There's the first lieutenant of the Naiad has a good chance. I saw him: a very sharp sort of gentleman, and carries his head remarkably high; but that won't do for me. I'll not allow any captain to play tricks in a ship that I'm aboard of. I know the rules and regulations of the service as well as any one, and that the captain shall see, if he attempts to go beyond his tether."

"Now, Tommy," replied I, "you know, that although you talk so big, if you had been appointed a lieutenant into a ship commanded by Lord de Versely, you would have been as much afraid of him as a lieutenant as you used to be as a midshipman."

"Lord de Versely," replied Tommy, who felt the truth of what I said: "he's a peculiar sort of man."

"Take my word for it, Tommy, you'll find all captains peculiar to one point; which is, that they expect respectful behaviour, and not cavilling, from their officers; and our service is so peculiar, that it is absolutely necessary that the officers should set this example to the men."

"Yes; that may be very well; but who knows but the captain of the brig may be some young fellow, who has seen no more service than myself— perhaps, not been to sea so long?"

"That is no reason that you should not obey his orders; indeed, if not experienced, you ought to do all you can to support him."

"Well, if he was to ask my advice, indeed—"

"But he may not require your advice, Tommy, he may prefer deciding for himself. Now, the first lieutenant of the Naiad is a great Tartar, and I'm certain, if he is your captain, that, on the first word, he would have you under an arrest. There's an old saying, Tommy, 'It's folly to kick against tenpenny nails;' and that every officer does who kicks against his superior. I can assure you, Tommy, that if ever I am a captain, my officers shall obey me implicitly. I will have no cavilling at my orders. I will always treat them as gentlemen, and support their authority, as they ought to support mine; but captain of my own ship I would be, and I suspect that it would go hard with any officer who ventured to dispute my rights."

"Well, I dare say you will be a martinet, or rather that you are one now, as you command a schooner. However, as I never intend to sail with you, that's nothing to me. I'm sure, from what has passed, that you and I should have a row before we were a week on board; for I'm not to be played with."

"Well, Tommy, I'm very glad we have had this explanation; for now we both know what to expect. I am resolved to be captain, you to resist my authority."

"No, no, I don't say that—I only say that I won't be played with—I won't be trifled with."

"Tommy, I will neither play nor trifle with you; nor will you ever play or trifle with me. We have done that as midshipmen; in our new relative situations it is not to be thought of for a moment. Read this." I handed him my appointment as commander of the Diligente: Tommy cast his eyes over it, and at once saw that his promotion did not prevent his getting into scrapes, as usual.

"You a commander! you captain of the Diligente! Why, I came to sea before you."

"I know you did, Tommy; but, although you have been in the service longer, you have not seen quite so much service as I have. At all events, I'm now your captain. I flatter myself I shall make a very tolerable one; and what is more, I have an idea that you will make a very good lieutenant, as soon as the vanity, with which you have been puffed up since your receiving your promotion, will have settled down a little, and that you will find it much pleasanter to be on good terms with your captain than to be eternally in hot water, especially with one who, you know, is not a person to be played with."

Tommy looked very confused; he said nothing, but kept his eyes on my commission, which he still held in his hand. I had no idea that Tommy Dott's being ignorant of my being captain of the brig would have occasioned such a conversation as this. I only wished to amuse myself with him, and surprise him at the last. Tommy perceived that he had made a mess of it, and he stammered out some explanation as he returned me the commission; and I replied: "The fact is, Dott, you were merely cutting a caper upon your new promotion; you never meant what you said; it was all talk. You always have been very obedient to proper authority since I have known you, and I am sure that you always will; so let's say no more about it. I wish you joy upon your promotion, and, what's more, I'm very glad that we are to sail together." Saying this, I held out my hand, which Tommy took very readily, and we then began to talk on other subjects.

Chapter Twenty Seven

I had written to Cross, informing him of my promotion, and his being appointed to the Diligente.

I had been a fortnight with the admiral when the Naiad arrived with the prizes in company, and, my wound being now cured, I took leave of the admiral, and went down, that I might superintend the fitting out of my new vessel. As there were supernumerary men expected out of England, the admiral, at my suggestion, allowed me to turn over the crew of the Firefly to form the nucleus of my ship's company, and made up my complement from his own ship.

In two months I was ready for sea, and most anxious to be off. The admiral perceived my impatience, but, as there was no other vessel in the harbour, he would not let me go until another arrived, to be at his disposal in case of emergency. The weariness of so long remaining in harbour was, however, a little relieved by a circumstance which took place, and which probably will make my readers imagine that my propensity for playing tricks was not quite eradicated.

I lodged at a sort of hotel, kept by a mulatto woman of the name of Crissobella, as the negroes termed her, originally Christobela. She was of Spanish blood by the father's side, and had come down from the Havannah. She was very portly; very proud and dignified in her carriage, and demanded as much attention from her lodgers as a lady would who had received us as her guests, so that, to gain and retain admittance into her hostelry, it was necessary not only to pay a large bill, but compliments to an equal amount. She was very rich, possessed numerous slaves, and was perfectly independent of keeping an hotel. I believed she preferred to have something for her slaves and herself to do, and moreover, probably, she felt that if she retired she should be thought a person of no consequence, whereas in her present position she received a great deal of attention. One thing was certain, that if those who lodged and boarded with her were very polite, and, on their return from any other place, brought her small presents, she was very indifferent as to their paying their bill; nay, to those who were her favourites, her purse was open, and a handful of doubloons was freely tendered, if required.

The living was the same as at a boarding-house. Breakfast was ready in the large hall by nine o'clock, and remained there until every one had come down at their own hour. Dinner was always ready at five o'clock, and then Crissobella presided at the table. She admitted civilians, army officers, and navy, down to midshipmen; but warrant officers and captains of merchant vessels were considered too low. On the whole, it was a very pleasant establishment, as the private rooms were well furnished, the slaves numerous, and the attendance very good. Considering the price of most eatables on that island, it could not be considered as very dear, although the wines, etcetera, made up a formidable bill at the end of the month.

This kind of exclusiveness on the part of Signora Crissobella made the hotel quite the fashion, and certainly it was by far the best in the town. The inmates of it at this time were besides me Lieut. Thomas Dott and Lieut. William Maxwell, both appointed to the Diligente; three or four young civilians, on mercantile speculations from New York; three midshipmen, who had been left behind on account of fever, and who were promising fair, by the life they were now leading, to be very soon sent to the hospital again; and one or two planters from the other islands. The latter and I were very well behaved, but the civilians were noisy, drinking and smoking from morning till night. The midshipmen were equally troublesome; and as for the new-made lieutenants, they were so authoritative and so disagreeable, and gave themselves such consequential airs, that Mammy Crissobella, as the slaves called her, was quite indignant—she had never had such a disorderly set in her house.

She complained to me, and I spoke to them, but that was of little use. I had no power over the young merchants, and the three midshipmen did not belong to my ship. As for my lieutenants, I could not say much at their giving themselves airs at an hotel where they paid for what they had. It was not an offence that a captain could remonstrate upon. I therefore merely said, that Mammy Crissobella could not have them in her house if they did not leave off their treatment of the slaves, and if they continued to give her so much trouble and annoyance. At last our hostess would stand their behaviour no longer, and ordered them all to leave the hotel, sending in their bills; but they all were unanimous in declaring that they would not go, and it was not very easy to use force on such occasions. I tried all I could to make matters right, but my efforts were of little avail. At last Mammy Crissobella became quite furious. She did not make any alteration in the meals, as that would be punishing all of us; but she refused wine and spirits; this they did not care for, as they sent for it elsewhere by their own servants, and there was nothing but noise and confusion all day along. Mammy often came to appeal to me, and wished to go to the governor, but I persuaded her not to do so; and the mutiny continued, and every day there was nothing but altercation at the meals.

"So help me God, gemmen, you no gemmen. You make wish me dead, dat you do. I tak obeah water some day. I not live like this," said Mammy Crissobella. "I take pepper-pot—I kill myself."

"Pray don't do that," replied Tommy Dott; "we shall be put to the expense of mourning."

"And I shall weep my eyes out," continued one of the mercantile gentlemen.

"Weep your eyes out—is that all? I shall blow my brains out," said another.

"And I will lie down on your grave and die," said the third.

"Dat all very well, gemmen; you say dat and laugh—but I no slave. 'Pose I not get you out my house, I ab *vengeance*, now I tell you, so look to that. Yes," continued Mammy Crissobella, striking the table with her fist, "I ab revenge."

"I have been thinking," said one of the mids, "what I shall do if Mammy Crissobella takes pepper-pot; I shall marry Leila, and keep the hotel. Mammy, you'll leave me the plate and furniture."

Leila was the head female slave—a very well-featured young mulatto girl, and a great favourite, as she was always laughing, always in good humour, and very kind and attentive. At this remark Leila laughed, and Mammy Crissobella, who observed her showing her white teeth, "You laugh, you huzzy: what you laugh for, Leila? Get away—get out of room. I give you nice flogging, by-by. You dare laugh—you take side against me, you nigger."

I must here observe that Mammy Crissobella had been closeted with me for some time previous to this scene, and that Leila and the two planters were in the secret; this was, of course, unknown, and the hostess's anger appeared now to be extended towards me and the two planters, with whom she had been on good terms.

Shortly afterwards Mammy rose and left the room, and then I spoke to the party, and told them that they were driving the poor woman to extremities. The planters agreed with me, and we argued the case with them, but the majority were, of course, against us, and the young merchants appeared to be very much inclined to be personal with me. At last I replied, "Very well, gentlemen—as you please; but as I happen to be well known both to the admiral and governor I give you fair warning that, if this continues much longer, I will report the affair. I should be very sorry to do so; but the house is now very uncomfortable, and you have no right to remain when the landlady insists upon your going."

At this reply of mine the naval portion of the guests were silent, but the civilians more insolent than before. I did not wish to come to open war, so I said nothing more, and left the table. After I was gone, the refractory parties made more noise than ever. Just before the dinner hour on the following day, Mammy Crissobella sent a circular round to the young men, stating that she could not receive them at dinner. They all laughed, and went down to table as before. The dinner was better than usual, and they complimented Mammy upon it. Mammy, who had taken her seat with a scowl on her brow, and had not spoken a word, merely bowed her head in reply to their observations.

Dinner was over, and then Mammy desired Leila to bring her a goblet which was on the sideboard, and a small white jug which was in the *buffet*. She appeared much distressed, and hesitated a good deal, putting the goblet to her lips, and then putting it down on the table without tasting it. This conduct induced us all to look seriously at her. At last she took it up, sighed deeply, and drank the whole off at a draught. For a few seconds she held her hand over her forehead, with her elbows resting on the table. At last she looked up and said, "Gemmen, I got a little speech to make—I very sorry dat I not drink your health; but it no use—dat why you see me drink; I tell plenty time you make me mad—you make me drink obeah water—make me kill myself. Now I ab done it—I drink pison water just now. In two hour I dead woman."

At this communication, the truth of which appeared confirmed by the woman's behaviour, all the company started from their chairs.

"Gemmen, I dare say you all very sorry; you be more sorry by-and-by. Captain, I beg your pardon; Mr W—, Mr G (the two planters), I beg your pardon; I not mean hurt you, but could not help it. Now I tell all company, all drink the pison water—because I not like die on the jibbit, I drink de pison water—Gemmen your dinner all pison, and you all pisoned. Yes, all pisoned," cried Mammy Crissobella at the highest pitch of her voice, and rushing out of the room.

At this announcement, I started from my chair and clasped my hands, as if in agony. I looked round me—never did I witness such a variety of horror as was expressed in the different faces at the hotel. The old planter; Mr D, who sat next to me, and who was in the secret as well as Mr G, laid his head on the table with a groan. "The Lord have mercy on my sins," exclaimed Mr G; Mr Lieutenant Maxwell looked me in the face, and then burst into tears; Mr Lieutenant Dott put his fingers down his throat, and with three or four more getting rid of their dinner as fast as they could.

At last I sprang up to ring the bell; no one answered. I rang again more furiously. At last a slave appeared.

"Where's my servant?"

"Not here, sar."

"Where's all the people of the house?"

"All with missy, sar; Mammy Crissobella die."

"Run down then to the beach, and desire the surgeon of the brig to come up immediately."

"Yes, sar," replied the negro, leaving the room.

"Oh, I feel it now—here," exclaimed I, putting my hand to my chest; "I'm suffocating."

"And so do I," replied one of the midshipmen, weeping.

The girl Leila now entered the room in tears. "Mammy dead," said she. "Oh Captain Keene, I very sorry for you: you come with me, I give you something. I know how stop pison."

"Do you, Leila? then give it me; quick, quick."

"Yes, yes; give it us quick."

"I not stuff enough but I make more when I gib what I ab to Captain Keene. You all stay still, not move; pose you move about, make pison work. I come back soon as I can."

Leila then took my arm and led me tottering out of the room, when I went to Mammy Crissobella, and laughed till I cried; but the punishment was not over. After remaining about ten minutes looking at each other, but neither speaking nor moving, in pursuance of Leila's direction, with the utmost despair in their countenances, they were gladdened by the return of Leila with a large jug, out of which she administered a glass of some compound or another to each of them. I watched at the door, and the eagerness with which they jostled and pushed each other to obtain the dose before the rest was very amusing, and never did they swallow any liquor with so much avidity, little imagining that, instead of taking what was to cure them, they were now taking what was to make them very sick; but so it was; and in a few minutes afterwards the scene of groaning, crying, screaming, writhing with pain, was quite awful.

After a time, the slaves came in and carried them all to their respective beds, leaving them to their own reflections, and the violent effects of the drugs administered, which left them no repose for that night, and in a state of utter exhaustion on the following morning.

At daylight I went into Mr Dott's room with the surgeon, to whom I had confided the secret. Tommy was a miserable object.

"Thank heaven! here is one still alive," said the surgeon to me.

"Oh! Captain Keene," said Tommy, "I'm glad to see that you are so well; but you had the remedy given you long before we had."

"Yes," replied I, "it was given me in good time; but I hope it was not too late with you."

"I feel very bad," replied Tommy. "Doctor, do you think I shall live?"

The doctor felt his pulse, and looked very grave; at last he said, "If you get over the next twelve hours, I think you may."

"How many are dead?" inquired Tommy.

"I don't know; you are the first that I have visited; it's a shocking business."

"I've been thinking that we were very wrong," said Tommy; "we ought not to have driven the poor woman to desperation. If I do recover, her death will be on my conscience."

"I'm glad to hear you say that, Tommy," replied I; "but the doctor says you must remain very quiet, and therefore I shall leave you. Good-bye; I will see you again this evening."

"Good-bye, sir, and I hope you'll forgive me for not having been so respectful as I should have been."

"Yes, yes, Tommy; we have been friends too long for that."

Mammy Crissobella's dose had certainly put an end to all Tommy's spirit of resistance. All the others who had been victims to our plot were kept in the dark as to the real facts, and, as soon as they were able to be moved, paid their bills to Leila, and left the house.

Chapter Twenty Eight

On the third day, Tommy Dott and Mr Maxwell went on board, imagining that they had had a miraculous escape, and the two old planters and I were left the only inmates of the house to welcome the resurrection of Mammy Crissobella, who was again as busy as before. She said to me, "Massy Keene, I really under great obligation to you; suppose you want two, three hundred, five hundred pounds, very much at your service; never mind pay back."

I replied that I did not want any money, and was equally obliged to her. But the affair had already made a great noise. It was at first really supposed that Mammy Crissobella had poisoned them as well as herself, and I was obliged to refute it, or the authorities would have taken it up. As the admiral sent down to make inquiries, I went up to him and told him the whole story; I was obliged to do the same to the governor, and it was the occasion of great mirth all over the island, and no small mortification to those who had been the sufferers. Mammy Crissobella was complimented very much upon her successful stratagem to clear her house, and she was quite in ecstasies at the renown that she obtained.

One day the admiral sent for me, and said—"Keene, I can wait no longer the arrival of another vessel. I must send you to England with despatches: you must sail to-morrow morning."

As I was all ready, I took my leave of the admiral, who promised me every assistance if on his station, and his good word with the Admiralty, and said that he would send down my despatches at daylight. I went on board, gave the necessary orders, and then returned to the hotel to pack up my portmanteau and pay my bill; but Mammy Crissobella would not hear of my paying anything; and as I found that she was beginning to be seriously angry, I gave up the point. So I gave the old lady a kiss as a receipt-in-full, and another to Leila, as I slipped a couple of doubloons into her hand, and went on board. The next morning shortly after daylight the despatches were on board, and the Diligente was under all the sail she could carry on her way to England.

The Diligente sailed as well as ever, and we made a very quick passage. I found my ship's company to be very good, and had no trouble with my officers. Tommy Dott was very well behaved, notwithstanding all his threats of what he would do. It was therefore to be presumed that he was not very ill treated.

We were now fast approaching the end of our passage, being about a hundred miles to the South West of the Scilly Islands, with a light wind from the southward when, in the middle watch, Bob Cross, who had the charge of it, came down and reported firing in the South East. I went up, but, although we heard the report of the guns, we could not distinguish the flashes. I altered our course to the direction, and we waited till daylight should reveal what was going on. Before daybreak we could see the flashes, and make out one vessel, but not the other. But when the sun rose the mystery was cleared off. It was a French schooner privateer engaging a large English ship, apparently an East-Indiaman. The ship was evidently a good deal cut up in her spars and rigging.

Bob Cross, who was close to my side when I examined them with my glass, said, "Captain Keene, that rascally Frenchman will be off as soon as he sees us, if we hoist English colours; but if you hoist French colours, we may get down and pin him before he knows what we are."

"I think you are right, Bob," says I. "Hoist French colours. He will make sure of his prize then, and we shall laugh at his disappointment."

As Cross turned away to go aft, I perceived a chuckle on his part, which I did not understand, as there was nothing particular to chuckle about. I thought it was on account of the Frenchman's disappointment, when he found that we were not a friend, as he might suppose.

"Hadn't we better fire a gun, Captain Keene, to attract their attention?"

"Yes," replied I; "it will look as if we really were Frenchmen." The gun was fired, and we continued to stand towards them with a good breeze. About seven o'clock we were within two miles, and then we observed the Englishman haul down her colours, and the schooner immediately went alongside, and took possession. I continued to run down, and in half an hour was close to her. Calling up the boarders, I laid the brig alongside the schooner; as half her men were on board the Indiaman, they were taken by surprise, and we gained possession with very trifling loss on our side, much to the astonishment of the crew of the privateer, as well as that of the Indiaman.

The captain, who was on deck, informed me that they had engaged the schooner for nine hours, and that he had some hopes of beating her off, until he saw me come down under French colours, upon which he felt that further resistance was vain. I told him I was afraid the schooner would escape, if I had not deceived him, and complimented him upon his vigorous defence. The schooner was a very fine vessel, mounting fourteen guns, and of three hundred tons burthen. In fact, she was quite as large as the Diligente.

While we were handing the prisoners over to the brig, and securing them, I accepted the invitation of the captain of the Indiaman to go into the cabin with him, where I found a large party of passengers, chiefly ladies, who were very loud in their thanks for my rescue. In another hour we were all ready. I left a party on board the Indiaman to repair damages, and my surgeon to assist the wounded men, and hauled off the brig and schooner. The latter I gave into the charge of Tommy Dott, and we all made sail.

As I was walking the quarter-deck, delighted with my success, Cross, who had the watch and was by my side, said, "I think, Captain Keene, you did very right in hoisting French colours."

"Why, yes, Cross," replied I; "she is a very fast sailer, that is evident, and she might have escaped us."

"That's not what I mean, Captain Keene."

"What then, Cross?"

"Why, sir, I would not tell you why I wished you to hoist French colours at the time, because I was afraid that, if I did, you would not have done so; but my reason was, that it would make a great difference in our prize-money, and I want some, if you do not."

Even then I could not imagine what Cross meant, for it never came into my head, and I turned round and looked at him for an explanation.

"Why, Captain Keene, if we had hoisted English colours, the schooner would have made sail and gone off, and, even if she had not done so, the Indiaman would have held out till we came down; but as he hauled down his colours, and was taken possession of by the enemy, he now becomes a recapture, and I expect the salvage of that Indiaman will be of more value to us than two or three of such schooners."

"That certainly did not enter my head when I hoisted the colours, Cross, I must confess."

"No, sir, that I saw it did not, but it did mine."

"It's hardly fair, Cross."

"Quite fair, sir," replied Bob. "The Company is rich, and can afford to pay, and we want it in the first place, and deserve it in the next. At all events, it's not upon your conscience, and that schooner is such a clipper, that I really think we should have lost her, if she had run for it; besides, as she is as strong as we are, we might have lost a good many men before we took her."

"That's very true, Bob," replied I, "and satisfies me that I was right in what I did."

The wind had sprung up much fresher from the westward, and we were now all three running with a fair wind; and as it continued, we did not put into Plymouth, but continued our course for Portsmouth, and on the third day, at a very early hour in the morning, anchored at Spithead.

Chapter Twenty Nine

As it was too soon to present myself to the admiral, I dressed, ready to go on shore, and hoisted the number of the Diligente as given by the admiral at Jamaica; but, as I expected, it was not known to the guard-ship, and there was much surmise among the early risers as to what might be the large ship, schooner, and brig-of-war, which had entered.

We had just finished the washing of the decks, and I was standing aft with Cross, who had the morning watch, when he observed to me, "Captain Keene, we are now at anchor as near as possible to where the Calliope was when you went adrift in the boat with poor Peggy. Some difference between your situation now and then."

"Yes, Bob," replied I; "I was thinking the same when I was dressing this morning, and I was also thinking that you would be very anxious to go on shore—so you may take a boat as soon as you please; I will order one to be given to you."

"Thankey, sir. I am a little anxious to see the poor girl, and I think matters will go smooth now."

"I hope so, with all my heart. Let the gigs be all dressed and cleaned, and the boat manned at six bells. Pass the word for them to get their breakfast."

As it was better that I should wait for the admiral's getting up, than that he should wait for me, I was on shore, and up at the office at half-past seven o'clock, and found that the admiral was in his dressing-room. The secretary was there, and I delivered my orders and despatches, with which he went up to the admiral. In about a quarter of an hour he came down again with the port-admiral's request that I would wait for him, and stay to breakfast. The secretary remained with me, extracting all the West India intelligence that I could give him.

As soon as the admiral made his appearance, he shook me warmly by the hand. "Captain Keene," said he, "I wish you joy: I see you are following up your career in the West Indies. We know you well enough by the despatches, and I am glad to be personally acquainted with you. This last business will, I have no doubt, give you the next step, as soon as you have been a little longer as commander. Mr Charles, desire them to make the signal for the Diligente and schooner to come into harbour. The Indiaman may, of course, do as he pleases. Now then, for breakfast."

The admiral, of course, asked me as many questions as the secretary, and ended, as I rose to take my leave, in requesting the pleasure of my company to dinner on that day. As the reader may suppose, I had every reason to be satisfied with my reception.

As soon as I had left the admiral's office, I put into the post-office, with my own hands, my letter to my mother, and one to Lord de Versely. In the latter I told him of my good fortune, and enclosed a copy of my despatch to the Admiralty. Although the despatch was written modestly, still the circumstances in themselves—my having recaptured an Indiaman, and carried, by boarding, a vessel of equal force to my own, and superior in men—had a very good appearance, and I certainly obtained greater credit than it really deserved. It was not at all necessary to say that I hoisted French colours, and therefore took the schooner unawares, or that at the time most of her men were on board of the Indiaman; the great art in this world is, to know where to leave off, and in nothing more than when people take the pen in their hands.

As soon as I had finished my correspondence—for I wrote a few lines to Mrs Bridgeman, at Chatham, and a postscript to my mother's letter—I went down to the saluting battery, when I found that the two vessels were just entering the harbour. I went up and reported it at the admiral's office, and the admiral went on board of both vessels to examine them himself, and he ordered a dock-yard survey. They were both pronounced fit for his Majesty's service, with the necessary dock-yard alterations. The crew of the Diligente were turned over to a hulk, preparatory to unrigging and clearing her out for dock. As soon as I left the admiral's house, I sat down at the George Hotel, where I had taken up my quarters, and wrote a long letter to Minnie Vanderwelt.

Cross called upon me the next morning. I saw by his countenance that he had good news to tell me. He had found his lady-love as constant as he could wish, and having explained to the blind old smuggler that he had been offered and accepted the situation of boatswain in his Majesty's service during the time that he was in the West Indies, he had received his approbation of his conduct, and a warm welcome to the house whenever he could come on shore.

"I have not put the question to the old chap yet, Captain Keene," said he, "but I think I will very soon."

"Don't be in too great a hurry, Bob," replied I. "Give the old fellow a little more 'baccy, and ask his advice as to what you are to do with your prize-money. You must also talk a little about your half-pay and your widow's pension."

"That's very good advice, Captain Keene," replied Cross. "Mercy on us! how things are changed! It appears but the other day that I was leading you down to this very hotel, to ship you into the service, and you was asking my advice, and I was giving it to you; and now I am asking your advice, and taking it. You have shot ahead in every way, sir, that's sartin; you looked up to me then, now I look up to you."

I laughed at Cross's observation, which was too true; and then we went into the dock-yard, and were very busy during the remainder of the day.

The following morning I received an answer from Lord de Versely, couched in most friendly terms. He complimented me on my success, and the high character I had gained for myself during so short a career, and added that he should be happy to see me as soon as I could come to London, and would himself introduce me to the first lord of the Admiralty. He advised me to request leave of absence, which would be immediately granted, and concluded his letter, "Your sincere friend and well-wisher, de Versely."

As soon as I had laid down the letter, I said to myself, I was right—the true way to create an interest in a man like Lord de Versely, is to make him proud of you. I have done well as yet—I will try to do more; but how long will this success continue? Must I not expect reverses? May not some reaction take place? and have I not in some degree deserved it? Yes, I have used deceit in persuading him of my mother's death. I began now to think that that was a false step, which, if ever discovered, might recoil upon me. I remained a long while in deep thought. I tried to extenuate my conduct in this particular, but I could not; and to rid myself of melancholy feelings, which I could not overcome, I wrote a letter, requesting leave of absence for a fortnight, and took it myself to the admiral's office. This depression of spirits remained with me during the time that I remained at Portsmouth, when, having obtained leave, I set off for London, and on arrival, put up at a fashionable hotel in Albermarle Street.

Chapter Thirty

The next morning I called at Lord de Versely's and sent up my card. I was immediately ushered up, and found myself in his presence. Lord de Versely rose from his sofa, and took my hand. "Keene, I am very glad to see you. I am proud that an *élève* of mine should have done me so much credit. You have gained all your rank in the service by your own merit and exertions."

"Not quite all, my lord," replied I.

"Yes, all; for you are certain of your next step—they cannot well refuse it to you."

"They will not refuse your lordship, I have no doubt," replied I.

"Sit down, Keene. We will have a little conversation, and then we will go to the Admiralty."

His lordship then asked me many questions relative to what had passed; and I entered into more detail than I had done in my letters. After an hour's conversation, carried on by him in so friendly—I may almost say affectionate—a style as to make my heart bound with delight, the carriage was announced, and accompanied his lordship down to the Admiralty. His lordship sent up his card, and was requested immediately to go upstairs. He desired me to follow him; and as soon as we were in the presence of the first lord, and he and Lord de Versely had shaken hands, Lord de Versely said, "Allow me to introduce to you Captain Keene, whose name, at least, you have often heard of lately. I have brought him with me because he is a follower of mine: he entered the service under my protection, and continued with me until his conduct gave him his promotion. I have taken this opportunity of introducing him, to assure your lordship that, during the whole time that he served with me as midshipman, his gallantry was quite as conspicuous as it has been since."

The first lord took me by the hand, and complimented me on my conduct.

"Captain Keene has strong claims, my lord. What can we do now for him?"

"I trust you will acknowledge that Captain Keene has earned his post rank, my lord," replied Lord de Versely; "and I shall take it as a particular favour to myself if your lordship would appoint him to a frigate, and give him an opportunity of doing credit to your lordship's patronage."

"I think I may promise you both," replied the first lord; "but when we meet in the house to-night, I will let you know what I can do."

After a few minutes' conversation, Lord de Versely rose, and we left the room. As soon as we were in the carriage his lordship said, "Keene, you may depend upon it I shall have good news to tell you to-morrow; so call upon me about two o'clock. I dine out to-day with the premier; but to-morrow you must dine with me."

I took leave of his lordship as soon as the carriage stopped; and as I wished to appoint an agent, which I had not yet done, I had begged his lordship to recommend me one. He gave me the address of his own, and I went there accordingly. Having made the necessary arrangements, I then employed the remainder of the day in fitting myself out in a somewhat more fashionable style than Portsmouth tailors were equal to.

The next morning I sat down to write to my mother; but somehow or another I could not make up my mind to address her. I had thought of it, over and over, and had made up my mind that in future I would always correspond with my grandmother; and I now determined to write to her, explaining that such was my intention in future, and requesting that all answers should be also from my grandmother. I commenced my letter, however, with informing her that I had, since I had last written, obtained leave of absence, and was now in London. I stated the kindness shown me in every way by Lord de Versely, and how grateful I was to him. This continued down to the bottom of the first page, and then I said "What would I not give to bear the name of one I so much love and respect! Oh, that I was a Delmar!" I was just about to turn over the leaf and continue, when the waiter tapped at the door, and informed me that the tailor was come to try on the clothes which I had ordered. I went into the bed-room, which opened into the sitting-room, and was busy with the foreman, who turned me round and round, marking alterations with a piece of chalk, when the waiter tapped at the bed-room door, and said Lord de Versely was in the sitting-room. I took off the coat which was fitting as fast as I could, that I might not keep his lordship waiting, and put on my own.

Desiring the man to wait my return, I opened the door, and found his lordship on the sofa, and then for the first time, when I again saw it, recollected that I had left the letter on the table. The very sight of it took away my breath. I coloured up as I approached his lordship. I had quite forgotten that I had addressed my grandmother. I stammered out, "This is an honour, my lord."

"I came to wish you joy of your promotion and appointment to a fine frigate, Keene," said Lord de Versely. "I have just received this from the Admiralty; and as I have business unexpectedly come to hand, I thought I would be the bearer myself of the good news. I leave you the letter, and shall of course see you to dinner."

"Many thanks, my lord," replied I. "I am, indeed, grateful."

"I believe you are, Keene," replied his lordship. "By the bye, you leave your letters so exposed, that one cannot help seem them. I see you are writing to your grandmother. I hope the old lady is well?"

My grandmother! Oh, what a relief to my mind it was when I then recollected that it was to my grandmother that I had written! I replied that she was very well when I last heard from her.

"If I can be of any use in arranging your money affairs, Keene, let me know."

"I thank you, my lord; but I found that my agent perfectly understands business," replied I. "I will not trouble your lordship, who has so many important affairs to attend to."

"Very good," replied he. "Then now I'll leave you to read what I have given you; and I shall expect you at eight. Goodbye." His lordship again shook me warmly by the hand, and left me.

I was quite giddy with the reaction produced upon my feelings. When his lordship left the room I dropped down on the sofa. I forgot the letter in my hand and its contents, and the tailor in the next room. All I thought of was the danger I had escaped, and how fortunate I was in not having addressed the letter to my mother, as I had at first intended. The agony which I felt was very great, and, as I remained with my hands covering my eyes, I made a vow that nothing should induce me ever to use deceit again. I then read over the letter. There was nothing but gratitude to Lord de Versely, and a wish that I had been born a Delmar. Well, if his lordship had run his eyes over it, there was nothing to hurt me in his opinion; on the contrary, it proved that I was grateful; and I then recollected that when I expressed my gratitude, he said he believed it. As for my saying that I wished my name was Delmar, it was nothing, and it let him know what my wishes were. On the whole, I had great cause for congratulation.

I was here interrupted by the tailor who put his head out of the bedroom door. I went to him, and he finished his work, and promised me that

I should have a complete suit at half-past seven o'clock in the evening, in time for dinner. I then returned to the sitting-room, and opened the letter which Lord de Versely had put into my hands. It was from the first lord, acquainting him that I might call at the Admiralty the next day, as my post-captain's commission was signed, and I was appointed to a thirty-two gun frigate which would be launched in two or three months. Well, then, thought I, here I am, at twenty-three, a post-captain in his Majesty's service, and commanding a frigate. Surely, I have much to be thankful for. I felt that I had, and I was grateful to Heaven for my good fortune. Now I had but one more wish in the world, and that was, instead of being Captain Keene, to be Captain Delmar.

The reader may say, "What's in a name?" True; but such was my ambition, my darling wish, and it is ardent longing for anything, the ardour of pursuit, which increases the value of the object so much above its real value. The politician, who has been manoeuvring all his life does not perhaps feel more pleasure in grasping the coronet which he has been in pursuit of, than the urchin does when he first possesses himself of a nest which he has been watching for weeks. This would, indeed, be a dreary world if we had not some excitement, some stimulus to lead us on, which occupies our thoughts, and gives us fresh courage, when disheartened by the knavery, and meanness, and selfishness of those who surround us. How sad is the analysis of human nature—what contradictions, what extremes! how many really brave men have I fallen in with, stooping to every meanness for patronage, court favour, or gain; slandering those whose reputation they feared, and even descending to falsehood to obtain their ends! How many men with splendid talents, but with little souls!

Up to the present I had run a career of prosperous success; I had risen to a high position without interfering, or being interfered with by others; but now I had become of sufficient consequence to be envied; now I had soon to experience, that as you continue to advance in the world, so do you continue to increase the number of your enemies, to be exposed to the shafts of slander, to be foiled by treachery, cunning, and malevolence. But I must not anticipate.

I remained in London till my leave was expired, and then went down to Portsmouth to pay off the brig, which had been ordered into dock, to be refitted for his Majesty's service.

Chapter Thirty One

The Circe, thirty-two, to which I had been appointed, was a small but very beautiful frigate and as far as I could judge by her build as she lay on the stocks, had every requisite for sailing well.

When I took my leave of Lord de Versely, he told me that he should come down on the first of the following month (September) to Madeline Hall, where his aunt, Miss de Versely, was still flourishing at a green old age. "Here is a letter of introduction to her, Keene," said he, "as she has not seen you since you were a few months old, and therefore it is not very likely that she would recognise you. Take my advice, and make yourself as agreeable to the old lady as you can; you will find Madeline Hall a very pleasant place, when you are tired of the dockyard and the smell of pitch and tar."

I thanked his lordship, and we parted with much more cordiality shown by him than I had experienced.

I hardly need say, that the first person who came to congratulate me on my arrival at Portsmouth was my old friend an adviser Bob Cross. "Well, Captain Keene," said Bob, as I shook him warmly by the hand, "I'm delighted at your success, and I know you will not be sorry to hear that I am getting on as well as I could wish in my small way; Jane and I are to be married in a few days, and I hope you will honour me by being present at the wedding."

"That I will, Bob, with pleasure," replied I; "let me hear all that has taken place."

"Why, sir, it's told in a few words. I took your advice, and brought the old gentleman presents, and I sat with him and heard all his old stories at least fifty times over, and laughed at his jokes as regularly the last time as the first; and he told Jane and her mother that I was a very pleasant, sensible and amusing young man—although he had all the talk, and I had none. The fact is, sir, it was he who first brought up the subject of my splicing his niece; that is to say, he hinted how he should like to see her well settled, and that if she married according to his wishes, he would leave her all he had.

"Well, sir, it was the opinion of Jane and her mother, that, as he was a whimsical, changeable old chap, it would be right for her to refuse me at first; and so she did, very much to the old man's annoyance, who then set his mind upon it, and swore that if she did not marry me, he would not leave her a farthing. After a few days of quarrelling, Jane gave in, and the old chap swears that we shall be married immediately, and that he will give us half his property down at once."

"Strike the iron while it's hot, Bob," replied I. "Is the day fixed?"

"Not exactly, sir; but we are to be put up in church next Sunday, and it takes three Sundays. I hope you won't part with me, sir," continued Bob. "The Diligente will be paid off on Tuesday, they say, and if you could get me appointed to the Circe—"

"Why, Cross, you are thinking of going to sea again, even before you are married. I should advise you not to be in such a hurry. You must not displease the old gentleman; besides, you must not leave a young wife so soon."

"That's very true, Captain Keene, but I don't think I should be comfortable if I knew you were afloat without me."

"I suppose you think that I cannot take care of myself."

"Yes, I do, sir; but still I know that I should fret; and, sir, it will be four months at least before the Circe is ready for sea and I may just as well be appointed to her, and I can decide whether I do go to sea or not when the time comes."

"Well, Cross, I will certainly apply for you; but, if you take my advice, you will give up the sea altogether, and live on shore."

"I have nothing to do, sir."

"Yes, you have; you have to cherish your wife, and look after the old gentleman."

"Well he is rather shakey, they say sir; the old woman is often called out to him at nights."

"Well, Cross, I will do as you wish, and time will decide how you are to act. I am going over to Southampton for a few days perhaps, and will take care to be back by the wedding. By-the-bye, have you heard anything about prize-money?"

"Yes, sir; it's payable for the Diligente and schooner, and all our recaptures in the West Indies when we were in the Firefly. The Dutch frigate has been for distribution some time; but as I was only petty officer then, it won't come to much."

"Well, I can tell you that the government have taken the schooner which we captured in the chops of the channel, and the East India Company have given us salvage for the ship. My agent has received already 7,400 pounds on my account, which I have ordered to be purchased into the funds. As there were so few warrant officers, your share will not be less than 1,500 pounds, perhaps more. As you said, the salvage of the Indiaman has proved more valuable to us than all the rest of our prize-money put together."

"Well, Captain Keene, if my prize-money comes to as much as that, I think I shall be nearly as well off as my little Jane will be. Will you have the kindness to let your agent put it by for me in the same way that you have done yours?"

"Yes, Cross, I will see to it immediately; I shall write to him to-morrow, or the day after."

After a little conversation, Cross took leave. The next day I took post-horses, and went over to Madeline Hall, having two or three days before received a note from the Honourable Miss Delmar, saying how glad she should be to see me as a friend and shipmate of her nephew, Lord de Versely; so that it appeared the old lady had been written to by Lord de Versely respecting me.

I arrived early in the afternoon, and the post-chaise drove up the avenue of magnificent chestnut-trees which led to the mansion.

Chapter Thirty Two

I must say that I was very much excited; I was now arriving at the site of my birth, and it brought to my mind the details given me by my poor mother, when, finding she could no longer conceal the truth from me, she entered into a narrative to extenuate her conduct, pointing out her temptations, and how fatal to her were opportunity and seclusion. Her form was before me with the tears running down her cheeks as she made her humiliating confession to her own son, and I could not help exclaiming, as I cast my eye upon the beautiful grounds, "My poor mother!"

The chaise stopped, and the boys dismounted and rang the bell. In a minute three or four servants made their appearance, and on inquiring, I found that the Honourable Miss Delmar was at home, and visible.

"Colonel Delmar, I presume, sir?" said the old butler.

"No," replied I—"Captain Keene."

The butler looked me full in the face, and earnestly; and then, as if recollecting himself, he bowed and went on.

"Captain Keene, madam," said he, as he introduced me into a large room, at the end of which sat a venerable-looking old lady, very busy with her knitting needle, and another, almost equally ancient, sitting on a low stool beside her.

As I advanced, the old lady made me a bow as she remained in in her chair, and looked at me through her spectacles. She certainly was the beau-idéal of old age. Her hair, which was like silver, was parted in braid, and was to be seen just peeping from under her cap and pinners; she was dressed in black silk, with a snow-white apron and handkerchief, and there was an air of dignity and refinement about her which made you feel reverence for her at first sight. As I approached to take the chair offered to me, the other person, who appeared to be a sort of attendant, was shuffling her feet to rise; but as soon as Mrs Delmar had said, "You are welcome, Captain Keene; sit still," she continued, "my child, there is no occasion to go away." I could scarcely help smiling at the old lady calling a woman of past sixty, if not even further advanced, a child; but the fact was, that Phillis had been her attendant as lady's maid for many years, and subsequently promoted to the position of humble companion.

As for Miss Delmar, as I afterwards found out from her own lips, she was upwards of eighty-seven years old, but still in perfect good health, and in full possession of all her faculties; Phillis therefore was much younger, and as the old lady had had her in her employ ever since she was twenty-two, it was not surprising that she continued to address her, as she had done for so many years, as a young person compared to herself; indeed I have no doubt but that the old lady, following up her association of former days, and forgetting the half-century that had intervened, did consider her as a mere child. The old lady was very chatty and very polite, and as our conversation naturally turned on Lord de Versely, of whom I spoke in terms of admiration and gratitude, I had soon established myself in her good graces. Indeed, as I subsequently discovered, her nephew was the great object of her affections. His younger brother had neglected her, and was never mentioned except when she regretted that Lord de Versely had no children, and that the title would descend to his brother.

She requested me to stay for dinner, which I did not refuse, and before dinner was over I had made great progress in the old lady's esteem. As, when dinner was announced, her companion disappeared, we were then alone. She asked me many questions relative to Lord de Versely, and what had occurred during the time that I was serving with him; and this was a subject on which I could be eloquent. I narrated several of our adventures, particularly the action with the Dutch frigate, and other particulars in which I could honestly do credit to his lordship, and I often referred to his kindness for me.

"Well, Captain Keene, my nephew has often spoken to me about you, and now you have done him credit in proving that he had made you a good officer; and I have heard how much you have distinguished yourself since you have left him."

"Or rather he left me, madam," replied I, "when he was summoned to the House of Peers."

"Very true," replied the old lady. "I suppose you know that you were born in this house, Captain Keene?"

"I have been told so, madam."

"Yes, I have no doubt your poor mother that's gone must have told you. I recollect her—a very clever, active, and pretty young woman (here the old lady sighed); and I held you in my arms, Captain Keene, when you were only a few days old."

"You did me great honour, madam," replied I.

Here the conversation took another channel, which I was not sorry for.

After tea, I rose to take my leave, and then I received an invitation from the old lady to come and spend some time at Madeline Hall, and to come a few days before the first of September, that I might join the shooting party. "I expect my nephew, Lord de Versely," said she, "and there is Colonel Delmar of the Rifles, a cousin of Lord de Versely, also coming, and one or two others. Indeed I expect the colonel every day. He is a very pleasant and gentleman-like man."

I accepted the invitation with pleasure, and then took my leave. The chaise drove off, and I was soon in a deep reverie; I called to mind all my mother had told me, and I longed to return to the Hall, and visit those scenes which had been referred to in my mother's narrative; and more than that, I wished to meet Lord de Versely on the spot which could not fail to call to his mind my mother, then young, fond, and confiding; how much she had sacrificed for him; how true she had proved to his interests, and how sacred the debt of obligation, which he could only repay by his conduct towards me.

On my return to Portsmouth, I found that orders had come down for the paying off the Diligente, and re-commissioning her immediately. As the men would now be free (until again caught by the impress, which would not be long), I turned up the ship's company, and asked how many of them would enter for the Circe. I pointed out to them that they would be impressed for other vessels before long, but that I could give them each three months of absence, upon which they would not be molested, and that by three months all their money would be gone, and if it were gone before that time, the guard-ship would receive them when they had had enough of the shore. By this method I proposed to myself to obtain the foundation of a good ship's company. I was not disappointed. Every man I wished to take with me volunteered, and I wrote leave of absence tickets for three months for them all as belonging to the Circe, reporting what I had done to the Admiralty. The brig was then paid off, and the next day re-commissioned by a Captain Rose, with whom I had some slight acquaintance.

As I was now my own master again,—for although appointed to the Circe, I had nothing but my pennant to look at,—I thought that, by way of a little change, I would pass a few days at the Isle of Wight; for this was the yachting season, and I had made the acquaintance of many of the gentlemen who belonged to the club. That I had no difficulty in getting into society may easily be imagined. A post-captain's commission in his Majesty's navy is a certain passport with all liberal and really aristocratical people;

and, as it is well known that a person who has not had the advantage of interest and family connections to advance in the service, must have gained his promotion by his own merits, his rank is sufficient to establish his claims to family connections or personal merit, either of which is almost universally acknowledged; I say almost universally, because, strange to say, for a succession of reigns, the navy never has been popular at court. In that region, where merit of any kind is seldom permitted to intrude, the navy have generally been at a discount. Each succession of the House of Hanover has been hailed by its members with fresh hopes of a change in their favour, which hopes have ended in disappointment; but perhaps it is as well. The navy require no prophet to tell it, in the literal sense of the word, that one cannot touch pitch without being defiled; but there is a moral pitch, the meanness, the dishonesty, and servility of Court, with which, I trust, our noble service will never be contaminated.

I have, however, somewhat wandered from my subject, which was brought up in consequence of a gentleman who had paid me every attention at a large club down at Cowes, to which I had been invited, inquiring of me, across the table, if I were connected with the Keenes of —? My reply was ready: "I did not think that I was; my father had died a young man in the East Indies. I knew that he was of Scotch descent (which he was), but I was too young to know anything about his connections, whom he had quitted at an early age; since that I had been educated and brought forward by Lord de Versely, who had, since the death of my mother, treated me as if I were his own son." This was said openly, and being strictly true, of course without hesitation on my part. It was quite sufficient; I had noble patronage, and it was therefore to be presumed that I was somebody, or that patronage would not have been extended. I mention this, because it was the only time that I was ever questioned about my family; it was therefore to be presumed that my reply was considered satisfactory.

I accepted an invitation on board of the yacht and sailed about for several days, very much amused and flattered by the attention shown to me by the noble commodore and others. One day I fell in with an old acquaintance. A small vessel, of about twenty tons, cutter-rigged, came down under the stern of the commodore's yacht; it was then very smooth water, very light wind, and, moreover, very hot weather; and one of the squadron, who was standing by me on the taffrail, said, "Keene, do look at this craft coming down under our stern—there's quite a curiosity in it. It is a yacht belonging to an Irish Major O'Flinn, as he calls himself; why the O, I don't know; but he's a good fellow, and very amusing; there he is abaft; he has the largest whiskers you ever saw; but it is not of him I would speak. Wait a little, and as soon as the square sail is out of the way, you will see his wife. Such a whapper! I believe she weighs more than the rhinoceros did which was at Post-down fair."

As the vessel neared, I did behold a most enormous woman in a sky-blue silk dress, and a large sky-blue parasol over her head; the bonnet having been taken off, I presume, on account of the heat. "She is a monster," replied I; "the major was a bold man; I think I have seen the face before."

"I am told that she was the daughter of a purser, and had a lot of money," continued my friend.

I recollected then, and I replied, "Yes; I know now, her name was Culpepper."

"That was the name," replied he; "I recollect now."

The reader may probably recollect Miss Medea, who knew so well how to put that and that together; and her mother, who I presumed had long ago been suffocated in her own fat, a fate which I thought that Mrs O'Flinn would meet with as well as her mother. The lady did not recognise me, which I was not sorry for. I certainly should have cut her dead. I walked forward, and my thoughts reverted to the time when my mother first brought me down to embark, and I was taken care of by Bob Cross. This recollection of Bob Cross reminded me that I had promised to be at his wedding, and that it was to take place on the following day, which I had quite forgotten. So that Mrs O'Flinn did me a good turn at last, as I should have neglected my promise, if she had not made her appearance, sailing along like an elephantine Cleopatra.

Chapter Thirty Three

I had not called upon old Waghorn, the uncle of Jane; as I was fearful that he might recognise the pretended agent of former days with the now captain of the Circe. The blind are very acute in all their other senses,—a species of reparation made by nature by way of indemnification for the severe loss which they have sustained.

As I grew older I grew wiser, and I could not help remarking, that the acts of deceit, which as a midshipman I thought not only very justifiable, but good fun, were invariably attended with unpleasant results. Even in this trifle my heart misgave me, whether on my appearance at the wedding I might not I be recognised, and be the cause of creating a breach, by raising suspicions on the part of the blind man which might prevent the wedding; and I had stated my fears to Bob Cross. "Well, Captain Keene, it was all done with good intentions, and I do not think that there is much fear. It's a long while back, and you were not so much of a man as you are now. They do say, that cheating never thrives, and I believe that it seldom does in the long run. Jane will be much disappointed if you do not come."

"There is no help for it, Bob; I must disguise my voice; I must cheat a little now to hide the first cheat. That's always the case in this world."

"I don't call it cheating, sir; my ideas are, that if you cheat to get advantage for yourself, then you do cheat; but when you do so to help another, there's no great cheating in the case."

"I cannot agree with you, Bob; but let us say no more about it. I will be with you at ten o'clock, which you say is the hour that you go to church."

This conversation took place on the morning of the wedding. About eight o'clock, I dressed and breakfasted, and then took a wherry over to Gosport, and in half an hour was at the house, which was full of people with white favours, and in such a bustle, that it reminded me of a hive of bees just previous to a swarm.

"Here's the captain come, sir," said Bob, who had received me; for the bride was still in her room with her mother.

"Happy to see you, sir; I wish you joy, Mr Waghorn," replied I, taking his hand.

"You're Captain Keene, then, whose letters to the Admiralty Jane has so often read to me in the newspapers. Where have we met? I've heard that voice before."

"Indeed sir," replied I, rather confused.

"Yes, I have; I always know a voice again; let me see—why, captain, you were here with Cross, the first time I ever heard him—you were an agent, and now you're a captain," continued the old man, looking very grave.

"Hush, sir," replied I: "pray don't speak so loud. Do you recollect what I came about? Do you suppose that when I was a party to the escape of a prisoner I could let you know, being a perfect stranger, that I was an officer in his Majesty's service?"

"Very true," replied the old man, "I cannot blame you for that. But was Cross an officer in the service at that time?"

"No, sir, he was not," replied I; "he was appointed boatswain to my ship by the admiral in the West Indies."

"I'm glad to hear that. I thought Cross might have deceived me also; every one tries to cheat a blind man—and the blind are suspicious. I'm glad that Cross did not deceive me, or I would have seen my niece in her coffin before—but say no more about it, you could not do otherwise; all's right, sir, and I'm very glad to see you, and to have the honour of your company. Sit down, sir, I beg. By the bye, Captain Keene, have you heard of the girl since?"

"My dear sir," replied I, glad to give him my confidence, "there are no secrets between us now; it was no girl, but the son of the captain of the Dutch frigate, and an officer, whose escape you assisted in."

"I don't wonder, then, at your not making yourself known," replied the old man. "Why, if I had known it had been an officer, I never would have had a hand in the job—but a poor girl, it was mere charity to assist her, and I thought I was acting the part of a Christian, poor blind sinner that I am."

"You did a kind act, sir, and Heaven will reward you."

"We are sad, wicked creatures, Captain Keene," replied he. "I wish this day was over, and my poor Jane made happy; and then I should have nothing to do but to read my Bible, and prepare for being called away; it's never too soon, depend upon it, sir."

The appearance of the bride with her bridesmaids put an end to our conversation, which I was not sorry for. The order of march was arranged, and we started off for the church on foot, making a very long and very gay procession. In half an hour it was all over, and we returned. I then had an opportunity of telling Cross what had passed between me and old Waghorn.

"It was touch and go, sir, that's sartin," replied Bob; "for if the old gentleman had not been satisfied, he is so obstinate that the match would have been broken off at the church door. Well, sir, I always said that you were the best to get out of a scrape that I ever knew when you were a middy, and you don't appear to have lost the talent; it was well managed."

"Perhaps so, Bob; but in future I do not intend to get into them, which will be managing better still." I then left Cross, and went to talk to Jane, who certainly looked very handsome. The tables for dinner were laid out in the garden, for it was a beautiful warm autumnal day. We sat down about twenty, and a merrier party I never was at. Old Waghorn was the only one who got tipsy on the occasion, and it was very ridiculous to hear him quoting scraps of Scripture in extenuation, and then calling himself a poor blind old sinner. It was not till eight o'clock in the evening that the party broke up, and I had then some difficulty to persuade some to go away. As for the old man, he had been put to bed an hour before. I staid a few minutes after all were gone, and then, kissing Jane, and shaking hands with Bob, I went back to Portsmouth.

Chapter Thirty Four

As soon as I was at home again, the events of the day, from association of ideas, naturally brought Minnie Vanderwelt into my head, and I recollected that I had not written to her since my promotion and appointment to the Circe; I therefore sat down and indited a long letter, ending with expressing my regret at not having received an answer from the many I had written, especially the last, which informed them of my arrival in England, and gave them the knowledge where to address me. I also requested to know what had become of young Vangilt, whose escape I had contrived. Having enclosed that letter to the agent, and begged him to have it forwarded to Hamburg, I went to bed, and, after the excitement of the day, had a variety of dreams, in which Minnie's form was continually making its appearance.

The following morning brought me a long letter from my aunt, Mrs Bridgeman, very lively and very amusing: the only news in it was the marriage of Lieutenant Flat to a tavern-keeper's daughter, which had given great offence to the marine corps, as she was said to be rather light of carriage. She begged me very much to pay them a visit, but that was not all to my wishes, I most candidly confess. My pride revolted at it; I even doubt if I would have fitted out a ship at Chatham where people could point their finger at me, and say—That post-captain's father was a marine in those barracks. Another letter from Lord de Versely, announcing his arrival at Madeline Hall, and requesting me to join him as soon as possible, was infinitely more to my taste, and I resolved to start next day, which I did. I was very cordially received by his lordship, and very graciously by the old lady, who expressed a hope that I would now make a long visit. About an hour after I had arrived, Colonel Delmar made his appearance: he was a cousin of Lord de Versely's, but I certainly should not, from his appearance, have supposed him to be a Delmar: for he was short, round-shouldered, and with a fat, rubicund face, apparently about forty years of age. I observed, after our introduction, that his eyes were very often directed towards me; but his manner was courteous, and, although his appearance at first sight was not prepossessing, his conversation was very agreeable, and he was very gentleman-like. Before dinner was over, I felt a great liking for him.

As the first of September had not yet arrived, the birds had still two days of peace and quietness, leading their broods through the stubbles, and pointing out to them the corn which had spilled on the ground, for their food. That the old birds had some idea of a gun, it is to be supposed, from their having escaped the season before; but the young coveys had still that pleasure to come; in two days more they were to be initiated into the astonishing fact, that fast as feathers could fly, lead could fly faster, and overtake them.

The two or three days before the shooting season begins are invariably very tedious in the country, and I passed my morning chiefly in roaming through the park and pleasure grounds, and I hardly need say that, during those rambles, my thoughts were chiefly occupied with the intimacy which had taken place between my mother and Lord de Versely. On the third morning after my arrival I had been strolling for more than two hours, when I came to a very retired sort of Gothic cell, formed of the distended limbs of an old oak, intermixed with stones and grass. It faced towards the park, and was built up on the green lawn amidst clumps of laurel and other evergreens. I threw myself on the benches. It was just the place for a man to select for a rendezvous: just the secret spot where a maiden could listen without trembling at intruders; and it struck me that this must have been the trysting place of my parents. For an hour I remained there, castle-building for the future, and musing on the past, when I heard a voice, close to me on the other side of the cell, the back of which was turned towards the hall. I knew the voice to be that of the old lady, who, it appears, had, as usual, come out in her garden chair, and was dragged by her attendant, Phillis: the wheels had made no noise on the velvet lawn, and, until roused by her voice, I was not aware of their approach.

"Nonsense, Phillis; why, child, what should you know about such things?" said the old lady.

"If you please to recollect, ma'am," replied Phillis, who certainly was old enough to recollect all the passages in a woman's life, "I was your maid at the time that it happened, and I was constantly in company with Bella Mason. She was very respectful towards you, but you did not know what her temper was; there never was so proud a young woman, or who considered herself of such consequence as she did—so much so, that she treated even Mr Jonas, the butler, and Mrs Short, the housekeeper, with disdain."

"Well, well, I know that she was proud; her mother was always a proud woman. Mr Mason, in his younger days, held property of his own, at least his father did, but he ran through it revelling and horse-racing; but what does that prove?"

"I only say, madam, what was said at the time by everybody, that Bella Mason never would have married that marine, whom she looked upon with contempt, although he certainly was a good-looking young man, if she had not been obliged to do so."

"But why obliged, Phillis?"

"To conceal her shame, madam; for, if you recollect, the child was born three months after marriage."

"I recollect that, very well," replied Miss Delmar; "it was a sad thing, and, as my nephew said, I ought to have looked out sharper after Bella than I did, and not have allowed her to be so much in company with that marine."

"That marine, ma'am! he was innocent enough; Bella was not likely to listen to one like him."

"Who can you mean then, Phillis?"

"Why, Lord de Versely, ma'am, to be sure. Everybody in the Hall was sure the child was his; he and Bella were for ever together for months before her marriage."

"Phillis, Phillis, you don't know what you are saying—it's impossible; indeed, I recollect talking the matter over with Lord de Versely, who was then Captain Delmar, and he was more shocked at the impropriety than even I was, and offered to give the marine a good whipping."

"That may be, madam, but still Captain Delmar was the father of that boy; for, if you recollect, old Mrs Mason came to the Hall, and went away almost immediately."

"Well, what of that? she was displeased no doubt."

"Yes, indeed she was, madam; but she had a private meeting with Captain Delmar; and Mrs Short, the housekeeper, overheard what passed, and I understand that the captain did not deny it to her. One thing is certain, that Mrs Mason, as she was going away, in her rage made use of language about Captain Delmar, which otherwise she never would have dared. And, then, madam, only look at Captain Keene,—why, he is the very image of his lordship."

"He is very like him, certainly," said the old lady, musing.

"And then, madam, do you think his lordship would have brought the boy up in the service, and made him a post-captain, if he had been the son of a marine? And then, madam, see how fond his lordship is of him; why, he dotes upon him; and would he ask the son of his own servant to come down to Madeline Hall, as fit company for you? No; so, madam, depend upon it,

Captain Keene is a Delmar, and no wonder his lordship is so fond of him, madam; for he is his only child, and I dare say his lordship would give him his right hand if he could leave him the barony and estates, instead of them going away, as they will, to his younger brother's children."

"Well, well, Phillis, it may be so. I don't know what to think of it. I shall speak to Lord de Versely about it; for if Captain Keene is a Delmar, he must be looked to. He is a Delmar, although with the bar sinister. I feel a little cold, Phillis, so drag me to the terrace, that I may get a little sunshine."

Phillis, I thank thee, said I to myself, as the chair wheeled away. Your love of chatting may be useful to me. Perhaps his lordship may now acknowledge my birth to his aunt, and good may come of it. I waited till the chair wheels were heard on the gravel walk, and then quitted the grotto, and bent my steps away from the Hall, that I might commune with my own thoughts without chance of interruption.

I had quitted the park, and was now pacing over several fields, one after another, walking as if I had some important business in hand, when in fact, my legs were only trying to keep pace with my thoughts, when I vaulted over a gate, and found myself in a narrow lane, sunk deep between two hedges. Indifferent as to the path I took, I turned to the right, and continued on my way, walking as fast as before, when I heard the low bellowing of an animal. This induced me to raise my eyes, and I witnessed a curious scene in front of me, which I will narrate in the next chapter.

Chapter Thirty Five

As I said before, the lane was very narrow, not admitting more than one vehicle to go along it, and was sunk between the hedges on each side, so as to render it not very easy to climb up the bank. The parties who presented themselves were, first a cow with her tail turned towards me, evidently a wicked one, as she was pawing and bellowing in a low tone, and advancing towards two people who were the object of her attack. One was a very little man, dressed in black, the other a stout burly young fellow in a shooting-jacket; but what amused me most was, that the stout young fellow, instead of being in the advance to defend one so much smaller than himself, not only kept behind the little man, but actually now and then held him by the shoulders before his own person, as a shield to ward off the expected attack of the vicious animal. It is true that the little personage expostulated, and spoke several times in a tone of command to his companion, but his words were unheeded, and the cow advanced, and they retreated in the order which I have described.

I quickened my pace, so as to gain rapidly upon them, and was soon but a few yards from the animal. I had no stick or weapon of any kind, but still I knew how to manage unruly cattle as sailors do when they were sent on board ship alive. Indeed I had more than once put it into practice myself; and although with a bull it was not a very easy matter, with a cow I felt certain that I could effect my purpose.

The animal appeared now determined to come to close quarters; and I therefore approached her until I was about a couple of feet from her flank, all ready for a spring, in case she should see me, and turn round. But she was too busy with the parties in front of her, and at last she made a run. The stout young man pushed the little man towards the cow, and then ran for it. The little one, in his attempt to recoil, fell on the turf, and the cow made at him. I sprang forward, and catching the horn of the animal farthest from me in my right hand, at the same time put my left knee on the horn nearest to me, threw all my weight upon it, so as to turn the animal's nose up in the air, and seizing it by the nostrils with the other hand, I held her head in that position, which of course rendered the animal harmless. In that position the cow went over the prostrate man without doing him any injury, plunging and capering, so as to extricate herself from my weight. I remained clinging to her for about ten yards further, when I perceived the stout fellow ahead, who hallooed out, "Hold her tight! hold her tight!" but that I would no longer do, as it was fatiguing work; so, as a punishment for his cowardice, I let go the animal, springing clear off, and behind it, the cow galloping away as fast as she could down the lane, and the fellow screaming and running before as fast as he could.

Having thus rid myself of the cow and the coward, I turned back to where the other party had been left on the ground, and found him standing up, and looking at what was passing. "You're not hurt, sir?" said I.

"No, thanks to you; but no thanks to that rascally clerk of mine, who wanted to shove me on the cow's horns to save himself."

"He has a run for it now, at all events;" replied I, laughing, "and I let the cow loose on purpose; for if I had held on, and used all my strength, I could have brought her down on her side and kept her down. Oh! there's a break in the bank, and he has climbed up it, so he is safe for a good fright," continued I; "and now we had better get away ourselves; for the animal may come back, and, although one can pin her in that way from behind, it is not to be done when she comes stem on to you."

"Well, sir, I have heard of taking the bull by the horns as not being a very wise thing; but taking a cow by them has probably saved my life. I thank you."

"We manage them that way on board ship," replied I, laughing.

"You are a sailor, then, sir," replied the little man. "Probably I have the pleasure of addressing Captain Keene?"

"That is my name," replied I; "but here is the cow coming back, and the sooner we get to the gate the better. I'm not ashamed to run for it, and I suppose you are not either." So saying, I took to my heels, followed by my new companion, and we very soon put the barred gate between us and our enemy.

"I will wish you good day now, sir," said I; "I am going to the Hall."

"I am also bound there, Captain Keene," replied my companion, "and, with your permission, will accompany you. Egad, we may meet another cow," said he, laughing, "and I prefer being in your company."

He then informed me that he was the solicitor and agent of the Honourable Miss Delmar, and had been sent for about some new leases, and that his name was Warden. During our walk I found him a very cheerful, merry little man, and a very good companion.

On our arrival at the Hall, Mr Warden was informed that Miss Delmar was not able to receive him just then, as she was very busy with Lord de Versely, who was with her in her private room. I therefore remained with Mr Warden for about an hour, when Lord de Versely came down and joined us. He appeared to be in a remarkable gay humour, and shook me warmly by the hand when he came in.

"Now, Mr Warden, you are to go up and receive your instructions, and recollect, the sooner everything is executed the better."

Mr Warden left the room, and I narrated to his lordship the adventure with the cow. Just as I had begun it, Colonel Delmar came in, and listened to my narration.

In about half an hour Mr Warden came down-stairs, and with a very smiling face.

"Well, Mr Warden," said his lordship, "have you your instructions?"

"Yes, my lord and I assure you that I never shall execute any with so much pleasure. Has Captain Keene told you how he saved my life this morning?"

"No, he did not say that," replied his lordship; "but he has told me about the cow, and your clerk putting you foremost in the breach."

"She would have made a breach in me I expect, if it had not been for the captain," replied Mr Warden; "and you may therefore believe me, my lord, when I say that I shall obey my instructions with pleasure. I wish you good morning. Good morning, Captain Keene. Colonel, your most obedient." So saying, Mr Warden left the room. I was very much struck with Mr Warden's observation, that he would execute his instructions with so much pleasure; and when I turned round, I perceived that Colonel Delmar was looking very grave; but the first dinner bell rang, and we all went to our rooms to dress. Well, thought I, as I was dressing myself, I presume the old lady has left me a thousand or two in her will. I cared little about that, and then I dismissed the subject from my thoughts; but as I sat by Miss Delmar after dinner, I could not help thinking that her manner towards me was more affectionate than it had been before; the *hauteur* with which her civility and kindness had hitherto been blended appeared to have been thrown aside; I presumed that Lord de Versely had been speaking in my favour, and felt grateful to him for his kindness. Perhaps, thought I, he has revealed to her the secret of my birth, and she now considers me as a relation; perhaps she may have left me more than I supposed. However, it is of little consequence.

Chapter Thirty Six

The next day, being the first of September, we were all very busy, and we continued to shoot every day for a week, when I thought it time to return to Portsmouth. I mentioned my intentions to Lord de Versely, and was pressed to stay until the following Saturday, it being then Tuesday. On Wednesday Mr Warden made his appearance, attended by his clerk, who carried a bag of papers. He remained half an hour and then went home; but, before he went, he asked me to dine with him on the following day, and I consented.

After we returned from shooting the next day, I changed my clothes, and, leaving word with the butler that I dined out, I took my way across the fields. I was walking very quietly on the grass, by the side of a high hedge, when I perceived two other men on the opposite side; one I recognised as Colonel Delmar; the other I could not at first make out; but, as I approached them, I perceived that the colonel was talking with the clerk of Mr Warden. I passed them without notice, for they were very earnestly engaged in conversation. What they said, I did not know; but I thought it singular that so proud a person as Colonel Delmar should be so engaged with an inferior; a little reflection, however made me consider that there was nothing very surprising in Colonel Delmar's entering into conversation with a man in the country. They might be talking about the game, or a hundred other things.

I had a very friendly dinner with Mr Warden, who, after dinner, gave me a hint that I should not be the worse for the papers signed the day before. He did not however, say anything positive, as it would have been a breach of trust. When I spoke of my soon being afloat again, he said that he would not fail to watch over my interests at the Hall during my absence, and he requested that I would write to him, and consider him as my sincere friend. "Of course, my dear Captain Keene, I do not expect that you will at present give me your entire confidence; but I trust you will when you know me, and at all events that you will not fail to do so when my advice may be of use to you. I have a debt of obligation to pay, and I shall be most happy to do so, if it is in my power!" I thanked Mr Warden for his kind offers, and promised to avail myself of them, and we parted great friends.

The next day, Friday, we had a large addition to our shooting party. I had not been out more than an hour, when, as I was standing near Lord de Versely, who was re-loading his gun, a report, close to us, was heard, and I fell down close to his feet, apparently dead. A keeper, who was with us, ran to see who had discharged the gun, and found that it was Colonel Delmar, who now ran up to us, stating, in hurried terms, to Lord de Versely, that his gun had gone off accidentally as he was putting on a copper cap, and bitterly lamenting the circumstance. Lord de Versely was at the time kneeling down by my side (as I was afterwards informed), showing the greatest anxiety and grief. My hat had been taken off; it was full of blood and the back of my head was much torn with the shot. I remained insensible, although breathing heavily; a gate was taken off its hinges, and I was laid upon it, and carried to the Hall.

Before the surgeon had arrived, I had recovered my senses. On examination, I had had a very narrow escape; the better part of the charge of shot had entered the back part of my head, but fortunately not any had penetrated through the skull. After a tedious hour, employed in extracting this load, my head was bound up, and I was made comfortable in my bed. I must say that Lord de Versely and Colonel Delmar vied with each other in their attentions to me; the latter constantly accusing himself as the author of the mischief, and watching by my bed the major part of the day.

This accident delayed my departure, and it was not until three weeks afterwards, that I was sufficiently recovered to leave my room. In the meantime, Lord de Versely, assured that I was out of danger, went back to London. The colonel, however, remained. His kindness and attention had given me great pleasure, and we had become very intimate. He had offered to go with me to Portsmouth, and I had expressed the pleasure I should have in his company. The Honourable Miss Delmar had shown the greatest feeling and anxiety for me during my illness; so had Mr Warden, who often called to see me; in fact, I found myself so surrounded by well-wishers and friends, that I hardly regretted my accident.

At the end of the fifth week, I was sufficiently recovered to be able to return to Portsmouth, where I was now very anxious to arrive, as the Circe had been launched and had already received her lower masts. I took my leave of Miss Delmar, who requested my early return to Madeline Hall, and, accompanied by Colonel Delmar, was once more established at Billett's Hotel.

Bob Cross was the first who made his appearance; for I had written to him to acquaint him with my intended return. He had heard of my narrow escape, as it had been put into the newspaper; his information was trifling, but to the purpose. All was right as to the frigate: she sat on the water like a duck; the rigging was far advanced, and the officers seemed of the right sort. All was right, also, as to his matrimonial affairs; his wife was every thing he wished; the old gentleman was as sweet as molasses, and he had laid the keel of a young Cross. We then entered upon business, and I gave him some directions as to the rigging, and he left me.

The next morning, the first lieutenant called to pay his respects, and his appearance and conversation proved him to be what he had been recommended as, a good seaman and a brave man. I went with him to the dockyard to look at the frigate in the basin, and afterwards on board the hulk to see the other officers and the men, who had been entered. I had every reason to be satisfied, and I then returned to the hotel, to dine with Colonel Delmar. This officer appeared to have taken a strong interest in me, and ever since the accident of his gun going off, which had so nearly been fatal to me, was unbounded in his professions of regard. I must say, that a more gentleman-like or more amusing companion I never met with. A great intimacy was established between us; he was constantly making me presents of value, which I would fain have prevented his doing; occasionally, when we were alone, he would hint something about my family and parentage; but this was a subject upon which I was invariably silent, and I immediately changed the conversation; once only I replied, that my father and mother were both dead.

On my arrival at Portsmouth, I found several letters waiting for me, and among them two or three from my mother, who had seen the report in the newspaper of the escape that I had had, and, of course, was excessively anxious to hear from my own hand how I was. Had I thought that it would have come to her knowledge, I certainly should have written to my grandmother from Madeline Hall; but I imagined that she knew nothing about it, until my return to Portsmouth, when her anxious letters proved the contrary; for in her anxiety she had quite forgotten her promise that all communication should be through my grandmother.

As soon as I had read the letters I locked them up in my desk, and hastened to reply to them, assuring my mother of my perfect restoration to health, and cautioned her not to break through the agreement we had made for the future, pointing out to her that had these letters been forwarded to Madeline Hall, her handwriting would have been recognised. I said, in conclusion, "I must say, my dear mother, that I now heartily repent that we should have resorted to the step we have done in pretending that you are dead. That some advantage was gained by it at the time, I really believe; but I have a feeling that eventually some mischief may occur from it. I hope I may be mistaken; but if I am not, it will only be the punishment which I deserve for an act of duplicity which I have repented of ever since."

Chapter Thirty Seven

My time was now fully employed during the day in fitting out the frigate; but in the evening I generally dined out at the admiral's or at the officers' mess. I received several invitations from the marine mess to dine with them; but I always contrived to be engaged, for I was fearful that something might be said relative to my putative father, Ben, which might hurt my pride. Not that I had any reason to suppose that any of the officers would have been guilty of any such rudeness; but as a great deal of wine was drank when company were at the mess, and there were many young men there, it was possible that, having the knowledge, they might in their cups say something which they never would have done when they were sober. The colonel very often dined there, and constantly asked me why I refused. My reply was certainly not the truth, for I said that I was not very partial to marine officers.

We had been three weeks at Portsmouth when Colonel Delmar received a letter from a friend of his, a Major Stapleton, which he read aloud to me at breakfast. It stated that the major would be down at Portsmouth the next day, and requested the colonel to procure him good rooms. "He is an excellent fellow, the major," continued the colonel, "and will be a great addition to our society. I will prevail upon him to stay a week or ten days."

On my return from the dock-yard on the following day, I found the colonel and Major Stapleton in our sitting-room, and was introduced to him. He was a small, neatly-made man, with handsome features, very well dressed, and of very fashionable appearance. Still there was something in his eye which did not please me; it was unsettled and wandering, and never fixed upon you for more than a second. He met me with great warmth and *empressement*, shook me by the hand, and declared what pleasure he had in making my acquaintance. We sat down to dinner, and were very merry.

The major had been with us a week, when we had a large party to dinner. The wine was passed freely, and we all were more or less elated. The major appeared particularly so, and very much inclined to be quarrelsome, and as he constantly addressed himself to me, I was very cautious in what I said, as I perceived that he was in the humour to take offence at anything. Several very offensive remarks were made by him, as if to pick a quarrel between us, but I parried them as well as I could, and I was making an observation, when the major started up, and told me that what I said was a lie, and that I was a scoundrel for having said so.

Now, as my observation was to my first lieutenant, and was in reference to the hold of the frigate, there could be no cause for this insult, and it could only be ascribed to his being in a state of intoxication. My reply was very cool and quiet: "Major, you do not know what you are saying; but we will talk about it to-morrow morning." I then rose and went to my bed-room, and the whole party broke up immediately.

Shortly afterwards, Colonel Delmar came into my room, and blaming the major very much for his conduct, ascribed it to intoxication and said that he would make him send a proper apology, which he had no doubt the next morning, when the major was informed of what he had done, he would be most anxious to offer himself.

I replied, that I presumed so; and he quitted my room. Indeed, so fully was I convinced of this in my own mind, that I gave it no further thought, and was soon fast asleep, and did not wake until Colonel Delmar entered my room at a late hour.

"Well, colonel," said I.

"My dear Keene," said he, "I have been to the major, and, to my surprise, when I stated to him what had passed at the table last night, his reply was, that he perfectly remembered all about it and that he would not retract what he had said. I remonstrated with him, but in vain. He says, that it is cowardly to retract, and that he will never make an apology."

"Then," replied I, "there is but one step for me to take."

"As our friend, I told him so, and pressed him very hard to acknowledge his error, but he continued steadfast in his refusal. I then took upon myself to say that I was there as your friend, and begged he would name an officer to whom I might address myself. Did I not right, my dear Keene?"

"Certainly; and I am very much obliged to you," replied I, putting on my dressing-gown.

"He must be mad, utterly and positively mad!" exclaimed Colonel Delmar; "I regret very much that he has ever come here. I know that some years ago, when he was younger, he fought two or three duels rather than make an apology; but in this instance it was so unprovoked, and I had hoped that he had got over all that nonsense and obstinacy. Are you a good shot, Keene? because he is a notorious one."

"I can hit my man, colonel; it is true that I have only fought one duel in my life, and would make a great sacrifice rather than fight another; but no alternative is left me in this case; and if blood is shed, it must be on the head of him who provoked it."

"Very true," replied Colonel Delmar, biting his lip; "I only hope you will be successful."

"I have no particular animosity against Major Stapleton," replied I; "but as he is such a good shot, I shall in my own defence take good aim at him. At all events, I have sufficient acquaintance with fire-arms, and have passed through too many bullets not to be cool and collected under fire, and I therefore consider myself quite a match for the major. Now, colonel, if you will order the breakfast, I will be down in ten minutes or a quarter of an hour."

As the colonel was going out of the room, his servant knocked at the door, and said that Captain Green wished to speak to him on particular business; I therefore did not hurry myself, but proceeded quietly with my toilet, as I was well aware what the particular business was, and that the conference might last some time. On my descending into the sitting-room I found the colonel alone.

"Well, Keene," said he, "everything is arranged, for the major is deaf to all expostulation. You are to meet this evening, and, to avoid interference, Captain Green and I have agreed to say that the major has apologised, and all is made up." Of course I had no objection to make to that, and we parted for the present, I walking to the dock-yard, and he remaining at the hotel to write letters.

The reader may think that I took matters very coolly; but the fact was, I had no preparations to make in case of accident, having no wife or family, and as to any other preparations at such a time, I considered them as mockery. I knew that I was about to do what was wrong—to offend my Creator—and knowing that, and sinning with my eyes open, much as I regretted that I was compelled to do so, I was still resolved upon doing it. How great may be the culpability in such cases when you are called upon to sacrifice all your worldly interests, and to be despised among men, or run the risk of involuntarily taking another person's life, I could not pretend to judge; but one thing was certain, that, however it may be judged in the next world, in this, among soldiers and sailors, it will always be considered as venial. I did, therefore, what most in my profession would have done under the same circumstances. I drove it from my thoughts as much as possible, until the time came to decide my fate. I considered that I must be judged by the tenor of my whole life, and that repentance, under chance of death, was of about the same value as death-bed repentance.

As soon as the dock-yard men were mustered out, I returned to the hotel, and sat down to dinner with the colonel. We had scarcely finished a bottle of claret when it was time to be off. We walked out of the town, to the place appointed, where I found my adversary and his second. The ground was marked out by the colonel, and, when I took my station, I found that the setting sun was in my eyes. I pointed it out to him, and requested my position might be changed. The other second heard me do so, and very handsomely agreed that I was entitled to what I asked, and the colonel immediately apologised for his remissness to my interests. The ground was then marked out in another direction, and the colonel took me to my place, where I observed that one of the white-washed posts was exactly behind me, making me a sure mark for my antagonist. "I am not used to these things, Keene," replied Colonel Delmar, "and I make strange mistakes." I then pointed out a direction which would be fair for both parties. The pistols were then loaded, and put into our hands. We fired at the signal. I felt that I was hit, but my adversary fell. I was paralysed; and although I remained on my feet, I could not move. Captain Green and the colonel went up to where my adversary lay: the ball had passed through his chest.

"He is dead," said Captain Green—"quite dead."

"Yes," replied Colonel Delmar. "My dear Keene, I congratulate you: you have killed the greatest scoundrel that ever disgraced his Majesty's uniform."

"Colonel Delmar," replied Captain Green, "the observation might well be spared: our errors and our follies die with us."

"Very true, Captain Green," replied I. "I can only express my surprise that the colonel should have introduced to me a person whose memory he now so bitterly assails." Somehow or another, from the commencement of the duel, Colonel Delmar's conduct had excited my suspicions, and a hundred things crowded into my memory, which appeared as if illumined like a flash of lightning. I came suddenly to the conviction that he was my enemy, and not my friend. But I was bleeding fast: some marines, who were passing, were summoned, and the body of Major Stapleton was carried away by one party, while I was committed to another, and taken back to the hotel. The surgeon was sent for, and my wound was not dangerous. The ball had gone deep into my thigh, but had missed any vessel of magnitude. It was extracted, and I was left quiet in bed. Colonel Delmar came up to me as before, but I received his professions with great coolness. I told him that I thought it would be prudent of him to disappear until the affair had blown over; but he declared to me that he would remain with me at every risk. Shortly afterwards, Captain Green came into my room, and said, "I'm sure, Captain Keene, you will be glad to hear that Major Stapleton is not dead. He had swooned, and is now come to, and the doctor thinks favourably of him."

"I am indeed very glad, Captain Green; for I had no animosity against the major, and his conduct to me has been quite incomprehensible."

After inquiry about my wound, and expressing a hope that I should soon be well, Captain Green left; but I observed that he took no further notice of Colonel Delmar than a haughty salute as he quitted the room; and then, to my surprise, Colonel Delmar said that, upon consideration, he thought it would be advisable for him to go away for a certain time.

"I agree with you," replied I; "it would be better." I said this, because I did not wish his company; for it at once struck me as very strange that he should, now that Major Stapleton was alive and promising to do well, talk of departure, when he refused at the time he supposed him to be killed. I was therefore very glad when in an hour or two afterwards he took his leave, and started, as he said, for London.

Chapter Thirty Eight

My recovery was rapid: in less than a fortnight I was on the sofa. The frigate was now rigged, and had taken in her water and stores, and was reported ready for sea in a month, as we still required about forty men to make up our complement. I saw a great deal of Captain Green, who paid me a visit almost every day; and once, when our conversation turned upon the duel, I made the same remark as I did when Colonel Delmar used such harsh language over the body of Major Stapleton. "Yes," replied Captain Green, "I thought it was my duty to tell him what Colonel Delmar had said. He was very much excited, and replied, 'The *greatest* scoundrel, did he say?—then is the devil better than those he tempts; however, we are both in each other's power. I must get well first, and then I will act.' There certainly is some mystery, the attack was so unprovoked, the determination so positive. Have you any reason to suppose that Colonel Delmar is your enemy, Captain Keene? for certainly he did appear to me to do all he could at the time of the duel to give your adversary the advantage."

"I really have no cause to suppose that he has grounds for being my enemy; but I cannot help suspecting that, for some reason or reasons unknown, he is so."

When Captain Green had left me, I tried all I could to find out why Colonel Delmar should be inimical to me. That he was the supposed heir to Miss Delmar I knew; but surely her leaving me a few thousands was not sufficient cause for a man to seek my life. Lord de Versely had nothing to leave; I could come to no conclusion that was at all satisfactory. I then thought whether I would write to Lord de Versely, and tell him what had happened; but I decided that I would not. The initials had been put in the papers at the announcement of the duel, and, had he seen them, he certainly would have written down to inquire about the facts. My mother had so done, and I resolved that I would answer her letter, which had hitherto remained on the table. I sent for my desk, and when my servant brought it me, the bunch of keys were hanging to the lock. I thought this strange, as I had locked my desk before I went out to meet Major Stapleton, and had never sent for it since my return; my servant, however, could tell me nothing about it, except that he found it as he brought it to me; but after a little time, he recollected that the doctor had asked for a pen and ink to write a prescription, and that the colonel had taken the keys to get him what he required. This accounted for it, and nothing more was said upon the subject. Of course, although it was known, no notice was taken of what had passed by the Admiralty. I had not even put myself down in the sick report, but signed my daily papers, and sent them into the admiral's office as if nothing had happened.

In six weeks I was able to limp about a little, and the Circe was at last reported ready for sea. My orders came down, and I was to sail with the first fair wind to join the squadron in the Texel and North Sea. I had taken up my quarters on board, and was waiting two days, while the wind still blew hard from the eastward, when my promise to write to Mr Warden occurred to me; and, as I had closed all my despatches to Lord de Versely — the Honourable Miss Delmar, to whom I made my excuse for not being able to pay my respects before my departure—my mother, and my aunt Bridgeman—I resolved that I would write him a long letter previous to my sailing. I did so, in which I entered into the whole affair of the duel, the conduct of Colonel Delmar, and my suspicions relative to him; stating, at the same time, that I could not comprehend why he should have sought to injure me. I finished this letter late in the evening, and the next morning, the wind having come round, we sailed for our destination.

Once more on the water, all my thoughts were given to the service. We soon fell in with the North Sea squadron, and the day afterwards the Circe was directed to go on shore in company with the Dryad, and watch the flotillas of gun-boats which had been collecting in the various rivers and ports; to sink, burn, and destroy to the utmost of our power. This was an active and dangerous service, as the enemy had every advantage in the sands and shoals, and hardly a day passed in which we were not engaged with the flotillas and batteries. It was, however, now fine weather, for the winter had set in early, and had passed away, and for two months we continued in the service, during which my skip's company were well trained. One morning a cutter from the fleet was reported from the mast-head, and we expected that we should soon have our letters from England, when the Dryad threw out the signal for six sail of praams in shore.

The two frigates made all sail in chase, leaving the cutter to follow us how she could. Our masters were well acquainted with the shoals on the coast, and we threaded our way through them towards the enemy. We were within gun-shot, and had exchanged broadsides with the batteries, when the flotillas gained a small harbour, which prevented our making any further attempts. The Dryad made the signal to haul off; it was quite time, as we had not more than four hours' daylight, and were entangled among the shoals. The breeze, which had been fresh, now increased very rapidly, and there was every appearance of a gale. We worked out as fast as we could, and by nine o'clock in the evening we were clear of the sands, and in the open sea; but the gale had sprung up so rapidly that we were obliged to reduce our sail to close-reefed topsails. With the sands under our lee, it was necessary to draw off as fast as we could, and we therefore carried a heavy press of sail all the night—at last, the wind was so strong that we could only carry close-reefed maintop-sail and reefed fore-sail; and with a heavy sea, which had risen up, we felt that we were in extreme danger.

Daylight once more made its appearance. Our first object was to ascertain the position of the Dryad. For a long time we looked in vain; at last, a partial clearing up of the horizon on the lee bow discovered her, looming through the heavy atmosphere, more like a phantom ship than the work of mortal hands. She was a deep grey mass upon a lighter grey ground. Her top-masts were gone, and she was pitching and rising without appearing to advance under her courses and storm staysails.

"There she is, sir," said Mr Wilson; "and if the gale lasts, good-bye to her."

"If the gale lasts, Mr Wilson," said I in a low voice, "I suspect you may sing our requiem as well; but we must trust to Heaven and our own exertions. Pass along the lead-line, Mr Hawkins."

"Aye, aye, sir," replied the officer of the watch; "how much out sir?"

"Forty fathoms."

The men ranged themselves along the lee-bulwarks, chains, and gangway and passed the deep sea-lines from aft to the anchor stock forward. The deep sea lead was taken forward, and as soon as it was bent and ready, the ship was thrown up to the wind so as to check her way. "Heave," and the lead was thrown, and as it descended the line was dropped from the hands of the men, one after another, as the line drew aft; but when it came to the hands of the master, who was on the quarter, instead of finding, as he expected, forty fathoms of water, he had to haul in the slack line for such a length of time, that the lead was astern and no proper soundings could be obtained.

One thing was, however, certain, which was, that we were in much shallower water than we had any idea of; and the master, much alarmed, desired the quarter-master to go into the chains and see if he could get soundings with the hand-lead while the men were hauling in the deep sea-line. The quarter-master was forestalled by Bob Cross who, dropping into the chains, cleared the line, and swinging it but twice or thrice, for there was little or no way in the vessel, let it go.

The anxiety with which the descent of the line was watched by me, the master, and other of the officers who were hanging over the hammock rails, it would be difficult to describe. When sixteen fathoms were out the lead sounded. Cross gathered up the slack line, and fourteen and a half fathoms was announced.

"Mr Hillyer," said I, "oblige me by coming down into the cabin." The master followed me immediately. The chart was on the table in the fore-cabin.

"We must have gone to leeward dreadfully, sir."

"Yes," replied I; "but the sweep of the currents in heavy gales is so tremendous, and so uncertain on this coast, that I am not surprised. We must have had a South East current, and probably we are hereabouts," continued I, putting the point of the compass upon the spot.

"It seems hardly possible, sir," replied the master; "but still I fear it must be so; and if so," continued he, drawing a deep sigh, "I'm afraid it's all over with us, without a miracle in our favour."

"I am of your opinion, Mr Hillyer; but say nothing about it," replied I; "the gale *may* moderate, the wind *may* shift, and if so we *may* be saved. At all events, it's no use telling bad news too soon, and therefore you'll oblige me by not saying anything on the subject. A few hours will decide our fate."

"But the Dryad, she is good four miles to the leeward of us, and the soundings decrease here so rapidly, that in an hour, with the sail she is under, she must go on shore."

"She has no chance, that's certain," replied I. "I only hope it may be so thick that we may not see her."

"Not a soul will be saved, sir," replied the master, shuddering. "I should say it were impossible, Mr Hillyer; but we all owe Heaven a death; and if they go first and we go after them, at all events, let us do our duty until the time comes—but never despair. As long as there is life, there is hope; so now let us go on deck, and put as good a face on it as we can."

Chapter Thirty Nine

I returned on deck followed by the master. "The barometer is rising," said I aloud, to the first lieutenant; "so I presume the gale will break about twelve o'clock."

"I am glad to hear of it, sir; for we have quite enough of it," replied the first-lieutenant.

"Do you see the Dryad?"

"No, sir; it's quite thick again to leeward: we have not seen her these ten minutes."

Thank God for that, thought I, for they will never see her again. "What soundings had you last?"

"Fourteen fathoms, sir."

"I expect we shall cross the tail of the bank in much less," replied I; "but, when once clear, we shall have sea-room."

As the captain is an oracle in times of danger, the seamen caught every word which was uttered from my mouth; and what they gathered from what I had said, satisfied them that they were in no immediate danger. Nevertheless, the master walked the deck as if he was stupefied with the impending crisis. No wonder, poor fellow; with a wife and family depending upon him for support, it is not to be expected that a man can look upon immediate dissolution without painful feelings. A sailor should never marry: or if he does, for the benefit of the service, his marriage should prove an unhappy one, and then he would become more reckless than before. As for my own thoughts, they may be given in a few words—they were upon the vanity of human wishes. Whatever I had done with the one object I had in view—whatever might have been my success had I lived—whether I might have been wedded to Minnie some future day, or what may have resulted, good, bad, or indifferent, as to future, all was to be, in a few hours, cut short by the will of Heaven. In the next world there was neither marriage nor giving in marriage—in the next world, name, titles, wealth, everything worldly was as nought—and all I had to do was to die like a man, and do my duty to the last, trusting to a merciful God to forgive me my sins and offences; and with this philosophy I stood prepared for the event.

About noon it again cleared up to leeward, but the Dryad was no longer to be seen: this was reported to me. As it was nearly three hours since we last had a sight of her, I knew her fate too well—she had plenty of time to go on shore, and to be broken up by the heavy seas. I did however point my glass in the direction, and coolly observed, "she has rounded the tail of the bank, I presume, and has bore up. It was the best thing she could do." I then asked the master if he had wound his chronometers, and went down into the cabin. I had not, however, been examining the chart more than a minute, when the officer of the watch came down, and reported that we had shoaled to twelve fathoms.

"Very good, Mr Hawkins; we shall be in shallower water yet. Let me know if there is any change in the soundings."

As soon as the cabin door was again shut, I worked up the tide to see when it would change against us; I found that it had changed one hour at least. Then it will be sooner over, thought I, throwing down the pencil.

"Mr Cross, the boatswain, wishes to speak to you, sir," said the sentry, opening the cabin door.

"Tell him to come in," replied I. "Well, Cross, what's the matter?"

"I was speaking to the first lieutenant about getting up a runner, sir—the fore-stay is a good deal chafed; that is, if you think it's of any use."

"How do you mean, of any use, Cross?"

"Why, sir, although no one would suppose it from you—but if the face of the master (and he is not a faint-hearted man neither) is to be taken as a barometer, we shall all be in 'kingdom come' before long. I've cruised in these seas so often, that I pretty well guess where we are, Captain Keene."

"Well, Cross, it's no use denying that we are in a mess, and nothing but the wind going down or changing can get us out of it."

"Just as I thought sir; well, it can't be helped, so it's no use fretting about it. I think myself that the gale is breaking, and that we shall have fine weather by to-morrow morning."

"That will be rather too late, Cross; for I think we shall be done for in three or four hours, if not sooner."

"Eleven fathoms, sir," said the officer of the watch, coming in hastily.

"Very well, Mr Hawkins; let her go through the water," replied I.

As soon as the cabin door was again shut, I said, "You see, Cross, the tide is now against us, and this will not last long."

"No, sir; we shall strike in five fathoms with this heavy sea."

"I know we shall; but I do not wish to dishearten the men before it is necessary, and then we must do our best."

"You won't be offended, I am sure, by my asking, Captain Keene, what you think of doing?"

"Not at all, Cross; it is my intention to explain it to the ship's company before I do it. I may as well take your opinion upon it now. As soon as we are in six fathoms, I intend to cut away the masts and anchor."

"That's our only chance, sir, and if it is well done, and the gale abates, it may save some of us; but how do you intend to anchor?"

"I shall back the best bower with the sheet, and let go the small bower at the same time that I do the sheet, so as to ride an even strain."

"You can't do better, sir; but that will require time for preparation, to be well done. Do you think that we shall have time, if you wait till we are in six fathoms?"

"I don't know but you are right, Cross, and I think it would be better to commence our preparations at once."

"Ten fathoms, sir," reported the officer of the watch.

"Very well, I will be on deck directly."

"Well, sir, we must now go to our duty; and as we may chance not to talk to one another again, sir," said Cross, "I can only say God bless you, and I hope that, if we do not meet again in this world, we shall in heaven, or as near to it as possible. Good-bye, sir."

"Good-bye, Cross," replied I, shaking him by the hand; "we'll do our duty, at all events. So now for my last dying speech."

Cross quitted the cabin, and I followed him. As soon as I was on deck, I desired the first lieutenant to turn the hands up, and send them aft. When they were all assembled, with Cross at their head, I stood on one of the carronades and said: "My lads, I have sent for you, because I consider that, although the gale is evidently breaking, we are shoaling our water so fast, that we are in danger of going on shore before the gale does break. Now, what I intend to do, as our best chance, is to cut away the masts, and anchor as soon as we are in six fathoms water; perhaps we may then ride it out. At all events, we must do our best, and put our trust in Providence. But, my lads, you must be aware, that in times of difficulty it is important that we should be all cool and collected, that you must adhere to your discipline, and obey your officers to the last; if you do not, everything will go wrong instead of right. You have proved yourselves an excellent set of men, and I'm sure you will continue so to do. It is possible we may not have to cut away our masts, or to anchor; still, we must make every preparation in case it is necessary, and I have, therefore, sent for you, to explain my intentions, and to request that you will all assist me to the best of your abilities; and I feel convinced that you will, and will do your duty like British seamen. That's all I have to say, my lads. Pipe down, Mr Cross."

The ship's company went forward in silence. They perceived the full extent of the danger. The first lieutenant and boatswain employed a portion in backing the best bower anchor with the sheet; the others roued up the cables from the tiers, and coiled them on the main-deck, clear for running. All hands were busily employed, and employment made them forget their fears. The work was done silently, but orderly and steadily. In the meantime we had shoaled to eight fathoms, and it was now nearly three o'clock; but as it was summer time, the days were long. Indeed, when the weather was fine, there was little or no night, and the weather was warm, which was all in our favour.

When everything was reported ready, I went round to examine and ascertain if the cables would run clear. Satisfied that all was right, I then picked out the men, and appointed those who were most trustworthy to the stations of importance; and, having so done, I then returned to the quarter-deck, and called up the carpenter and some of the topmen to be ready with the axes to cut away the masts and lashings of the booms and boats. Just as these orders were completed, the gale blew fiercer than ever. We were now in seven fathoms water, and pressed heavy by the gale.

I stood at the break of the gangway, the first lieutenant and master by my side, and Cross a little forward, watching my eye. The men in the chains continued to give the soundings in a clear steady voice, "By the mark seven," "Quarter less seven," "And a half six." At last, the man in the chains next to me, a fine old forecastle man, gave the sounding "By the mark six," and he gave it with a louder voice than before, with a sort of defiance, as much as to say, "The time is come, let the elements do their worst."

The time was come. "Silence, fore and aft. Every man down under the half-deck, except those stationed. Cut away the boom lashings, and clear the boats." This was soon done, and reported. "Now then, my lads, be steady. Cut away the lanyards in the chains."

One after another the lanyards and backstays were severed; the masts groaned and creaked, and then the fore-mast and main-mast were over the side almost at the same time; the mizen followed, as the frigate broached to and righted, leaving the ship's deck a mass of wreck and confusion; but no one was hurt, from the precautions which had been taken, the mast having been cut away before we rounded to, to anchor, as otherwise, they would have fallen aft and not gone clear of the ship.

"Stand by the best bower. Stand clear of the cable. Let go the anchor."

As soon as the best bower cable was nearly out, the sheet anchor and small bower were let go at the same moment, and the result was to be ascertained.

Chapter Forty

The frigate was head to wind, rising and pitching with the heavy sea, but not yet feeling the strain of the cables: the masts lay rolling and beating alongside.

The ship's company had most of them returned on deck, to view their impending fate, and the carpenters, who had already received their orders, were battening down the hatchways on the main-deck. In a minute the frigate rode to her anchors, and as soon as the strain was on the cables, she dipped, and a tremendous sea broke over her bows, deluging us fore and aft, nearly filling the main-deck, and washing the carpenters away from their half-completed work. A second and a third followed, rolling aft, so as to almost bury the vessel, sweeping away the men who clung to the cordage and guns, and carrying many of them overboard.

I had quitted the gangway, where there was no hold, and had repaired to the main bitts, behind the stump of the main-mast. Even in this position I should not have been able to hold on, if it had not been for Bob Cross, who was near me, and who passed a rope round my body as I was sweeping away; but the booms and boats which had been cut adrift, in case of the ship driving on shore broadside, were driven aft with the last tremendous sea, and many men on the quarter-deck were crushed and mangled.

After the third sea had swept over us, there was a pause, and Cross said to me, "We had better go down on the main-deck, Captain Keene, and get the half-ports open if possible." We did so, and with great difficulty, found the people to help us; for, as it may be imagined, the confusion was now very great; but the carpenters were again collected, and the half-ports got out, and then the battening down was completed; for, although she continued to ship seas fore and aft, they were not so heavy as the three first, which had so nearly swamped her.

I again went on deck, followed by Cross, who would not leave me. Most of the men had lashed themselves to the guns and belaying pins, but I looked in vain for the first lieutenant and master; they were standing at the gangway at the time of the first sea breaking over us, and it is to be presumed that they were washed overboard, for I never saw them again.

We had hardly been on deck, and taken our old position at the bitts, when the heavy seas again poured over us; but the booms having been cleared, and the ports on the main-deck open, they did not sweep us with the same force as before.

"She cannot stand this long, Bob," said I, as we clung to the bitts.

"No, sir, the cables must part with such a heavy strain; or if they do not, we shall drag our anchors till we strike on the sands."

"And then we shall go to pieces?"

"Yes, sir; but do not forget to get to the wreck of the masts, if you possibly can. The best chance will be there."

"Bad's the best, Cross; however, that was my intention."

The reader will be surprised at my having no conversation with any other party but Cross; but the fact was, that although it was only occasionally that a heavy sea poured over us, we were blinded by the continual spray in which the frigate was enveloped, and which prevented us not only from seeing our own position, but even a few feet from us; and, as if any one who had not a firm hold when the seas poured over the deck, was almost certain to be washed overboard, every man clung to where he was; indeed, there were not fifty men on deck; for those who had not been washed overboard by the first seas, had hastened to get under the half-deck; and many had been washed overboard in the attempt.

The most painful part was to hear the moaning and cries for help of the poor fellows who lay jammed under the heavy spars and boats which had been washed aft, and to whom it was impossible to afford any relief without the assistance of a large body of men. But all I have described since the anchors were let go occurred in a few minutes.

On a sudden, the frigate heeled over to starboard, and at the same time a sea broke over her chesstree, which nearly drowned us where we were clinging. As soon as the pouring off of the water enabled us to recover our speech, "She has parted, Cross, and all is over with us," said I.

"Yes, sir; as soon as she strikes, she will break up in ten minutes. We must not stay here, as she will part amidships."

I felt the truth of the observation, and, waiting until a heavy sea had passed over us, contrived to gain the after ladder, and descend. As soon as we were on the main deck, we crawled to the cabin, and seated ourselves by the after-gun, Cross having made a hold on to a ring-bolt for us with his silk neck-handkerchief.

There were many men in the cabin, silently waiting their doom. They knew that all was over, that nothing could be done, yet they still contrived to touch their hats respectfully to me as I passed.

"My lads," said I, as soon as I had secured my hold, "the cables have parted, and the ship will strike, and go to pieces in a very short time; recollect that the masts to leeward are your best chance."

Those who were near me said, "Thank you, Captain Keene;" but the words were scarcely out of their mouths, when a shock passed through the whole vessel, and communicated itself to our very hearts. The ship had struck on the sand, and the beams and timbers had not ceased trembling and groaning, when a sea struck her larboard broadside, throwing her over on her beam-ends, so that the starboard side of the main-deck and the guns were under water.

It would be impossible after this to detail what occurred in a clear and correct manner, as the noise and confusion were so terrible. At every sea hurled against the sides of the vessel the resistance to them became less. What with the crashing of the beams, the breaking up of the timbers, and the guns to windward, as their fastenings gave way, tumbling with a tremendous crash to leeward, and passing through the ship's sides, the occasional screams mixed with the other noise, the pouring, dashing, and washing of the waters, the scene was appalling. At last, one louder crash than any of the former announced that the vessel had yielded to the terrific force of the waves, and had parted amidships. After this there was little defence against them, even where we were clinging, for the waters poured in, as if maddened by their success, through the passage formed by the separation of the vessel, and came bounding on, as if changing their direction on purpose to overwhelm us. As the two parts of the vessel were thrown higher up, the shocks were more severe, and indeed, the waves appeared to have more power than before, in consequence of their being so increased in weight from the quantity of sand which was mixed up with them. Another crash! the sides of the after-part of the vessel had given way, and the heavy guns, disengaged, flew to leeward, and we found ourselves without shelter from the raging waters.

The part of the wreck on which Cross and I were sitting was so completely on its beam-ends that the deck was within a trifle of being perpendicular. To walk was impossible: all that we could do was to slide down into the water to leeward; but little was to be gained by that, as there was no egress. We therefore remained for more than an hour in the same position, wearied with clinging, and the continual suffocation we received from the waves, as they deluged us. We perceived that the wreck was gradually settling down deeper and deeper in the sand; it was more steady in consequence, but at the same time the waves had more power over the upper part; and so it proved; for one enormous sea came in, blowing up the quarter deck over our heads, tearing away the planking and timbers, and hurling them to leeward. This, at all events, set us free, although it exposed us more than before; we could now see about us, that is, we could see to leeward, and Cross pointed out to me the mainmast tossing about in the boiling water, with the main-top now buried, and now rising out clear. I nodded my head in assent. He made a sign to say that he would go first after the next wave had passed over us.

I found myself alone, and as soon as I had cleared my eyes of the salt-water, I perceived Cross in the surge to leeward, making for the floating mast. He gained it, and waved his hand. I immediately followed him, and, after a short buffet, gained a place by his side, just behind the main-top, which afforded us considerable shelter from the seas. Indeed, as the main-mast was in a manner anchored by the lee rigging to the wreck of the vessel, the latter served as a breakwater, and the sea was, therefore, comparatively smooth, and I found my position infinitely more agreeable than when I was clinging on the wreck. I could now breathe freely, as it was seldom I was wholly under water; neither was it necessary, as before, to cling for your life.

On looking round me, I found that about twenty men were hanging on to the mast. Many of them appeared quite exhausted, and had not strength left to obtain a more favourable berth. The position taken by Cross and myself was very secure, being between the main-top and the catharpings, and the water was so warm that we did not feel the occasional immersion; five other men were close to us, but not a word was said,—indeed, hardly a recognition exchanged. At that time we thought only of immediate preservation, and had little feeling for anybody else.

Chapter Forty One

The night was now coming on; the rolling waves changed from the yellow tinge given by the sand to green, and then to purple: at last all was black except the white foaming breakers.

Exhausted with fatigue, it had not been dark more than two hours, when I felt an irresistible desire to sleep, and I have no doubt that I did slumber in this position, half in and half out of the water, for some time; for when I was roused up by losing my balance, I looked above and perceived that the sky was clear, and the stars shining brightly. I then looked around me, and it was evident that the water was not so agitated as it had been; the wind too had subsided; its roaring had ceased, although it still whistled strong.

"Cross!" said I.

"Here I am, Captain Keene, close under your lee."

"The gale is broke; we shall have fair weather before the morning."

"Yes, sir; I have thought so some time."

"Thank God for His mercy; we must trust that He will not leave us here to perish miserably."

"No, I hope not," replied Cross; "let us trust in Him, but I confess I see but little chance."

"So have many others, yet they have been saved, Cross."

"Very true, sir," replied he: "I wish it was daylight."

We had, however, three or four hours to wait; but during that time the wind gradually subsided, and then went down to a light and fitful breeze. At dawn of day the mast rose and fell with the swell of the sea, which still heaved after the late commotion, but without any run in any particular direction, for it was now calm. I had been sitting on the mast with my back against the futtock-shrouds; I now rose up with difficulty, for I was sorely bruised, and stood upon the mast clear from the water, to look around me. About thirty yards from us was the wreck of the foremast with many men clinging to it. The mizen-mast had broken adrift. The fore part of the frigate was several feet above water, and the bowsprit steeved in the air; of the after part there were but three or four broken timbers to be seen clear of the water, so deep had it been buried in the sand.

Cross had risen on his feet, and was standing by me, when we were hailed from the wreck of the fore-mast, "Main-mast, ahoy!"

"Halloo!" replied Cross.

"Have you got the captain on board?"

"Yes," replied Bob; "all alive and hearty;" a faint huzzah which was the return, affected me sensibly. That my men should think of me when in such a position was soothing to my feelings; but as I looked at them on the other mast and those around me, and calculated that there could not be more than forty men left out of such a noble ship's company, I could have wept. But it was time for action: "Cross," said I, "now that it is calm, I think we shall be better on the fore part of the frigate than here, half in and half out of water. The forecastle is still remaining, and the weather bulwarks will shelter the men; besides if any vessels should come in sight, we should more easily be able to make signals and to attract their attention."

"Very true, sir," replied Cross; "and as there are many men here who cannot hold on much longer, we must try if we cannot haul them on board. Do you feel strong enough to swim to the wreck?"

"Yes, quite, Cross."

"Then we'll start together, sir, and see how matters are."

I dropped into the sea, followed by Cross; and as the distance from us was not forty yards, we soon gained the wreck of the fore part of the frigate; the lee gunnel was just above the water; we clambered over it, and found the deck still whole; the weather portion as white as snow, and quite dry: we gained the weather bulwarks, and looked in the offing in case there should be any vessel, but we could see nothing.

"Now, sir, we had better hail, and tell all those who can swim to come to us."

We did so, and six men from the main-mast and nine from the fore-mast soon joined us.

"Now, my lads," said I, "we must look after those who cannot get here, and try to save them. Get all the ends of ropes from the belaying pins, bend them on one to another, and then we will return and make the men fast, and you shall haul them on board."

This was soon done; Cross and I took the end in our hands, and swam back to the main-mast. One of the top-men, with a broken, arm was the first that was made fast, and, when the signal was given, hauled through the water to the wreck; six or seven more followed in succession. Two men swam back every time with the rope and accompanied those who were hauled on board, that they might not sink. There were many more hanging to different parts of the main-mast, but on examination they were found to be quite dead. We sent on board all that showed any symptoms of life, and then we swam to the fore-mast, and assisted those who were hanging to it. In about two hours our task was completed, and we mustered twenty-six men on the wreck.

We were glad to shelter ourselves under the bulwark, where we all lay huddled up together; before noon, most of the poor fellows had forgotten their sufferings in a sound sleep. Cross, I, and the man with the broken arm, were the only three awake; the latter was in too much pain to find repose, and, moreover, suffered from extreme thirst.

A breeze now sprang up from the southward, which cheered our spirits, as without wind there was little chance of receiving any assistance. Night again came on, and the men still slept. Cross and I laid down, and were glad to follow their example: the night was cold, and when we lay down we did not yet feel much from hunger or thirst; but when the morning dawned we woke in suffering, not from hunger, but from thirst. Everybody cried out for water. I told the men that talking would only make them feel it more, and advised them to put their shirt sleeves in their mouths, and suck them; and then I climbed upon the bulwarks to see if there was anything in sight. I knew that the greatest chance was that the cutter would be looking after us; but, at the same time, it was not yet likely that she would come so near to the sands.

I had been an hour on the gunnel, when Cross came up to me. "It's banking up, sir to the southward: I hope we are not going to have any more bad weather."

"I have no fear of a gale, although we may have thick weather," replied I; "that would be almost as bad for us, as we should perish on the wreck before we are discovered."

"I am going to lower myself down into the galley, Captain Keene, to see if I can find anything."

"I fear you will not be successful," replied I, "for the coppers and ranges are all carried away."

"I know that, sir; but I have been thinking of the cook's closet we had built up above the bowsprit. I know that he used to stow away many things there, and perhaps there may be something. I believe the shortest way will be to go to leeward, and swim round to it."

Cross then left me, and I continued to look out. About an hour afterwards he returned, and told me that he had easily opened it with his knife, and had found eight or nine pounds of raw potatoes, and a bucketful of slush. "We are not hungry enough to eat this now, sir; but there is enough to keep the life in us all for three or four days at least; that is, if we could get water, and I expect we shall feel the want of that dreadfully in a short time. I would give a great deal if I could only find a drop to give that poor fellow Anderson, with his broken arm; it is terribly swelled, and he must suffer very much."

"Did you find anything in the closet to put water into, Cross; in case we should get any?"

"Yes; there's two or three kids, and some small breakers, Captain Keene."

"Well, then, you had better get them ready; for those clouds rise so fast, that we may have rain before morning, and if so, we must not lose the chance."

"Why, it does look like rain, sir," replied Cross. "I'll take one or two of the men with me, to assist in getting them up."

I watched the horizon till night again set in. We were all very faint and distressed for water, and the cool of the evening somewhat relieved us; the breeze, too, was fresh. The men had remained quietly in the shade as I had advised them; but, although patient, they evidently suffered much. Once more we all attempted to forget ourselves in repose. I was soundly asleep, when I was woke up by Cross.

"Captain Keene, it is raining, and it will soon rain much harder; now, if you will order the men, they will soon collect water enough."

"Call them up immediately, Cross; we must not lose this providential succour. It may save all our lives."

The men were soon on the alert: the rain came down in a steady shower; and as soon as they were wet through, they took off their shirts, and dabbling them into the water as it ran down to leeward, squeezed it out into their mouths, until their wants were satisfied, and then, under the direction of Cross, commenced filling the three breakers and four tubs which had been brought up. They had time to fill them, and to spare, for the rain continued till the morning. The tubs and breakers were securely slung under the fore-bitts for future use, and they then continued to drink till they could drink no more.

Chapter Forty Two

The sun rose and chased away the clouds, and the heat was overpowering. What would have been our situation if it had not pleased Heaven to refresh us?

The consequence of their thirst being appeased made the demand for food imperative, and a raw potato was given to each man. The day passed, and so did a third, and fourth, and our hopes began to fail us, when at daylight the next morning I spied a sail to the westward. The breeze was light but the vessel was evidently coming down towards us, and before noon we made it out to be the cutter.

We then sat on the bulwarks, and held out a white shirt, as a signal to attract their attention. When about three miles from us, the cutter rounded to, not appearing to notice us, and for two hours we were left in this state of maddening anxiety and suspense, when at last we perceived her bows pay off, and she again stood towards us. They had at last seen us, and as soon as they had run down to within three cables' length, the boat was lowered and sent to take us off. In three trips we were all on board, and devoutly thanked Heaven for our preservation.

The lieutenant of the cutter said that at first the sun prevented his seeing us, which I believe was the fact; but he acknowledged that he had no idea that we had been wrecked, although he thought that the Dryad was, as he had seen a mast floating, and, sending a boat to look at it, found her name on the cross-trees. We were, however, too much exhausted to enter into much conversation. As soon as we had been supplied with food, we were all put to bed in their hammocks; the first lieutenant resigned his standing bed-place to me. A long sleep recovered me, and I felt little the worse for what I had suffered, and sat down to a breakfast at noon on the following day with a good appetite. The cutter had, by my directions, shaped a course for the island of Heligoland, where we should find means of returning to England.

"I have letters for you, Captain Keene," said the lieutenant, "if you are well enough to read them."

"Thank you, Mr D—; I am now quite well, and will be happy to have them."

The lieutenant brought me a large packet, and I took a position on the sofa to read them comfortably while he went on deck. I first opened those on service—those, of course, had little interest for me, now that I had lost my ship—I skimmed them over, and then threw them on the table one after another. There were three private letters from England, one of which was in Lord de Versely's hand-writing; I opened it first. It was very kind, but short, complaining that he had not been very well lately. The second was from my mother. I read it; it contained nothing of importance; and then I took up the third, which had a black seal. I opened it; it was from Mr Warden, acquainting me that Lord de Versely had expired very suddenly, on his return from the House of Lords, of an ossification of the heart.

In my weak state this blow was too much for me, and I fainted. How long I remained in that state I cannot say; but when I came to my senses I found myself still down in the cabin. I rallied as well as I could, but it was some time before I could take up the letter again, and finish it. He stated that his lordship had left me all his personal property, which was all that he could leave—that the library and wines were of some value, and that there would be about a thousand pounds left at the banker's, when the funeral expenses and debts had been paid. "Oh! if he could but have left me his family name!" I cried, "it was all I coveted. My father! my kind father! I may really say who will lament your loss as I do?" I threw myself on the pillow of the sofa, and for a long while shed bitter tears, not unmixed, I must own; for my grief at his death was increased by my disappointment in having for ever lost the great object of my wishes.

The lieutenant of the cutter came down into the cabin, and I was compelled to hide my emotion. I complained of headache and weakness, and, collecting the letters, I again lay down in the standing bed-place, and, drawing the curtains, I was left to my own reflections. But there was a sad tumult in my mind. I could not keep my ideas upon one subject for a moment. I was feverish and excited, and at last my head was so painful that I could think no more. Fortunately exhaustion threw me again into a sound sleep, and I did not wake till the next morning. When I did, I had to recollect where I was and what had happened. I knew that there was something dreadful which had occurred; again it flashed into my memory. Lord de Versely was dead. I groaned, and fell back on the pillow.

"Are you very ill, Captain Keene!" said a voice close to me. I opened the curtains, and perceived that it was Cross, who was standing by my bedside.

"I am indeed, Cross, very ill; I have very bad news. Lord de Versely is dead."

"That is bad news, sir," replied Cross—"very bad news, worse than losing the frigate. But, Captain Keene, we must have our ups and downs in this world. You have had a long run of good fortune, and you must not be surprised at a change. It is hard to lose your frigate and your father at the same time—but you have not lost your life, which is a great mercy to be thankful for."

I turned away, for my heart was full of bitterness. Cross, perceiving my mood, left me, and I remained in a state of some indifference, never rising from the bed-place during the remainder of the time that I was on board.

On the second day we arrived at Heligoland, and I was requested by the governor to take up my quarters with him, until an opportunity occurred for my return to England. My spirits were, however, so much weighed down that I could not rally. I brooded over my misfortunes, and I thought that the time was now come when I was to meet a reverse of the prosperity which I had so long enjoyed.

The sudden death of Lord de Versely, at the age of fifty-six, left me without a patron, and had destroyed all my hopes centred in him. The object of my ambition was, I considered, for ever lost to me. There was now no chance of my being acknowledged as a member of his family. Then the loss of so fine a frigate, and such a noble ship's company. That I should be honourably acquitted by a court-martial I had not a doubt; but I had no chance of future employment; for, now that Lord de Versely was dead, I had no one to support my claims. My prospects, therefore, in the service were all gone, as well as the visions I had indulged in. I dwelt with some pleasure upon the idea that Lord de Versely had left me his personal property—it proved his regard; but I wanted his family name, and I preferred that to thousands per annum. The second day after our arrival Cross called, and was admitted. He found me in bad spirits, and tried all he could to rouse me. At last he said, "As for the loss of the frigate, Captain Keene, no human endeavour could have saved her, and no one could have done his duty better than you did, as the court-martial will prove; but sir, I think it would be proper just now to show that your zeal for the service is as strong as ever."

"And how am I to do that, Cross?"

"Why, sir, you know as well as we all do how the Frenchmen are going to the wall; that they have been thrashed out of Russia, and that they are retreating everywhere. They say that they have left Hamburg, and I understand that the gun-brigs here are going on an expedition from this island, either to-morrow or next day, to storm the batteries of Cuxhaven, and so create a diversion, as they call it—and very good diversion it is—

licking those French rascals. Now, Captain Keene, if I may take the liberty of saying so, would it not be as well to take as many of your men as are able to go and join the storming party? Much better than sitting here all day, melancholy, and doing nothing."

"It's the first I've heard of it, Cross; are you sure you are correct?"

"How should you hear it, sir, shut up here, and seeing nobody? It's true enough, sir; they were telling off the men as I came up, and I think they start at daylight to-morrow."

"Well, Cross, I will think of it, and let you know my decision if you call here in half an hour."

Cross left me, and I was still undecided, when the governor called to pay me a visit. After the first exchange of civilities, I asked him if the report was true that there was an expedition about to proceed to Cuxhaven. His reply was that the Russians had entered Hamburg, which the French had evacuated on the 11th, and that the French garrisons at Cuxhaven were reported to be in a very distressed state, and, in consequence, the Blazer, and another gun-brig, were about to proceed to attack the forts.

Hamburg! thought I; why, Minnie Vanderwelt is at Hamburg with her father. I will go and try if I cannot get to Hamburg. The remembrance of Minnie gave a spur to my energies, and created a new stimulus. I then told the governor that I had a few men doing nothing; that I would join them to the expedition, and serve as a volunteer. The governor thanked me for my zeal, and I left him to go down and communicate my intentions to the commanding officer of the gun-brig, who expressed himself most happy at my assistance and co-operation.

Chapter Forty Three

As neither my men nor I had any luggage to hamper us—for we had just the clothes we stood in—we were not long getting ready. We started next morning; and on entering the river, found that the French had destroyed their flotilla, and soon afterwards we were invited by the people to come on shore and take possession of the batteries which the French had evacuated. I remained with Cross and my men on shore at Cuxhaven, while the brigs went up the river, in pursuit of a privateer.

After a day or two, tired of inactivity, and anxious to arrive at Hamburg, I proposed to Cross that he should accompany me, which he cheerfully acceded to. I had drawn a bill at Heligoland, so that we were in no want of money, and we set off on our expedition. We had not, however, proceeded far before we were informed that the road to Hamburg was so full of French troops, scattered about, that it would be impossible to gain the city without we made a *détour*. As we knew that our throats would be cut by these disorganised parties, we followed the advice given to us, walking from village to village, until we had put Hamburg between us and the river. But when there, we found that we could not approach the imperial city, but were obliged to direct our steps more inland. At last, we heard that the inhabitants of the town of Lunenburg had risen, and driven out the French garrison, and I resolved to proceed there, as it was more advisable than being continually in danger of being picked up by the French stragglers, who were committing every enormity that could be imagined.

We arrived safe; stated who we were to the authorities, and were well received; but we had not been there more than two days, when the rejoicings and braggings of the town's-people, on account of the late victory over the French garrison, were turned to consternation by the intelligence that General Moraud was advancing with a considerable force to re-take the town. The panic was so great, that all idea of defence was in vain; and at the very time that I was entreating them to make a stand, the French troops poured in, and two cuirassiers galloped up, and seized upon Cross and me. A few minutes afterwards, General Moraud came up, and inquired, in a rough tone, who we were. I replied in French, that we were English officers.

"Take them away," said he, "and secure them well; I'll make an example here that shan't be forgotten."

We were taken to the guard-room, where we remained shut up for the night. The next morning one of the cuirassiers looked into our cell. I asked him whether we could not have something to eat.

"Cela ne vaut pas la peine. Mon ami, vous n'aurez pas le temps pour la digestion; dans une demie-heure vous serez fusillés."

"May I ask the English of that, Captain Keene?" replied Cross.

"Yes, it is very pleasant. He says that it's not worth while eating anything, as we shall be shot in half an hour."

"Well, I suppose they'll shoot us first, and try us afterwards," replied Cross. "Won't they give us a reason?"

"I suspect not, Cross. I am sorry that I have got you into this scrape; as for myself, I care little about it."

"I am sorry for poor Jane, sir," replied Cross; "but we all owe Heaven a death; and, after all, it's not worth making a fuss about."

Our conversation was here interrupted by a party of French soldiers, who opened the door and ordered us to follow them. We had not far to go, for we were led out to the Grand Place, before the prison, where we found the French troops drawn up, and General Moraud, with his officers round him, standing in the centre. At twenty yards' distance, and surrounded by the troops, which did not amount to more than three hundred, were thirty of the principal inhabitants of the town, pinioned, and handkerchiefs tied over their eyes, preparatory to their being shot; this being the terrible example that the governor had threatened.

"Look, Cross," said I, "what a handful of men these Frenchmen have retaken the town with. Why, if we had resisted, we might have laughed at them."

"They won't laugh any more, I expect," replied Bob.

"*Allons,*" said the corporal to me.

"Where?" replied I.

"To your friends, there," replied he, pointing to the town's-people, who were about to be shot.

"I wish to speak to the general," replied I, resisting.

"No, no: you must go."

"I will speak to the general," replied I, pushing the corporal on one side, and walking to where the general was standing.

"Well," said the general, fiercely.

"I wish to know, sir," replied I, "by what law you are guided in shooting us. We are English officers, here on duty to assist against the French, and at the most can only be prisoners of war. Upon what grounds do you order us to be shot?"

"As spies," replied the general.

"I am no spy, sir; I am a post-captain in the English navy, who joined with the seamen saved from the wreck of my frigate in the attack upon Cuxhaven, and there is my boatswain, who came up with me to go to Hamburg. At all events, I am fully justified in siding against the French: and to shoot us will be a murder, which will not fail to be revenged."

"You may pass yourself off as the captain of a frigate, but your dress disproves it, and I have better information. You are two spies, and smugglers, and therefore you will be shot."

"I tell you before all your officers that I am Captain Keene, of the Circe frigate, belonging to His Britannic Majesty, and no spy; if you choose to shoot me now, I leave my death to be revenged by my country."

At this moment an officer in naval uniform stepped forward and looked me in the face.

"General Moraud," said he, "what that officer says is true: he is Captain Keene, and I was prisoner on board of his vessel; and I also know the other man as well."

"Captain Vangilt, I do not request your interference," replied the general.

"But general, as an officer in the marine of the emperor, it is my duty to state to you, that you are deceived, and that this officer is the person that he states himself to be. Messieurs," continued Captain Vangilt, addressing those about the general, "I assure you it is true, and I am under the greatest obligation to this officer for his kindness and humanity when I was his prisoner."

"I recognise you now, Mr Vangilt," replied I; "and I thank you for your evidence."

"You see, general, he knows me by name: I must demand the life of this British officer."

The other officers then spoke to the general, who heard all they had to say, and then, with a sardonic grin, replied,—"Gentlemen, he may be an officer, but still he is a spy." At that moment an orderly came up on horseback, and, dismounting, gave a note to the general.

"*Sacré bleu!*" cried he; "then we'll have our revenge first at all events. Soldiers, take these two men, and put them in the centre, with the others."

Vangilt pleaded and entreated in vain: at last, in his rage, he called the general "a coward and a madman."

"Captain Vangilt, you will answer that at some other time," replied the general; "at present we will carry our will into execution. Lead them away."

Vangilt then covered his face with his hands, and all the other officers showed signs of great disgust.

"Farewell, Vangilt," said I in French; "I thank you for your interference, although you have not succeeded with the *scoundrel.*"

"Take them away!" roared the general.

At that moment the report of musketry was heard in dropping shots.

"Well, if ever I saw such a bloody villain," said Cross. "Take that, at all events;" continued Bob, shying his hat right into the general's face. "I only wish it was a 32-pounder, you murdering thief."

The rage of the general may easily be imagined. Once more he gave his orders, drawing his sword in a menacing way at his own soldiers, who now forced us towards the part of the square where the other victims were collected. As soon as we were there, they wanted to blind our eyes, but that both I and Bob positively refused, and a delay was created by our resistance. The musketry was now approaching much nearer; and a few seconds afterwards the general gave the order for the party to advance who were to execute the sentence.

The other prisoners kneeled down; but I and Cross would not; and while we were resisting, the general repeated his order to fire; but the men were confused with the advance of the enemy, and the impossibility to fire while Cross and I not only resisted the soldiers, but held them so fast, that had the party fired they must have shot them as well as us. A cry "To arms" was given, and the troops all wheeled round in front to repel the enemy. A loud hurrah was followed by an inpouring of some hundred Cossacks, with their long spears who, in a few seconds charged and routed the French, who retreated in the greatest confusion by the different streets which led into the Grand Place.

"Hurrah! we are saved," cried Cross, snatching up a musket that had been dropped by a soldier. I did the same, and pursued the retreating French, till a bullet through my leg put a stop to my progress. I called to Cross, who came to my assistance, and he helped me back to the Grand Place, which was now clear of troops.

Chapter Forty Four

The Cossacks having divided, and gone in pursuit of the French, I pointed out to Cross a hotel, and requested him to help me there. As we crossed the square, strewed with the dead and wounded, we passed close to General Moraud, who was breathing his last.

"See, Cross," said I, "there is retribution. He intended that we should fall where he now lies."

The general recognised us, gave a heavy groan, and, turning on his back, fell dead.

As soon as I gained the hotel, I was taken up into a room, and made as comfortable as I could be until my wound could be dressed.

"We're well out of it this time, sir," said Cross.

"Yes, indeed, Bob; this has indeed been a miraculous preservation, and we ought to thank Heaven for it."

"Why, Captain Keene, I thought just now you did not care whether you lived or died."

"No more I did at that time, Cross; but when we are so wonderfully preserved, we cannot think but that we are preserved for better things; and as Providence has interfered, it points out to us that it is our duty to live."

"Well, I'm glad to hear you say that, sir. There's all the troops coming back. What queer-looking chaps they are, with their long lances and long beards!"

"Yes; they are Cossacks—Russian irregular cavalry."

"Irregular enough I don't doubt; but they spitted the French men nicely. They look exactly what I thought the Pope of Rome was like."

"Cross, call the master of the hotel, and tell him to come here." When the man came, I desired him to let the commander of the allied troops know that an English captain was wounded, and required surgical assistance. The master of the hotel went to the burgomaster, who was one of those who had been ordered to be shot; and the burgomaster, who was now in company with the Russian commander, made known what I required. In about an hour a surgeon came, and my wound was dressed. The burgomaster called soon afterwards, and expressed his obligation to me. "For," said he, "if you had not created the delay—which you did by your resistance—it would have been all over with us by this time."

"You have to thank a Dutch naval officer of the name of Vangilt," replied I; "it is he who saved us all; and if he is not hurt, you must be kind to him, and bring him to me. I will get him his parole, if he is a prisoner. Will you see to it, burgomaster?"

"I will," replied he, "as soon as we are a little more tranquil; but, what with fright and confusion, none of us know what we are about. You were right, sir, in persuading us to defend ourselves. We might easily have beaten off the small force of General Moraud; but we thought he had ten thousand men, at least. We will do better another time; but the French are now in full retreat everywhere."

That night, after dusk, Captain Vangilt came into my room: he had been a prisoner; but the burgomaster made inquiries, and let him out, which, as chief magistrate, he had the power to do. Vangilt embraced me with much warmth, and expressed his regret that he could not persuade that wretch, Moraud, from his murderous intentions.

"It came to the same thing, Vangilt. I owe you my life; for if you had not created the delay, we should have been shot."

"That's true," replied he. "How fortunate it was, that, as my squadron of gun-boats were destroyed, I consented to join Moraud with what men I could collect, to surprise the town. Are you badly wounded?"

"No, not seriously, I believe; I hope to be able to get to Hamburg in a few days."

"There is more than one there who will be delighted to see you."

"Is Mr Vanderwelt alive and well?"

"Oh yes; and Minnie, my pretty cousin, is still unmarried." Vangilt smiled as he made this reply.

"I must ask for your parole, Vangilt, and then you can go to Hamburg with us."

"With all my heart," replied he; "for we are tired of war, and as I am a Dutchman and not a Frenchman, I care little for the reverses we have met with; all I hope is, that Holland may become a kingdom again, and not a French state, as it is now."

The next day, I was visited by the Russian commandant, who very willingly granted me the parole of Vangilt. In a week I was well enough to travel by slow journeys to Hamburg, lying on mattresses in a small covered waggon, and escorted by Cross and Vangilt. A few hours before my arrival, Vangilt went ahead to give notice of my coming, and on the evening of the second day I found myself in a luxurious chamber, with every comfort, in the company of Mr Vanderwelt, and with the beaming eyes of Minnie watching over me.

The report of Minnie's beauty was fully warranted. When she first made her appearance, the effect upon me was quite electrical: her style was radiant, and almost dazzling—a something you did not expect to find in the human countenance. Their reception of me was all that I could desire; their affection shown towards me, their anxiety about my wound, and joy at once more having me under their roof, proved that I had not been forgotten. After a short time, Vangilt left the room, and I remained on the sofa, one hand in the grasp of Mr Vanderwelt, the other holding the not unwilling one of Minnie. That evening I made known to them all that had taken place since I last wrote to them, winding up with the loss of my frigate, the death of Lord de Versely, and my subsequent capture and rescue.

"And so it was in attempting to come and see us that you were wounded and nearly murdered?"

"Yes, Minnie; I had long been anxious to see you, and could not help availing myself of the first opportunity."

"Thank God you are here at last," said Mr Vanderwelt, "and that there is now every prospect of a conclusion to the war."

"And you won't go to sea any more—will you, Percival?" said Minnie.

"They won't give me a ship, Minnie, after having lost the one I commanded; to be unfortunate is to be guilty, in those who have no interest."

"I'm very glad to hear it; then you'll remain quietly on shore, and you will come and see us."

As I had been rendered feverish by travelling, and my wound was a little angry, as soon as it was dressed for the night, they left me to repose; but that I could not—the form of Minnie haunted me; to sleep was impossible, and I lay thinking of her till day dawned. The fact was, that I was for the first time in love, and that in no small degree—before morning I was desperately so. Indeed, there was excuse sufficient, for Minnie was as winning in her manners as she was lovely in her person, and I was not at all surprised at hearing from Vangilt of the numerous suitors for her hand.

Chapter Forty Five

The next morning I was pale and feverish, which they observed with concern, Minnie was sitting by me, and Mr Vanderwelt had left the room, when she said, "How very pale you are, and your hand is so hot; I wish the doctor would come."

"I could not sleep last night, Minnie—and it was all your fault."

"My fault!"

"Yes, your fault; for I could not sleep for thinking of you; I thought you were looking at me as you do now the whole night."

Minnie blushed, and I kissed her hand.

As soon as my wound was dressed, I requested writing materials, and wrote to the Admiralty, giving an account of what had occurred since I quitted Heligoland. (I had written to inform them of the loss of the frigate when I was on the island). I stated in my despatches that my wound would probably confine me for some weeks; but as soon as I was able to be moved, I should return to England to await their orders. I also wrote to my mother and Mr Warden. I informed the latter of what had passed, and the delay which would be occasioned by my wound, and requested him to write to me more fully as to the death of Lord de Versely, and any other particulars which might interest me.

Having sealed these despatches, and entrusted them to the care of Mr Vanderwelt, my mind was relieved, and I had nothing to do but to think of and talk to Minnie. That my progress in her affections was rapid, was not to be wondered at, her attachment to me having commenced so early; and as her father was evidently pleased at our increasing intimacy, in a fortnight after my arrival at Hamburg, Minnie had consented to be mine, and her father had joined our hands, and given us his blessing.

As I now had no secrets from them, I detailed my whole history, the cause of Lord de Versely's patronage, and the mystery of my birth. I opened the seal-skin pouch to show them Lord de Versely's letter to my mother, and stated what had been the object of my ambition through life, and how great was my disappointment at my hopes being overthrown by the death of his lordship.

"My dear Percival," said old Mr Vanderwelt, after I had concluded my narrative, "you have been pursuing a shadow, although the pursuit has called forth all your energies, and led to your advancement. You have the substance. You have wealth more than sufficient, for you know how rich I am. You have reputation, which is better than wealth, and you have now, I trust, a fair prospect of domestic happiness; for Minnie will be as good a wife as she has been a daughter. What, then, do you desire? A name. And what is that? Nothing. If you do not like your present name, from its association with your putative father of low origin, change it to mine. You will receive the fortune of an heiress, which will fully warrant your so doing. At all events, let not your pride stand in the way of your happiness. We cannot expect everything in this world. You have much to be thankful to Heaven for, and you must not repine because you cannot obtain all."

"I have so ardently desired it all my life; it has been the sole object of my ambition," replied I, "and I cannot but severely feel the disappointment."

"Granted; but you must bear the disappointment, or rather you must forget it; regret for what cannot be obtained is not only unavailing, but, I may say, it is sinful. You have much to thank God for."

"I have indeed, sir," replied I, as I kissed his daughter; "and I will not repine. I will take your name when you give me Minnie, and I will think no more about that of Delmar."

After this conversation, the subject was not renewed. I felt too happy with Minnie's love to care much about anything else; my ambition melted away before it, and I looked forward to the time when I might embrace her as my own.

My wound healed rapidly; I had been a month at Hamburg, and was able to limp about a little, when one day Cross came in with a packet of letters from England.

There was one from the Admiralty, acknowledging the receipt of my two letters, one announcing the loss of the Circe, and the other my subsequent adventures, desiring me to come home as soon as my wound would permit me, to have the cause of the loss of the Circe investigated by a court-martial; that of course: one from my mother, thanking Heaven that I had escaped so many dangers with only a bullet in my leg, and stating her intention of going up to town to see me as soon as she heard of my arrival; the third was a voluminous epistle from Mr Warden, which I shall give to the reader in his own words.

" My dear Captain Keene :—

"I received your two letters, the first, acquainting me with your miraculous preservation after the loss of your frigate, and the other with your subsequent adventures on *terra firma*. You appear to me to have a charmed life! and as there is now every prospect of a speedy termination to this long and devastating war, I hope you will live many days. I did not enter into many particulars as to Lord de Versely's death, as it was so sudden; the property left you is not perhaps of so much value in itself, as it is as a mark of his regard and esteem. Nevertheless, if ever you sit down quietly and take a wife, you will find that it will save you a few thousands in furnishing and decorating; the plate, pictures, and objects *de vertu*, as they are termed, are really valuable, and I know that you will not part with them, bequeathed as they have been by your friend and patron.

"I must now refer to particulars of more consequence. You know that, as a legal adviser, my lips are supposed to be sealed, and they would have remained so now, had it not been that circumstances have occurred which warrant my disclosure; indeed, I may say that I have permission to speak plainly, as you have to repel charges against you which, if not disproved, may seriously affect your future interests. Know then, that when you were last at Madeline Hall, I was sent for to draw up the will of the Honourable Miss Delmar, and I then discovered that the will which had been made in favour of Lord de Versely, to whom Miss Delmar had left everything, was by his express desire to be altered in your favour; and at the same time the secret of your birth was confided to me. You will see, therefore, that Lord de Versely did not neglect your interests. The de Versely property he could not leave you, but he did what he could in your favour. This will was signed, sealed, and attested, and is now in my possession; and as the old lady is very shakey, and something approaching to imbecile, I considered that in a short time I should have to congratulate you upon your succession to this fine property, which is a clear 8,000 pounds per annum.

"You must also know, that Colonel Delmar, whom you also met here, and who accompanied you to Portsmouth, has always hoped that he would be the heir of the old lady; and, indeed, had you not stepped in, I have no doubt but eventually such would have been the case. It appears that he has, by some means, discovered that you have ousted him, and since you sailed he has returned to Madeline Hall, and has so unsettled the old lady, by reporting that you are an impostor, and no relation by blood, that she has given me instructions to make a new will in his favour. By what means he has prevailed upon her I cannot tell: the chief support of his assertion rests upon some letters, which he has either surreptitiously obtained or forged, written by your mother and addressed to you. Now that your mother has been supposed to be dead many years I knew well for Lord de Versely told me so. The old lady has shown me these letters, which certainly appear authentic; and she says, that if you have deceived her and Lord de Versely as to your mother's death, you have deceived them in everything else, and that she does not now believe that you are the son of her nephew. As I hinted before, the old lady is almost in her dotage, and cannot well be reasoned with, for she is very positive. I argued as long as I could with her, but in vain. At last she consented to stop proceedings until I heard from you, saying, 'If I can have any proof under my nephew's own hand that Percival is his son, I will be content; but without that I sign the new will.'

"Such is the state of affairs, that you have little chance if such a document cannot be produced, I feel certain; at all events, I have gained delay which we lawyers always aim at. I only wish the old lady would take a sudden departure, and leave the question as unsettled as it is. Had Lord de Versely not been so suddenly called away, this would never have happened; as it is, we must make the best fight we can. At present the colonel has it all his own way. Pray write immediately, and explain as much as you can of this strange affair and let me know what steps you think it advisable to be taken.—Yours very truly,

" *F. Warden* ."

Chapter Forty Six

The receipt of this letter was extremely mortifying to me. I could not help feeling that if I lost the fine property which had been intended for me, I lost it chiefly by the deceit practised relative to my mother's supposed death, and that if I did lose the estate in consequence, it was a proper punishment. At the same time, I felt not a little indignant at the conduct of Colonel Delmar. I now understood why it was that he was talking with Mr Warden's clerk when I passed by them; and I also felt certain that he must have taken advantage of my situation at Portsmouth, and have opened my desk and stolen the letters from my mother. For this I resolved to call him to account, under any circumstances (that is, whether he or I became the heir to the old lady), as soon as I could fall in with him. Although I was far from despising the property which I was now likely to lose, yet I was more actuated in my wish to regain it by my enmity towards him, and I immediately resolved upon what I would do.

As I was still unfit to travel, and, moreover, was resolved not to leave Hamburg without Minnie as my wife, I sent for Cross, and telling him in few words, what had taken place, asked him if he would immediately start for England, which he gladly consented to do. "The old lady requires, it seems, proof from Lord de Versely's own hand that I am his son; fortunately, that is in my power to give; so do you take this, and as soon as you arrive in England make all haste to Mr Warden's and put it into his own hands." I then took off the seal-skin pouch containing Lord de Versely's letter to my mother, and confided it to his care. At the same time I wrote a long letter to Mr Warden explaining as far as I could the means which the colonel had used to get possession of the letters, and the reason which induced me to make his lordship believe that my mother was dead. I did not attempt to extenuate my conduct; on the contrary, I severely blamed myself for my deception, and acknowledged that if I lost the estate it was nothing more than I deserved.

Cross made all haste, and sailed the next morning. Having put this affair in train, I had nothing to do but to give all my thoughts to Minnie. In another fortnight I was completely recovered, and then I mentioned to Mr Vanderwelt my anxiety that the marriage should take place. No difficulties were raised; and it was settled that on that day week I should lead my Minnie to the altar. I thought that the week would never expire; but, like all other weeks, it died a natural death at last, and we were united. The *fête* was over, the company had all left us, and we were again alone, and I held my dearest Minnie in my arms, when Mr Vanderwelt brought me in a letter from England. It was from Mr Warden, and I hastily opened it. Minnie shared my impatience, and read over my shoulder. The contents were as follows:—

" *My dear Captain Keene* ,

"Most fortunate it was for you that you have preserved that letter; but I must not anticipate. On receiving it from Cross I immediately went with it to the old lady, and presented it to her. I did more,—I read over your letter in which you stated your reasons for making Lord de Versely believe that your mother was dead. The old lady, who is now very far gone in her intellect, could hardly understand me. However, her nephew's handwriting roused her up a little, and she said, 'Well, well—I see—I must think about it. I won't decide. I must hear what the colonel says.' Now, this is what I did not wish her to do; but she was positive, and I was obliged to leave her. The colonel was sent for; but I do not know what the result was, or rather might have been, as fortune stood your friend in a most unexpected way.

"As I went out, I perceived two gentlemen arrive in a post-chaise. One of them appeared very ill and feeble, hardly able to walk up the steps. They inquired for Colonel Delmar, and were shown into a sitting-room, until he came out of Mrs Delmar's apartment. I saw him come out; and there was so much satisfaction in his countenance, that I felt sure that he had gained over the old lady. And I went home, resolving that I would burn the new will, which had not been signed, if it were only to gain the delay of having to make it over again. But the next morning an express arrived for me to go immediately to the Hall. I did so, but I did not take the new will with me, as I felt certain that if I had so done, it would have been signed that day. But I was mistaken: I had been sent for on account of the death of Colonel Delmar, who had that morning fallen in a duel with Major Stapleton, the officer who fought with you. It appears that Captain Green had informed the major of the language used by the colonel when Major S was supposed to be dead; and that the major, who has been very ill ever since, only waited till he was able to stand to demand satisfaction of the colonel. It was the major with his friend whom I met as I left the Hall the day before. They fought at daylight, and both fell. The major, however, lived long enough to acknowledge that the duel with you had been an arranged thing between him and the colonel, that you might be put out of the way, after the information the colonel had received from my clerk, and that the colonel was to have rewarded him handsomely if he had sent you into the other world. I suspect, after this, that the fowling-piece going off in the cover was not quite so accidental as was supposed. However, the colonel is out of your way now, and the old lady has received such a shock, that there is no fear of her altering the will; indeed, if she attempted it, I doubt if it would be valid, as she is now quite gone in her intellect. I have, therefore, destroyed the one not signed; and have no doubt, but that in a very few weeks I may have to congratulate you upon your succession to this property. I think that the sooner you can come home the better, and I advise you to take up your quarters at Madeline Hall, for possession is nine points of the law, and you can keep off all trespassers.—Yours most truly,

" *F. Warden* ."

"Well, Minnie dearest, I may congratulate you, I believe, as the lady of Madeline Hall," said I, folding up the letter.

"Yes, Percival, but there is a postscript overleaf, which you have not read."

I turned back to the letter.

"PS. I quite forgot to tell you that there is a condition attached to your taking possession of the property, which, as it was at the particular request of Lord de Versely, I presume you will not object to, which is—that you assume the arms and name of Delmar."